The Wicked City

Beatriz Williams

HARPER LUXE

An Imprint of HarperCollins*Publishers*

FIRST HARPERLUXE EDITION

ISBN: 978-0-06-264399-5

HarperLuxe™ is a trademark of HarperCollins Publishers.

Library of Congress Cataloging-in-Publication Data is available upon request.

17 18 19 20 21 ID/LSC 10 9 8 7 6 5 4 3 2 1

The Wicked City

ALSO BY BEATRIZ WILLIAMS

A Certain Age

Along the Infinite Sea

Tiny Little Thing

The Secret Life of Violet Grant

A Hundred Summers

Overseas

To New York City, you ambitious, resilient, breathtaking, wicked creature

The Wicked City

New York City, 1998

Ella visited the laundry room for the first time at half past six on a Saturday morning at the beginning of March. Not that the timing really mattered, she decided later, when her life had taken on its new, extraordinary dimensions and she'd begun to consider the uncanny moment of that beginning. Certain things— let's call them that, *certain things*—had a way of tracking you down and finding you, even when you thought you were just going to wash some clothes in a Greenwich Village basement.

She'd moved into the building a week ago, and the hamper in the corner of the bathroom seemed pitifully empty without all the bulk of Patrick's things. Still, it was time. Standards must be upheld. You couldn't keep laundry in a hamper for more than a week, whatever catastrophe had interrupted your life. Too seedy. Too regressive. Anyway, Ella's mother was bound to call her up soon for the morning welfare check, and she would surely ask whether Ella had done her laundry yet, and Ella wanted to be able to say *yes* without lying. (Woman could smoke out a lie like a pair of shoes on sale at Bergdorf's.)

She'd already gone out for a run in the damp charcoal streets, but she hadn't showered yet. (Terrific thing about insomnia: you could do things like go running and do your laundry without having to confront your fellow tenants in a state of squalor.) As she descended the cold stairwell to the basement, she realized that its strange odor was actually the fug of her own sweat—salt and skin, not yet turning to stink. Her hair, badly in need of washing, whirled in a greasy knot at the back of her head, held from collapse by a denim scrunchie that had not been fashionable even during the heyday of scrunchies. Loose gray sweatpants, looser gray T-shirt emblazoned with her college logo—she'd peeled off her running clothes to fill out the wash load—and on her feet, the shearling L.L.Bean slippers Patrick always hated, because they were crummy and smelled like camping. Teeth furry. No bra.

She remembered all these details because of what occurred inside that laundry room the first time she entered. Six thirty in the morning, the first Saturday of March.

A *starter* marriage, her mother called it. Ella had never heard the term before.

"There was an article in the Style section just a month or two ago," Mumma said. "It made me think of you."

"But we only split up the week before last," Ella said, staring at the cluster of U-Haul boxes in the center of her new bedroom.

"I never trusted him."

"You could have fooled me."

Mumma leaned back against a stack of towels and made one of those gestures with her right hand, like she was flicking out ash from a cigarette that no longer existed. An amputee with a phantom limb. "Oh, I *liked* him well enough. What wasn't to like? I just didn't trust him."

"I didn't realize there was a difference."

"Well, there is. Anyway, it seems the term was coined by a fellow named Douglas . . . Douglas something-or-other, in some sort of novel he wrote about your generation."

"Douglas Coupland?"

"Yes! Coupland. Douglas Coupland. Have you read it?"

"*Generation X?* Or else *Shampoo Planet.*"

"No, the first one."

"Read them both in grad school. But I don't remember anything about starter marriages."

"It was in a footnote, apparently. I expect you missed it. You're all in such a *rush,* your generation. You miss the details."

"I might have read it and just forgotten."

"You should take your time. The footnotes are the best part."

Ella rose from the bed and picked up the X-Acto knife from the clutter on her chest of drawers. Her mother had a way of saying everything like a double entendre. The suggestive throatiness of the *take your time*. And *footnotes*. What were footnotes, in her mother's secret vocabulary? Better not to know. For one thing, there was Daddy. "Starter marriage, Mumma? You were saying?"

"A first marriage, made for the wrong reasons, or because you didn't have enough experience to judge the merchandise. Like a starter home or a starter car. You trade up."

"You and Daddy didn't have to trade up."

"We were lucky. *I* was lucky. The point is, it's nothing to be ashamed of. As long as you haven't got kids, you just move on. Move on, move up."

The X-Acto knife had one of those retractable blades, and Ella couldn't seem to make it work. The edge came out halfway and stuck. "Look, could we not talk about moving on for another week or so? I haven't even talked to a lawyer yet."

"Why not? I gave you the number."

"And the fact that you have a divorce lawyer on speed dial kind of stresses me out, by the way."

"He's not on speed dial, and he's not a divorce lawyer. He's a colleague of your father's. He can give you advice, that's all." Ella's mother uncrossed her legs and rose from the bed so gracefully, she might have been Odette. Or Odile. "God knows you won't take it from me."

"That's not true."

"Isn't it? What about your wedding dress?"

"That was four years ago!"

"And was I right?"

Ella banged the bottom of the X-Acto knife on the toaster oven. "You were right about the dress. But you might have warned me about the groom."

"Oh, darling." Mumma plucked the knife from her fingers, flicked out the blade with a single nudge of her thumb, and sliced delicately along the seam of a box labeled SWEATERS, CASHMERE. "You wouldn't have listened to that, either. You were in love."

———

In love. Ella could still remember what it felt like, falling in love. Being in love. She remembered it as a certain moment, the first really warm day of that year, a month or two after she met Patrick, when he was away on a business trip in Europe and she was alone for the first Saturday in weeks. She'd put on her favorite cotton sundress, which had lain squashed in her drawer since October and reminded her instantly of Granny's house on Cumberland Island. The smell of summer. She'd gone outside into the innocent sunshine, bought an iced coffee, and walked by herself in Central Park, entering near the Museum of Natural History and making her way southeast, without any particular goal. As she strolled past the entwined couples drowsing in the Sheep Meadow, she'd gazed at them, for the first time, in benevolence instead of envy. She'd thought—actually *spoke* inside in her head, in conscious words that she still recalled exactly—*I'm so happy, it's the end of May and I'm in love, and the whole summer lies before us.* An immaculate joy had quickened her feet along the asphalt paths, the conviction that the world was beautiful (she'd even sung, under her breath, a few bars of that song—*And I think to myself, what a wonderful world*—to which she ended up dancing with her father at her wedding, two years later) and that the rest of her life was just falling into its ordained pattern before her. The life she was meant to live, unfolding itself at last. Courtship, marriage, apartment. Exotic, self-indulgent vacations. Then kids, house in Connecticut, school runs and mom coffees. Less exotic, more wholesome vacations. Which shade of white to paint the trim in the dining room. Later that day, she had dinner with her sister and spilled out every detail, every silvery moonbeam over pasta and red wine at Isabella's. And not once that entire love-struck Saturday did she suspect that Patrick was doing anything other than working—working really hard!—throughout *his* Saturday in Frankfurt. Thinking of her the whole time. Not once did the possibility of disloyalty enter her head. They were in love! Hadn't he told her so, before he left on Tuesday? In between kisses. Naked in bed. Warm and secure. *I've finally found you*, he said, his actual words, while he held her face in his hands. What could be more certain than that?

Now she had to go back and recall all those old business trips, every late night at work, every client dinner, and wonder which ones he was lying about. A painfully detailed revision of history and memory.

And that was the worst part. Because she could still remember how wonderful it was to be in love with him.

But that was six years ago. Now she had this too-light basket of laundry and this dark, chilly stairwell on Christopher Street, painted in gray and moist against her skin. Only blocks away from the sleek SoHo loft conversion she had shared with Patrick, which had its own washer and dryer and required no stair-climbing of any kind, except on the row of StairMasters in the residents' gym: eternally occupied, unlike the building stairwells, because you weren't climbing those steps to *go* anywhere. My God, of course not. Just to stay skinny. (Sorry, to *keep fit.*)

Of course, in the cold light of reason, Ella should have been the one to kick Patrick out. Damn it. *He* should have been the one cramming his belongings into a studio apartment in the Village—*It's charming,* Mumma said last Sunday, picking her way between the boxes to peer out the window, into the asphalt garden out back—while Ella, crowned by a nimbus of moral superiority, enthroned herself on one of the egg chairs inside the two-thousand-square-foot loft on Prince Street.

He should have been the one bumping a laundry basket into a damp basement in search of a rumored laundry room, while *she* flicked her sweaty running clothes into the washing machine off the granite kitchen and sipped an espresso from the De'Longhi. (Not that Patrick would ever do his own laundry, even if he knew how; in his bachelor days, he sent it out for wash-and-fold.)

He should have been spending his weekend unpacking boxes and contemplating the miniature kitchen in the corner. The way you had to step around the toilet to exit the shower. The way you had to open said shower door and prop your foot on said toilet in order to shave your legs. (Not that Patrick shaved his legs, either; at least not since his brief but expensive flirtation with a carbon-framed racing bicycle.)

But she'd been too shocked and angry to consider her rights as the Wronged Wife, hadn't she? No, wait. That wasn't right, *shocked and angry*. Not visceral enough. She'd felt as if a loud steam whistle were blowing inside her skull. As if her insides were melting. As if her legs and arms had no nerves. And how could you think straight when your body was in such disarray?

So instead of waiting to confront Patrick, send Patrick to the doghouse as he deserved, she'd fled into the bedroom—trying not to look at the bed itself—and packed a few things into a gym bag and rushed to Aunt Viv and Uncle Paul's apartment in Gramercy. Stammered an explanation she didn't fully comprehend herself. Spent the next week in their guest room, searching the classifieds for no-fee apartments and fending off her friends' sympathy and her parents' advice. Fending off the manic trill of her cell phone every few hours, which she refused to answer.

And now here *she* stood, instead of Patrick, in a Christopher Street basement before a metal door labeled LAUNDRY, at six thirty in the morning.

Balancing the basket on her hip while she fumbled with the door handle.

Thinking, *At least I've got the jump on everyone else, washing clothes this early on a Manhattan Saturday morning.* The one time when the damn city actually does sleep.

But as the door cracked open, and Ella stuck in her shameful shearling-lined foot to push it out the rest of the way, a wondrous and unexpected noise met her ears.

The sound of four industrial washing machines and two industrial dryers, all churning in furious, metallic frenzy.

Not only that. Each machine bore a basket of laundry on top, claiming dibs, waiting to pounce at the end of the cycle. Ella's eyes found the clock on the wall, just to make sure that she hadn't somehow missed daylight savings time.

Nope. Six thirty-four.

She let the basket slide down to the concrete floor. Put her hands on her hips. "What the *hell?*" she wailed. "Who *are* you people?"

"Oh, hello," said a male voice behind her, appallingly sunny. "You must be the new one."

Ella turned so quickly, she kicked over the basket. Jogbra spilled out. Sweaty running shirt. Seven days' worth of lace panties in various rainbow hues. (Patrick scorned boring underwear.) She bent down and scooped desperately. "Yes, I am. Four D. Moved in last weekend."

A pair of legs strolled into view, clad in blue jeans and a battered pair of nylon Jesus sandals. "Geez, I'm sorry! Didn't mean to startle you. Let me—"

"No! I've got it." Ella scooped the last article back in the basket. Tried to find something innocuous to go on top. Something without lace. Something that wasn't hot pink. Something that didn't smell. She straightened at last and looked up. "I just wasn't expecting . . . wasn't expecting . . ."

The man laughed at her dangling sentence, as if he had no idea what had scattered her train of thought, no idea at all that he was young and dark-haired and wore a force field of tousled happiness that fried away the dampness in the basement air. "Not expecting all the washing machines full at this hour of the morning? Sorry about that, too. Just one of the quirks about life inside Eleven Christopher. I'm Hector, by the way. Top floor." He held out his hand.

Ella transferred the basket to her opposite hip and grasped his palm. Firm, steady, brief. "Hector?" she said.

"My mom's a classics professor. Was."

"She's retired?"

"No. Died a few years ago. Breast cancer."

"Oh, my God! I'm so sorry."

"Me too." He turned away and moved to the second washing machine, which had just finished a thunderous spin cycle and now sat in stupor. "Tell you what. Special deal for the newbie. You jump the queue and take over my machine, and I didn't see a thing."

"That would be so unscrupulous. What if I get caught?"

Hector tossed her a luminous grin. "In that case, I guess I'd just take the blame. Pull rank. I have seniority around here. Well, except Mrs. McDonald on the ground floor. She's been here since the Second World War. Gets an automatic laundry pass."

"Sounds like you all know each other."

"We *are* kind of a tight crew, you might say." He

moved away with his basket of wet clothes. "All yours, Four D."

"Thanks so much. I really appreciate it."

"So, that was your cue, by the way."

"My cue?"

"You're supposed to tell me your name. Unless it really *is* Four D."

"Oh! Sorry. I'm a little slow on weekends. It's Ella? Ella Gilbert."

"Nice to meet you, Ella Gilbert. Welcome to the neighborhood." He set his palms on the edge of the folding table along the opposite wall and hoisted himself up. "Don't mind me. Just waiting for that dryer to finish up."

Ella looked at the two machines, clunking in hypnotic circles.

"So what if the owner doesn't turn up in time? Is there a protocol?"

"Oh, you know. We just take the load out and fold it."

"No, seriously."

"Seriously."

"*We*, as in the other tenants? You fold each other's *laundry* around here?"

"Like I said. Tight crew."

"I guess so."

"Once you get to know everyone, I mean."

To this, Ella made a noncommittal *hunh*—get to *know* everyone? What was this, *college?*—and studied the instructions on the lid of the washer. Realized she was supposed to add the soap first. Started to unload.

"What's up? Something wrong with the washer?" Hector asked.

"Nothing, just . . . I guess you add the soap first on this model."

"Ella, I hate to have to break this to you, but it really doesn't matter. Soap first or soap after. Unless there's a soap drawer, I guess, which there isn't. Pretty basic machine."

Ella stopped with her hand on a T-shirt. "But it says—"

"So break the rules. It's okay. What's the worst that could happen?"

"I don't know. The whole laundry room floods with soap?"

Hector laughs. "You are awesome, you know that? Go ahead. I dare you. Be bad."

Ella overturned the basket into the drum, added half a cup of liquid Tide, and slammed the lid. "There. Are you happy?"

"I am. Felt good, didn't it?"

"Maybe." She turned and leaned her bottom against

the washer, an act of supreme courage because it brought her back in direct communion with Hector's face, which had the kind of fresh, animal beauty that made your eyes sting. She'd forgotten what that was like, instant attraction. Not that she hadn't encountered beautiful men since meeting Patrick; this was New York, after all, colonized by the beautiful, the brilliant, the rich. Sometimes all three in one hazardous, electromagnetic package. But falling in love with Patrick had somehow, blessedly, immunized her against fascination for somebody else. She could appreciate a man's gleaming charisma—she could say to herself, *Well, that's certainly a good-looking guy, nice style, great sense of humor*—without feeling any meaningful desire to have sex with him, even in the abstract, even in fantasy. So it was strange and shameful and utterly unsettling that when she tried to meet Hector's lupine gaze, she felt her skin heating up and her mind grasping for wit. Like some membrane had dissolved in her sensible, grown-up, married brain, unleashing an adolescent miasma. Wanting to say something sensible and thinking, *Your eyes are the color of cappuccino, can I drink you?*

"My mom was a rule-follower, too," Hector said. "It's okay. I get it. Nothing to be ashamed of."

"I'm not ashamed. You guys seriously fold each other's laundry?"

"Sure. I mean, when we *have* to. Not just because. That would be weird."

"What about—well, you know—"

He grinned again. "Unmentionables? If you feel that strongly, Queen Victoria, you can always take them up to your room and dry them on a chair arm. Me, I've got nothing to hide. Just tighty whities. Pretty boring stuff."

"You do realize we're in New York City, right? A rental building? We're not even supposed to make eye contact in the hallway."

Hector shrugged. He wore a fine-gauge V-neck sweater, charcoal gray, cashmere or merino, a bit shabby, exposing a triangle of white T-shirt at the neck. The sleeves were pushed halfway up his forearms. The blue jeans were likewise worn, but to an honest fade: not the awkward, fake threads of a pre-shredded pair. He had enviable olive skin, and maybe that was the key to his strange luminosity—this smooth, golden sheath of his that didn't show a single line, not even in the fluorescent basement lighting. Just a shadow of stubble on his jaw. Because of course he rolled out of bed like that. Stretched, shook himself. Probably drank a shot of wheatgrass and did fifty naked push-ups. "Just the way we operate around here," he said. "Band of brothers. And sisters."

"But folding laundry. Really? That's—I don't know, it's so personal."

"It's just laundry. And we *are* kind of personal around here. Anyway, you can't just dump your buddy's clothes in a pile and leave the scene. That would be wrong."

"Why wrong?"

"Do unto others, Ella. Who wants wrinkled T-shirts?"

"Then just do your laundry some other time. After work. What's with everyone jamming up the laundry room at dawn on a Saturday? I feel like I've walked into some kind of cuckoo commune."

"It's not that bad, I swear."

"Yeah, it is. It's totally a commune. And I'll bet you're the mayor."

"I don't think communes have mayors, do they? I mean, by definition?"

"You're dodging the question."

"Sorry." He hung his head a little. "Like I said, I have seniority, that's all."

"Seniority? You?"

He ran a hand through his hair, which was shaggy and dark and thick, contributing hugely to Ella's overall impression of Hector as a handsome, unkempt wolfhound. "Is it that bad? I guess I should clean up my act a little more. That's what happens when you don't spend all day working for the Man."

Ella threw up her hands. "Fine. Don't tell me anything. I'll just have to figure out all the house rules on my own. Or do my laundry on Monday nights after work."

"Actually, no. You don't want to do that. Nights are bad."

"Bad? Bad how?"

Across the room, the first dryer switched off and let out a series of frantic beeps. Hector jumped from the table. "Oops! That's me."

"Should I give you a hand?"

"Naw, I've got it."

"Are you sure? I'm feeling a disturbing need to contribute somehow."

"Ah, see? Drinking the Kool-Aid already."

Drinking something, that's for sure, Ella thought. Realized—the horror!—she was staring at Hector's backside as he bent to remove the clothes from the dryer. Like a teenager. And then she remembered, like an electric shock, *Jesus, I'm married!* The way she would sometimes have nightmares, early in her marriage, in which she was in bed with some faceless man, nobody in particular, having sex, and realized halfway through that she had a husband and she was cheating on him, and she would startle awake and stare, heart thumping, at Patrick's sleeping shoulder and feel such a drenching, horrified guilt that she actually cried. As if she had genuinely, consciously, in real life committed the crime of adultery.

Except this wasn't a dream. Hector was real. Hector and his pert backside, his unemployed, slacker hotness, stood a few yards away, had a name and a face, and now, in this altered landscape of her life, unexpected and unsought, she had no nearby husband to immunize her. No one to keep her safe from the wolfhounds of New York City.

She turned swiftly for the door. "Guess I'll be going, then!"

"Wait! Hold on a second."

Unless he wasn't real. Unless he was an actor or something, installed here as an instance of charity, or maybe a test. Or occupational therapy. She wouldn't put that kind of trick past her mother. She wouldn't put anything at *all* past her sister, even though Joanie was supposed to be studying in Paris right now.

He certainly looked like an actor. If this happened in a movie—vigorous, raven-locked guy prowls into post-breakup laundry room and purrs all the right things—you would roll your eyes and say, *Nice try.* Or you would think it was some kind of porn.

"I can't," she said over her shoulder.

"Please?"

Ella paused, hand on knob. "You're a big boy. Don't beg."

"Not begging. Just polite, like my mama taught me. So do you have a minute?"

"Not really. I've got a lot of unpacking to do."

"Wow. The brush-off. Was it something I said?"

"No, I'm sorry—"

"Don't say sorry. If I accidentally shot off some kind of sexist bullshit, just call me on it, okay? My bad."

"No! It's not that. I just—" *I'm married,* she finished in her head. Wronged, scorned, cheated upon, humiliated, separated: all those things. But also, technically, married. And I don't know if you're hitting on me or not. It's only been five minutes. But I think I might have been hitting on you. Was I? And if I was, is that morally wrong or just really, really stupid? Or something else, something that would take a therapist to explain properly and at great length and expense.

"I mean, I don't want to hold you up or anything. Just tell you about a few things. Rules of the road. In case I don't see you around, over the next few days. And you end up bringing your laundry down here at night."

"What do you mean? Are there rats or something?"

"Um, no. Not rats. I mean, there might be rats. Who knows? But probably not. No droppings or whatever." Hector's voice had turned a little uncertain, or maybe *apologetic* was a better word, and the change was so interesting that Ella now swiveled to face him. In doing so, she caught a glimpse of herself in the mirror that hung, inexplicably, above the folding table on which Hector's problematic backside had recently been resting. The greasy hair. The flushed, bare face. The baggy T-shirt.

Jesus Christ, Ella, you fucking idiot. (She never swore aloud, but her inner monologue could flame along like a Tarantino movie, when she was angry enough.) What the hell were you thinking? Of course he's not hitting on you. Unless someone's paying him to do it. Unless he pities you.

She smiled gently. "You know what? I'm sorry. Didn't mean to be rude. Just got a lot on my mind, that's all."

"No hard feelings. Moving's stressful. Right up there with death and divorce, they say. I just wanted to say that it's not Kool-Aid."

"Sorry? What's not Kool-Aid?"

"The whole thing." He slammed the dryer door on his load of wet laundry and straightened. Turned to her. Folded his arms across his lean chest. He had a loping, tensile shape to him, in keeping with the wolf-hound aspect. Patrick was more muscular, gym honed, though not quite as tall. "The Eleven Christopher thing. It's not rats, either. It's the speakeasy."

"The speakeasy? You mean like a bar?"

"Like a bar, sure." He pulled apart his arms and pointed his thumb to the wall, the one with the table and the mirror. Cinder blocks covered in gray paint. "Right there, in the basement. The other side of that wall. Starts up at night. You can hear the music and the voices. People laughing and having a good time. Sometimes you can actually feel the walls vibrate, you know, from the dancing and all that. And sometimes other stuff."

"Wow. Really? I didn't see a storefront or an entrance or anything."

"Well, that's kind of the point, with a speakeasy. You have to know it's there."

Hector fastened on her face as he said this. Giving her his full, charged attention. That friendly gaze had gone narrow, more serious, and instead of pressing the necessary buttons on the dryer he just folded his arms back across his chest and waited for her to reply. And she thought—or really, the thought arrived in her head, unsolicited—Why, he isn't young at all, is he? His eyes, they're antiques, they were born old and tanned and heavy. *Where did you come from, little old soul?* Except those were Ella's mother's words. Tucking her into bed, leaning in to kiss her forehead. The smell of Chanel. *Where did you come from, little old soul?*

She realized he was expecting a reply. She wasn't sure what to say. Was she supposed to care about the bar next door? Were the residents upset? Was there some kind of petition he wanted her to sign? This was New York; if you couldn't stand the constant interruption of the city around you, the sirens splitting your ears and the bridge-and-tunnel crowd vomiting outside your window at three in the morning, you packed up and left for the suburbs pretty fast. So what was the deal?

She asked, "Is the noise really bad? The super didn't say anything. I mean, I'm a pretty sound sleeper. More importantly," she went on, trying for a lighter note, "will they give us a house discount?"

The chuckle he returned seemed a little too nervous. Broke the strange earnestness between them. He turned to the dryer and pressed his thumb on one of the buttons. It was an old model; the buttons were large and stiff and stuck down when you pushed them. There was a click, a faint buzz of electric engagement, and then the drum began to turn, *bang bang bang.*

"House discount," Hector said. "That's a good one. But sorry, no can do."

"Bummer. What is it, some kind of secret celebrity hangout?"

"Nope. I mean, no one *we* would know. It's more of a—"

The door swung open, hitting Ella in the arm, and a small, dainty girl bounded through behind an old-fashioned wicker laundry basket. Her skin was fresh and peachy, and her hair was the color of organic honey.

"Oh my *God*! I'm so *sorry*! Are you *okay*?"

Ella rubbed her arm. "Fine."

"No, *really*. I should've looked first. I'm such a *klutz*!"

"I'm okay, really. Just leaving."

"You're the new girl, right?" She put her basket on her hip and stuck out her hand. "I'm Jen. Three C."

"Hi, Jen. I'm Ella."

Jen turned to Hector in a whip of honey hair. "Hello up there! Up to no good?"

He spread out his hands. "You know me. Sleep well?"

"All right." She ruffled his forelock. "I heard you playing."

"Just for you, babe."

"Me and all the others. Wait, isn't that machine done yet? Put my stuff on top, like, an hour ago."

"My bad. Jumped ahead of you."

"You *what?*"

"You snooze, you lose, right?"

Jen smacked him with the wicker basket. "You *creep*! That is like so *wrong*! We have a *thing* here in this building! Where's the *trust?*"

"Ow!" Hector said, rubbing his shoulder. "All right! Mea culpa. Won't happen again."

Ella spoke up. "Actually, he's covering for me. It was my laundry."

"*Your* laundry?"

"But I put her up to it," Hector said.

Jen shook her head in sorrow. "I just don't know what to say. This is so disappointing."

"I was just trying to be nice."

"Look," said Ella, "I'm sorry about the laundry. I owe you one, okay?"

"Oh, I'm not mad at you. It's *this* one." Jen jerked her thumb at Hector. "Watch out. He's notorious. Definitely can't be trusted with cute new tenants."

Ella reached for the door handle. Her stomach hurt, like she'd just taken a fist. "Yeah, um. I'll just be going now. Nice to meet you both."

"Ella, wait—"

But Ella pretended not to hear him. Let the door close on notorious Hector and dainty Jen and the four busy washing machines and two busy dryers. The table where you folded your neighbors' clothes and the wall separating you from some kind of weird, exclusive underground bar with no signage outside.

The mirror that said you were nobody's cute new tenant. Just the kind of woman who couldn't keep her husband safe in his own bed.

Saturday nights were the worst. You could keep yourself busy unpacking all day—and Ella did, until the last box was empty and broken down for recycling, until the last book was on the shelf and the last spoon in the drawer, and only the few pictures needed hanging—but once you opened the shrunken fridge and began to contemplate your few alluring options for dinner, you realized how much you took for granted in marriage.

Not that Ella hadn't before found herself alone on a Saturday night. Sometimes Patrick was overseas—some Europe junket, or else paying calls on Asia—and sometimes he had client dinners. Sometimes out with the boys. (Anyway, that was the story, which she'd never doubted until now.) But these absences were infrequent enough that she actually—if she was honest with herself—relished the freedom. She might have had dinner with Joanie (at least until Joanie left for

Paris) or her aunt and uncle (whom she adored) or even gone down to Washington to stay with her parents.

For the most part, though, she hung out with Patrick. Dinner, movie, TV. Sex. Usually sex. She took pride in keeping the electricity in her marriage. *Her* husband would never have to saw on the old chestnut that he wasn't getting any at home now that Ella had a ring on her finger. Oh, no. She almost always said yes, even when she was tired or busy with work. Ella's father looked eternally on her mother like she was Ginger and Mary Ann all rolled in one—Ella had caught them at it more than once, so embarrassing—and that was her model. That was the marriage she wanted to have. The kind everybody envied. She wanted the radiant, satisfied skin her mother had. The adoring gaze that followed her mother around the house.

Tonight, however, and for all the Saturday nights stretching into the imaginable future, there would be no sex. No cabernet and steak frites at the bistro around the corner. No twilight movie theater, laughing together at the same jokes, hands bumping in the popcorn. Just this half-empty fridge, this leftover baked ziti from the pizza place next to the subway stop. This TV set. These books. This studio apartment, the sprawling, affluent contents of her life compacted back into a single room, as if the past six years had never really occurred, as if they were just some play she had watched, some theme park she had visited, and now she was back in her rightful life.

This clock, ticking steadily into bedtime.

She ate the ziti and washed the dishes. She picked up a book she was supposed to read last year, for that book club she went to for a while, and poured herself a glass of wine. And another. Went to bed at eleven and stared at the dark ceiling. Somewhere in the building, somebody was playing a jazz CD, solo trumpet, Wynton Marsalis or something. Long and lonely and melancholy, rolling up and down the scale like it was reaching for something that didn't exist.

And then she remembered. She'd left her laundry downstairs.

The building was irredeemably old-fashioned, even though the paint was fresh and the staircase sturdy, maybe because it seemed to have largely escaped any horrifying postwar renovations or—worse—ersatz period details added back later. When she'd inspected the place last week, Ella had liked that. She wanted something different from the sleek SoHo loft she had just escaped, which they had bought two years ago when Patrick got promoted to managing director and came home with his first really serious bonus, and whatever your preference for traditional design or new, you certainly couldn't detect the handprints of some visionary, wall-demolishing architect on this place. She loved all the authentic, handmade moldings and the creaky floorboards, the quirky layout and the low-voltage lighting.

Of course, that was during the afternoon, when the winter sun had flooded softly through the old windows and turned the air gentle. Now, at nine o'clock on a Saturday night, Ella felt she was creeping downstairs through some kind of gothic novel. Or maybe that was the wine and the book—*In Cold Blood,* not the best choice for your lonely Saturday night—and the nocturnal melancholy of discovering your husband was having sex with other women. Or possibly the ziti, which sat unsteadily in Ella's stomach, like it knew it wasn't wanted.

And there was something else, something she'd noticed on her first visit. Something that had made her turn to the super and pull out her checkbook and say, *I'll take it.* Something vibrant in the air, something that lived inside the walls. Her parents' house had it. Her first apartment had had it. Her junior-year dorm had had it. The SoHo loft—gutted and cleared out and renovated to the studs from a derelict warehouse, everything old replaced by everything new—had not. Until now, turning the last corner of the stairwell, she hadn't realized just how dead that apartment was. How she'd missed the company.

So maybe it wasn't fear that she felt, reaching for the laundry room door. Maybe it wasn't dread of the unknown, or of Hector's strange warning about rats and noise from the bar and vibrating walls.

Maybe it was anticipation.

She opened the door.

ACT I

We Meet
(and it's a doozy)

NEW YORK CITY

1924

1

There's this joint on Christopher Street, a joint I'd know like the beat of my own heart, if I happened to have one. They used to call it the Christopher Club, and now it's just Christopher's. When you enter through a door in the basement of the grocery next door, you first smell the rotting vegetables and the cat piss, but never worry: all that stink clears up when the cigarettes and the liquor engulf you. And the music. The best jazz south of Ninety-Sixth Street. The bass player's a good friend of mine. Bruno. I don't know his last name; nobody does. We don't deal in surnames unless absolutely necessary.

Now, I don't inhabit the place every evening—I'm a working girl, you know, and I need my beauty sleep— but as I happen to live on the other side of said grocery, in a tiny room at the back of the fourth floor, I like to drop in from time to time, friendly-like, for a drink and a dance and a smoke and a gossip. As I'm doing now. Right there at the corner table—no, the other corner, next to the music—wearing a black dress and crimson lips and a head of strawberry hair. (The hair's natural, the lips aren't.) And that darling rosy-scrubbed black-and-white fellow I'm flirting with, the one who's taken the trouble to dress like a gentleman? That's Billy Marshall, my latest. A Princeton boy. You know the type. He's reading me this poem he's written in my honor—a real sweetie pie, my Billy-boy—but I'm afraid I'm not listening. A man's just walked through the door like a prizefighter looking for a prize, the kind of fellow who demands your immediate attention. Square shoulders, bony jaw. Plain gray suit, sharp felt hat. You know the type.

The thing is, you don't see him around a joint like this, a joint in the Village, long wooden bar and no chandelier, starving artists and starving artists' models, queers and poets, Jews and Negroes, swank babies like Billy-boy descending southward in search of local color. We haven't seen a gray suit around here since that stockbroker last year who lost his way back to the IRT station from a Bedford Street brothel on the down-low, if you know what I mean. Where he got the password, God knows. Anyway, this particular suit is cold sober, overcoat over his arm, nose as monochrome as the rest of him. Wouldn't know a good time if it kissed him on the kisser and unbuttoned his starched white shirt.

Right away, I give the eyebrows to the owner, the

man behind the bar—we call him Christopher, nobody knows his real name—and he gives the eyebrows right back, only more in the nature of a question mark. I flick the gaze back to the newcomer. Christopher makes this tiny nod and strolls down the bar, directly in the fellow's line of sight, and braces two hands on the edge of the counter, like the knots of a terribly thick rope.

"Darling," says Billy, "are you listening?"

"Of course I'm listening, sweetie. Go on."

By now, the stranger has reached the bar, along a line right down the center of Christopher's wingspan. He sets one foot on the rail and one elbow on the counter and he asks for something, I can't hear what. Over the rim of his shoulder, Christopher's eyebrows glide upward.

"You don't like it."

"I adore it! I think it's awfully clever. And those rhymes. Why, you could have Bruno here set it to music."

"It's a *sonnet*, Gin, an English sonnet. Not a music-hall song."

"You can make a lot of bread from a music-hall song."

"Who cares about money?" He seizes my hand on the table. "I care about *you*, darling. I care about taking you away from all this."

"And what if I like *all this* just fine? It sure beats the place I grew up in. Why, a joint like this is paradise compared to back home."

"You're too fine and good to be sitting here in this lousy dump. You deserve a better life, out in the country, where you don't have to lift a finger, where you don't have to spend eight hours a day in slavery to some lecherous banker, where you don't have to think about anything so crass as—"

"You know something, Billy-boy? I generally find that people who say they don't care about money are the exact same people who've never had to earn any."

"You're right. You're quite right. And that's what I want for—"

"Cherub," I say kindly, returning his hand, "will you excuse me a moment? It seems my company is required at the bar."

2

Now, before you go forming any ill opinions of me, let me assure you I've never taken a cold dime from Billy the Kid. A drink or two, maybe, but no kale.

I don't allow any gentleman to pay for the privilege of my company. I've seen too many girls get into hot water that way, and anyway Billy's such a dear fellow. We met several weeks ago at some uptown party or another—I think Julie Schuyler introduced us, she's a friend of mine, if you can call it that—and he looked at me and I looked at him, and he had this lovely sheepish clean-eared handsomeness, this scrubbed jaw and pink cheek and full lower lip, this brown eye just waiting for a match to set it smoldering. Lean, straight shoulders and new skin, his shirtfront as white and flat as pure marble, his head tilted forward and his mouth cracked open, his pink tongue fumbling for a greeting. I said, *Hello there, I'm Gin,* and he said, *I'm Billy,* and I said, *Pleased to meet you, Billy the Kid,* emphasis on the *pleased,* and he just blushed into his blond, curling hair and I fell in love. I took his hand and we danced a bit, and then we went out into the cold Manhattan morning and kissed right there on the corner of Fifth Avenue and Sixty-First Street, while the frozen branches of Central Park scratched against the nearby wind, and his lips were exactly as soft and warm as I feared. Later, he asked me if my name was really Gin, and I said no, it was Geneva, but people called me Ginger because of my hair, and Ginger became Gin. His face showed relief. I guess he was afraid I might be a drunk.

3

Unlike Billy—that tall, slender sapling, full of promise—the stranger at the bar is a live oak. Limbs thick, neck like a trunk. Ears planted on each side of his head. His shorn golden-brown hair puts me in mind of a pelt. Next to his elbow, atop the plain black overcoat, his hat contains the perfect curves of a Fifth Avenue haberdashery, the kind that charges you a mint and sends you out a gentleman. Next to his other elbow sits a glass of sweet milk, straight up.

"Evening, Gin." Christopher nods to the stranger. "Fellow was asking for you."

I point to the milk. "Make it two, will you?"

Christopher turns away, and I hold out my hand. "Ginger Kelly. I couldn't help admiring your shoulders. Do you swing from trees?"

"Not since I was ten." (Voice like a bass drum, beaten by a knotted rope.)

"Crush coconuts between your bare palms?"

"That depends on what you mean by coconuts." He takes my hand. "Oliver Anson."

"What a civilized-sounding name. Irish?"

"English."

"My mistake."

The milk lands on the counter. Christopher adds a look that asks whether I require any assistance, and I return a look that says, *Keep an eye on Billy for me, will you?* I lift my glass. "Cheers."

"Cheers."

Clink.

Drink.

The band starts a new piece, drawling, full of blues. Bruno's bass thrums up and down. The milk is ice-cold and creamy and pure on the tongue, the taste of childhood, and as I study Anson's face over the rim of the glass, I consider the contrast between his genteel clothes and his rocky, tanned face. His eyes, so dark a blue they are almost without color at all. I can usually take down the measure of a man at first glance—it's a talent of mine, the way some folks can whip up a soufflé or paint someone's face—but this one isn't adding up. A cop doesn't have the dough to dress like that. A gangster doesn't have the taste. Anyway, he's young. Not as young as Billy, but younger than I thought. The few lines on his face are new and kind of faint, as if sketched by a needle. I set down the milk.

"Tell me something, Mr. Anson. Just how did you come to know my name and whereabouts?"

"Does it matter?"

"It might. A girl making her way in the big city can't be too careful."

"I quite agree."

"And you can't trust a living soul, I've found. Always some do-gooder skulking around, you know, the vice patrol, looking to catch a girl out on the town for the crime of having a good time."

"You think I'm some kind of bull?"

"Now, what kind of question is that? We're just standing here, drinking our milk like good little boys and girls. Nothing wrong with that."

He glances at Billy and back again. "Is he yours?"

"Maybe he is and maybe he isn't. I don't believe that's any of your business."

"I think he's about to make it my business."

So Billy storms up, flushed to the temples, neck pink against his white collar, and inserts himself between me and Anson. Demands to know what the devil he thinks he's doing. They're the exact same height, maybe six feet and a hair of the dog, but I believe Billy weighs about half as much. Anson replies to this perfectly legitimate question with the polite tolerance you might lay on a stale doughnut. Says something about having a private word with me.

"Well, you *can't* have a private word with her."

"Can't I?"

"No. Miss Kelly has *nothing* to do with you, nothing at all. She's here with *me*, do you understand? Minding our own business."

"I see." Mr. Anson finishes his milk, lays a dollar bill on the counter. Collects his hat and his overcoat. Nods to me in such a way that you could almost call it a bow. "A pleasure, Miss Kelly."

"All mine, Mr. Anson."

He walks away, leaving that whole dollar bill unchanged on the counter, straight up the steps and out the door, and Billy turns to me, all bright and crackly with triumph, the dear young thing.

"Well! I sure as hell showed *him*, didn't I?"

4

The powder room at the back of Christopher's isn't much to speak of, and I've seen a crapper or two in my time. I mean, it's a basement of a basement. What are you going to do? There's about enough room to swing a cat, if you're the kind of damned brute who swings cats, and your cat belongs to a pygmy tribe. The tiles are black and white, the mirror's chipped, the sink bears the stains of a thousand furtive cigarettes. The toilet's liable to flush you down whole, if you're not careful. In the corner, there's a narrow ventilation shaft—I use the term loosely—leading to the stinking back garden of the next-door grocery, and I am presently contemplating said shaft as a means of possible escape. Not from poor Billy—whose bravery in the face of Tarzan has just about melted down the sides of that place in my chest where the heart's supposed to lie—but from the nearby army of New York's finest, who, I feel certain, await only a flicker of Tarzan's eyelashes to storm the building in thunderbolts of moral righteousness.

Now, if I stand on the toilet, the pig might just fly. I've got the figure for it, thanks to poverty and cigarettes. On the other hand, who wants to die in a ventilation shaft?

You may be surprised to hear this, but when I first arrived on Manhattan Island two years ago, wearing my heart on my sleeve and ten additional pounds around my hips, I had never once sipped the nectar of juniper nor breathed the leaf of tobacco. It's true! My dear mother had scraped and saved to send me to a nice Catholic school fifty miles away, and I'll be damned if those nuns didn't have their wicked way with me. A year of college didn't improve matters, what with the

Wagnerian dorm mother and the scarcity of men. So there I stood in the middle of Pennsylvania Station, in a hat and a sweet pink coat, clutching the tiny valise that contained my all, just like every starlet who's ever set foot in her land of dreams, and I thought I had made a terrible mistake, that I would never belong in this sea of stink and vice, this hive of determined bees lining their cells with honey. And then I tasted the *honey, honey,* and I started to understand what New York City was all about. Hallelujah. I started to glimpse my place in the hive, how each tiny insect contributed her mite of pollen, how grand it was to live in a hive like this at all, even if your cell measured one inch square and lacked proper ventilation, even if you had to pawn your favorite shoes each month to pay the milkman for a quart of milk, even if—well, you get the idea. The point of Manhattan is that you occupy a cell in the hive at all. That you belong. That you have your seat at the Christopher Club bar, and that seat, if you're clever, can propel you from a typing pool downtown to a swank party uptown to the front of a camera in a tatty Village studio, so any man with a nickel in his pocket can admire the tilt of your tits.

And I'll be damned if I'm ready to give up my seat just yet.

I set one foot on the lid of the toilet. Brace my hand

on the wall. Hoist my bones upward and upward to the hole in the ceiling, fill my lungs with the reek of sewage, and then, of course, comes the exact second the boots clamor down the hallway and the door flies open, and the powder room fills with gentlemen of blue suits and billy clubs, unamused by my predicament.

5

About those nuns.

Maybe I was a little unfair, a moment ago. There's nothing like a good convent education, as I often tell my gentleman friends, and even my lady ones. Your knuckles may suffer and your knees may burn, but the poetry and the multiplication tables are yours for eternity. Along with the guilt, but who doesn't need a little shame from time to time, to keep her on the straight and narrow? Anyway, there was this one sister, Sister Esme, who loved me best, and to prove it she rapped my knuckles the hardest and sent me to penance the longest. When I turned seventeen, she called me into her office—about as inviting as an Assyrian tomb—and gave me a beautiful Bible, in which

she had painstakingly marked all the passages she
thought relevant to my character, such as it was. You
can imagine. She told me that of all the girls who had
filtered through her classroom, I was the most unruly,
the smartest-mouthed, the least tractable, the most ir-
religious and argumentative, and she fully expected to
hear great things from me. She also said (assuming a
terribly serious mien) that she had one single piece of
advice for me, which was this: I owed confession only
to God. Not to my fellow man, not to my instructors,
not *even* to my parents (this accompanied by a signifi-
cant slant to the eyebrows). And most especially (her
voice grew passionate) not to any person, howsoever
persuasive, howsoever threatening, belonging to the
judiciary branch of the government, whether local,
state, or federal. My conscience belonged to my Maker,
and to Him alone. Did I understand?

Well, naturally I didn't. Lord Almighty, I was only
seventeen! I had so little experience of the world outside the walls of that school. But—in the usual way of
childhood advice—Sister Esme's words return to me
with new meaning as I slouch upon a metal bench in
my cell at the Sixth Precinct, cheek by miserable jowl
with the other female patrons of the Christopher Club
that January midnight.

Now, I don't mean to startle you, but I've never

landed in the pokey until tonight, though you might say the visit's overdue. I guess the place is about what I expected. We're a tawdry lot, sunk into nervy, silent boredom. Dotty's chewing her nails; Muriel's worrying a loop of sequins on her sleeve, such as it is. One girl, gaunt and ravishing, leans cross-armed against the damp concrete wall, staring right through the bars to the tomato-faced policeman on the chair outside. She's too beautiful for him, and he knows it. Looks everywhere but her. I don't know her name, but I've seen her around. She's wearing a shimmering silver dress, ending in a fringe, and her arms are white and bare and cold. Someone once told me she was Christopher's girl, and I guess it might be true. Nobody ever bothers *her* for a smoke and a dance, for example. She sits by herself most nights at the end of the bar, staying up past bedtime, sipping cocktail after cocktail, trailing a never-ending cigarette from her never-ending fingers, disguising the color of her eyes behind ribbons of smoldering kohl. The kohl's now smudged, but the smolder remains. Liable to ignite the poor cop's tomato head any second. She gave her name as Millicent Merriwether—I pay close attention to these details, see—but then none of us told the booking rookie our genuine monikers. Where's the fun in that? And I'll be damned if this vamp is a Millie.

There's a clock on the wall, above Tomato-Head's cap. A damned slow clock, if you ask me. For the past half an hour, I've amused myself in priming my nerves for every twitch of the minute hand, moving us sixty seconds farther into the morning, and each time I'm early. Each time I teeter on the brink, unable to breathe, thinking, *Now!* and *Now!* and *Now!* until finally the stinking hand moves. As amusements go, it's a real gas. Millie the Vamp turns her head and regards me from the corner of one pitying eye. I shrug and resume my study. By the time three o'clock jumps on my spinal cord without any kind of notice from our hosts, without any sign at all that anyone's left alive in the rest of the Sixth Precinct station house, I've had it. I call out to Tomato-Head.

"I don't guess a girl could bum a cigarette, if she asks nicely?"

He makes this startling movement. Clutches his cap. Turns from tomato to raspberry.

"No? I guess rules are rules." I lift my hands and stretch, an act that creates an interesting effect on my décolletage, don't you know. "I don't mean to be a nuisance, officer, but I do have a breakfast appointment I'd rather not miss. And this fellow happens to prefer me scrubbed up and smiling, if you know what I mean."

Tomato-Head looks to the ceiling for relief.

"Now, don't be embarrassed. We're just a mess of girls, here, the nicest girls in the world. It's a shame, the way they turn honest girls into criminals these days, don't you think?"

"Oh, shut your flapper, Gin," Dotty says crossly. "It ain't his fault."

"No, of course not. Poor little dear. He's just doing his job. Why, I'll bet he's seen the inside of a juice joint or two himself, when he's not on duty. He doesn't look like teetotal to me, no sir. He looks like the kind of fellow who enjoys a nice time on the town, likes to make a little whoopee—"

"Says you."

"Don't you think? A friendly-faced cop like that? I'll bet he's on our side."

"Him?"

"Sure. Because why? Because it's the first time the joint's been raided, isn't it? And Christopher's been around since the start of the Dark Ages. So—"

"Oh, give it up."

"So I say there's a rat. A rat in the house. Somebody squealed, didn't they? Hmm, officer?"

Tomato-Head chews his lips and looks ashamed.

"You see? Someone ratted Christopher out. I'll bet it's someone on the inside, too. I'll bet—"

Millie turns so fast, her fringed hem takes a minute

to catch up. "Be quiet, Ginger, for God's sake. You don't know a thing."

In all the excitement, my legs have come uncrossed. I sit back against the wall and lift the right pole back over the left. Slide my arms back together over my cold chest. Bounce my shoe a little. Bounce, bounce. "Seems I'm right, then. The question is who."

She narrows her eyes until they just about disappear between the charcoal rims. Turns away and says, into thin air, "No. The question is whom."

"La-de-da. Someone's got an education."

"So do you, Ginger. I'm just not ashamed to show it."

There's the littlest emphasis on the word *Ginger,* which those of you born with fire in your hair will recognize. I consider the back of Millie's neck, and the exact tender spot I'd stick a needle, if she were one of those voodoo dolls they sell in seedy little Harlem shops. Behind my shoulders, the wall is cold and rough and damp, and the air smells of mildew. Our guard yanks a packet of cheap cigarettes from his breast pocket and starts a smoke. The brief illumination of the match scorches my eyes. Three oh four. Ticktock. As the familiar scent of tobacco drifts across my teeth, the eyelids start to droop. The vision of Millie's pale, smooth neck starts to blur. Not ashamed to show it, Ginger. Not ashamed, Ginger. *Ginger. GINGER!*

An elbow cracks my ribs.

"Ginger! Jesus! Wake up, will you?"

I straighten off somebody's shoulder. Adjust my jaw. Blink my eyes. Test my bones for doneness. You know how it is.

"Ginger Kelly?" A man's voice, a man from Brooklyn or someplace.

"I'm afraid I don't know anyone by that name."

"Tell that to the judge," Brooklyn replies, and the next thing I know the keys jingle-jangle, the cell clangs open, the handcuffs go snap around my wrists, and let me tell you, when a girl hears that much metal rattling around in her neighborhood, she'd better start sending up every prayer the nuns ever taught her, sister, because the devil's at the door and the Lord don't care.

6

My thoughts turn to Billy as this uniformed meathead drags me down the corridor, past this cell and that cell, contents murky and unknown. I wonder where they put the poor boy, whether they let him off because he's a Marshall, whether he's frantic about me now. Of course he is. That's the kind of fellow he is. Dear Billy-boy. I guess I shouldn't feel this kind of regret; after all, I didn't exactly lead him blindfolded down the path of debauchery. Debauchery found him before I did. That first kiss wasn't his first, and he knew one end of a martini glass from the other. Still. But for me, he might have spent the evening in the convivial atmosphere of his eating club, idly debating such innocent matters as the blackballing of unsuitable freshers and the prospects of the Tiger baseball team for the season upcoming, instead of getting himself arrested for consumption of Gin.

But no lovesick voice wails my name—either real or assumed—as I stumble past the cages of the Sixth Precinct station house, and when we reach the stairs at the end of the corridor I conclude I'm simply *sola, perduta, abbandonata.* The old story. The stairs lead rightward up to the booking desk, but Officer Brooklyn turns left instead, opening a metal door with a metal key, and the sharp garbage breath of a late January alleyway strikes my nose like a billy club.

"Say! What's the big idea?" I demand, but Brooklyn takes no notice, just tightens his paw around my bare upper arm and hauls me up the steps to alley level, where a black sedan rattles and coughs next to the sidewalk, rear door open, exhaust clouding the atmosphere in a great gasoline fog.

And you'll forgive me for hoping that the dear, familiar head of my Billy-boy will pop free from the smoke of that backseat—the final death of my native optimism is still some weeks away—but there's only room for two on the leather bench, and Brooklyn, pushing me inside, clambers in right behind me. *Go,* he grunts, and the tires squeal and the car lurches from the curb, and my forehead hits the front seat, and nobody says *Sorry* or even *You all right?* Nobody offers me a cigarette or an overcoat. We just zigzag down the frozen, bitter streets of the Village, straightening out at Fourteenth Street, while my teeth chatter and my brain aches, and a thousand smart remarks rise to my lips. I bite them all back, of course, because for one thing I can tell Officer Brooklyn hasn't got the intellect to appreciate them, and for another—well, anyway. I merely observe aloud that we seem to be headed to the Hudson River piers—obvious enough—and Brooklyn grunts something or other that might mean *Yes* or else *Shut your yap,* and silence reoccupies the cab, except for the hum of the engine and the steam of our breath. I sit back and make myself small against the cold. When we slam to a stop outside a rusty tenement at Tenth Avenue and Twenty-Second Street, I permit myself a tick of triumph. You can hear the shouts of the stevedores, the busy clang of ocean liners obtaining coal and stores. If I'm not mistaken, those three black-tipped funnels over there, finding the moon above the triangular tips of the Chelsea docks, belong to the great RMS *Majestic* herself. Bound for England tomorrow morning. Lucky bitch.

But for now. The tenement. That's my real concern, because Officer Brooklyn is opening the door and dragging me across the seat to the crumbling sidewalk outside, and those sallow brick walls aren't looking any more inviting on second glance. An old saloon occupies the ground floor, windows all boarded up, and a few piles of hardened gray slush decorate the flagstones outside. My pretty shoes slide right out from under me. I don't think Brooklyn even notices; he just carries my weight on the slab of his right arm as I glissade across the granite. Behind us sounds the imperative whistle-chug of a New York Central steam engine, hauling freight up the middle of Tenth Avenue. He doesn't notice that, either. Just bangs on the door next to the boarded-up saloon until it opens.

"Oh, no," I say. "Not on your life."

Brooklyn turns his head at last. He's not a pretty fellow, our Brooklyn, all jaw and no forehead, eyes like a pair of walnuts begging for a nutcracker. Shoulders about to burst from a plain uniform-type navy over-coat. The raw color of his nose and cheeks suggests either excessive cold or excessive whiskey, though you can't rule out both. Or even possibly some kind of emotion. Those walnut eyes goggle almost out of his skull, and who can blame him? I'm about half his size, a third his weight. My hands are cuffed at the back, and I can't feel my toes.

"I bite, you know," I add.

Brooklyn shakes his head and pulls me through the doorway. A sign flashes by, one of those brass plaques, sort of tarnished, but you don't stop to read plaques when someone's hauling you into a tenement to commit the Lord only knows what foul crimes on your person. Your mind spins, your stomach lurches. Your eyes fasten instead on inconsequential details, like the rough woolen texture of Brooklyn's sleeve, and the overlapping pattern of scuffs on his brown shoes, and the worn-out sway in the center of each step, right where your foot goes, and the cold, moldy smell of the joint. You think, Damn it, this might be my last sight on earth, why can't I find something beautiful? As if it matters. And all those taxis and fancy private automobiles will be lining up in the dawn smoke, one by one, to disgorge humanity onto the gangplanks of the god-damned *Majestic*, and no one will notice the item in the newspapers the next day, about a woman found dead in a Tenth Avenue tenement: some kind of prostitute, the detectives believe, and from the state of the corpse she must have put up a good fight.

Because I will, by God. Put up a good fight. I'm putting up a fight right now, kicking and biting, deboning my limbs such that I slither momentarily from the shelf of Brooklyn's arm, only to be scooped up again and hauled into oblivion. But there's nothing to bite except wool and glove, nothing to kick that actually notices it's been kicked. We swing around the landing and up another flight, and I'm breathless now, panting and jabbering, while the stained walls slide past, the color of misery, lurid bare electric bulbs, linoleum hallway, door thrown open by muscular hand, Gin thrown inside, toe catching on edge of Oriental rug, crash splat. Voice like a hurricane. "What the devil, Bulow? She's not a sack of grain."

"She's a damned hellcat. Bit my cheek."

"I expect you deserved it."

Have you ever donned a narrow dress and metal handcuffs, laid yourself out flat on a beery Oriental rug, and then tried to rise? Well. It's not as easy as it sounds, believe me. All the dignity of an eel on a hook. Still. I've just about got my knees under me when a pair of hands clamps around the joints of my shoulders and lifts me straight into the air and back down on my feet. Spins me around, demands a key from Brooklyn. Brooklyn delivers, though his face suggests he'd rather swallow it whole. Seems he's right, I did bite his cheek. What do you know. Fresh, new blood trickles to his jaw. The handcuffs loosen. Brooklyn steps back and folds his arms across his three-foot chest. I hate to boast, but he does look sort of mauled. Nasty scratch on the side of his neck. I stretch my wrists and wriggle my nerveless fingers and turn to face his boss, whose face bears down on mine like a mountainside. Not that I'm the kind of girl who backs down from mountains. Not me.

I tap his chin with a schoolmarm finger.

"Tarzan. I had a hunch you were up to no good."

7

The first thing Tarzan does is return to his desk and press some kind of button. Then he rests one haunch on the desk, folds his hands together, and asks me if I want coffee. I say why not. Door opens, feminine voice makes inquiry. Coffee for Miss Kelly, please. Door closes. No word from Brooklyn; maybe he's gone.

Tarzan gestures stage left. "Please sit down, Miss Kelly. I expect you're exhausted."

"No, thanks. I'd rather stand."

"You're certain?"

"Quite. Is this your office? I love what you've done with the place. All those padded armchairs and old masters. And that thrilling modern wallpaper! Or have you got a leak?"

"It's a place of employment, not a parlor."

"Oh, *employment*! I'm glad you mentioned it. What exactly *is* your line of work, Mr. Tarzan?"

"My name is Anson."

"Mr. Anson."

"And my job, put simply, is to intercept the illegal transportation and sale of intoxicating liquors."

"Lord Almighty. You're a Revenue agent."

He shrugs.

"Well, that's a relief. I can confidently say that you've got the wrong girl, Agent Anson. I'm more in the consumption line, if you know what I mean. Transportation and sale is not my concern."

"Not at the moment, maybe," he says, "but it will be."

"Now, see. That's just exactly what I didn't want you to say."

"Your choice, of course. But I do hope you'll help us. Good, here's the coffee."

Thank the Lord for the pause that ensues. Allows me to haul in my breath, corral the runaway gallop of my heartbeat. Wipe my palms on my sequins while everyone's turned to the poor young secretary in the navy suit and cream blouse who carries in the coffee on an old enamel tray, the kind your parents might have brought out to entertain callers in a more civilized age. As it turns out, Brooklyn hasn't left the room after all. He's taken a chair near the door, a poor spindly thing that shudders under his weight. (The chair, I mean, not the door.) I take my cup—cream, one lump—and carry it to the seat I refused earlier, which looks as if it were bought cheap from the shuttered saloon downstairs.

"Are you cold, Miss Kelly?" Anson asks as the door closes behind the minion.

"Not at all."

"You look blue."

"I'm just mad."

He removes his jacket, walks around behind me, swings the old thing over my shoulders. I consider shrugging it off, just on principle, but a jacket like that trumps any principle you care to possess. Wholesome silk lining, sensuous warmth, scent of shaving soap. Is there anything more delicious than a gentleman's wool coat cloaked around your shoulders? Even when the gentleman's not yours.

"Why are you angry?" he asks, returning to the desk.

"Let me count the ways."

He casts a cool look in Brooklyn's direction. "I apologize for my methods."

"As you should. I'm bruised all over. I'd show you where, if I weren't a lady."

"But aside from the physical harm—"

"Oh, aside from little old *that*—"

"I had no choice. I couldn't just ask you to come of your own free will. You wouldn't have agreed, for one thing, and frankly I needed a little of what the financiers call leverage."

"Leverage?"

He places a thumb next to the corner of his mouth and brushes away an imaginary something-or-other. "Mr. Marshall."

"*Billy!* What have you done with Billy?"

"He's not in any danger. Not at the moment, anyway."

"You've got no right. He's as innocent as a lamb."

"A lamb. And you, Miss Kelly? Are you innocent as a lamb?"

"I have the feeling you already know the answer to that. I'm as innocent as the next girl, I guess."

Anson gives the ceiling some mature consideration.

"Now, see here, Mr. Anson. We both know you've got no business persecuting a working girl like me for taking a sip or two of this and that. I'm not the crook. It's those gangsters out there on the Lincoln Highway in the middle of the night, it's that hillbilly with a dozen stills blowing off the roof of his barn—"

Snap go the fingers of Anson's right hand. "Is that so, Miss Kelly? *Hillbillies?* What do you know about hillbillies?"

I could swear the lightbulb flickers in its socket above my head. But maybe it's just the lightbulb going off inside my head, the *Jesus Mary, Gin, you dumb cluck!* hollering up from my unconscious mind: the part of your head that does all your best thinking, everybody says. Too late now. Outside the window, New York lies nice and quiet, the dark night speckled with various pinpricks of human activity, of people not giving a damn what happens here in this room at this particular hour of the twenty-four. A few feet away, Anson's granite face stares and stares, no expression whatsoever, calm as you please.

Just a word. But what a word. *Hillbillies*, Miss Kelly. What do you know about hillbillies?

"Nothing," I lie.

"Nothing at all?"

"Nope."

"Because you sounded, just now, like a woman who knows something."

"I'm a working girl, Mr. Anson. A New York working girl. I get my news like everyone else. The morning paper. You can learn a lot about the world from the morning paper, but it doesn't mean you know one single mite more than the next girl."

Anson shifts position, leaning back against the desk, both hands curled around the edge. It's the kind of angle that displays the girth of his quadriceps to their absolute maximus, such that you imagine they might rip free from all that civilized wool and sock you in the stomach. Absent a coat, his shirtsleeves show up like snow in the gray, dark room. I would say there's something colorless about him altogether, like he's put on a mask of ice: that good, thick Adirondack ice they haul down from those lakes upstate. You could pick and pick and never draw blood. A fine pair, we are. The coffee cup sits untouched on his left side, sending up steam.

"But every New York working girl comes from somewhere, doesn't she, Miss Kelly?" He lifts one hand away from the desk and gestures to the window. "Nobody's born here."

"That's not true. A lot of girls are born here."

"Not you. You're a country girl, aren't you? The far end of Maryland, isn't that right? Small town called River Junction, I believe."

At this point, the edges of the room go a little dark.

I'd like to take a sip of coffee—poor thing's getting cold, sitting there in my lap like that—but I'm afraid my hand will tremble. So I just clench the handle with my right thumb and forefinger, while I clench the saucer with the left. Sew my lips into a smile. Focus my vision on the tip of Anson's oversized nose. The cleft at the tip of his damned chin, chipped from ice.

He moves. Picks up his coffee with a steady hand. Sips, savors. Savors what, I don't know. It's just black coffee, nothing else. You have to be a brute to drink coffee like that, a brute as bitter as the brew you're swallowing.

"Tell me, Miss Kelly," he says, setting down the cup in the saucer and resuming his pose against the desk, legs crossed at the ankles, not a care in the world, "when was the last time you saw your stepfather?"

8

As it so happens, I can name the exact hour I last saw my stepfather, though I'm not going to inform Special Agent Oliver Anson of the Bureau of Internal Revenue of that fact. I'm not going to inform Anson of anything, see, because the word *informer*, where I come from, carries about the same ugly weight of blasphemy as the word for a man who engages in a certain intimate act with his nearest maternal relation, from time to time. (Yes, that word.) So what I'm about to say remains right here betwixt you and me, understand? Nobody likes a rat.

The hour was dawn. End of August, nineteen hundred and twenty. Hot as the dickens. Yours truly was up early, gathering the eggs from the miserable henhouse out back, while the sunlight crept down the mountainside and the warm mist coated the grass. In another week, I was supposed to be heading back to college, and by God I should have been counting down the seconds. Not that I especially loved college and the sneering razor-nosed girls who inhabited the joint, oh no. You see, by the time of that burning August of 1920, River Junction had taken on all the aspects of an earthly perdition for me. That's why I woke up early—not because the eggs needed gathering, although they did, but because nobody else was up. You could stand there in the middle of the chicken coop and watch the creeping of the sun, the stir of the mist, the slow, deliberate greening of the landscape, and your only company was the hens. The birds whistling good morning from the branches of a nearby birch. The damp earth smelling of loam and chicken shit. You know the feeling. Your feet planted firm in the center of all Creation.

Until *he* turned up, anyway.

He. Him. My mother's husband. Name of Dennis, but everybody calls him Duke. Duke Kelly. The dear soul was so kind as to bequeath me his surname when he married my mother, and I do believe he's been aiming to collect the debt in installments ever since.

Now, first and foremost, you have to understand that everybody in River Junction loves Duke. Loves him! He's not the mayor, but he's the next closest thing: the mayor's best pal. Friendly fellow, every brick of him mortared with charm. Dresses in clean, neat clothes; brushes back his dark, curling mane with just the right dollop of peppermint hair oil. You'd like him too, if you happened to be stopping in River Junction for a cup of coffee at the depot café, and he happened to be sitting at the next table drinking his own cup of coffee and smoking a cigarette he'd rolled himself right then. He would strike up a conversation with you, ask you where you were headed, tell you that's a right nice-looking car you got out there, or else if your car's a jalopy, remark on your right nice-looking wife. Offer you a cigarette and a light. If you needed directions, say, he would sit down with you and your map and show you the exact best route to your destination, where to pick up a couple gallons of gas if you need them, and you would leave town thinking that River Junction was an awful nice place, nice people, that's what's grand about America, don't you think, small towns like River Junction and the folks who live there. Salt of the earth. And I'm not saying you'd be wrong.

So I was standing in the chicken coop, as I said, basket of eggs hooked over my elbow, armpits a little damp already even though the sun hadn't yet touched us, there in the holler of two mountains that constitutes the geographic boundaries of River Junction. I heard the soft tread of footsteps on wet grass, the wiry squeak of the chicken coop door. My stomach fell.

"Hello there, Geneva Rose," he said. "You's up awful early this morning."

"Eggs wanted gathering."

"That so?"

"Every morning."

"You need a hand, maybe?"

"No, thanks."

"Lemme give you a hand."

"I said no thanks. I like to stand out by myself, in the morning."

"Well, now. That ain't too friendly, honey."

I shrugged.

"Why don't you just turn about and look at me, Geneva Rose? Turn about and say good morning to your old daddy."

"You ain't my daddy," I said, but I turned around anyway, kind of slow, so I might fix my face in just the right expression as I went. Stiff and stony, so he couldn't see what I was thinking. Couldn't tell the revulsion coiling around my guts at the sight of his shining hair, his smooth, tanned skin, his blue eyes like the color of summer. His full lips stretched in a smile, just wide enough that you could see the tips of his teeth, golden with tobacco, right upper incisor chipped at the corner from a fall out the saloon door four years back. Or that was the story, anyway. I never was there when it happened.

"You ain't got no call to speak to me like that, Geneva Rose Kelly. When I reared you up like you was my own. Sent you off to school like your mama wanted. Never asked no questions. Never treated you no different."

Well, I could dissect the falsehoods in that speech one by one, the way they taught me in college: how to disassemble somebody's argument like you might disassemble a chicken for frying. Not that any of the other girls at college had ever fried a chicken, my goodness no, let alone plucked it and pieced it and dipped it in flour. But I didn't pick those words apart. Not out loud. Dear reader, I am no idiot.

"And I appreciate that kindness, Duke. I really do. But I'm not your daughter, and that's a fact. And I never was any good at pretending things that aren't true."

"Just listen to you, baby girl. Sounding like some kind-a lady. Like one-a them grammar books or something. You learn to talk that way at college? You set to thinking you're too good for your old daddy?"

"Course not."

"Because that's how it sounds to me, Geneva Rose."

"Well, that ain't how it is."

"Now, that's better." He nodded and reached for my cheek. "That's more like my baby girl. You was but two years old when I laid eyes on you. When your mama come back home from New York City. Prettiest baby I ever seen."

I turned my head away. Took a step back. The smell of his hair oil stung my nostrils. The smell of his shaving soap. He wore a blue checked shirt, same color as his eyes, tucked into dungarees held high by plain black suspenders. Sweat already beading at his temples. Lips red and damp.

"Don't you go a-larking off, baby girl," he crooned. "Ain't nobody up around here excepting you and me. Your mama's still abed."

"She won't be long."

"Sure she will, sugar. She don't rise herself up till noon sometimes. Just a-drinking and a-staring at the ceiling, your mama."

His breath smelled like cigarettes. Wee dram of brown skee, too, if I wasn't mistaken. Liquid courage, to use another word for it, which maybe explained what he was doing there in that chicken coop, in the thick August dawn while my mother slept in her bed, one week less a day before I should have been leaving for my second year of college.

"Baby girl," he said. "Don't you be shy, now. I'll treat you right. You know I will. I treat everybody right that treats me right."

"I think you best be fixing to get back inside that house, Duke Kelly," I said. Edging to the right. Clear line for the frail wire-screen door of the coop. The patch of sun on the opposite slope was falling fast now. The air turning to a foggy gold. "You best fix to get back inside before somebody sees you out here."

"Who's a-going-a see us? Ain't nobody up. Not on a hot old morning like this-un."

I kept on staring at his nose without looking, imagining some kind of shade between our two faces, I guess, some kind of blind, so I wouldn't be giving myself away. Another rightward step.

"Johnnie's up, I reckon. Johnnie's always up early."

"Johnnie don't know from nothing. Now just you stop yourself a-moving about like that, Geneva Rose. Let me get a look at you. See how you filled out this summer. Almost a woman grown now, ain't you? Just almost."

So I froze up, and you would, too, if you'd heard his voice like that, like the purr of an African cat, chilling your young bones from the inside out, worrying down your spine. Or maybe you wouldn't. Maybe I'm the only one who hears that bass snarl of malice in Duke Kelly's voice. Everybody else just thinks he's a real nice fellow. Anyway, I froze up, paralysis of fear, muscles all stuck in their joints, such that I didn't even flinch when Duke's big hand came to rest on the collar of my dress.

"That's better," he said. "That's my good baby girl."

I waited and waited while that hand crawled all over my bosom, pinching and squeezing. While that voice crawled over my ears. I waited until he came in close with his mouth open, panting hot on my face, cheeks smudged red, and then I drove my fist into his stomach hard as I could, knocking his rank skee breath right from his belly, and then I ran. Ran straight through the door of that chicken coop, ripping the wire, ripping my skin, and then I did a stupid thing. See, I should have gone into the house, where Mama and the boys lay asleep, where Johnnie sat eating his porridge at the kitchen table, spoon by spoon with a drop of molasses, but I was so scared I wasn't thinking straight. I ran for the creek instead, dumb bunny as I was back then, ran for the creek and the old fishing hole where we used to spend our summer afternoons, me and the boys, when I was home from school. Of course, the creek was screened by willows and thick with skeeters, and nobody came down there at that time of day, nobody at all, and you couldn't hear nobody talking or screaming from down there, either, on account of the trees and the way the creek makes a holler betwixt two sloping banks, see, into which all these sounds find themselves trapped like crawdads at the bottom of a wooden barrel.

So why did I make for the creek? God knows. Just a young, dumb bunny as I was back then. Not thinking straight.

9

Anyway. I'm nobody's bunny any longer. What I tell that nice special revenue agent is this: "I'm afraid I don't recollect exactly, Mr. Anson. Why do you ask?"

"You've had no relations at all with your family since you left River Junction in the summer of 1920?"

"Say. That's a personal question."

He shrugs those shoulders of his. Checks his wristwatch. Sips coffee, sighs, turns his head to the window as if to make certain that Manhattan still exists out there, rattling and shouting and drinking and fornicating. A delicate glow passes across the bridge of that hefty nose. Headlights of some nocturnal automobile.

"Have all night, do you?" I say.

"If necessary."

"My goodness. Is old Duke so important as that?"

"Yes."

"Can't you give me a hint?"

He turns back to me. "Do I need to give you a hint? You seem like a clever woman, Miss Kelly. I'm sure you've already guessed the nature of my interest in your stepfather."

"I haven't laid eyes on River Junction in nearly three and a half years, Mr. Anson. If my stepfather's set himself up in a little business since then, taking advantage of the difference between what one half of the country wants and what the other half doesn't want them to get, why, I don't know a thing about it."

Anson places his cup and saucer back on the desk and walks across the few yards of thready Oriental carpet to where I sit in my chair, all folded shut like a clam at low tide. The silk lining over my shoulders responds with an electric ripple. Or maybe that's the nerves underneath. Each button of Anson's plain waistcoat is done right up, not a stitch loose, not a single flaw in the weave of fine gray wool, and the reason I can report these details is because he's come to rest about a foot away, not even that. I do expect I can tell you the brand of starch stiffening the cuffs of his sleeves. From this angle, his head looks like a prehistoric skull, all bone.

He sinks to one knee, right there next to my chair, and lays his right forearm over his thigh. His eyes are larger than I thought, more charcoal than blue, the color of winter.

"Not a *little* business, Miss Kelly. Your stepfather has built a network of distilleries across Allegany County and beyond, and nobody will say a word against him. I don't know if they love the man or if they're plain scared, or if they're on the take."

"All three, I do expect."

"In two years, the Bureau hasn't been able to make a dent in his business, not a single arrest. A few months ago, two of our best men disappeared out there."

"My condolences. What's the world coming to, when a Prohi can't just take a little lettuce in his back pocket and keep his blood on the inside?"

"*My* agents don't accept bribes, Miss Kelly."

"You don't say? Because a little birdie tells me they'd be the first."

"They're good men with families. Wives and children."

"Well, I'm sorry to hear that. Do *you* have a wife and children, Mr. Anson?"

A slow blink, like a reptile. "That's a personal question, Miss Kelly."

"Oh, I *see*! *I'm* the one who's supposed to spill all the beans in this room, isn't that right, while you get to keep your beans to yourself. Seems you've got a nice little racket of your own, Anson. A nice little racket."

He breathes in slow, regular drafts from a pair of gargantuan lungs. Fresh coffee on his breath and nothing else, not tobacco nor liquor nor money, just good clean virtue.

"You see? It's all a matter of perspective, isn't it? There was this painter I used to sleep with, when I first came to New York. A real wisenheimer. He taught me about a lot of things. He taught me all about perspective. How you can change the essence of an object, the soul of it, you can change this thing entirely just by looking on it some different way. But you know what? I'll bet you already knew that. Something tells me you know a lot about art, don't you, Mr. Anson? Expensive art, the kind they hang in museums and fancy Fifth Avenue apartments. You know from perspective, I'll bet."

"I understand the concept."

"You think you're the good guy, don't you, Mr. Anson? You think you're some kind of honest-to-goodness knight, riding into River Junction on your fine white charger to do away with that dastardly villain with the twirling mustache. Cover yourself with medals. Laurels on your head, damsels on your arm. I wonder what you'd say if you knew how it looks from where I'm sitting."

"So tell me."

I turn a little on my hip on that chair, so we're face-to-face, terribly intimate, the way you turn to your lover in bed. Prop my elbow on the back of the chair. Drape one leg over the other. His knee's no more than an inch from my own.

"Why, you look exactly the same, you and my stepfather. You take me by surprise. Haul me to your lair. Corner me where I can't strike back. Hold someone dear over my head, just to make sure I play along. You and Duke, you just want to get a little something out of me, whether I like it or not, and you don't ever mean to pay me back for my trouble."

Well, if I was hoping to get a little flicker out of him, some sign of impact, forget it. You might as well chip emotion from a glacier. Just those wintry eyes, staring at me. Those fingers hanging downward from his thigh, thick and knobbled. Scar on his chin. On his forehead. Lashes black and plentiful. The room throbs around us, the city throbs around the room. A block or two away, the boats skate silently across the Hudson River, hauling in booze, hauling in contraband everything in an unstoppable swarm, like the skeeters back home, too small and quick and clever for you to swat.

Without warning, the fingers flex. A few quick strikes, like the twitches of a dying man.

"I have neither wife nor children, Miss Kelly," he says. "Your turn."

"All right. Here's my turn: Duke Kelly's a cold-blooded bastard, and I'll turn myself in at the nearest precinct before I trundle back to River Junction like some poor sucker and help you catch him."

"I see. And what if *you're* not the poor sucker heading for jail?"

"Then I don't give a damn either way."

"Are you sure about that? Isn't there someone in this town you care about?" He leans forward an inch or two and says, low and slow, "Someone even now enjoying the hospitality of the New York City Police Department."

"You mean Billy."

He doesn't answer that. Why should he? Just returns

my stare. Exchanges my breath for his. I'll say one thing: he's got a handsome set of eyelashes, the only soft thing about him. So light at the tips, I want to dust them with my pinky finger, ever so gently. For some reason, this idea soothes the pulse at the base of my neck, the one that has a nervous tendency to gallop off like a runaway horse at the mention of my stepfather's name. The ringing clears from my eardrums. Thoughts fall back into place. Bright, crisp, useful little thoughts.

"Now, Mr. Anson. We both know you can't make a thing stick to my Billy-boy. Don't you know what family he belongs to? The Marshalls?"

There is a slight pause. "I have an idea."

"Pillars of society. Patrons of every charity between here and Albany. Pals with every pol at every poker table in town. All Billy has to do is make a telephone call to dear old Pater and he's a free man. Why, I'll bet you a bottle of genuine Dewar's he's a free man already. Trundling on back to Princeton, New Jersey, this minute, in the backseat of Pater's Packard limousine. What do you say to that?"

Anson shoots straight to the ceiling. Plants his hands on his hips. Ignites the nerves behind his eyeballs. Parts his lips like he's got a *lot* to say to that, sister, and none of it good.

But the seconds tick on, one after another, and nothing comes out from between those two poised lips. Just the furious whir of second thoughts in the tumblers of his brain. Then the slow unstiffening of the muscles of his face, not what you'd call movement, not even a change of expression—he hasn't got any of those, remember?—but a kind of deflation, a loosening of the skin. Maybe his shoulders sink a little, I don't know. But the eyes stay bright.

"I guess I'd say you're probably right about that."

"So you got nothing."

"Maybe I don't."

"In fact, I do believe this entire hullaballoo constitutes nothing more than a bluff on your part, doesn't it, Mr. Anson? Be honest, now. Just a noisy show to try and scare a poor working girl who's done nothing worse tonight than order herself a glass of honest sweet milk from the wrong establishment."

Long, lazy pause. Like the ocean holding its breath before the turn of the tide. And then. So quiet, it's almost a whisper:

"If that's what you want to call it."

I rise slowly, untangling my legs as I go, allowing my skirt to fall back into place and my limbs to lengthen. I cross my hands behind my back and keep on rising, right up to my tiptoes, so my nose nearly brushes the brute end of Mr. Anson's chin.

"Why, if I wanted to raise a big stink, I could take this whole affair straight to the top, couldn't I? I could show off all my bruises. Weep and wring my little old hands. If Billy were to hear of this, for example . . ." I shrug my shoulders, such that Mr. Anson's silk-lined jacked slides across my skin.

He stares down his nose and mutters, "Good old Billy."

"Yes. So what do you say we come to a little arrangement, Mr. Anson? A little proposal of my own."

"What kind of arrangement, Miss Kelly?"

"So simple, even an honest fellow like you can understand it. It's like this. *You* take me home this minute, and *I* promise not to give Billy Marshall your name."

10

Anson drives me back to Christopher Street himself. He doesn't say much, just busies himself with the matter of negotiating the narrow, cold streets, the patches of slush and garbage. The buildings are tense and shuttered, as if laid under siege. The brakes squeal faintly in front of the Italian grocery.

"What have you done with Christopher?" I ask.

"Christopher?"

I jerk my head. "The owner."

Anson's thumbs meet at the top of the steering wheel. "I expect he'll have to go up in front of a judge. Pay a fine."

"And what about me? Do I have to see a judge?"

"No. You're free. For now, anyway."

I look over his shoulder, through the window. It's begun to snow: the minute, tender flakes at the vanguard. "You know he'll be back in business tomorrow night. A week at the most."

"I know that. It's not him I'm concerned with."

"You can't stop any of it. You'll die trying."

"Maybe I will."

"A fellow wants a drink, he's going to have it."

Anson lifts his hands from the wheel and sets the brake. Reaches inside the pocket of his overcoat and produces a calling card.

"You'll telephone me if you change your mind?"

"If I change my mind? Why, sure."

"Take the card, then."

"I don't need to." I tap my forehead.

"Now, that's funny. An hour ago you could scarcely remember your own name. Now you've got a photographic memory."

"When I need it."

He presses the card into my hand. "Take it anyway. In case someone knocks you on the head and gives you a spell of amnesia."

"Does that happen often in your line of work?"

"All the time."

I pinch the wee board between my two fingers and study it again. The plain Roman letters. Oliver Anson. Exchange and number. By the time I'm finished, Anson's opened the door of the automobile and strode around the hood to let me out.

"Thanks. I can find my way from here."

"I'm escorting you inside, Miss Kelly."

"No, you're not."

"Statistically speaking, it's the most dangerous time of night."

"No kidding? Then I guess I must be statistically dead by now."

He shuts the car door behind me and straightens. His gaze falls on my chin, which sticks right out there into the Manhattan night, at an angle those nuns used to abhor.

"All right. Good night, Miss Kelly. Thank you for your time."

"Don't mention it."

My shoes slip and clatter on the paving stones. The headlights flare against the glitter of my dress, against the tiny whir of snowflakes. I reach the sidewalk and the door. Pull out my latchkey, like any modern, independent girl in New York City. The snow coats the stoop like a layer of dust, and mine are the first footprints. The knob turns, and I remember something.

"Anson! Your jacket."

"Keep it."

I shrug the garment from my shoulders and trip back down across the sidewalk to where Anson stands next to the driver's-side door, in his overcoat and a plaid muffler, probably cashmere wool, like the girls at college used to wear, only sleeker. Hat pulled down low over that slanting forehead. The car's parked right in the middle of two street lamps, nice and dark, so I can't see his face all that well.

I say, "No, you take it. Or else you'll be coming back for it, won't you? And that wouldn't do at all."

He takes the jacket and folds it over his arm, while the snow stings my bare skin and lands in my hair. And you know something? For a single crazy instant, I imagine myself asking him upstairs. You know. For a cup of coffee or something. Chase away the winter.

Anson nods, like he's imagining the same thing. His hand reaches out to land on my shoulder, and the leather feels wet on my skin, cold: the fresh, sweet meltwater of New York snowflakes.

"Now get inside before you freeze to death."

11

I suppose you imagine, after a night like that, I'd be looking forward to a long winter's nap in my own clean bed. And I am. I might sleep all February, if you let me.

But I can't, you see. Because in the first place, I'm shortly due at a typing pool in the underwriting department of Sterling Bates & Company on the corner of Wall and Broad, come snow or come revenue agents; and second of all, the light's shining forth from underneath my door.

And it turns out, Special Agent Anson was wrong, after all.

12

D arling!"
"Billy! Wh—" (Word ends in *oomph* against
the lapels of Billy's dinner jacket.)

"Darling. I've been worried *sick*." (Into my hair.)
"Where have you been? I telephoned the precinct, I
telephoned everyone I could think of—"

"You telephoned *what*?" (Extracting self from lapels.)

"Dearest love." He takes my face between his hands
and kisses my mouth. His breath smells of cigarettes
and Scotch whiskey and anxiety. "Did they hurt you?
If anyone hurt you—"

"Nobody hurt me."

"That agent. The agent who called in the raid."

"What about him?"

"He didn't try anything, did he?"

"I don't know what you're talking about."

Billy holds me out at arm's length—which is to say,
about the length of the entire room—and examines my
eyes for truth. "But you were away all night."

"That sometimes happens in a police raid."

"You look exhausted."

"Of course I'm exhausted. I've just spent the night

in jail. And *you're* supposed to be in New Jersey by now. Don't you have some lecture or something tomorrow? Some professor requiring your presence?"

He blinks. Exhibits a sort of disheveled aspect altogether, collar loose and tie undone, hair spiking madly into his forehead. Waistcoat all unbuttoned. A fine few lines have grown in around the corners of his eyes, pointing out the reckless black throb of the pupils. "My God. *Lectures?* Who gives a damn about college?"

"Why, your parents, I'll bet. For one thing."

"My *parents?*"

"Yes. Those. The ones picking up the check for the whole racket, if I'm not mistaken."

"Ginger. Darling. How can you possibly think I'd leave you to rot in some stinking jail while I—I—*slink* back to college like some damned little rat and listen to some damned little professor—as if *that* matters, next to you—"

"Of course it matters! I'm just some dame you know in the city, you silly boy. I can take care of myself."

"You shouldn't have to. You wouldn't, if you would just *allow* me—"

"Billy." I stroke his cheeks a little, the way you might stroke a Labrador puppy to calm him down. How I worship those cheeks. He's got the loveliest bones up there, high and sturdy and dusted with pink on most occasions, as now. Hasn't got much beard to speak of—shaves but once a day—and the skin's as tender as any velvet, curving deliciously downward to his jaw and his plump raspberry mouth, presently pursed with worry. The room is cold, and he's so warm. Scintillating with distress. "How awfully touching. You sweet, dear thing. But you have a future, remember? A nice, bright, shining future. And futures like yours require a college education."

"I don't want any kind of future that doesn't have you in it, Gin. That's the kind of shining future for me."

"Oh, Billy. Go home, sweetie. Go home and get some sleep."

"It's too late to go home." He kisses me again, more softly. Hands sliding down my shoulders to the small of my back. Voice running lower, like an engine changing gears. "Hudson ferries've been in port for hours. And I don't want to sleep."

"I mean uptown. Your parents' place."

"They'll ask too many questions if I turn up now. Four o'clock in the morning. And I'll wake up the baby."

"You know, for such a tender sprout, you're awfully persuasive, Billy-boy."

"My uncle's a lawyer, remember?"

"Is he a good one?"

Billy laughs into the hollow behind my ear. "Not really."

"What about you? Do *you* want to be a lawyer?"

"I don't care what I am, Gin darling. Not right now. I'm just so glad to see you. Glad you're safe and free. Let's not go down to that club anymore, all right? Let's find a place somewhere, place of our own—"

"Now, Billy."

"Aw, I mean it this time. You don't know what it's like, riding that stinking ferry back to New Jersey, knowing what kind of stew I'm leaving you in. I can't stand it any longer." (He's unbuttoning my dress by now, nimble long aristocratic fingers, touching the base of my spine in the way that makes me shiver and forget things.) "Wherever you like, Gin. Upstate or down south or Timbucktoo. We can get married and raise a bunch of kids."

"Says who?"

"Says me."

"And what are we going to live on, Billy-boy? Moonshine?"

"I'll find something."

The dress is history. He picks me up and sort of crashes backward down on the bed. The mattress heaves and settles. Releases the musty lavender smell of old sheets. Dear Billy-boy. Bones like a sapling. Sweet lips kissing the sense right out of my skin. The night unwinds and spills around us. The snowflakes hurl against the window. I've got no more fight in me. I kick off my shoes and loop my arms around his safe, warm neck and say all right, whatever you like, sweetie pie. Take me away.

And he does.

13

A word about the few square feet of bedroom I call home.

I'm sure you've heard about those nice, respectable, wallpapered boardinghouses for professional young ladies. The ones uptown, where anxious matrons keep watch over fragile female reputations, and gentleman callers are to be kept strictly downstairs.

This isn't one of those boardinghouses, I'm afraid. Although the landlady does her best, she really does! Mealtimes regular and nourishing, visiting hours established if not enforced. Sheets changed once a week, and possibly even washed during that interval, though certainly not ironed. But the hard truth is you can't attract the same kind of boarder on Christopher Street as you can on, say, East Sixty-Ninth Street, and a boardinghouse is only as respectable as the boarders it contains, wouldn't you say? I suppose the speakeasy next door doesn't exactly elevate the tone, either. Anyway, to preserve appearances, Billy always climbs up the fire escape and enters through a window I keep unlatched (nothing to steal, after all), and he tips Mrs. Washington a dollar a visit because he's a gentleman. I believe he enjoys the adventure.

He certainly doesn't enjoy the furniture. Have you ever tried to entertain a lover on a single bed? Fosters intimacy, I'll say that.

14

I mention all this because I don't want you to misunderstand when I describe how, upon waking later that morning, I find myself enjoined in a lovers' knot of baroque configuration: pinned to the sheets by Billy Marshall's heavy right thigh across the two of mine, my mouth encompassed by his shoulder, our limbs snarled together. His damp lips dangle along my ear, and his hair shadows my eyes in a kind of brilliantine curtain. The tempo of his respiration suggests utmost satisfaction. (As well it should.) The tempo of mine suggests— well, otherwise.

I heave Billy's body aside and sit straight up, gasping for air, gasping for freedom. The air's dark but not black, and the illumination behind the thin calico curtain warns of a snow-streaked dawn. Next to my hip, Billy continues in exquisite slumber, embracing my shingle of a pillow. The familiar dimensions settle around me: walls, window, chair, washstand, bureau. Not much space between them. I reach for my kimono from the hook on the wall and slither over Billy's corpse to stand on the cold floor. It's bare. I have a horror of dirt.

We did not take long to express our physical longing, Billy and I, in the pit of a New York winter's night. Short and brisk and effective. My nerves still course from the aftermath, and when I peer at my watch, laid out on the bureau in a perfect vertical line next to Billy's silk top hat, I discover there's a good reason for that: I have slept only two hours. Dear Miss Atkins at Sterling Bates will expect me at my typewriter at nine o'clock, mind sharp and fingers swift. I cast another gaze at Billy. White skin glowing in the gray sunrise. Mouth parted and smiling at the corner.

I wrap myself in the kimono and lift the extra blanket from the foot of the bed. If I'm lucky, I'll wake again before Billy does, so he doesn't catch me in the old paisley armchair, all by myself.

15

But when my eyes open again, the bed contains no Billy. No strewn clothes, no shining silk top hat perched on the bureau, no handmade leather shoes tumbled on the floor. No sign of life whatsoever.

16

He's left a note. He's a gentleman, after all. I won't quote it here; it's too intimate. To summarize: he had hoped, after such a night between us, after such a declaration on his part, after such kisses and so on and so forth. You get the general idea. And I have disappointed him. I have kept my soul to myself, while taking all of his. He is going back to New Jersey, and wishes my future happiness with all his heart. Billy likes to *feel* things, you see. He likes to feel them *deeply,* to experience life at its absolute *rippingest,* to italicize every thought and emotion that rises inside him. After some consideration—that is to say, gnashing of teeth and rending of hair and scribbling of yet more midnight letters—he'll be back for more. And I'll snatch him in my arms and whisper my thanks to the Lord. In the meantime, I'm due at the corner of Wall and Broad in twenty minutes.

I expect you're disappointed. A typing pool. You figured I was employed in some more extravagant capacity, didn't you? Something glamorous and immoral. And it's true, I do have a small but picturesque sideline in the immoral. Immorality pays so much better. (About which, more later.) But my mama's example rusts before me as a cautionary tale, and since Sterling Bates had the goodness to hire me two years ago, as a pink-coated college dropout with eight nimble fingers and a pair of opposable thumbs, I find I can't quite let poor Miss Atkins down. So many girls let her down. Anyway, who can resist the allure of a regular paycheck?

My room contains no closet, properly speaking. I keep my dresses and suits on the hooks on the wall, neatly pressed, and my shirts folded in order in the second drawer of the bureau. Stockings and girdles and brassieres up top. I wash myself with the water from the pitcher and apply my navy suit, my white shirt, my dark stockings and sensible shoes. My small, neat hat over my shining hair. No cosmetics, not even a smear of lip rouge. Company orders. Banks. They've awfully conservative.

Downstairs, Mrs. Washington has laid out breakfast. Some of the other girls are there, Betty and Jane and Betty the Second, drinking coffee and spooning porridge. Nobody speaks. The newspaper hasn't been touched. The room contains its usual atmosphere of java and drugstore perfume. I pour myself a cup of coffee and spread a layer of jam over a slice of cold toasted bread. Pick up the paper and take in the headlines. Izzy and Moe led a raid the other night, fancy joint up on Fifty-Second Street. Eighty-six arrested, including forty-one ladies. (The paper drops the term *ladies* with conspicuous irony.) No mention of doings on Christopher Street, but I suppose Special Agent Anson charged in and ordered his milk well after deadline for the early morning edition. Anyway, I haven't got time to read past page one. I stuff the crust in my mouth, gulp the last of the coffee, blow a good-bye kiss in the direction of my sisters (I'm getting the silent treatment these days because of Billy, and I can't say I blame them), and as I whirl around the corner, thrusting arms in coat sleeves, fingers in mittens, I run smack into Mrs. Washington herself, wiping her hands on an apron.

"Oh! Miss Kelly. There you are *at last.*"

"Mrs. Washington. Can't stop. Late for work!"

"But, Miss Kelly—"

"I'll be back at six!"

"—telegram?"

Halt. Hand on doorknob. Skin prickling beneath muffler. Mouth going dry. I think, *That door surely does want painting, doesn't it?*

"Telegram?" I repeat.

"Arrived last night. Put it under your door. Didn't you see? Western Union."

"When?"

"Oh, about eight o'clock or so. I hope it's not bad—"

Well, I brush right past Mrs. Washington's hopes and on up the stairs, first flight second flight third flight, panting, fumbling for latchkey in pocket, there it is, jiggle jiggle, door squeaks open.

Floor's bare. Of course. I would have noticed a damned yellow Western Union envelope on my nice clean floor, wouldn't I? Even enrobed by lovey-dovey. So Billy must have picked it up for me and put it somewhere. Forgotten to mention that fact, in the heat of things. Dear Billy-boy. Never would open the envelope and peek inside, because he's a gentleman. The snow's turned to sleet, clicking hurriedly against the window glass. The room's in perfect order, every last meager object occupying its ordained place. Where would Billy put a Western Union envelope not intended for his own eyes? The bureau.

But no splash of yellow interrupts the nice clean surface of my battered thirdhand bureau. Just the mirror and the hairbrush and the vanity tray. Washstand is likewise pristine. Heart goes thump thump, pushing aside my ribs. Hand clenches mittens. Where the devil, Billy? Where the devil did you put that telegram? Darling, love-struck Billy, consumed by worry, all of twenty years old and not thinking straight. Books lined up in rigid order on the wall shelf. Bed all made, flat as a millpond. Above my head, someone thumps across the attic floor and slams a door shut, and the furniture rattles gently.

Rattles. Gently.

Thump thump thump goes my neighbor down the stairs, around the corner of the landing, down the next flight. The washbowl clinks its porcelain clink. The way it does in the pit of a New York winter's night, when you are expressing your carnal need for another human being, no matter how regardful you are of the walls and furniture and sleeping boarders.

I sink to my hands and knees, and there it is, wedged upright between the wall and the bureau. A thin yellow envelope. Yank bureau away from the wall a couple inches, stick arm in gap. Miss Geneva Kelly, 11 Christopher Street, New York City. And I am correct about Billy Marshall's principles. The glue's undisturbed.

For the smallest instant, I just sit there, back against the wall, legs splayed. Envelope pinched between my fingers. Black ink staring back. My name. The large Roman capitals WESTERN UNION TELEGRAM. As if I didn't know.

But no little black stars. Nobody's dead. That's something, isn't it?

I stick my index finger in the crease and rip.

```
1924 JAN 31 PM 6 41
MISS GENEVA KELLY
11 CHRISTOPHER STREET NEW YORK CITY
MAMA SICK STOP ASKING FOR YOU STOP COME
HOME EARLIEST STOP LOVE JOHNNIE
```

New York City, 1998

Ella always hated how, when you went to a cocktail party in Manhattan, or met someone over drinks or dinner or brunch with friends, the first question was always: *So what do you do?*

Meaning, your job.

She understood why, of course. New York was the city of dreams; it was where you went to chase those dreams, if you wanted them badly enough. In New York, of all places, your career defined you; people understood you on the basis of what you did for a living. If your dream was money, you worked on Wall Street. (Ella had yet to meet any investment banker who pursued his career because of a single-minded childhood desire to help companies meet their capital needs.) If your dream was also money, but you weren't so good with numbers, you worked for a law firm. If your dream was money and you were okay at numbers but were only willing to work eighty hours a week instead of a hundred, you went into management consulting. If your dream was . . . well, come to think of it, Ella had yet to meet anyone in New York whose dream wasn't money. But they were there. She saw them in restaurants and at Starbucks and on street corners. The actors and singers and writers and dancers and musicians and models. Whose dreams were also money, but in service to some other, more complicated dream.

As for Ella. She wasn't sure why she came to New York, really. She always dreaded that question—*What do you do?*—because the answer was so boring. *I'm an accountant.* Cue the eyes shifting around the room, seeking an opportunity elsewhere. The dull, automatic *Uh-huh* as she explained that she was actually a *forensic* accountant, parachuting from dead company to dead company, dissecting the carcass to figure out what had gone wrong and who was to blame. Which was kind of like solving a complicated murder mystery, except with numbers. But by then, her new acquaintance wasn't really listening. The word *accountant* turned a switch in people's brains, so that anything else you said just made a garbled *Blah bla-bla-blah* in the air, like Charlie Brown's teacher.

Whatever. Why did Ella come to New York? She came to New York because she got a job offer after college from a large Manhattan accounting firm, with health insurance and a 401(k) and a starting salary generous enough to afford her very own tiny walk-up apartment on the Upper West Side, close to the park, not too many crack vials on the stairs outside and—most importantly—no roommate to ask her how her day went and eat all her leftover ziti in the fridge. End of story. End of dream.

Of course, once she met Patrick, she thought she knew what had brought her to Manhattan. Fate! She was fated to meet Patrick there, fated to fall in love with him. She'd been *so* close to taking a job with that firm in Boston—and really, Boston was a better fit for her, felt more like home to her—and she hadn't. So she was meant to be a New Yorker. Meant to be Patrick's wife. Her dream was love.

Thank God, then, she had a backup dream. Her job. Sure, she'd veered off the partner track long ago, once she realized that making partner basically meant spending all your time trying to win new business and manage client expectations. But she liked what she did. In the first place, every few months, she got assigned to a new carcass, and if Tolstoy had been a forensic accountant, he would have said that thriving companies were all alike, but each company failed in its own way. Usually because somebody was doing something illegal.

This was especially true in the financial services industry, in which Ella had ended up specializing, partly because she worked from the New York office and partly because she ended up knowing Wall Street so intimately: the inevitable result of marrying someone who worked there. So many scoundrels, so much greedy ingenuity. (That was the second reason she liked her job. Matching wits against all those greedy, scoundrelly minds.) So she looked forward to being called into a partner's office at the start of a new gig. You never knew where you might get sent, or why.

Today in particular. She'd been on the beach for four weeks now, waiting for a new assignment. Doing routine internal business—PowerPoint slides for business pitches, interviewing college students, that kind of thing—that left far too much of her intellect free to wallow in the forensic analysis of her failed marriage. She preferred numbers. So orderly, so incapable of deceit. She stared at the family photo on the credenza behind Travis's desk—kind of artsy, black and white, silver Tiffany frame, smiling wife and clean-cut twin boys of maybe five or six years, wearing white polo shirts and chinos—and wondered, for the first time, if Travis had ever cheated on them.

Until three weeks ago, she would have said no. Of course not. Travis was a solid, decent guy, not the cheating type at all. Never made a pass at her. Never treated the PAs with anything other than professional courtesy. Profoundly boring middle-aged haircut. But then, three weeks ago, she would have said the same thing about Patrick. Earnest, romantic. Loved his mom. They'd been trying for a baby for almost a year, a baby Patrick really wanted. And then—

"—get in a taxi now?"

"I'm sorry. Lost my train of thought. Taxi where?"

"Is everything okay, Ella?"

"Sure! Fine. Just need another cup of coffee, I think."

Travis stared at her and spoke slowly, patiently, like he probably spoke to his twins when they weren't paying attention. That was the kind of guy he was. Never lost his cool. Just like Patrick. "To Wall Street, Ella. Corner of Broad. You'll be working right at the bank's headquarters this time."

"Oh. Right." Ella knew better than to ask which bank. Instead, she glanced down at the spiral-bound briefing book on her lap, which lay unopened, navy blue cover flat over an inch-thick stack of white paper, held shut by two remarkably tensile, white-rimmed thumbs.

The title seared her eyeballs.

STERLING BATES INC.

MUNICIPAL BOND DEPARTMENT

"Ella? Everything okay?"

"Fine!"

"There's no issue here, is there? Conflict of interest? Because this is a sensitive project, like I said. Some big names involved. And the whole thing could blow up on us, depending on what we find, which is why we want you on the team. We need our best people, and we need them at their best. We can't afford a single mistake on this. Got to have your head in the game. Are we clear, here?"

Ella laid her left hand flat on the surface of the briefing book, obscuring the cutout white rectangle of black block text.

"Absolutely clear," she said.

Ella's cell phone vibrated at a quarter to midnight, while she lay flat on the folding table in the laundry room, listening to the sounds from the other side of the wall.

She picked up the phone and looked at the caller ID. Set it down again. The table buzzed beneath her back, at soothing, regular intervals, before lapsing back into stillness. Immediately after it stopped, Ella felt the familiar twinge of guilt. Imagined Patrick flipping his own phone closed, staring despondently at the reclaimed-wood floor in the living room or the tight, golden sisal weave in the bedroom. Or, just as easily, the industrial carpet in his twenty-ninth-floor office at Sterling Bates.

He called every day, sometimes twice. He also e-mailed, not as frequently. Most of those messages sat unopened in her inbox, but not all. Last week, the morning after she met Hector and Jen and came down to the laundry room in the middle of the night, she had such a terrible insomnia hangover at work, she actually forgot she was separated from her husband, forgot what had happened the last time she saw him, and clicked on his name. Automatic response. Started reading before she could help herself.

I AM SO SORRY. I'll keep saying it, over and over, until you believe me. If you could just see what a wreck I am right now. I know I have a problem. I'm getting help now. I just want to see you and try to explain and apologize. I swear to God it will never, ever happen again. I love you. I love our marriage. You are the most important thing in my world. Please—

She'd clicked away to a spreadsheet. Looked down at her keyboard and tried to breathe. Sipped some coffee while her heartbeat rippled her silk blouse and her head ached and her stomach swam.

Do not reply, she'd told herself. Do not reply.

She'd sent back the flower deliveries that arrived daily at Aunt Viv's apartment, each one more fragrant and costly than the last. She'd filed the cards and notes in the circular. She'd let her cell phone vibrate into voice mail. She'd restrained her mouse from clicking on any one of the e-mails, until now. She hadn't even told him her new address. She knew better. There wasn't an argument Patrick couldn't win, a deal he couldn't close. All he needed was a foot in the door.

The phone buzzed again. This time she turned it off entirely and concentrated instead on the music drifting through the walls, a jazz tune of exuberant syncopation, in which a trumpet and a bass and a clarinet chased each other in dizzying circles, making her think—God knew why—of forest animals. That was it. Scurrying up and down trees. This was real jazz, not the junk they played in tourist traps. Sound, bluesy, inventive jazz, and the patrons knew it. They laughed and chattered and danced—Hector was right, the vibration of heels sometimes rattled the floor—and while Ella couldn't distinguish any particular voice, she was starting to feel like she knew them, these people, communing by night in a Greenwich Village basement. Hiding from the rest of the world, experiencing this elemental music in the shared marrow of their bones.

The first night, she had listened for maybe an hour, standing the whole time, not moving a muscle for fear she might lose. Like the sound would dissolve if she reached out to touch it, or even to approach the gray cinder-block wall that separated her from them. She caught a glimpse of herself in the mirror above the table, and the sight of her own mesmerization startled her. Eyes soft and lips round. If the image were of anyone else, she'd have said it was the look of someone in love. When she turned at last and climbed the stairs, five long prewar flights back to her apartment, she went to bed and fell right asleep to the pensive, delicate notes of a piano.

And she knew that she hadn't chosen this apartment, after all. The apartment had chosen her.

The music next door was already having its effect. Her brain settled into a comfortable trance; she wasn't ready for sleep yet, but she was close. The images shifting in and out of focus behind her eyes, the scenes and ideas, they weren't the frightful thoughts about Patrick—about Patrick and other women—about her vast, unfamiliar future—about the once-sturdy mile-stones now scattered about that future like bowling pins—but about other things. People she didn't know. A champagne bottle tottering on a sofa, next to a man's black tuxedo leg. Another man, playing a nimble clari-net, except he's not a stranger, he's someone you know, and you're trying to tell him something. Now driving a narrow, tree-bordered highway while a sunset burns behind you. (Somehow Ella knew that Manhattan lay between her and that sunset, though she couldn't say why.) Sitting down for a drink at a bar, where you know the bartender; you're commiserating about something. The colors, the colors are so beautiful. A rich, red-streaked mahogany. Gold something. The taste of salt.

Time to go to bed now, Ella. You've had your fill. Jazz and conversation. She lifted her head and rose to her elbows, groggy, jostling the cell phone so that it crashed to the floor. She leaned over the edge of the table and reached to the floor, but the phone lay just beyond the tips of her fingers, and for some reason she didn't want to get down from the table altogether, which was the logical solution, but to snag the phone from her current position, and while she was attempting this awkward maneuver, some woman next door started to scream bloody murder. The music broke up. Ella, startled, fell right off the table to the gray linoleum floor.

For several seconds, she didn't do anything. Just listened in shock to the sound of that screaming woman, the long, excruciating rip of vocal cords, the bang of furniture turning over. Or was that a gunshot? A man shouted something terse, and the screaming stopped.

Ella rose on her hands and knees. Her heartbeat crashed in her ears; her arms shook. Somewhere in her chest, a gash opened up, as if someone had taken a knife and sliced right down the center of her sternum.

She braced her hands on the table and staggered to her feet. Spots broke out before her eyes, and she realized she wasn't breathing, that her terror and the downright physical pain assaulting her had frozen her rib cage. *Breathe*, she whispered. Forced her lungs to act. The cavity inside to expand—painfully—and contract.

On the other side of the wall, silence had fallen. Not a sound, not a note. She thought, *I have to call the police.* She picked up her phone, which was blank and dark, and pressed the power button.

The light came on. She flipped it open. No bars. No bars, when there had been three or four a moment ago.

Go upstairs, she thought. Go see if anyone needs help.

She turned around, still clutching her phone, waiting for it to find a signal, and ran for the laundry room door. Up the dark staircase, around the corner, down the dim hallway to the front door. She flung the door open and ran down the steps to the wet sidewalk. The drizzle fell softly on her hair and nose and hands; the smell of rotting garbage lay in the air, though the sanitation pickup had come yesterday and the pavement was clear. She wrapped her fingers around the railing that surrounded the basement next door. Not a sound, not a light, not a single sign that anyone lived there, let alone ran an exclusive jazz club into the small morning hours.

"Hello?" she called. "Anyone there?"

No reply. Ella became conscious of all the windows stacked up around her, the curious New York eyes behind them. On the other side of the street, a pair of men walked briskly, heads bent under the drizzle. Probably glancing her way and thinking she was some kind of crazy, some kind of loony, out this late in her bathrobe and slippers, maybe locked herself out, maybe tossed out by her jealous boyfriend. A taxi turned the corner of Bedford and crawled down the street, between the rows of parked cars.

She tried again, a little more loudly. "Does someone need help? Can I call the police?"

Ella knew she was dancing along a fine, narrow line. Seven or eight million people crammed into one city with any number of wackos and crackheads, you had to look out for each other. On the other hand, you also had to know when to mind your own business and walk on, walk on. Let people take care of their own. Let the secrets stay secret, the hidden stay hidden. Lest you find your own business ripped open and exposed to the world.

The taxi's headlights flashed by. The street lay quiet around her. She turned away from the railing and went back up the steps, and that was when she realized that the two strangers were right about one thing.

She'd run straight out of the building without her key.

"Can I make you a cup of coffee or something?" Hector asked as they climbed the stairs.

Ella opened her mouth to decline. "Sure," she heard herself say. "I mean, no. It's so late."

"No worries."

"I'm sorry if I woke you up, buzzing you like that."

"Like I said, no worries. I wasn't asleep."

"It was such a stupid thing to do."

Hector stopped, forcing her to turn around on the narrow stairs and look at him. "Ella, has anyone ever told you that you apologize too much? It's no big deal. Everyone gets locked out sometime. You buzz your neighbor. Your neighbor lets you in. It's the code. Okay?"

"Okay."

"Now," he said, prodding her in the small of her back, "you get on up there. I'm going to make coffee. You can join me or not."

She resumed climbing. "Okay."

"Okay, you'll join me?"

"No point wasting good coffee."

"I also have a bottle of good Kentucky bourbon, if that works better for you."

"Do I look like I could use a shot of bourbon?"

He chuckled behind her. "Ella, you don't take a *shot* of bourbon. You drink it from a glass, nice and slow. With or without ice. You take your time and savor it."

"Oh. Sure."

"And *yes*, by the way. You do look like you could use a glass of bourbon. Didn't I warn you about going down to that laundry room at night?"

"Yes."

"And did you listen?"

"Obviously not."

They'd reached the last landing, on the fifth floor. Ella hadn't been up this far; she'd glanced, over her shoulder, just before she fit the key in her lock. Just out of curiosity, of course, and not because she was hoping for a glimpse of Hector leaving his apartment, Hector entering his apartment, beautiful Hector taking a pizza delivery in his boxer shorts. But she'd never climbed that last flight of stairs. Nothing up there but Hector's pad. He didn't even have a letter after his apartment number; it was just APT 5 on the list of buttons in the vestibule.

His door lay at the end of a short hall, where the stairwell met the wall. He slipped past her and reached inside his pocket. A furious scratching started up on the other side of the door, like something was trying to dig a hole.

"Do you have a dog?" Ella asked.

"That would be Nellie. Vicious attack animal. Watch out."

Hector opened the door, and a brown-and-white blur shot through the crack and hurled itself into his legs, licking and whimpering, making small, delighted yaps like the bark of a seal. "Nellie! Nellie, babe. There you are. Who's a good girl? Whoa, take it easy, babe, only been away five minutes, you big numbskull. Down, Nellie. Mind your manners. Look, we got a guest."

The dog turned—a King Charles spaniel, Ella saw—and unleashed another fusillade on Ella's knees.

"Get down, Nellie. Jeez. I'm sorry, it's like she loves everybody. Hope you're a dog person."

Ella bent down and stroked Nellie's long ears, like a pair of brown corn-silk tassels. Angled her face so that the desperate kisses landed just to the left of her mouth, instead of square on the lips. "I totally am a dog person," she said. "Nellie as in Nell Gwyn?"

"Very good, Sherlock. You're the only one who's picked that up."

"I love history. Kind of funny, actually. My full name's Eleanor, too. How old is she?"

"Four." He crouched down next to Ella and put his hand on the spaniel's wriggling back. "She was my mom's dog. We got her a puppy to cheer her up, before her final round of chemo."

"So you're a very special dog, aren't you, Nellie?" Ella watched her twist about and return to Hector, calmer now, snuggling her nose into the corner of his elbow.

"Very special." He straightened and pushed the door fully open. "After you. Yeah, you, too, Nellie. Come on. Don't give me the puppy eyes, babe. We both know you already had your walk. Shoo. In you go. Show Ella inside. Atta girl."

The first thing Ella noticed inside Hector's apartment was the piano, a full-size grand Steinway that stood before the row of three windows overlooking the street. The lid was closed, and a thick plaid blanket covered the entirety of the case. A brass instrument lay on the lid's edge. Ella stepped closer and saw it was a trumpet.

"Wow," she said. "You're a musician."

"Guilty. Hope it doesn't bother you. I try to keep it muted late at night, but luckily the other residents actually like hearing my stuff, for some strange reason."

Ella turned. Hector was already in the kitchen area, opening a cabinet door while Nellie circled his feet. He was wearing a short-sleeved gray T-shirt and sweatpants, his dark hair strewn carelessly back from his face, looking like a canine early in the era of domestication. "Wait. Is that you? Playing at night?"

"Damn. Is it bothering you?"

"No, not at all. You're amazing. I thought it was— well, coming from downstairs."

Hector set down a bottle, half-full of amber liquid, and a bag of coffee. "What'll it be, Ella? Uppers or downers?"

She crossed her arms. "So I have to confess something. I've never drunk bourbon before."

"No kidding?"

"No kidding."

"Then I kind of think you should give it a try. Not that I'm pushing you in any one direction. You probably have to go to work in a few hours, right?"

"True. But I'm really, *really* not looking forward to it. So . . . ?"

"So . . . bourbon?"

"What the hell."

"Atta girl." He unscrewed the lid and walked toward her. "First, you have to smell it."

"Like wine?"

"Naw. Nothing so snobby as that." He stopped before her and tilted the neck of the bottle in her direction. The room was lit by a pair of antique wall sconces—probably original, to the building if not to the room itself—and the glow turned his olive skin an even deeper shade of gold. The two lights appeared as small white dots in his pupils. "Just breathe it in. For your own enjoyment. Preview of coming attractions."

She leaned forward and sniffed delicately at the opening. "Holy cow. How strong is that?"

"Eighty proof, I guess. But it's the flavor you're going for. Bourbon has this distinctive smell. Made mostly from corn mash, instead of rye or barley, like your typical Scotch malt."

"It's kind of spicy? Warm?"

Hector tilted the bottle back toward his own nose, right where hers had been, and breathed deep. "Ahh. Almost as good as drinking it. Ice or no ice?"

"Which do you recommend?"

"I like it without. Room temperature. You really get the flavor that way. But if you like your drinks cold . . ." He walked back to the corner of the room that formed the kitchen and pulled two lowball glasses from an open shelf. It was a funny kind of kitchen, neither modern nor traditional. Simple wooden surfaces and shelves, unadorned cabinets. Almost homemade looking, except everything fit together in perfect lines. A single pendant lamp hung from the ceiling, which must have been at least nine or ten feet high.

"No," Ella said slowly. "I think I'll try it warm."

"Awesome. Hang tight." He crouched a few inches as he poured, staring carefully at the bourbon as it streamed into each glass. The pendant cast a pair of sharp, thick shadows under his cheekbones, which were maybe a little *too* high and wide, now that she thought about it, throwing his face out of the fine proportion required for textbook beauty. But Ella admired them anyway. In a completely nonsexual way, of course. Hector straightened, set down the bottle, and lifted a glass in each hand. "Ready?"

Ella moved closer to the counter and reached over to take her glass from Hector's fingers. "Ready as I'll ever be. Cheers."

"Cheers. Now, hold on, there, Silver. Sip slow. Just a taste to start. You won't like it at first. You have to give it time. Kind of like getting acquainted with someone complicated."

Ella set her lips on the edge of the glass and brought the bourbon forward, until it touched the tip of her tongue.

"That's right," Hector said, watching her closely. "What do you think?"

"It's—it's great."

"Liar."

She laughed and tried again. "Okay. It's like being hit by a club."

"That's more like it." Hector took a drink and turned around to lean back against the counter, palming the glass and swishing the liquid gently along the sides.

"Nice kitchen, by the way."

"You like it? I actually put it in myself."

"No. Way."

"Way."

"You're a carpenter?"

"I'm a musician, Ella. Actually a composer, which is even worse. So I had to find another trade to keep me solvent, right? Didn't want to sponge off my parents all my life."

"You know what? I don't think I've ever met a carpenter in New York. Not one who lives in Manhattan, anyway."

"I made a deal with the landlord when I took the place. I do all the carpentry-type fix-it stuff around here, and I get a deal on the rent. So what do you think? Feeling better now?"

"Much."

"You were pretty freaked out, there, for a minute."

"Yes, Hector. I was pretty freaked out by the screaming woman in the basement next door."

"Fair enough. But it's all good now, right? We went back down, didn't hear anything. If someone was really in trouble, you'd be hearing something, trust me. Plus, Nellie would go nuts, right? Dogs are sensitive to all that stuff. Smarter than we are."

"I guess so."

"That's why the other tenants don't mind me playing at night," he said. "Drowns out anything from downstairs."

"Like screaming?"

He shrugged. "Some weird shit goes down sometimes."

"I don't understand. Why don't the police get involved?"

"Who knows? Maybe the owner has an arrangement. Look, it's New York, right? We cater to every taste in this town. As long as it's consensual, you can have your letch as long as I have mine."

"I don't know. That screaming didn't sound consensual to me."

Hector shrugged. "Look, my bedroom window overlooks the back. If I see anyone bleeding or hiding a body, I'll call the police. Is it getting any better? The bourbon?"

Ella looked down at her glass, which was less full than she thought it would be. "Actually, it kind of is. Like drinking fire, but in a good way." She pushed off from the counter and wandered back to the piano. Nellie, who had settled into an alert, silken pile at Hector's feet, leapt up to follow. Her claws scrabbled like jacks on the wooden floor.

"You like music, then?" Hector called after her.

"Love music. My grandmother's a cellist. She taught me how to play the piano first, then she let me play her instrument."

"No kidding? You can play the cello?"

"Played it all the way through college. But I was never going to be as good as her. I mean, I loved it. I was a passionate player, you know? I just couldn't get my fingers to move like hers."

"You want to jam a little?"

"Jam? Right now?"

"Sure." Hector moved past her and set his glass on the piano lid. "No cello, but I've got a string bass you can try."

"You mean, like, jazz?"

"If you like. Jazz, whatever. I can do pretty much anything." He flipped open the keyboard cover and stood there, washed by the yellow street lamp outside, bare arms lean and poised, head turned a little to one side. His fingers started to run along the keys, awakening a ripple of delicate sound that went straight to Ella's belly. He nodded to the corner. "Bass is over there."

Ella took a deep breath and swallowed down the rest of the bourbon. Her throat burned, her brain gasped for air.

"How about some Beethoven?" she said.

An hour and another couple of glasses of bourbon later, they were sitting side by side on the piano bench, thigh by thigh, playing Gershwin. Laughing. Ella had discarded her bathrobe, and her bare arm moved next to his bare arm. Muscles plucking in rhythm. Nellie lay curled under the bench, snoring softly in the rests between measures.

"See, the thing about Gershwin, which I love,"

Hector said, "is that he isn't one or the other. He's deep, so deep. I mean, the notes are, like, revolutionary. But he's talking about you and me. He isn't afraid to connect at an emotional level."

"He's not trying to show off to the academy," Ella agreed. "He writes for his audience. He wants to move you."

"He gets you right here." Hector makes a quick fist and presses it to his chest, almost without missing a note. "Lyrical. But complicated and unexpected, right? And it's so effortless, you don't realize how genius it is until you take it apart."

Ella made a last arpeggio and lifted her hands away. "I once acted in a school production of *Porgy and Bess,* believe it or not."

"No kidding. Who did you play?"

"Bess. We only had one African-American girl in my class, and she hated singing. It was kind of weird, but it worked."

"Awesome." He closed his eyes and flowed into "Summertime." "You must have lived in some serious white-bread suburb."

"Yeah. Grew up in Arlington. My dad's a lawyer."

"And your mom?"

"Law professor. And she models, believe it or not. Just for fun, and I guess to keep her ego stroked. Not that it needs stroking. She's like this glamorous fifty-something who looks good in everything."

"Ha. I love your mom. My girlfriend's a model."

Ella, in the act of swallowing the very last drop of bourbon, started to cough. "Wow. Nice."

Hector laughed. "It's not like that. What do I look like, some kind of smarmy modelizer? Hanging out in clubs?"

"I don't know. Maybe."

"Naw, I don't have the bank for it. They're expensive, those girls. Also kind of young. No, she's a hand model, actually."

"A hand model."

"You know, like Nivea advertisements. Gloves and jewelry. Especially jewelry. She's in that Tiffany engagement ring ad on the subway right now."

"Wait, I've seen those. The big solitaire? She's pulling a ribbon?"

"That's the one."

"Seriously? Those are her hands?"

"Wild, huh? She had, like, a six A.M. call for that one. So she doesn't stay over often. I wouldn't get any work done."

"Hmmm."

"I *mean*, Ella, if you would get your mind out of the *gutter*"—he bumped his gray jersey shoulder against hers—"that she has to be in bed at ten o'clock with her oven mitts on. And that's exactly when my brain starts making music."

"Oh. That's a pain."

"Yeah, I don't think we thought that one through very well. What about you? What's your story?" He shifted abruptly into something else, kind of jaunty. Ella didn't recognize the tune. "What twist of fate brought you here to Eleven Christopher?"

"Oh, you know." Ella stared at her bare, ringless fingers. "Just needed a new place to live, that's all. Look, I should really get going. I do need to be at work tomorrow morning."

"Oh, yeah? Doing what?"

"I'm an accountant," she said, and this time remembered to add quickly, "a forensic accountant."

"Forensics, huh? You get to find out where all the dead bodies are buried?"

"Pretty much. And where they hid the money first."

"Well, that is some seriously cool shit. You're like Sherlock Holmes."

"I keep a pipe and a deerstalker in my desk drawer."

"Don't forget the opium."

"Cheaper than therapy, I always say."

He chuckled and moved into another tune, gentle

and tickling, which Ella didn't recognize. "So do you like what you do?"

"Most of the time." She paused. "Actually, it kind of sucks right now. I just got assigned to the same company as my ex. So I kept expecting to see him in the lobby or the elevator."

"Man. Stressful. Big company?"

"Pretty big. Luckily, it's not his department or anything. I'll just deal."

"Be strong, like you are."

The words took a strange shape inside her ears. Ella had never thought of herself as particularly strong. Her mother was strong. Her sister was strong. Her father had a quiet, unshakable strength that awed her. But Ella? She only felt strong from the inside of a piece of music. Or a spreadsheet.

"Yeah, wish me luck." She rose from the piano bench and manufactured a gigantic stretch. "Thanks for the bourbon."

Hector rose, too, in the middle of a measure, and closed the keyboard. The sudden absence of music made the room grow huge. Made the space between the furniture yawn, made the air turn thick.

"Nerves all settled?" he asked, looking at her seriously. Like a doctor. His breath smelled of bourbon.

She held up her hand, palm down. "Do you see me shaking?"

"Cool as a cucumber, Sherlock. Good news. Off you go, then. Get your beauty sleep." He held his arm to the side. "Want a bottle of water or something to take down with you?"

"No, I'm good." The room swam a little around her. "Actually, maybe the water's a good idea."

Hector went to the fridge while she threw on her bathrobe and went to the door. He handed her the bottle of water and asked if she wanted him to walk her down.

"Thanks," she said, "but I'm fine."

"I know you are. You are as fine as they come. I mean that."

"Thanks. I guess it's good night, then."

"Good night, Ella. And if you need anything, just let me know, okay? If there's any weird stuff downstairs. I'm the house doctor."

"The mayor, you mean?"

"Ha. Touché." He raised his fist, and Ella bumped his knuckles. "Watch those stairs. And take some aspirin."

"Will do." She turned to leave. Took a few careful steps down the hallway and stopped. "Wait a second, Hector."

"What's up?"

Ella stared at the ecru wall, on which the light overhead made a strange, lurid pattern. Or maybe not. Maybe the pattern was just the bourbon smoking her eyeballs. She licked her lips. "So. I had fun tonight."

"Yeah. Me too. Knew you were kindred, under that suit you wear out the door in the morning."

"Kindred?"

"You know. Certain people. You can just sit down at a piano together and play."

"Right." She blinked hard. "Also. I kind of lied to you back there."

He didn't reply.

Ella gathered her breath. Didn't turn around; that would be too much. Anyway, the floor was already unsteady beneath her. *Kindred.* "Not exactly lied, I guess," she continued. "About why I moved here, I mean. I just didn't tell you the truth."

"The whole truth, and nothing but the truth?"

"Sort of."

"Big deal or small deal?"

"I don't know. I guess it's a big deal to me."

"Well, I guess we all have secrets, right?"

Ella turned after all. Gripped the stair railing for balance. Hector stood tall in the doorway, sturdy and wiry and remarkably still. His face was heavy with fatigue.

Nellie had wandered over and now stared in sleepy curiosity from between his legs. Yawning, showing off a set of small, sharp teeth. Hector braced one hand on the door frame and waited for her.

"So it's like this," she said. "I left my husband three weeks ago because I caught him having sex with a prostitute."

ACT II

We Come to an Understanding
(of sorts)

RIVER JUNCTION, MARYLAND

1924

1

Now the B&O branch line into River Junction runs a passenger train but once a day, and even so I find myself in possession of a carriage nearly empty, except for a middle-aged woman in widow's weeds who stares through the window the entire journey, though a book lies open in her lap.

I don't blame the folks who aren't present. Why should you travel into the frigid crook between two godforsaken mountains in the middle of far western Maryland in the middle of winter, unless you have urgent business calling you there? No reason at all. Like the widow, I observe the passing drifts of snow, the pastures all tucked under smooth white blankets, the gray horizon bleeding into the gray sky, the mounting hills and the small, broken-down houses huddled between them, and I cannot raise the slightest whiff of longing. Just a sick weight growing in my stomach, fed by the rattle of wheels and sight of the smoke trailing from all those lonely chimneys. The smell of burning Pennsylvania anthracite.

2

The last time I saw my mother, she lay in bed. She spent a lot of time in bed, my mother, with one thing or another. Nine and a half months after marrying Duke Kelly, she heaved out ten pounds of Johnnie from between her narrow hips, and she never really was the same after that. Not that Duke seemed to care much about Mama's state of health, I guess, because she went on to whelp three more boys, one after another, like a crumbling sausage factory that somehow continues to churn out sausages, and then twin girls who died a month later, and then—well, I lost track by then, because I was mostly at the convent, getting an education. All I know is that she kept falling sick, which is the name we give to a miscarriage out here in the country, and lastly had another girl the year I started college. That's Patsy. She'll be rising five years old now, if she's made it this far. My baby sister. Anyhow. The last time I saw Mama, she was sitting up in bed, nursing wee Patsy, and when I told her I was quitting college and running off to New York City right that very morning, she didn't even look up. Didn't even meet my eye. Just brushed back a bit of limp hair from her temple and told me not to be getting myself in trouble, and I thought, *You're one to talk*, not in a sour vein but rather a pitying one. I asked if I could hold Patsy and say good-bye, and she said no, baby's nursing, so I just leaned over and kissed Patsy's velvet crown and then Mama's temple, and breathed in the scent of milk and skin. And I said I'll be going now, and funny thing, when I straightened up my eyes I found the window, and right through the middle of that dirty square marched Duke himself, doing something to the buttons of his trousers, and I turned away so Mama wouldn't see my face. And you may be sure I departed the premises directly that minute, carrying my little carpetbag in one hand and my coat in the other, running out the front door so he wouldn't spot me. Heat rising from the grass. Train whistle crying down the tracks. Sent my address two weeks later not to Mama but to Johnnie, because Duke always opens Mama's mail but doesn't give much damn about any business of Johnnie's.

Speak of train whistles. There it goes, thin and short, and two seats ahead of me the widow starts in her seat. Glances over her shoulder in my direction, under guise of looking for the conductor. Her face is plump and well fed, not a trace of want.

"Excuse me," she says, "is you Geneva Rose Kelly?"

I reply cagily, "I am."

"Why, they Lord. Don't you know me?"

"Should I know you?"

"It's Ruth Mary Leary, you old so-and-so! We was at school together, recollect?"

"Ruth Mary! Of course." (Laying on a thick, false coating of enthusiasm as I pick through the old stacks of memory.)

"Course, I was just Ruth Mary Green back then, before me and Eddie ran off to Baltimore to get hitched. You remember *that,* I reckon!" She laughs.

"Course I do. Talk of the town."

"Mama liketa murdered Eddie."

"She surely did. How are you these days, Ruth Mary?" I say these words with knowing tenderness, because her costume suggests that someone dear— likely Eddie, whoever the devil he is—must have gone and turned toes-up in the recent past, and I can see she expects I've heard all about her sorrows and joys over the years. That I make it my habit to keep current on the patter of River Junction elopements and birthings and passings on. Ruth Mary Green. I have some general impression of bony knees and a dirty, wan face. Long, straight hair worn in two braids. A blue calico dress. The River Junction schoolyard, which I last inhabited when I was but eight years old.

Ruth Mary's face sinks a little. "Course it was awful when Eddie passed on."

"Course."

The train makes that first soft lurch, braking down for the River Junction station, the lurch that tells you it's time to gather your things and make your apologies. Ruth takes no notice.

"But your daddy's taken right good care of us. Right good care. He's a right good man, your daddy."

I make for my pocketbook and my little satchel, so she can't see my face as I reply. "He surely is."

"I'm a-coming from Hagerstown. Calling on my sister. You recollect Laura Ann? Done had herself another baby girl. Doing just fine. You here to see your mama?"

"I am."

"I hope she ain't took a turn for the worse."

"She has, I'm afraid. Johnnie wired me last night."

"They Lord. I'll send something over. Poor Mr. Kelly. He does dote on her."

This time, when I reply, my smile is tacked on with care and attention, bright as you please. "Like bees on nectar."

3

Ruth wants to know if anyone's meeting me at the station, and I tell her no, I didn't have time to wire ahead, I thought I'd walk.

"*Walk!* You can't walk in this, Geneva Rose. My brother Carl's a-meeting me in the Ford. Be more than pleased to give you a lift."

"You needn't bother. I like the walk."

"Why, don't talk nonsense. You know Duke'd liketa have our hides if we let his baby girl walk home from the station in all this." She nods to the piles of dirty snow creeping past the window. The platform appears suddenly, crisp and gray, giving me some kind of startle, because there never was a platform at River Junction station before, let alone one shoveled free of precipitation. Just limp grass and beaten mud. The clapboard corner of the depot edges into view and stops, concurrent with the final lurch of the train and the sigh of the steam. Here we are, says Ruth. Home again. Sight for sore eyes, ain't it?

Not yet four years gone altogether, I collect, since I parted ways with River Junction, and I have tried not to give the place another thought since. Easy enough, when you are living in the bosom of Manhattan, encircled by an urban landscape of buildings and more buildings, mounting into the sky, stone and pavement and patches of stubborn parkland, jumbles of enchanting humanity in all its various states of dress and undress, wealth and unwealth, cathedrals and skyscrapers and mansions and slums, monuments to snatch your heartbeat, tenements to choke the breath right down in your lungs, and above all that the restless, reckless churn of motion. New York City is one thing never, and that is standing still. But here. Here at the River Junction railway depot, a brief western outpost on a meager branch line of the Baltimore & Ohio Railroad, as the train rests and sighs and Ruth Mary Leary reaches out a widowy black arm to push open the door and hump her suitcase across the step to this interesting brand-new platform, the whole world around us is just plain frozen. Frozen and empty. Same station house sleeping in the snow, strange in its old familiarity, an exact replication of a building I knew in another life: a life I did my best to forget.

Except, if I'm not mistaken, the clapboard siding has been painted a bright new red, and the beaten-up row of stores across the street—Cathy's Café, the five and dime, Ned MacDonald's hardware store—share an unaccustomed sharpness in their general demeanor. As if a smart-mouthed nun from an especially strict order marched up and told them to straighten their signboards and fix their windows and wash away all the dirt. (Not that I speak from experience, you understand.) And is that fellow with the shovel actually clearing snow from the sidewalk?

Is that actually a *sidewalk*?

I seem to have come to a stop, there on the unexpected railway platform, staring at the unexpected purity of River Junction's center of commerce, such as it is. The wind blows cold on my cheek. My fingers clench around the handle of my satchel. Someone taps my shoulder and says something, and he has to repeat his words—*Excuse me, ma'am, is this your pocketbook?*—before I startle out of my thoughts and turn.

The conductor. Burly fellow, holding out a plain black pocketbook in his gloved right hand. I nod my head and snatch the pocketbook and say thank you, brusque with embarrassment, and he says, My pleasure, ma'am, will there be anything else? And something about the tone of that voice makes me look up at his face and the dark blue eyes watching me steadily beneath the round brim of his conductor's cap.

"They Lord," I say.

"Let me know if you need any help, ma'am," he says, stony voiced, no expression whatever.

"No help needed, *thank* you."

Ruth tugs at my arm and tells me her brother Carl's right over there in the Ford, come along. Won't take no for an answer.

So I oblige. Turn away from that aggravating damn conductor and march down the platform at Ruth's side. Satchel banging against my leg. Wouldn't do to be rude, now, would it?

4

The ride is short. As I said, a mere half mile separates Duke Kelly's ramshackle abode from the railway depot, and Ruth Mary Leary's brother Carl has acquired himself a fine new Model T Ford, engine purring like an overfed cat: the kind of automobile that makes easy work of a country road, even in wintertime. Carl's delighted to see me. Seems he went to school with Johnnie.

"Recollect how we used to catch them crawdads in the old fishing hole, down by the creek? You was covered in dirt back then, Geneva Rose. Knees all skinned, dress up to here." (He points to his shinbone.) "Fixed to steal a kiss from you once, and Lord Almighty did you let me have it. Never did try again."

"Wise decision."

He laughs. "Always knowed you was going to bust outta River Junction for good. You was that kind of girl. Reckon you own half New York by now."

"Not quite. It's a big town, after all. An island unto itself."

"Reckon you got some high-class fella to step you out these days, that right? Reckon your knees ain't skinned no more, no ma'am. You done cleaned up right smart, Geneva Rose, just like I knowed you would."

Ruth Mary spears his ribs with her elbow. "Now, you quit your teasing, Carl Green. Geneva's back home on account-a her mama's sick."

"Aw, I'm sorry. Forgot about all that. Didn't mean to offend." Looks back at me, over his shoulder, and his blue eyes are kind.

"Oh, that's all right, Carl. Laughter's the best medicine, they always say."

Already we've turned the corner of Front Street, and Duke's abode stands but seventy-five yards ahead, on the rightward side of the road. Me, I happen to be staring leftward, toward the astonishing sight of a brand-new house getting itself built: a large house made of red brick, full dozen busy workmen crawling all over its skin, almost as if it weren't the middle of winter and this the middle of River Junction.

"Why, whose house is that?" I cry out, from the backseat.

"Which-un, sugar?"

"The brick one, the one that's getting built."

"Why, don't you know? That there is your brother Angus's house. Fixing to get married in June. That house be his wedding present. From your daddy."

"Here we are!" sings out Ruth.

Carl brakes hard, sending the flivver into a bit of skid across the firm-packed snow covering the road, and Ruth screams a little. Carl just laughs.

As for me. So discombobulated am I from the sight of Angus's grand brick house and the precarious sliding of the Ford's new tires, I turn my head right bang in the direction of my childhood abode to fill my eyes, a mistake I hoped never again to make in this life.

But the sight that strikes my eyeballs isn't the sight I expect, and maybe I should have expected that. Maybe I should have taken note of the spruced-up railway depot and the spruced-up businesses, and the grand new house getting built as a wedding present for my worthless brother Angus. Maybe I should have thought more thoroughly through the implications of what Special Agent Anson disclosed to me last night (was it just last night?) in his shoddy little office along the rim of Tenth Avenue.

Not a little *business, Miss Kelly. Your stepfather has built a network of distilleries across Allegany County and beyond, and nobody will say a word against him.*

Now the first time I came home from the convent on a school holiday, it was a day much like this. Winter. Christmas around the corner, and the first fall of snow had newly hit the ground, covering the rotting re- mains of autumn. Mama and Johnnie came to the sta- tion to walk me home. I wore my shabby little clothes, my threadbare coat through which the wind whistled and froze on my skin. Wee satchel in one hand, carry- ing my all. Fingers still stinging by the wrong end of Sister Esme's ruler. Mama clutched Johnnie's wrist and waved as I stepped from the train. She was great with child, coat straining mightily over the weight of her belly, eyes all hooded and weary. Hat full of holes. I ran up to her and she bent and hugged me, and then she straightened and looked me up and looked me down, and I remember the expression on her face, because I couldn't decide was she happy or was she sad. Some frictional combination of the two, I guess, peculiar to grown-ups.

Anyway, we trudged home through the darkening snow and arrived at the house, Duke Kelly's house, and

Johnnie opened the creaking gate and I looked up and took it in, the house of my childhood, and I saw things I hadn't seen before. I saw the peeling white paint and the sagging boards, the bricks crumbling from the chimney and the way the porch slanted downward by a few unhappy degrees. And I thought something sort of strange for a little girl to think, an idea made unusually of clear, distinct words that still ring in my head: *This is not my home.* Just like that. *This is not my home.*

As I stood there by the gate, experiencing this alienation, the front door opened and there stood Duke, wearing his neat suit of brown wool, the lord of this dilapidated little manor. Looking us over as if he owned us, as if we were cattle wandering in from the cold. And the thought—*This is not my home*—flared up stronger and fiercer, almost fixing me to vomit with its clarity. *This is not my home.*

You cannot go back from a thought like that. You cannot return to a state of childlike trust in a building, a state of affection for all its faults, just because that house represents some kind of refuge from the outside world. Once you reject that house—or maybe that house rejects you, I don't know—your hatred can only mount and mount, until the walls themselves seem to poison you, the very surfaces of the furniture to fester under your touch. The day I passed through that front door for the last time, it was like a layer of foul skin peeled away from my body and slithered to the porch behind me, and I have never looked back, I never once turned my head for a last look.

Now it's gone.

That sagging white house, home to Kellys since about the Revolution, where Duke Kelly himself entered the world in the same upstairs bedroom as his daddy before him and his own sons after, has disappeared. In its place stands a building that might as well be the town hall, so far as I can see: faced in limestone, crammed tight with every architectural feature you can imagine—Palladian windows and Jacobean parapets and friezes and bay windows and God knows. Stretches fifty feet in either direction from a front door like the entrance to a cathedral.

"Lord Almighty," I say. "What's that?"

"Why, it's your daddy's new house! Ain't they sent you no pictures? Mr. Kelly's right proud of that place."

"No."

Carl sets the brake and jumps out to hump my carpetbag. "Well, there it is."

"Ain't it grand?" sighs out Ruth. "Just like that Morgan fella in New York."

"Just exactly like." I take the bag from Carl, whose

face wears an expression of intelligent mischief, and what do you know, I actually recall him. Recall an afternoon down by the creek, full of heat and mud and blood-drunk skeeters, and a boy with an unusual pointed face, like an elf, who snatched me out of the water and tugged me into the bushes and held his hand over my mouth, grinning and grinning, and I was so mad and helpless, imprisoned by his skinny arms, until I heard my stepfather's voice floating down the grassy bank and realized that this boy had actually rescued me. Staring at me just as he stares now. Blue eyes twinkly and all-knowing, like they see right through the substance of my little troubles. That was my first kiss. Didn't last long. I slapped him for it a second later. Carl Green. What do you know. I hold out my hand and say thank you, and I'm not talking about the ride home.

Well, the mischief fades a little. He takes the hand and shakes it. Warm palm melts through my glove. "You take care of yourself, Geneva Rose."

"I surely will."

A big voice roars from between the pillars on the brand-new portico.

"Carl Green, you sonofabitch! Get your lousy hands off my sister."

(That's Johnnie. As if you couldn't guess.)

5

My kid brother wraps me up in a hug that might turn a weaker mortal into a diamond. Johnnie always was two sizes bigger than the other boys, even when he was born. They used to get up games of football in the schoolyard and Johnnie just plowed right over everybody.

"Where's Mama?" I ask when he lets me go.

"Upstairs. How's yourself, sis? You look different."

"I *am* different. So're you. What kind of joint is this?"

"You should see the inside."

"I would if you'd invite me through the door."

Big old familiar belly laugh. Johnnie's laugh can cure any trouble. He takes my carpetbag and turns to usher me through the door, and I tilt away to wave good-bye to Carl and Ruth, but they're already gone, smell of gasoline exhaust fouling the air behind them.

The door stands open, allowing expensive gusts of warm air to escape into the winter afternoon. Johnnie sends me into the foyer and follows, shutting the door behind us, and I'll be damned if a fellow in a black-and-white uniform doesn't appear from the doorway to the right, hair all slicked back, asking me for my coat in broad country cadence. As I obey, I peer into his scrubbed face and dark eyes. "Why, Tommy Leary! Is that you?"

Tommy sort of flushes and says it sure is, how is you, Geneva Rose? I hand him my coat and say I'm just fine, stopped by to see my mama. Around us, the foyer takes shape, polished wood paneling and white marble floor, a god-awful chandelier bursting from the ceiling twenty feet above, twin staircases curving upward to form some kind of gallery. I nod toward them. "That way?"

"Turn right at the top. Johnnie'll show you."

He speaks in a tone of hushed reverence, or so near to hushing and reverence as a fellow like Tommy Leary can manage, and the very respect in his voice sends my pulse throbbing like a dynamo. I toss my coat into his arms and stride across that slippery damn marble to the rightmost staircase, and as I bound upward and wheel right and race down the corridor, I take no notice of the statuary and the portraiture and the red-and-gold wallpaper, nor yet the plush crimson carpet and the scrolling plasterwork on the ceiling above.

I just think, *Mama, poor Mama, left to decay in a mausoleum like this.*

6

No expense spared on Mama's bedroom, I'll say that. If Duke Kelly is the new king of River Junction, this chamber is fit for his queen. Twelve-foot ceilings and a canopied bed. French furniture gilded up right. She's even got a lady-in-waiting, some kind of uniformed nurse who hovers near the window, eyes snarling at me as I bend over Mama's sleeping body.

"She mustn't be disturbed," snaps the nurse.

I send her a glance, no more. "Pardon me. I'm Geneva Kelly, Mrs. Kelly's daughter, and I expect I'll do what is damned well best for her."

Behind me, Johnnie makes a coughing noise.

Mama may be sleeping, but not in peace. Her eyelids twitch, her fingers claw the glossy satin counterpane. Her skin is pale and fine, such that I can follow the disturbing passage of blood along the network of arteries and capillaries and veins, back to her heart, pulsing through again.

Someone once told me—I can't remember whom— that Mama was a great beauty in her youth. I suppose she must have been. After all, she ran off to New York when she was but sixteen and joined some kind of show, dancing and singing for the entertainment of ladies and gentlemen. Mostly gentlemen, I suspect. Inevitably, one of them sired me, but the funny thing is, she didn't return to River Junction right away after this disgrace. She stayed on in Manhattan for two more years, and when she returned, she was still bright and well fed, as her wedding photograph attests. How I used to stare at that photograph of Mama, snapped just before Duke got into her. The only glimpse I had of the real Mama, clean and untainted. Her eyes are hooded, mysterious, her brows a pair of long, elegant arches, slightly bent at the ends. Smooth dairy skin, lips set in a melancholy young pout entirely unsuited to the happy occasion of a respectable marriage meant to save her from mortal sin. But she's lovely, no doubt about that, and what's more, there exists no hint of my own existence in that photograph, either hiding coyly in her big white skirt or disturbing the perfection of her small white waist. Just her smirking new husband at her side, a head taller, eyes a little blurred as if recovering from a blink.

The point is, she was beautiful once, and you can still trace the contours of that beauty in her bones. Perhaps better than before, because her skin now sinks like a drape along her skeleton, exposing the angles of symmetry, exposing the loving hand of God in her creation. Maybe she feels my breath on her cheek, because her eyes crack open for an instant, her head turns in my direction, and then the lids fall back twitching and a sort of moan slips free from her desiccated lips.

The carpet rustles. "See what you've done," says the nurse.

"What's the matter with her?"

"She's in the last stages of a consumption, as you can see."

"What kind of consumption?"

"Aw, now, Geneva Rose," says my brother softly. "You know she been like this for years. Just a-getting worse and worse."

"Having so many babies, I guess. That kind of consumption."

Nobody says a word. Mama's breath bubbles in her lungs. Offers the nurse: "It's God's will."

"Or Duke's will, I guess, which is much the same thing." I place my hands over hers, hoping to still that goddamned clawing, but the knuckles keep on sliding beneath my palms, all bone, and another moan slips out, more like a sigh. My mama's dying. I remove my hands and straighten the counterpane and turn to Johnnie. "I could use a drink."

7

S eems Duke's house has a special room for such purposes, drinking and smoking and what have you. I guess most folks would call it a library. There's bookshelves, anyway, with real books in them, from all appearances. Smell of smoke and leather and tobacco. Maybe a hint of good country whiskey. Winter sun poking between the curtains. Johnnie mixes me something while I stand next to a baronial marble mantel and light a cigarette. "Have a seat," he calls—the room is wide—but I shake my head. The fire's made of coal and burns hot. Melts the stockings right off my legs. I have no intention of moving away from such delicious, unending warmth as that.

"We never used to have such fires," I observe.

"Things have changed around here."

"No kidding." I flick a little ash into the fire and turn to face Johnnie, who's making his way across the acre or so of Oriental carpet, bearing a lowball glass in each hand. "Your daddy's special recipe?"

"It ain't going to kill you, if that's what you mean."

"No, I guess not. He's not the kind of fellow to poison his own well, is he?" Nonetheless, I sniff before sipping. Rye whiskey, pure and pungent. Neither one of us proposes a toast. Doesn't seem proper, with Mama dying upstairs. Johnnie drinks about half in one gulp and lifts his massive elbow to the fireboard. Peers into my face in his mute, slow way. I sip again and say, "How long has Mama been sick like this?"

"Ain't she always been like this?"

"Don't say *ain't*, Johnnie. I raised you better than that."

He finishes the drink and pulls a cigarette case from his pocket. A gold one that reminds me of Billy's cigarette case, except Johnnie's is more ornate. Swirls and curlicues all embossed around the sides. His monogram in letters so complicated I take their identity on faith.

"Nice box. So you're on the take, I guess."

He pulls out a cigarette and lights up clumsily. "Last month—about Christmas—I reckon she fell sick again."

"The usual?"

He nods. Turns to the fire and rests both paws on the edge of the fireboard. Cigarette burns quietly from between two meaty fingers. "Some kind of infection got in. Couldn't shake it. Dad called in all kinds of doctors."

"I'll bet."

"He did, though."

"I don't doubt it. And where is the great humanitarian now?"

"Business meeting."

"Does he know I'm here?"

Johnnie straightens and snatches a drag from his cigarette. His long, broad nose looks a little pink to me. "Reckon he does now."

"You don't say. He's reading minds, is he?"

"Geneva Rose, the first thing you got to understand, ain't nobody comes in or out of River Junction these days without Duke Kelly knows it."

We stand there staring at each other, absorbing the heat of the fire. Johnnie's got this funny thing about his eyes, one kind of blue and the other one greener. Also the pupil's larger in the blue one—you have to be standing close to notice this—and the effect, combined with his giant frame and strange bony face, can give you a regular case of the willies if you aren't already acquainted with the fact that Johnnie Kelly is a gentle old pussycat, sweetest honey-heart in Allegany County, wouldn't hurt a flea unless it was carrying a football toward the wrong set of goalposts. God only knows where he gets his nature from. Not his daddy.

"How long has he been running this racket?" I ask.

"Since right about the day you left, I guess. Near enough, anyway. Figured out Carl Green's daddy was cooking up rye mash in his barn and making a few nice dollars on the side, selling it on to some outfit in Hagerstown. Well, Duke went straight to Hagerstown and convinced that fellow to let *him* run the business instead—"

"Did he now? Did he shoot the poor sucker dead, or just wave the gun in his face?"

"Naw, Geneva. You know Duke don't like guns."

I toss the end of my cigarette into the fire and hand Johnnie my empty glass. "Refill, dearest?"

Johnnie ambles back off across the rug, wrinkled suit jacket swinging from his wide shoulders, and I light another cigarette and start off along the row of bookshelves lining the wall, each one crammed tight with rigid new leather-bound volumes. Mahogany gleams under the electric light. I run my finger along a gold-stamped spine—*Tristram Shandy,* blow me down—and ask Johnnie where Duke got all the damn books. Rob the wrong storefront in Baltimore?

"Hired a dealer, I guess. Said he wanted the best library in the county."

I allow a low whistle. "How much lettuce is he clearing, do you think?"

"Aw, I don't keep the books."

"You can guess. A hundred thousand? Two hundred?"

"Maybe something like that. Maybe more."

Another whistle. "Three hundred large a year."

Johnnie walks up and hands me my second rye whiskey. "A month."

"Three hundred thousand dollars a *month*?" (Sputter of whiskey.)

"Something like that. Less expenses."

"Oh, naturally. Expenses. You've got to pay everybody off, for one thing. All those revenue agents and policemen don't come cheap, I'll bet. To say nothing of butlers and country estates and mahogany bookshelves full of books you can't even read. And a nurse to tend the wife you've fucked into an early grave."

To Johnnie's credit, he doesn't flinch at this little speech, not even the filthy, staccato word that punctuates it. Just a long, slow blink, as if he doesn't quite recognize my face, after all. The ceiling creaks above us. Lights in the electric chandelier give off a shiver. I suck on my cigarette and take a drink.

"Well? Aren't you going to answer me, you big dumb ox? Or are you on that bastard's side now, instead of mine?"

"Now, Geneva Rose," he says softly, "that money's done a lot of good around here."

"Oh, I can see that, all right. Smart new houses. Buildings all cleaned up. I see Carl Green's driving himself a nice new flivver, right off the lot. I'll bet everybody in River Junction's got an automobile now, and a garage to put it in."

"No. I mean folks can eat regular. Folks can get a doctor when they're sick. Get medicine and coal for the winter."

"And fancy gold cigarette cases."

"Aw, Geneva." He shakes his head. Nudges his glass against mine. "Anyway, where do you think *this* comes from? All that moonshine you're drinking in New York City. Don't tell me you ain't a-drinking hooch in some joint most nights, you and your friends. It's Duke's hooch you're drinking, ain't it? He's just giving you what you want. What you demand from somewhere. Anywhere."

"Goddamn it, Johnnie." I hurl my glass into the fireplace, hard, so it shatters good. Makes the coals hiss like a snake. "Goddamn the pair of you."

"Geneva Rose. You always was a hothead."

"I've got a right, don't you think?"

He doesn't answer.

"You know what? I should have done something about him years ago. Should've had the nerve to just walk up while he was sleeping, and bam! Right in his ear." I make my fingers like a revolver, cigarette sticking in a diagonal line from the imaginary trigger.

"Then I might have just stayed right here with you and Mama in River Junction. Never had to leave."

"Law woulda found you, though."

"Now, don't go spoiling my dream, Johnnie-boy. Don't say it never did cross your mind, neither."

He rolls his shoulders and stares at me piteously. "Lot of folks woulda starved or froze to death, then. Lot of widows woulda had nowhere to live."

"Got his finger in every pie, hasn't he? A thousand little insurance policies to make sure he never goes to jail."

"Folks round here'd die for him now, honey. Remember that."

"What about you, Johnnie? Would you die for him?"

He furrows his two thick brows into one, making my stomach knot up. But before he can open his mouth to answer this important question, a sweet voice pipes up from the doorway.

"Johnnie! Johnnie! Who're you talking to?"

And I turn my head to find a little girl bearing Mama's hooded eyes and Duke Kelly's dark hair, wearing a pink dress and black patent leather Mary Jane shoes, and Johnnie's big voice rolls out from beside me in an entirely different tone.

"Why, Patsy-pet, don't you know your own sister, come home this minute from New York City?"

8

I know I'm supposed to say something, call out some greeting, open up my arms so I can embrace this baby sister of mine, who is growing fast into a beauty far more breath-stopping than even her mama. But my limbs seem to have taken on some strange disease of paralysis, some untoward stiffening, while my belly contracts into a hard and sickening ball. Only my heart moves, knocking dizzily into my ribs.

Patsy-pet displays no such symptoms of physical malady. She skips right on across all that Oriental rug and into Johnnie's chest—he's lowered himself to his knees to accommodate her tiny frame—and just sort of peers round his ear and into my face like she can't decide am I friend or am I foe.

I sort of squeak, "Well now. I was wondering where you got to."

Patsy whispers something in Johnnie's ear, just exactly the way he used to whisper in mine, and he nods that head of his and lifts her right up into the air, settling her on his hip, and turns to me.

"Say hello to Geneva Rose," he tells her.

"Hello, Geneva Rose."

Somehow I force my right arm into movement. I shift the cigarette into the other hand and lift her little fingers and kiss them. Tiny, perfect nails like chips from a pearl. "Hello, Patsy darling. I used to rock you to sleep when you were a tiny baby."

She smiles. Ducks her head into the safety of Johnnie's shoulder. (Can't fault her for that, can I?)

Johnnie says, "Tell your big sister what you been doing today."

"Reading," she whispers.

"Reading what?"

"Books."

"Big-girl books, ain't that right?"

"Isn't," I say. "We say *isn't* instead of *ain't*. *Isn't* that right, Patsy?"

Patsy giggles into Johnnie's jacket.

"She's a swell reader," Johnnie says. "Took to her letters right away. We got a teacher in here, just for her. No schoolhouse for Miss Patsy."

"What about your numbers, Patsy? Numbers are important, too."

"Does her numbers, too. Regular little Einstein, this sweet child."

"But mostly you like to read, don't you, darling?" I touch her fingers again. I can't help it. Her eyes are a bright, clear blue, the same shade as Mama's. Same shade as mine.

Patsy nods and moves her thumb against mine, and I'll be damned if that slight little caress doesn't start my eyes stinging.

"Yes." I mimic her nod. "I can tell. You know why?"

Her eyebrows lift up. I lean in close.

"Because I was just the same way."

9

Now I'm getting sloppy, aren't I? I apologize. Too little sleep, maybe, or else the sight of my mama dying in her luxurious bed upstairs. Or the sight of Patsy's pretty eyes, as I said, just exactly like those in Mama's wedding photograph I mentioned earlier, except full of color instead of sepia, and all new and unspoiled.

And she likes to read. Well, she doesn't get that from her daddy, for certain. Duke can't read. He'd kill me for telling you that, but it's true. I remember how I used to hide inside the library—not *this* one, obviously, but the decrepit room tacked onto the dilapidated old shack we call a town hall—baking all afternoon in the chair next to the hot window, until you could stick four and twenty blackbirds into me and call me a pie. Miss Tweed was the librarian then. She was the preacher's daughter and awfully young, maybe seventeen or eighteen. The nearest I had to a sister, though we never fixed to speak. We didn't need to. One time, afternoon in the infernal center of July, so hot you might burn your palm just setting it against the window glass, Duke came looking for me, steaming from the ears. Miss Tweed saw him through the door and flicked her finger at me, and quick as a tick I ducked under her desk, next to her legs, and I listened to that young lady inform my step-daddy in her calm librarian's voice that no, she hadn't seen me today, must be too warm indoors. I was more likely cooling off in the creek with the other small fry. And such was Duke's fear of book-learned women, of libraries in general, that he turned away right then. Didn't even question her. And when the coast was clear I crawled out from her desk and we sort of looked at each other, and I saw that her cheeks were as pale as mine, even in that blazing room. She got married soon after, nice young fellow visiting the parsonage from Baltimore, and the library fell into neglect. When I tried to sneak inside the following summer, the door was closed and locked, and nobody seemed to have a key.

10

Composure restored by cigarettes and rye whiskey, I'm ready to climb back up the colossal staircase and sit with Mama until dinnertime. Johnnie takes Patsy out to play in the snow, and I watch them through the window of Mama's bedroom. There seems to be some kind of formal garden out there, replacing the henhouse and the corncrib and the rusting remains of farm machinery, though you can only just trace its neat, boxy edges beneath the snow and imagine how it looks in spring. Down where the trees stick up and the white ground bends south toward the creek, I keep my eyes away.

The nurse fidgets a moment and leaves, without saying a word, and I draw the chair closer to the bed and sit down. Mama's hands are quieter now, her eyelids more peaceful. A smell of medicine hangs over her, and the peculiar sour-sweet scent of death, and I swallow down a mite of bile and open a book on my lap. *Little Women*. Stolen from Duke's new library downstairs, pages crisp and new, binding rigid with glue. Mama always loved that story. I guess she liked to think that in another time, maybe married to a different man, she might have been some kind of Marmee herself. All hoopskirts and wisdom and fortitude and faith.

At the sound of my voice, however, her fingers start up the twitching again. Her eyelids churn, her lips spasm. I keep on reading in my most soothing voice, thinking maybe it's just the change in the air, the additional stimulation, but her agitation grows and grows and at last I drop the book on the plush carpet next to the chair legs, and I lay my head on the counterpane next to her thin and struggling chest. I take her cadaverous hand and hold it against my cheek. I don't know which of us I'm trying to quiet. The heat of her fever seeps past my skin. I can't stand the bubbling in her lungs, the death smell of her, the frail, febrile state of her bones in my palm. I want her just to die already, and then my throat and my eyes fill with remorse, which is wet and tastes of salt.

In the end, I expect I fall asleep, because when the door bangs open, startling me to my feet, the space behind the curtains has gone entirely dark.

"By the good Lord God," says Duke Kelly, "if it ain't the prodigal daughter."

11

As far as I can remember, my step-daddy never held down a regular job. Maybe when he was younger; I don't know. He used to say that was because there wasn't no jobs going here in River Junction, but other men found some kind of work, everhow menial, or scratched out a bit of food from the earth for fear of starving otherwise. Or else fear of watching their wives and children starve, which most fellows consider even worse.

Not Duke, however. Never packed a lunch pail so long as I knew him. Sit and brood, or else meet the other boys for checkers or rye whiskey at the saloon, smoking and flapping their gums all afternoon and sometimes all night. Every so often he would disappear for a day or two and come back with money—I don't know how much—and that's what we lived on, near as I can tell. But a regular job? Not enough for Duke. He was like a man waiting around for a train, a train that didn't come but once a day. Except that you didn't know the exact hour of its arrival, no timetable for a train like that, so there you sat, all day long, doing just enough to keep your heart still beating. Just passing time.

Now it seems Duke was right about the train. He certainly wears that air into Mama's bedroom: the air of a man who's been proved right about the most important question in his life. Physically, he's just the same. Hair as black and sleek, not a gray strand daring to touch daylight. Eyes as hard, chin as cleft, shoulders as boxy. Maybe a little rounder around the jowls, but prosperity will do that. The only thing changed is his clothes. He's dressed in a dark, expensive suit, made from the same rarefied grade of cashmere wool as that worn by the partners back at Sterling Bates on the corner of Wall and Broad, and his starched white cuffs are linked in solid gold. From his collar sticks the same stout, tanned, country neck, like that of a prize bull, and his thick lips press into the kind of smile that makes me want to leap out the window into the new-fallen snow.

I turn back to Mama. "Be quiet. She's dying."

"I know that, sugar."

He walks up behind me and comes to rest just over my right shoulder. I keep my back straight and my eyes on Mama's face. She's turned her head a little, as if hearing Duke's voice, and her fingers twitch against my hand.

"Poor thing," he says. "Never did have much strength."

"Because you kept filling her up with babies. Sucking her life away."

"Now, just what was I supposed to do, honey? We was man and wife. I never did run around after other women, did I? I kept to your mama just like I vowed."

"That's not how I remember it."

He laughs. "Now, that's different. Ain't you her own flesh and blood?"

"You disgust me."

"Fine words." He reaches past me and presses the backs of his fingers against her temple. Her eyes open. She turns her head into his touch. "Where's the nurse gone? Nurse ain't supposed to leave her for a single minute."

"I'm here. I'm nursing her."

"Well, now, Geneva Rose." He lifts his hand away and brings it to rest on my shoulder, just under the lobe of my ear, pinky finger pressing intimately against the bare skin of my neck. "That ain't your job, is it?"

I knock his hand away and bolt from the chair. "You stay away from me. You stay away from the both of us."

"She's my wife. I ain't a-going nowhere."

"If you touch her again, I'll kill you."

He curls his hand around the back of the chair I've just left. "You got no call to speak those words to me, Geneva Rose. I gave you my name and my home. Your mama's had the best money can buy. Just look at her. You want her dying in some damn cot in a boarding-house, all covered over with fleas?"

"Better than being bitten by a flea like you."

Duke doesn't move. Stands there next to Mama's bed, breathing and staring inside his fine suit of cash-mere wool. The radiators hiss at the windows. Around the topmost slat of that chair, his fingers flex and curl, flex and curl. "Look at you, baby. So fine and pretty, your hair all soft. Lips all red. Dress all short. Tell your daddy the truth, now. How many men you had since you moved to the city?"

"Dozens. Took me dozens to scrape off the stain of your hands on my skin, Duke Kelly, and I ain't fin-ished yet. I'm here to say good-bye to my mama, and then I'm going back to New York, where I am aiming to take up with the first man I see."

He reaches into the inside pocket of his jacket and pulls out a fine gold cigarette case, much like the one Johnnie showed me earlier. Takes his time lighting a cigarette with one of those new butane contraptions, also plated in gold. "No, you ain't either. You is going back to that nice young fella you been stepping out with, ain't that right? That swell college boy you keep tucked up in your bed. That cheap little room-a yours. That cheap little room on—now, what was it? Christopher Street."

No way to describe the sensation that strikes through me at those words. Like an icy bucket over the head, I guess, so cold it freezes your nerves in an instant, numbs the very reflexes that are supposed to save you.

I sort of squeak, "What do you know about that?"

"Aw, sugar. I know everything about you. You think I'd let my baby girl go off to New York City without a-keeping a tender watch over her? I been watching you all along, Geneva Rose. Keeping my eye on you." He winks. Shoots his cuff. Takes a long drag on his cigarette and turns his head to gaze down at his wife. "Just like I watch over your mama. What's money for, if you can't take good care-a your women and children?"

"You haven't taken good care of her. You've killed her."

"Now, that ain't fair. The good Lord God be taking her back to His bosom, that's all. Plenty-a women had more babies than her. Having babies is natural. What she was put on this good earth to do. Now He be a-calling her back." He bends over Mama's body and strokes her forehead. "I'm just here to see as she gets the best-a everything before she goes. Best money can buy."

"Blood money, you mean. Every dollar of it made outside the law."

"What do you care? You been drinking your share. Don't you fix to tell me you ain't. Don't fix to tell me you think a fella shouldn't enjoy himself a damn glass-a whiskey at the end of a hard day, just on account-a the government says he can't. You just mad on account-a it's me getting rich, instead-a some other racket? Look what I done for this town." He spreads out his arm. "Every man employed. Every woman got a chicken in her pot, shoes on her feet. You want to take all that away?"

"No."

"Good, then. Because I ain't going nowhere, Geneva Rose. You remember that."

He holds my mama's hand as he gazes at me, and the look on his smooth face curdles the atmosphere. The fire hisses in the fireplace, piling more heat atop the infernal output of the brand-new radiators, and the sweat trickles right down my spine to dampen the back of my girdle. Make my stockings prickle on my legs. Make my dress feel like a hair shirt, like I want to jump right on out of it. Jump on out of myself entirely.

"You can do as you like, I reckon. Just stay away from me."

He makes a smile. "You sure about that? You been living in a rat hole there in New York. A rat hole. You might could live in a castle, if you like."

Mama makes a little coughing sound. Legs go thrashing. I bound to the bed. Elbow my stepfather aside. Lift up her head a little, reach for the glass of water on the bedside table. The coughing stills. She turns her face toward my inner arm, like she's catching my scent, and I wet her lips with the water so she can lick it off. I don't imagine she can properly swallow. The bed's hung in heavy red damask, window curtains too, the color of slow insanity.

Duke says softly, "Don't need to be this way, sugar. You know I can be a right good friend."

"You must be tetched. I already told you. You touch me again, and I'll kill you."

He laughs. "Baby girl. I don't mean that kind-a friends. Not no more. You is soiled goods, Geneva Rose, you been soiled *good* in that city-a yours, no mistake, and you can say what you like, but I don't never follow where other men-a gone."

"Except with Mama."

"Well, that there was different. And your mama and I, we had an understanding betwixt us, see."

I stare down at Mama's tormented chest, beneath that satin counterpane, sawing up and down in a syncopated jazz rhythm. I hate the proximity of Duke's body, the muscular tension of his shoulders. The smell of his breath, laden with rye whiskey and good Virginia tobacco. My loathing is so vigorous, so native, that the act of standing next to him requires an extreme exercise of will, the same way you have to force the north pole of one magnet into the north pole of another.

"Some understanding," I mutter.

"You always was so contrary." Breath hot on the top of my head. "You never did comprehend what was good for you."

"What was good for *you*, you mean."

"What's that, baby girl? Can't hear you."

"Go to hell."

And that's when his hand encircles my throat from behind, without any kind of sound or ceremony: just those sharp-nailed fingers digging knowledgeably in between the tendons, pressing against the ridges and bumps of my voice box. The cigarette burns a hair's breadth from my skin. He says gently, into my ear, "Don't you go doing nothing stupid, baby girl. You know I don't take kindly to that. There's one thing I can't stand on this earth, and that's a damn Judas. You understand me?"

I can't exactly speak, so I just nod up and down against the washboard of his chest, while my stomach boils and my ears roar.

"Good," says Duke.

The door bangs open behind us, and he releases me like a spring. I pitch forward into the bed, just saving myself from landing atop poor Mama's belly, while the nurse, reeking of rye whiskey, makes some anxious, disjointed apology about visiting the lavatory.

12

Sometime in the night, Mama wakes up lucid. I am dozing beside her in the bed, and I bolt straight up.

"Mama?"

"Geneva Rose. That you?"

"It surely is, Mama."

"Thought I done heard you there, somewheres."

"You surely did. Right here next to you on the bed, Mama."

"That's right good-a you, sugar. So pleased you came."

"Course I came. You're my mama, aren't you?"

She doesn't answer. She's been whispering, like the sound of paper moving against paper, and I can't see her real well in the dark like this. Only the coals for light. I reach out and find her hand, and for some reason I am overcome by the memory of those hands braiding my hair when I was small, before she sent me away to the convent. I used to stare at her lively fingers in the scrap of mirror above the washstand, darting in and out of my uncooperative copper mane, whipping those strands into nice neat overlapping order on either side of my head. Mouth full of pins. She used to tell me how she did the other girls' hair back in New York, she was real good at it.

"You was reading *Little Women*, wasn't you?"

"Your favorite. Remember how we used to read together, Mama? You had all the voices just right."

"You was always such a good reader, Geneva Rose. You read still?"

"When I can."

"You all right in New York? You ain't got yourself into no trouble, have you?"

"Never once. I take good care of myself."

"Knowed you would. That's why—"

(Voice lapses away.)

"Why *what*, Mama? Why you let me leave for the city?"

"Yes. Had to, didn't I?"

I run my fingertips along the bones of her hand. "I reckon so."

My pulse is striking wildly. My lips are dry. I do recall reading that the dying sometimes discover a moment of final clarity, just before the reaper bends down and snatches them away. Feel as if my eyes are scraping the shadows, looking for a sickle gleaming in the moonshine. Feel as if the seconds are ticking away. No way to ask what needs asking. No way to say what needs saying. And she's gone quiet. Maybe it's over already. I press her knuckles.

"So sorry," she whispers.

(Relief.)

"You got nothing to be sorry for. Did all you could. You're a good mama."

She says something I can't quite make out. Something that sounds like negation.

"Why, yes, you did, Mama. You found a way to send me away to the convent. To college—"

"No!"

This word, unlike the others, comes out by force. Sort of a strangled little shout. I lie there on my side, facing her, smelling her medicine sick-sweet smell, the damp heat of her nightgown, holding her hand. Realizing that the smell of medicine is really the smell of alcohol, only more pure. I touch her hair, which is softer than I guess I was expecting, thin and fine next to her head, like somebody's been brushing it all day. Her head is moving a little, from side to side.

"Now, Mama. You just rest."

"That was your daddy. Your poor dear daddy."

I place my hand on her opposite cheek and turn her face an inch or two in my direction. "Mama! You mean Duke? That was *Duke's* idea? My education?"

"He did love you so."

"Oh, Mama. I don't know about that. Duke—"

"Your *daddy*," she insists, fervent emphasis, and I realize, in the darkness, her eyes are wide open, and she's staring at me like you might stare at an apparition of some kind, a vision from another universe.

"My daddy," I repeat.

The eyes close. "Loves you so."

Now, I've never given much thought to the man who sired me. I guess that might surprise you. All the Fifth Avenue psychologists say that I ought to have some kind of complex about my real daddy, some kind of fixation, most especially since the fellow who took his place turned out so rotten. Well, that might be true for some girls, but not for me. I don't spare him a single consideration, most days. Why should I? I don't reckon he spares one for me. And just look what he did to my mama! Leaving her to die away like this, stuck inside her poor old broken-down childbearing body. Inasmuch as I mind him at all, I figure he's some Manhattan swell who spotted my mama and thought he might have himself a good time with a pretty girl from the revue, and so he did.

So I can't quite explain why that tender whisper—*Loves you so*—causes such a bubble to swell up in my chest. Squeeze out all else. Breath and heart and everything.

"You mean my real daddy, Mama? That who you mean?"

She's moving her lips, but the words aren't coming forth, and I give her hand a squeeze, kind of sharp, to bring her back to River Junction. Her eyelids make this spasm. She says, "Laura Ann," except it all runs together, *Laurann*.

"Who's Laurann?"

"Laurann."

I pick my thoughts a bit. Stroking her hand. "You mean Laura Ann *Green*, Mama?"

"Laurann," she says once more, nodding, and she closes her eyes again, like in rapture, and goes all still, just her lips moving and moving without making a sound, and there's nothing I can do to rouse her.

Though I do realize, some time later, that her fever is gone. Skin as cool and dry as yesterday's washing.

13

Mama's dead by morning. The nurse and I wash her frail body and lay her out on the bed in what Johnnie says is her favorite dress, though I don't recognize it. Course not. I guess it must be one of the new ones Duke bought her. Velvet the color of midnight. Fashion that from before the war. Her skin is terribly pale against that dress.

Soon after comes the undertaker, neat and respectful in his black suit. He and his assistant load my mama into the van, and the assistant drives the van away while the undertaker disappears with Duke into some kind of private study on the first floor. By now it's gone ten o'clock. Too late to go back to bed and get some sleep, even if I could, though I haven't slept more than three or four hours in the past forty-eight. Can't even imagine the act of closing my eyes. Too many thoughts jumping around behind them. I wander around the first floor, heels clickety-clack on the fields of pale marble, looking for the kitchen and a possible pot of good black coffee. Figure it's got to be around here somewhere. Round the back, out of sight, a rich man's kitchen.

I pass through the door at the corner of the dining room and down a long corridor of a butler's pantry and there it lies, good glory, a kitchen about the size of the entire first floor of the old house, inhabited by a cook and a kitchen maid, cleaning up the breakfast dishes. The maid wipes her apron and fetches me toast and coffee. Her face is familiar. I expect I went to school with her too, in that time I try generally not to remember about. Before they sent me off to the nuns. I stand about awkwardly, thinking of something to say to the cook, who stares at me under her eyebrows like I'm some kind of exotic new fruit she's fixing to chop up and serve at luncheon. Duke Kelly's missing daughter, turned up on the eve of her mama's passing on. You don't see that kind of thing walking through your kitchen door every day.

So I stand there staring at the ceiling, arms crossed behind my back. Cook sets to work. Toast arrives crisp and buttery, coffee hot and thick. Maid says softly, "I'm awful sorry about your mama, Geneva Rose," and I put my face into grievous position, the kind of expression I guess you're supposed to return to a statement like that, and I thank her for her sympathy. Still can't remember her damn name.

Since I am so patently in the way, here inside this brand-new kitchen of Duke's, staffed by staff, brand-new Garland range, brand-new icebox, pantry the size of Pennsylvania Station, I pour myself a little more coffee and wander back upstairs to Mama's room. The door to the study is still shut tight. Nobody stirring. The house has got that heavy, unsettling quiet lying atop the floors and the furniture, like you don't even dare to whisper. My mama's dead. My mama's gone. Just her room left behind, her relics. What used to be Mama. Still, I climb back up those stairs, bearing my coffee cup in its saucer, looking for her. As if, when I push open that heavy, carved door, she's going to be lying there again, containing some scrap of life left, some bit of blessed spirit on this earth.

Bedroom's empty. Maids haven't started the cleaning yet. Counterpane a little rumpled, betraying a wee hollow where her body lay before the undertaker and his stone-faced assistant loaded her up and carried her off. I set down the coffee and crawl in. Curl myself into the hollow of Mama's body. Smells like medicine and sweat, and I guess I will smell that particular combination all my life now, all my life I will carry that scent in my head and it will bring this moment back to me, this void, this terrifying absence of my mama from this earth. This air on my skin, where her soft arms should rest, holding me safe from harm.

14

And then a funny thing happens. I don't know if you believe in ghosts. I sure enough don't. I believe in what I can see and touch. What exists. Why, there's times I can't say for certain I believe in God Himself. He does have a habit of making Himself scarce around here.

Anyway, I am lying in my mama's bed, in the cool hollow of the counterpane formed by what was my mama's living body, a short time ago, and I imagine I hear my mama's voice. Not inside my head, where it regularly belongs, but outside. From no particular direction. Just there. Clear words. Laura Ann.

I open my eyes.

Nothing there.

Just the furniture, French, topped in marble, one Looey or another, gilded an inch or so thick and bought at great expense, I reckon, from some dealer in Baltimore or Philadelphia, bearing no attachment whatsoever to my mama's past, or mine.

Still. I sit up. Swing my legs to the floor. I am unwashed, wearing yesterday's dress, could not yet bother myself to open my wee satchel and freshen up. I catch my reflection in the opposite mirror, the one stuck above the drawer chest, except that it isn't my reflection at all, it's my mama's. Mama's gentle face inside a frame of my own bobbed ginger hair, except younger somehow, the way she looks in her wedding photograph, smooth dairy skin and playful hooded eyes, lips parted a half inch, gazing right directly at me, Geneva Rose Kelly, like she's got something stuck inside her she wants to let out.

"What is it, Mama?" I ask her, even though I don't believe in ghosts.

I guess my eyesight returns to normal just then, or maybe I've blinked, because it's just my own ordinary face in the mirror now. Not beautiful at all, only sort of striking, the kind of face that photographs well, almost downright ugly since I haven't slept in so long. Wide face and slanted blue eyes, large sharp nose and full mouth and chin descending to a point like a witch's hat. Not my mama at all.

Still. I rise to my feet and walk across the room to that damn mirror above the gilded drawer chest, and

I reach out my hand and touch the surface, as if that might summon her back. Summon back the illusion of her. But my fingers meet only the cold, smooth surface of my own image, just below the scared right eye, and though I wait and wait, I don't hear anything more, nor does the face in the mirror change to anything more agreeable or straightforward than my own imperfect mug. I let my hand fall, right down next to the small ormolu clock ticking under the exact center of the mirror, and the square enamel box before it.

And my gaze drops too, right down there to where my hand rests, and naturally my curiosity and my despair sort of direct themselves into the smooth, expensive surface of that box. Not one she had before, that's for certain. Not trimmed and hinged and fastened in gold. I expect Duke must have given her that box, to keep all her—what? Trinkets? Mama never did have any trinkets. None that didn't get pawned at one juncture or another.

I stand there for some time, staring at that pretty box. At my long, slender hand resting next to one corner. I don't go in for lacquer—just you try keeping your nail lacquer shiny while your fingers go tappity-tap on a typewriter all the livelong day, and besides, they don't allow nail lacquer at Sterling Bates, heavens no—but I take nice care of the nails anyway, file them regular, rub my cuticles with cream. A fine-looking hand, by any standard. And I swear that hand does not move. Does not so much as twitch one single fingertip.

But the lid of that enamel box does slowly rise into the air.

15

On the other hand, I am so damn tired. (You recollect, perhaps, that I have not slept four hours in the past forty-eight.) So I might well be dreaming. Or I might be observing this sequence of strange events as a kind of mirage, the way desert travelers imagine things that aren't there: things they desire to see, things for which they thirst and long and crave, like water. Like shelter. Like the green shade of a date palm.

So I stand there and listen to the tick of that ormolu clock, nice and steady, though my heartbeat strikes about twice for every second. I stand there staring at that enamel lid, gaping wide like the mouth of an alligator. Box is about eight inches square. Delicate gilt motif of an Oriental type, painted in small, precise repeats, and you would not believe the intricate gold trim along the edges, simply could not have been wrought by human hands, howsoever nimble. There is not enough light that I can see what lies inside. Not a glimmer or a shadow or a hint. So I stand there, ears peeled, concentration absolute, waiting for some kind of instruction, I guess, that never does arrive. Ticktock. My pulse settles. I move my finger.

"Now, then. I just thought I might find you here, Geneva Rose. Picking through the loot."

I expect the jump of my nerves does me no credit.

"You get on out of this room, Duke Kelly. You got no business here."

He just laughs, free as you please. Wearing a black mourning suit, black tie. Collar all white and stiff against his bull neck. He steps forward and settles himself in the armchair before the fireplace—fire's gone out, nobody's come to lay more coal—and crosses one leg over the other. Nods to the drawer chest and my guilty body, shielding the open box. To my arms folded over my drumming heart. Tells me: "You can take that, if you want. Take whatever you damn please."

"I'm not taking anything from here."

"You sure about that? There's a fortune laying here in this room with us. Jewelry inside the safe right there. Clothes from Paris. I know you like pretty clothes, Geneva Rose. Pretty things."

"I don't want your things."

Shrugs. "As you like, sugar. You change your mind, it's all right here waiting for you. Not going nowhere."

"You set a date for the funeral?"

"Friday noon. You fixing to stay?"

"Course I am. She's my mama."

"You be needing a room to sleep in."

All of a sudden, I wish I had a cigarette. Something for my fingers and mouth to do. I uncross my arms. Brace my hands against the drawer chest behind me. "I can stay with a friend."

"*Friend*, Geneva Rose? What friend? You ain't got no more friends in River Junction. Nobody seen you in years."

"Ruth Mary Leary would have me."

Duke smiles and reaches inside his jacket. "Now, baby girl, ain't no need for that kind-a thing. Ruth Mary's got four wee babes-a her own. She ain't got the room for you. And folks'll talk, won't they? You don't want folks a-talking, do you?"

"I guess they've been talking plenty already. Don't make any difference if they talk some more. Anyway, I don't give a damn if they talk or not. I gave that up long ago. I don't give two cents what folks here think about me."

He takes a long first drag of his cigarette, and when

he pulls his mouth away and blows out a pleasurable big gust of smoke, he tells me I'm a damn fool.

"I'd be a damn fool to stay under your roof another night."

"Now, there you go again, Geneva Rose. Thinking I desire any more piece-a you, when you been spreading those pretty legs-a yours all across New York City the past four years."

"So you say. When did I ever trust a word from your mouth?"

He shakes his head slowly and pipes a little more smoke from his gasper. Considers the ceiling, twelve feet high. "I ain't never broken my solemn word, Geneva Rose, and that's the truth. You can rest easy under my roof. That ain't what I want from you no more. All grown up as you are."

"I don't care what you want from me. You're not getting it. I am leaving River Junction for good, the second my mama's grave is covered over. You won't be seeing me around here again, not ever. You won't be hearing from me. Not a single word, do you hear me? I'm done with you."

"What about your brothers and your sister? You done with them, too?"

"They know where to find me."

"Your baby sister don't. She is but five years old.

Why, she won't even know you, by the time she's grown." My stepfather leans back in the armchair now, black on crimson. Smokes all comfortable. Says quietly, still gazing at the ceiling, "Fixing to be a beauty, your sister, ain't she? An almighty beauty."

What a throat he's got. Tendons all stuck out, thick and round and pink as a watermelon. Adam's apple does this jig up and down as he swallows back spit. From his hand trails the cigarette, which I crave right now as I crave water to drink. Air to breathe. Bed to sleep in. But I don't say so. Would rather skin myself. I just shrug and say I guess she is, hard to tell at her age. But she sure does dote on Johnnie, and he worships her right back. Wouldn't let a fly touch a strand of her hair, I'll bet. I'll bet he'd kill the fellow who touched her, sure enough. Cut that fellow's throat and leave him for dead. Leave him to choke on his own blood.

Duke closes his eyes and smiles at the ceiling. The silk-hung ceiling, as crimson as hell.

"Geneva Rose," he says, "I do sometimes feel that the two of us might-a got off on the wrong foot together."

"No such thing as *together* with you and me, Duke Kelly. No such thing."

"Baby girl. You just settle your sweet self down. You ain't thinking clear. I'm talking about business."

Chin lowers at last. Eyes open to meet mine. "Business, that's all."

"Business? You and me?"

"That's what I said."

My palms are sweating against the edge of the drawer chest. Head's got that sick feeling, like I might pass out. Feel some kind of weight pressing right between my shoulder blades, a kind of poking and prodding, something trying to make itself known. I stick out my chin and say, "I've got no interest in your line of business."

"Now, that is plain unkind-a you, Geneva Rose. You ain't even heard me out."

"I don't need to hear you out. You're a damn bootlegger, is what you are, and I may trickle a little refreshment down my throat from time to time, but I don't like to think about how it got in my hand, and I especially don't like to think about the men like you who put it there. You can keep your business to yourself. I don't want any part of it. Any part of you."

I say this all impassioned, sort of a fury, and Duke, my stepfather, my dead mama's husband, the daddy of my brothers and my sister, he just sets his elbow on the arm of that chair and curls his meat hand into a fist and leans his cheek into the knuckles of that fist. He doesn't blink. Doesn't twitch. Curtains be shut tight out of respect, only an electric lamp burning by the side of the bed, and his skin's all smooth and dusky and his eyes are empty. He is like a man someone carved out of wax.

"You believe you're too good for me, Geneva Rose? Too good for this family and this town? That it? Because myself, I do happen to believe that we are all God's creatures, sugar, all of us here created in His precious image, and there ain't none of us no better than the other. And the people-a this town, they is mighty grateful for this business you don't want no part of. Mighty grateful. They ain't starving and they ain't falling sick like they did. You want these good people to starve, Geneva Rose? You want them to die-a the ague and the pneumonia and the bearing-a children?"

"You mean like Mama did?"

Well, he does flinch at that. A little bit of pink seems to stain his cheeks, if I'm not mistaken in this somber-lit room.

"Sweetheart. Your poor mama never was strong. Ain't nothing we could-a did for her, except to make her comfortable. Done all we could for her until the good Lord seen fit to gather her back into His loving arms."

Now the hair is prickling on the nape of my neck and the skin of my arms. Now the electricity tingles my scalp. Damp and nervy. Air seems fit to burst all around us, like some kind of fireworks contained in the atoms and molecules striking against me. The angry pressure between the blades of my shoulders just squeezes away my breath. I'm afraid to turn my head back to that mirror. Back to that open enamel box.

I move my hand a little, thinking I might shut the lid again, push all this mad energy back in its place, and you know how it feels when a bee stings you out of nowhere?

Well, a bee stings me, right out of nowhere, right on the back of my hand.

"Something the matter, baby girl?" asks Duke.

"Nothing's the matter."

"You need to sit down?"

"No, I don't need to sit down. I need some peace and quiet, that's all. I am mourning my mama."

Duke regards me a minute. He lifts his head from his knuckles and rises from his chair. "That's true."

"Haven't slept in days."

"Ain't you? Then I reckon you best get some rest."

"I best."

"But you think about what I said, all right? You just think on it. I ain't a-talking about no heavy work. I ain't a-talking about carrying in moonshine up the Lincoln Highway and that kind-a thing. I got plenty-a men for that, Geneva Rose, plenty-a men for that kind-a work. Just require you to deliver a package or two, from time to time, to some gentlemen I know in the city. That's all. You and your pretty face, you can do that easy as winking. And I'd pay you good."

"You could pay me the moon, Duke Kelly, and I wouldn't take it."

"I ain't a-talking about the moon. Who needs a dang moon? I mean real money. Money you can buy things with." He takes a few steps toward me, so I can smell his teeth and his hair oil and his cigarette burning from his left hand. See the ripple of his skin as he talks. "Hundred dollars a time, Geneva Rose. Give up that job-a yours, a-typing all day long. Give up them dirty photographs you do. So you just think on it. You think on it and let me know."

Can't breathe. Can't think. Heart's racing like a Thoroughbred. I gasp out something or other. Tell him I will surely think on it and let him know. He takes his hand and places it on my cheek, covering my bones, covering my ear and my jaw, and he leans close and kisses my hot, electric forehead.

"Now, I just knowed you'd come around, Geneva Rose. Just like the good, sweet daughter you always been."

16

Three and a half years have passed since I ran away from Duke Kelly into the hot blue morning, toward the fishing hole, not thinking straight, and I reckon I have been trying to atone for my folly ever since. To cleanse my skin of the stain of his touch. *The good, sweet daughter you always been.* My God, I want to scrub myself raw. Peel myself bloody all over again.

I don't remember what happened all that well, you understand. There are times I think, Lord Almighty, I must have dreamt it. The memory has that quality of dreams, all impression and emotion, such that you only really recall an instant or two, a sharp encounter, and you have to piece everything else together, and that's when you realize the whole thing doesn't make any sense. That maybe you imagined it after all.

I do recall running from that henhouse. Skin burning from the slice of the chicken wire. I recall that I reached the creek and fell down on my knees and washed my face and hands and neck in the cool, clear water; disturbed the long-legged bugs that skated on the surface, smelt the good smell of mud and creek rot. My heart banged against my eardrums. My breath hurt my throat. I recall that I crawled all the way into the water, hands and legs sinking in the silt, until I was almost submerged, until I began to float in the lazy, wide pool where the creek spread itself out under the shade. Until I felt a pair of cold eyes on my skin and I turned, arms flailing, to find Duke sitting on a boulder near the water's edge, lighting himself a cigarette.

Now, Duke can't swim, any more than he can read the words in a book. Least I never saw him inside of the water, that I can recollect. But you wouldn't have known this fact to look at him right then. No, sir. He just sat there on that boulder, smoking his cigarette, staring at me while I shivered and paddled in that pool of creek water, keeping myself afloat, considering my options. Or so I must have done, because I don't remember that part. Just him staring and the smell of his cigarette, and the way I felt like a naked she-rabbit trapped in a snare. Couldn't swim downstream, on account of the footbridge. Couldn't swim upstream, on account of the springhouse sitting right there atop the narrowing of the creek bed. Water was mountain-fed and already my skin was turning numb, my brain icing over. I recall that very well—how my head hurt with cold. And then I must have made my choice, because I remember darting for the opposite bank, swimming as fast as ever I could, but I could not swim faster than Duke crossed that bridge, because as soon as I lurched ashore, dripping and gasping, he did take me by the shoulders and pull me into the tall summer grass. Pinned me down with his knees while he fixed our clothes, I don't remember how, don't remember whether he first yanked up my skirt or undid his trousers, whether he ripped my blouse open or whether it was already loose. I recall his paws on my breasts, the purple sight of his organ bursting free from all that nest of black hair. Some kind of pain on my thighs, where he held me down somehow. White panic laying down on my brain, my arms and legs too stunned to move, just my fingers twitching and twitching while he spread me apart and then the sharp edge of a rock meeting the tips of the fingers of my left hand, like the Lord God saying in my ear, *Take this in remembrance of Me.*

I don't remember exactly what happened then. I just remember running all the way up that hill from the fishing hole, shuddering and bloodstained, and the way Duke's face looked that last and final morning, heavy and handsome, blocking out the sky, before he obtained that scar now spearing out white from beneath the hair near his right temple.

And I recall thinking I had better leave town before he woke up, and never ever return, because he surely would kill me. He would surely to God find a way to kill me for whatever it was I had done to him.

17

When Duke leaves Mama's bedroom, when the door closes boom behind his black-suited body, I sink on down to the rose-patterned carpet and I sit there for some time, while all that electromagnetism settles down around me, sizzling into nothing, the way a coal fire goes to sleep during the night. Wrap my arms around my legs and rest my forehead on my knees. Eyes shut tight.

I whisper, *Mama? You there?*

No answer. No words, nor even the sense of words, inside my head or outside. Just a clean, cool silence. Pressure on my back has gone. Sting on my hand soothes away. The dark, sweet air fills the cracks between my ribs. I untangle my arms and legs and slowly rise, bracing my hands on the gilded edges of the drawer chest, and by the time I've reached my full five feet seven inches of unruly height, the terror has left me entirely, though my every muscle is sapped of strength. I turn to face the mirror. The open box. I grasp it between my fingers and tilt it forward, so I can see the contents, and what I find there is not jewels or trinkets or anything a lady might hold dear, but buttons. Big, solid, round, expensive buttons of a masculine type, some gold and some silver and some horn, about a dozen in all, enough to line the bottom of the box and no more.

I close the lid and crawl back in my mama's bed and fall straight to sleep, and this time I stay that way, deep and heavy, until hunger wakes me at suppertime.

18

Everybody in River Junction goes to Mama's funeral. You'd think she was their patron saint, martyred in some kind of modern auto-da-fé, the way they weep and carry on. I just stand there in my black dress and black coat and black hat, tall lump of white-faced New York City coal, watching them lower her flower-strewn coffin into the frosted earth. Duke paid a dozen men to dig that hole in the ground, to clear away the snow and pour boiling water on the ground to make it thaw. A big to-do. Church full of hothouse lilies, which were Mama's favorite flower, thousands and thousands of them hanging in wreaths and stuck in bouquets, such that you almost felt drunk on the scent of them.

And now we are standing here in the ancient church cemetery, cold as blue blazes, near to freezing the hair on our behinds, while they pile dirt on Mama's coffin and everybody weeps except me and Johnnie and Patsy, who stands between us clutching our two hands, shocked into stillness. Preacher's preaching something pitiable and comforting. I look up suddenly and gaze across the graveyard to the edge of the trees, where a man stands in a long, dark coat, gazing back, maybe just at me, maybe at the whole group of us, Angus's wife sobbing in great theatrical gusts of melancholy. When I lower my head again, I catch the corner of Duke's stare, but I don't acknowledge it. Already given him all the satisfaction he's going to get.

19

The gathering afterward is fixing to be a long one, and I don't stay above a half hour. Just a glass of milk punch and a neat triangle of a ham sandwich, trimmed of its crust. I've got a train to catch, after all. That's what I tell Johnnie when he stops me, suitcase in hand, in the hallway near the door.

"You oughta stay another day," he says. "It ain't respectful, leaving in the middle like this."

"I've already done my mourning. Anyway, those old cats'd be disappointed to see me stay, don't you think? Can't gossip about me if I'm standing right there in front of them, drinking milk punch and dabbing my eyes."

"Still."

I set down the suitcase. "Say, Johnnie-boy. I do have a question for you, before I go. I was hoping to catch sight of Laura Ann Green here today. You didn't happen to see her about, did you?"

"Laura Ann Green? You mean Ruth Mary's sister, out in Hagerstown? She's married now, Geneva Rose. Fellow named Benwick. Had herself a brand-new baby, couple-a weeks ago. She can't come to no funerals."

"No, I mean her mama."

Johnnie's face goes a little heavy. "Mrs. Green?"

"That's right."

"Aw, Geneva Rose, poor old Mrs. Green passed on two years back. Didn't you know? Some kind-a 'flu, it was."

"Passed *on*?"

"Awful thing. Near enough broke poor Mama's heart. Like sisters, them two."

"*Those* two. For the Lord's own sake, Johnnie."

"*Those* two. What kind-a business you got with Laura Ann Green?"

"Nothing." I pick up the suitcase. "You keep a good

eye on Patsy for me, you hear? You don't let a thing happen to her. Not a damn thing."

His eyes sit tight on mine. He nods. "I surely will, Geneva Rose. I can promise you that."

"Good." Rise on tiptoe. Kiss his cheek. "Good-bye, then, Johnnie. You need anything, a place to stay or whatever else, you and Patsy, you come right to me."

"That I will, sis." He takes my shoulders and squeezes them good. "The Lord watch over you, now. Don't you do nothing stupid, back there in the wicked city."

"Would I ever?"

He swears a little and kisses my forehead and lets me go. Offers to walk me to the station. I tell him no, he needs to get back to the party. Back to our Patsy. Watch over her innocent wee self, the way the good Lord God tends to His lambs in their pastures.

20

Train's a half hour late, so I wait inside the station house, wrapping my hands around a cup of hot, sweet coffee, trying not to cast my eyes toward either the clock or the doorway. Each little noise sets my nerves to jump. Next to my feet sits my old leather satchel, containing my two skirts and blouses and my underthings, which have been washed and pressed by the diligent new laundry maid who now finds employment at the Kelly abode. Also contains Mama's enamel box and the buttons inside it, all wrapped up in tissue, but the laundry maid doesn't know anything about that. It's my little secret. My one small inheritance. Square box half-full of buttons.

Whistle screams softly through the windows. I set down my coffee on the little table and leave a dime for the stationmaster's wife who served it to me. (*Real sorry about your poor mama, Geneva Rose. You fixing to leave so soon?*) An old potbellied stove warms the air in the station house, so that when I step through the doors to the new concrete platform, the shock of cold makes my chest tighten. Sucks the air tight and safe inside my lungs. I hunker down into my muffler and my coat and stare beneath my lashes at the white clapboard buildings opposite. Cathy's Café. The five and dime, all shut up, CLOSED sign propped in the window out of respect for Duke Kelly's dead wife.

Whistle screams again. Rails sing. Steam engine chugs and sighs and stops in a grand squeal of brakes. A single door flings open at the front of the second car (there are but two altogether) and I grasp the handle of my suitcase and trudge down the platform to meet it.

I spare no glance for the sturdy, navy-suited conductor as I bang my way down the aisle to the end of the empty car. Not another soul on board except him and me, and he closes the door and disappears into the first car as soon as I'm up the step. Smells of sour things, sweat and soiled leather and God knows. Tobacco. Train lurches forward just as I slide into the next-to-last bench on the right, setting my satchel upon the seat between me and the aisle, and I turn my head to the window and watch everything slide away, the new platform and the white clapboard buildings and the neat-painted sign that says RIVER JUNCTION. Gaining speed now. Past the crossing and the church and the graveyard where Mama lies buried—a clutch of men still hard at work, filling that hole—and then the manse, big and square and gabled, grandest house in town until Duke Kelly started making his fortune. Now it's a dollhouse by comparison. Not even the Lord God takes precedence over Duke in River Junction, these days.

At the front end of the car, the door opens. Conductor appears, wearing a cap trimmed in tarnished braid. I open my pocketbook and ready my ticket. His shoulders are burly and his cap pitched low, so I can't see his face. I look away, heart going thud, and stare out the window at the thinning buildings, the gathering white fields. The heavy tread of his feet makes my blood whir. He stops beside me and says *Ticket, please,* and I look up in surprise, because the voice is too high and twangy, not the right voice at all, and now I perceive that his belly is round and his chin pointed, his height too short by a couple of inches. I hand over the ticket. He nicks it and hands it back and treads slowly up the aisle, and when he's gone I rummage back in my pocketbook until I find the note placed in my hand on the River Junction train platform a week ago.

B&O
last carriage
2nd row from rear
right side

There's no signature. No mark of any kind. Handwriting brusque and sharp, in the fine purple-black ink of an expensive fountain pen. I tuck it back inside my pocketbook and lean my head against the seat and close my eyes to the rhythmic clackety-clack of the wheels on the rails, the faint vibrating chug of the engine, the whoosh of my own blood in my ears. Feel as if I'm crushed under the pressure of a massive hand, smashing right there into the center of my chest, ribs creaking and bending, breath thinning, thick fingers curled around my left shoulder with such insistent warmth that I startle upward and realize that I must have fallen asleep, because a man stands next to me, staring down in deep concern from a pair of dark blue eyes.

"May I join you, Miss Kelly?"

"Suit yourself, Tarzan."

He moves the satchel to the floor and sits down beside me. I imagine he's going to offer his condolences, the usual platitudes, and I will answer him in kind. But he doesn't speak. Just sits there next to me, one leg crossed over the other, holding a folded newspaper between his two hands at such a still, lifeless angle that I don't believe he's actually reading it. After a while, the heat from his body leaks into mine, and I stare out the window until my eyelids fall and my thoughts soften. The train stops and starts, picking up passengers as it makes its way into Baltimore, and still he doesn't speak. His body is like a barricade, holding back the chattering world outside.

The train begins its long, staggering approach into Union Station, where I will transfer to the Pennsy, carrying me back into the safe embrace of Pennsylvania Station in New York City, my hustle and bustle, my wicked chaos, my Billy-boy. The sun is settling a cloth of late gold on the dirty rooftops of Baltimore. The electric lamps inside the car flicker and dim.

I turn to the man beside me and say, "You've got yourself a deal."

New York City, 1998

Ella had been investigating the municipal bond department at Sterling Bates for six days (not including the weekend, during which she'd also worked) when she finally ran into Patrick. She was walking into the marble lobby at a quarter past eight in the morning, towering vanilla latte gripped in her left hand, and he was walking out. They saw each other's amazed faces through the glass of the revolving door. Ella tried to make it to the elevator, but he caught up.

"Ella! Ella, please!"

She turned. "I have to be at work, Patrick."

"Work? Are you *kidding* me?"

He looked the same. Wasn't that strange? Somehow it didn't make sense that this was the same Patrick she'd known for six years: the same square, regular, dependable face and fine brown hair, brushed back with the same styling cream (she could see it on the bathroom counter) into the same short, corporate silhouette. The same features she'd seen a million times, a million ex-

pressions, sharing her home and her life, as recogniz-
ably hers as the furniture. The art on the walls. The
Patrick she thought she knew, who was in fact an entirely different Patrick, containing a whole segment
(like an orange, she thought) that didn't belong to her,
and was in fact completely unknown to her.

So how in God's name did this new Patrick manage
to look exactly like the old one? It wasn't fair. Because
she was trained to love that face. To look on that face
always with forgiveness and compassion. To share the
burdens on those sharp navy shoulders. That was what
she'd vowed, after all, on the beach at Granny's place on
Cumberland Island, in front of an unsettlingly mixed
crowd of friends and family and strangers. For better
or worse.

They'd had sex on the very first date. Not because
she'd fallen headlong in love over the course of chicken
saltimbocca and a decent Sangiovese at some red-sauce
Italian restaurant on the Upper East Side, but because
Ella was young and inexperienced and Patrick had that
natural ability to close a deal. She'd met him a week
earlier at work, back when Patrick was finishing his
analyst gig at JP Morgan, and her firm had been called
in to sort out a mess. A little flirting led to an invita-
tion for the following Saturday. He was handsome and

smart and engaging, wore the invisible coating of a man who was going places. She said yes. After dinner and a long walk, they went to his apartment and discovered a rapport. Some common interests, a shared affinity for numbers and puzzles. Started kissing on the sofa. Ella got caught up in the excitement and forgot she was supposed to hold back on a first date.

The sex itself was short and unremarkable, which she always regretted. Shouldn't your first sex with your future husband be monumental? Shouldn't you experience every moment, every kiss and touch and lunge, with the consciousness that you were having sex with the last person you'd ever have sex with? *Wow, that was amazing,* Patrick had said, rolling away and shucking off the condom, heading for the bathroom, and Ella lay there and thought, *That was quick.* But instead of shooing her home, he came back to bed and said—toying with her hair, sizing up her breasts in his palms—*Who knew you were such a hot package, sweet Ella Dommerich from Parkinson Peters?* They got to talking, had sex again, and within a couple of weeks they were calling each other boyfriend and girlfriend. And then May arrived, and they were officially in love. The sex got much better, sometimes seriously hot, before it slid inevitably into a certain territory of staleness and routine, reinvigorated occasionally by weekend trips to luxury resorts, but maybe more satisfying for its very predictability. At least Ella had thought so. Clearly, Patrick had not.

"Look," **Patrick** said earnestly, switching into deal-closing mode, "you can't just ignore this forever. We're married. We have to talk sometime."

"I need time to process this."

"It's been four weeks. I don't even know where you're living."

"I'm in the Village."

"Ella," he said, cajoling, lowering his voice to that old intimate croon of his, looking down at her soulfully, "please. Just coffee or something. I miss you. Every single minute, I miss you. Just seeing your face right now."

Ella's face, right now, was hot and red. She wanted to yell, *Well, maybe you should have thought of that before you stuck your dick inside a prostitute,* but she was Ella, not her mother, not her sister or her aunt Viv. Instead, she whispered, "Well, it's been hard for me, too."

"I know. I know. What I did, it was unforgivable. So I'm not asking you to forgive me. Just—just coffee, okay?" He glanced around the lobby. "Not here. Somewhere we can talk."

Ella hiked up the strap of her shoulder bag. "Patrick. I don't know. I don't know if I can talk to you yet. I really don't."

He touched her elbow. Closed his eyes briefly, like he was praying for guidance, like his feelings were too much for him to bear. Or so Ella had always thought, when Patrick did his closed-eyes thing, usually at moments of high emotion, like when she accepted his proposal and when he first told her he loved her. Except now Ella wondered if he'd really felt anything at all. Whether he closed his eyes to disguise instead of reveal. Wasn't there just the slightest whiff of the theatrical about those checked eyeballs? Something studied, the way you might consider how to express an emotion, instead of just expressing it?

"Please, Ella," he said. "I swear, it hasn't happened again. It won't happen again. It was a stupid, stupid mistake I will never make again. Therapy, whatever it takes. I will spend the rest of my life making it up to you. If you just give me the chance to start over and prove myself. Just coffee."

Ella's mouth froze. She was aware of curious glances, of the way people were stepping carefully around them, like dogs around an invisible fence. Her skin was so flushed, she couldn't think.

"Ella, it's me," he said. "It's Patrick. Remember our

honeymoon? That beach on Capri? I want that back. I just want to be your husband again."

Ella stepped away from the familiar smell of his clothes. "Fine," she said. "Coffee. Tomorrow afternoon, the Starbucks around the corner, on Broad. Three thirty."

"Why not today?"

"Because I have a meeting today, Patrick. A very important meeting with the head of the department."

She turned around and made for the elevator bank, drinking down her latte so no one would see that her lips were trembling with the lie she'd just told.

As it turned out, she couldn't have made a coffee date that afternoon anyway, or even a meeting with the department head. Right after lunch, her cell phone rang with the news that a pipe had burst in her apartment.

Wonderful, she thought. My wonderful life.

And yet. That little surge of pleasure that hit her blood at the sight of Hector standing in the middle of her flooded kitchen, wearing the same gray T-shirt as that night she'd first visited his apartment, conferring with the super and somebody in stained clothes who was probably the plumber? Not *un*-wonderful.

Then she noticed the rest of the kitchen.

"Oh, my God." She set her bag on the counter and stared at the water puddling around her heels.

"Wet vac's on its way," said Hector. "I lifted as much stuff as I could onto the tables and counters. The furniture's not looking great, though. The bed's all right— it's high enough up—but the sofa's got a skirt . . ."

Ella didn't really care about the furniture. She'd bought most of it off a showroom floor near the Flatiron, the cheapest she could find. She stared at the bed, which she made tight every morning, sheets and quilt tucked in hospital corners under the mattress, duvet stacked at the foot. Thank God. Imagine the humiliation of an unmade bed at a moment like this. "But what happened?" she said.

"Pipe burst," said the super, in the voice of a man talking to a very stupid female.

"I can *see* a pipe burst," she said, "but which pipe? Where? How?"

"Under the sink," said Hector. "Some of the plumbing's pretty old, from when the building was first converted from a boardinghouse into apartments, right after the war. The joint just gave way. Rusted out. Want to see?"

"Not especially."

"The good news is, I can make you a whole new

kitchen. Roll up the carpeting and replace any floor-boards that couldn't take it. Refinish, good as new."

She looked up at his face, which was obscenely cheerful. "You sound as if you're happy about this."

"Ah, but I've been wanting to get my hands on your kitchen for a while now."

"That sounded kind of pervy."

"Only because your mind's in the gutter, as usual." He turned his head to the door, where a steady banging announced the arrival of the wet vac, up several flights of stairs. "Here we go. Get you dried out in a jiffy."

All right. Yes. She was falling a little in love with Hector, in a totally platonic way. What wasn't to love? He had an adorable dog. He was smart and funny and absolutely brilliantly talented. They had a frisson be-tween them—a pleasant, easy, undemanding frisson—but he hardly so much as touched her, because of Claire.

Ella had met Claire last weekend, after trudging home from Sterling Bates at six thirty on a Saturday evening. Claire and Hector had knocked on her door right after she changed into her pajamas and invited her upstairs for pizza and wine and a movie. Ella had inspected those valuable hands and proclaimed them stunning. The rest of her was pretty, too. Petite and curvy, in comparison to Ella's angularity, with a gamine French face like Winona Ryder. And she was clever and funny and charmingly self-deprecating about the hands thing. She held them up to the light and said, *Would you believe I have to insure these things? In case they get caught in a car door or something?*

Well, they *were* terrific hands. Long in the fingers, smooth in the skin, delicately curved nails trimmed to a perfect eighth of an inch. No veins popping out anywhere. (*Yet,* Claire sighed.) The three of them arranged themselves on a piece of furniture that could only be described as a rustic sectional, Hector and Claire together on the long side, Ella on the short side with Nellie on her lap, and watched a movie on video. *The English Patient.* Claire's choice. "He wouldn't see it with me in the theater," she said, pursing her lips, curling a sidelong look at Hector. Not quite a pout.

He spread his hands. "I had a gig!"

"You had a night off every week."

"Had to catch up on my sleep, right? Anyway, you saw it with Heather."

She threaded her arm comfortably around his elbow. "Not the same thing as seeing it with your boyfriend."

Ella turned away to watch the opening credits. Juliette Binoche in the field hospital or whatever it was, wounded men pouring in, shellfire. She'd seen the movie last year at the Ziegfeld with Joanie, right before Joanie left for Paris (Patrick was away on business), and while Joanie had loved it—loved Ralph Fiennes in his Tiger Moth or whatever it was, loved Kristin Scott Thomas and her upper-class beauty, loved the whole vintage star-crossed lovers thing—the film had left Ella unsettled. Disconnected. Maybe because she still thought of herself as a bit of a newlywed, maybe because Patrick was away. She wanted Kristin Scott Thomas to remain true to her husband, even if he was a dud. She wanted Ralph Fiennes to—well, she wasn't sure—resist temptation or something. Not to steal another man's wife. She wanted the marriage to endure, she wanted that vow to remain sacred.

Now, of course, things were different. And maybe the movie would feel different, too; maybe it was the kind of movie that meant one thing when you were happily married, and something else when you were not.

Either way, she didn't have much chance to find out, because Claire was a Movie Talker. Had something to say about Juliette Binoche's hair, had something to say about the green of Kristin Scott Thomas's eyes. Nellie fell thoroughly asleep in Ella's lap, not even twitching, and Ella stroked the dog's ears while her own right leg went numb under the dead weight pressing against some nerve or another.

"Hey." Hector reached behind Claire to tap her shoulder. "She's not bothering you, is she?"

For a moment, Ella thought he meant Claire. "Oh, no. I'm used to it," she replied, thinking of Joanie, who also had plenty to say about whatever was on the screen.

"Okay. But you can kick her off, if you want. She's not really supposed to be on the sofa."

"Oh, come on," Claire said. "You let her on the sofa all the time."

Hector didn't reply, just gave Ella a sheepish look and returned his attention to the screen before them, and Ella went on stroking Nellie's ears while the dog snored and drooled into her pajamas. At one point, Hector silently handed her another slice of pizza. Refilled her wine. Claire refused both—alcohol was bad for the skin, she said—and reached for the tube of Neutrogena hand cream on the coffee table, next to the pizza box.

When the movie was finished, Ella had risen and stretched and said she'd better head back downstairs and get some sleep. Thanks so much for the pizza. Left them lounging on the cushions, talking about the movie, which Claire adored. *Great to meet you, Ella!* Claire called cheerfully, in the voice of a girlfriend who knows she has nothing to fear.

And she really did have nothing to fear, because

Hector was full of banter but never once made a pass of any kind, even the ambiguous kind that you could take up or ignore at your pleasure. Last night, for example, he'd called her cell phone and asked if she would come up and hear something he'd just written. She'd listened in awe. Drank a little bourbon. Laughed and took over the piano while he played trumpet. At one point he stopped and asked, without warning, whether she'd talked to her husband yet. She said no, she wasn't ready.

You gotta talk sometime, Sherlock, he said. Can't put a thing like that off forever. Then put the trumpet back to his mouth and played some more. Something slow and midnight, while a bit of moon slipped around the edge of the window to touch the points of his face. She'd slipped back downstairs a half hour later, warm and happy, conscience clear, not so much as a peck on the cheek. Just a nod from the blue shadows near the piano, and a reminder—the one he always made—to let him know if she needed anything.

Well, now she needed something. She needed a new damn kitchen, and someone to remove the ruined carpeting in the living room.

Which Hector was doing right now, as a matter of fact, exhibiting the kind of enthusiastic male relish for destruction that reminded her of her brothers and their Lego sets. "Breaks my heart when they cover up floorboards like this with cheap ugly-ass poly fiber," he said, tossing another section in the hallway. Whipping out the X-Acto knife for another barbaric slice.

"Seriously, you don't have to do this," Ella said.

"Actually, I do." He straightened and winked. Grinned like a lightning bolt. "Pays the rent."

"It's not carpentry, though."

"Oh, close enough. Anyway, I like the company."

Ella's cheeks were already warm from the grin. She looked down at the spreadsheets before her—she'd printed them out hastily before she dashed home—and said, "So what's the landlord like? Typical greedy bastard?"

"Not too bad. To be honest, he's my dad."

"*What?*"

"Yeah. I know, right? Nepotism's the way to go in this town. How else could I afford the entire top floor to myself?"

"Because you're an awesome carpenter?"

"Nice try. It's a sweetheart deal, there's no getting around it. But I put in all the renovation work myself. It was just storage before. Couple of narrow rooms, no plumbing." He gripped the edge of the carpet section in his hand and started to rip. "Truth is, I could probably afford market rent by now. I just like working with my dad."

"Wow. Did you sell some music or something?"

"Didn't I tell you? I'm scoring a movie."

"*What?*" she screeched, for the second time.

"Seriously? I didn't tell you that?"

"No, you didn't tell me that! Are you kidding me? That's *amazing*! What movie?"

"Oh, nothing you'd have heard of. An indie flick. But"—his muscles flexed hard; he took in a breath—"it's a pretty cool break. What I always wanted to do."

Ella stared at the twin columns of figures before her, representing underwriting revenues for 1995 and 1996, broken down by client. Municipalities up and down the Eastern Seaboard, even a few on the West Coast, raising money for schools and parks and community centers and sewer systems and everything else. She had been a newlywed while those revenues were being earned. When those bonds were being issued. Just back from the Amalfi coast. Hunting for a new apartment with Patrick, who was flush and cocky with his first bonus as a managing director. "That, Hector," she said, "is a bona fide spectacular dream."

"Well, you know, if you look at folks like me a century ago, you know, starving composers, we were writing operas. Or trying to, anyway. Look at Wagner.

Listen to Wagner. It's like hearing a film score, parts of it. He was the original score composer. He revolutionized the whole game; he was all about fitting the music to the action, creating a drama out of music. Harnessing the power of music to tell a story. Wagner, Verdi, Massenet, Puccini, they were rock stars. Household names. And now, modern opera, I mean the stuff being composed today, it's practically irrelevant. Have you heard of *The Ghosts of Versailles*? Of course you haven't. People go to movies instead. But the music's still essential. Try watching a movie when the score's stripped out." He straightened and shook his arms out. Stretched his fingers to the ceiling, outlined by the sunshine, and for an instant he was so beautiful, so full of promise, that Ella forgot to breathe.

"Actually," she said at last, "I've seen *The Ghosts of Versailles*. At the Met, a few seasons ago."

"Jesus. I love you."

"But I see what you mean. It's an insider's critique of opera convention. It's an opera about opera. I mean, it's musically interesting, it's incredibly accomplished, it's clever and complicated and the production was amazing, but as far as *storytelling*, as far as reaching deep and *moving* an audience, not just of music geeks but of human beings—"

"Exactly!"

She set down the spreadsheets and stood from the sofa. "Look at me. I'm being a total jerk, just sitting here while you do all the work. Let me help."

"No need. It's my job."

She took off her suit jacket. "Music's your job. Your real job. And the sooner you get back to it—"

"Nah, I like ripping up carpet. It's cathartic. Sends me back to the piano like a mad beast."

"Well, what if I want to rip carpet, too? Go back to my stupid numbers like a mad beast?"

He laughed. "Can't argue with that, Sherlock. Okay, then. Grab a corner."

Ella took the carpet in her hands, and it was heavier than she thought. Stiff and waterlogged, unwilling to separate itself from the floorboards below. "So when did you decide you wanted to compose? Or *what* you wanted to compose?"

"I don't know. College, maybe. I guess I knew early on that I didn't just want to write songs, even though that's the bread and butter. I wanted to tell a whole story in notes. I wanted to—"

Hector's entire body came to a stop midrip. Ella nearly tripped over the slackened carpet.

"What's wrong?" she asked.

He looked up. "Nothing."

But she was already leaning over the spot where he'd

been looking, newly uncovered by the soggy carpet. "There's a floorboard loose," she said.

"It happens. Hold on, I'll get a hammer." He dropped the carpet back down over the board and went to the toolbox spread out on the kitchen counter.

Ella knelt on the exposed floor, which was covered with carpet scuz and smelled like sap, and stared at the ripple of wet carpet covering the loose board. Already the water had loosened the stink of decades from the fibers. The apartment really needed airing, but the weather outside remained chilly and damp, the kind of stubborn, miserable March that just wouldn't end, and Ella hated the cold. She placed her palm on the wood next to her knee and wondered how long it had been covered like this. Whose feet had last trod those boards. Whether you could connect with a person from another age, just by touching the dirt left by a long-ago shoe.

Hector returned with the hammer and lifted the carpet. Ella craned her neck to see. "That's funny," she said. "There's no nail or anything."

"There wouldn't be. Nails aren't so good for feet."

"Then what are you hammering—" she began, and then, "Wait!"

Hector's arm was already raised. He startled and looked at her. "What's wrong?"

"I think there's something under there."

"Sure there is. The ceiling in three D."

"No, seriously." Something surged along Ella's nerves. Stung the hair at the back of her neck. The way she sometimes felt, late at night or inside some borrowed office, when she was poring over figures and spotted an anomaly, a gap in the logic, a flaw in numbers that could not, without human assistance, deceive you. Something occupying what ought to be an empty space. She put her index finger in the crack between the loose floorboard and its firm neighbor, and as she did so, she thought that the whole thing didn't look right, the floorboard was much shorter than the others. Didn't fit flush. Wasn't *right*.

"Oh, come on," Hector said. "There's nothing there, all right? Can we get a move on? I have to take Nellie for her walk."

"Just give me a second." Ella scooted closer to the board and wedged a few more fingernails in the crack. Now her nerves were really singing, her head almost sick with certainty. Like someone was yelling truth into her ear. Like someone had hooked a pair of electrodes to her neck. "Give me that hammer."

"I'm not going to give you my hammer! Do you even know how to use it?"

"Do I *know* how to use a *hammer*? Um, so remember when you told me to call you on any of your sexist bullshit?"

Hector frowned and handed her the hammer. "Just be careful, all right? Don't split the board in half."

"I won't. Jeez." She inserted the prongs into the crack, felt the instant give of the wood. "It's so loose; it's like someone did it on purpose. I'll bet it's treasure. No. A murder weapon!"

"Okay, Sherlock. But before you get too worked up, remember that wood is an organic substance, expands and contracts—holy crap, what are you doing?"

Ella lifted the board away—it was only a foot long—and stuck her hand in the cavity.

"Aw, don't do that . . ." Hector groaned.

Ella withdrew her hand, which now contained a small black enamel box, decorated in a delicate Oriental motif, edged in tiny gold lace, as fresh and new as if it sat on the shelf of some Madison Avenue trinket shop. All the tingling in her nerves and her follicles swept down into the skin of her hand, where it met the box's surface.

"Treasure, me hearties," she said.

"Let me see that."

"Hold on. There's something inside."

"How do you know?"

"Because I can *feel* it, duh." She tucked the box in

her left palm and opened the lid. The damp, smelly air seemed to gather up and sigh around her.

Hector peered over her hand. "Wow. Some treasure."

"Shut up. It's cool. Think how old they are."

"You're excited about a boxful of old *buttons?*"

"Don't dis my buttons. I'd have thought *you,* of all people, would see how amazingly awesome this is."

"Why *me of all people?*"

"Because you're Hector." She lifted out one of the buttons, the largest, made of some kind of brass. "Isn't that a crest?"

"Sure. Whatever. Look, can you put the pwetty wee buttons aside for a second and help me with this damn rug?"

"I thought you didn't need any help."

"I do if you're sitting on the carpet."

"Oh! Sorry." Ella stood up and stepped away. Her knees were all wet; she hadn't noticed. "You know what? I think it's the Harvard school crest. Look. VE RI TAS. Truth."

"You know it that well?"

"Patrick went to Harvard. He's got the crest everywhere. It's practically tattooed on his forehead."

"Ironic," said Hector. "Also typical. Most people

I've met from Harvard, it's the first fucking thing they tell you."

She laughed. "Sometimes, if you don't ask, they get frustrated and try to slip it into conversation. *When I was at school in Cambridge . . .*"

"Status markers. Look, are you going to carry that box around all day, or are you going to take out your anger on some helpless carpet?"

"I'm not angry."

"The devil you aren't. You're pissed as hell. You are one seething, bubbling cauldron of righteous rage, Ella Gilbert, and the sooner you break loose and sound your barbaric yawp, the better. Now grab hold."

"Carpet diem?"

"Exactly."

Ella closed the lid and set down the black enamel box on the kitchen counter. "Ouch!" she said, jerking her hand away.

"What happened?"

"Like something stung me!"

"What? Let me see."

She rubbed the back of her hand. "I'm fine. Just startled me, that's all."

"Ella, let me see it."

The sharp tone of his voice surprised her. He held

out his hand, palm up, and the compulsion to touch him was so strong, Ella didn't bother to resist. She stepped forward and placed her hand in his. He drew it close to his face and ran his finger along the skin.

"Here?" he said.

"Right in the middle. Below the knuckles."

"There's no mark."

She pulled her hand back. "Like I told you. It's nothing. I'm fine. Probably just a nerve twitching or something."

"You're sure?"

"Hector, you doofus," she said, "do you see any blood?"

"Smart-ass. All right. Let's finish this job up so we can play a little music before the sun sets. Deal?"

Ella picked up the X-Acto knife and flicked it open. "Deal."

The sun had long set by the time they finished playing and lay, side by side, on the floor of Hector's apartment, staring up at the skylight.

"So. I feel kind of guilty about something," he said.

"About what?"

"I shouldn't have said that stuff about your husband."

"What stuff?"

"About his going to Harvard. And the irony thing, you know, *veritas* meaning 'truth.' Totally out of line."

"Out of line how? I mean, you were right. Right about his lying, cheating ass." She poked him with her elbow.

"Maybe, but it's not my place. That's between you and him. You're still married. You haven't even talked to a lawyer yet, have you?"

"No," Ella whispered.

"So I shouldn't have said anything. I just—well, it really pissed me off, when you told me what happened. And sometimes I have a hard time keeping my righteousness on the inside, you know?"

"Understood. No worries. Didn't change my opinion, if that's what you're worried about."

They weren't touching. Ella lay just close enough to sense the heat of his body without actually feeling it. Overhead, the rectangle of sky was clear and silvery with moonlight. She was drowsy and content and still faintly electric, almost dizzy, having eaten an obscene amount of pasta and drunk a glass of red wine. She wondered what would happen if their fingers touched, and then she remembered Claire and lifted both hands to her chest and stuck them firmly together. She could still feel a slight echo of the sting she'd received in the kitchen. Pressed her thumb against the spot.

"So I saw Patrick today," she said.

"You did?"

"In the lobby. On my way in. We're supposed to have coffee tomorrow."

Hector allowed a few seconds to pass before he replied. "You okay?"

"Sure. I'm fine. It wasn't as bad as I thought. He hadn't grown horns or anything. Same old Patrick." She paused. "He just really wanted to talk. Which is fair. I think I'm ready."

"Good. That's good. You two need to start talking. Figure out where to go with this."

"You know, I can almost hear your wheels creaking. Trying to be fair."

He laughed. "I just hate to see a friend unhappy, that's all."

"Well, I appreciate that. And I appreciate that you're so cool about it. For some reason it's easier to talk to you than my family."

"What about your girlfriends?"

She snorted. "*What* girlfriends? I'm pretty much surrounded by men at work. And between work and husband, I guess I haven't really had much time for anything else, lately. Just a few friends left over from college, and none of them live in the city. Plus the wives of Patrick's friends, I guess, but that's just superficial social stuff, you know, making conversation over the seven-layer Super Bowl dip."

"But you have a sister, right? What about her?"

"Joanie? She's great. We love each other and all that, but we're kind of different. And she up and left for Paris a couple of years ago, and she's not that good at e-mail, so . . ."

There was another pause. "So . . . what? You're saying I'm like the New York City girlfriend you've been missing all along?"

Ella started laughing. "Oh my God. You are the best, you know that? God. I don't know what you are. You're something else. I'm just glad you're there, that's all. I mean, glad you're here. It's just been really . . . really"—her giggles switched over into sobs—"really *sucky* these past few weeks, you know? And—shit, I'm sorry—" She was crying into his chest, and his arm was around her. She wasn't sure if she'd turned into him or he'd pulled her over. Maybe both. "And the only good—the only good thing—"

"Shh. Just shut up, okay? Shut up and cry a little. You don't need to explain. I get it. I got your back, Sherlock."

So she let go. Let go and let him have it, all the tears, soaking up into his T-shirt. No words—thank God, no fucking *words*—just wet, salt tears.

———

When she was done, lay curled up at his side, head on shoulder, staring at the wall, Hector finally spoke.

"So you're staying the night, right?"

"*What?*"

"Jeez, Ella. Mind in the gutter *again*. I meant the *sofa*. No offense, but your apartment smells like the armpit of a wet sheep. Also, we had to shut off your water."

"Oh. I guess that's a problem."

"Plumber's coming tomorrow to get you hooked up again. But in the meantime, you're welcome to stay here. Or just to pee and shower, if you don't think you can resist my smoking-hot proximity all night. Your call."

"Uh-huh. I think the question is whether *you* can resist *mine*."

"Oh, Gilbert. I think we both know which one of us hasn't had sex in a month."

Ella rose to a sitting position. "Oh, Murray. You are *so* on."

In the end, Ella slept seven hours straight on the sectional in Hector's living room, covered by a blanket that smelled exactly like him, and she woke up hearing his voice in her head, repeating those words, *I got* *your back,* which had always struck her as a masculine promise, strictly man-to-man, until now.

So it wasn't until she slipped downstairs the next morning to dress for work that she realized the black enamel box was missing from the kitchen counter.

ACT III

We Get Down
to Business
(and how!)

NEW YORK CITY
February 1924

1

Monday morning after my mama's funeral, I dress as usual and clatter down the IRT to the Wall Street station, in order to discover whether I am still in possession of a desk and chair in the typing pool of Sterling Bates & Co.

Naturally, on the morning of my departure for River Junction, I wired an explanatory telegram to the attention of Miss Atkins, and I sent a further wire— this one bordered in black, so as to give emphasis to my grief—on the actual evening of my mama's death. But Miss Atkins is the kind of woman who expects all family tragedies will be approved in advance, if you understand my meaning, and you don't ever want to disappoint Miss Atkins's expectations. Girls have a way of disappearing around here.

So you might say that frozen February air lies a little loose in my lungs as I shuffle through the dark-coated nine o'clock herd, down the slope of Wall Street to the trio of bronze revolving doors cornering the stock exchange, each of them topped by inspiring scenes of battle carnage in bas relief. I enter beneath the siege of Troy and make for the elevators. Clackety-clackety-clack go our heels on the vast marble floor. The smell of cigarettes surrounds us. Bronze doors slide open, herd moves forward. Minute groans of frustration from those cut off. My palms are damp inside my gloves. Blood all cool and light. The needle moves slowly, stopping at every damn floor, until we arrive at the fourteenth—really the thirteenth, as I remind myself daily—and three of us file out, all women, dark coats and cloche hats, valuable hands sheathed in leather. Meat for the grist, and by grist I mean Miss Atkins.

Or perhaps I'm unfair. After all, her task can't be easy, directress of a typing pool smack in the center of downtown Manhattan. Our band of sisters, each one tappity-tapping away in hopes of better things, clothed in cheap dark suits and ambition of various stripes, like Stella who sits to my right. Miss Stella DeLucca from Brooklyn, Crown Heights or someplace, dreams of sharing an elevator with a Sterling Bates partner and the elevator breaks down and there they are, stuck together for an enchanted hour while the engineers work to get the car moving, and three months later she becomes the wife of a banker and takes a honeymoon tour through Italy and comes back pregnant to an estate on the North Shore of Long Island, Oyster Bay or someplace, housekeepers and maids at her bidding, husband whisked by Packard limousine to Wall Street each day, garden parties and Pony Club and what have you. But in the meantime she wants to enjoy herself. In the meantime she's telling her parents she's taking a night secretarial course at Katie Gibbs, when in reality she's stopping by the coffee shop ladies' room after work to put on kohl and crimson lipstick and a sequined dress, and she's heading off to some joint or another for an evening of no good. Because why? Because life is short. Because the night is long. Because it doesn't even matter why anymore. A girl wants to have some fun, she should have some fun. She's got a right. And poor Miss Atkins has to keep all of us girls typing in tappity-tap, error-free unison for eight hours a day plus a half-hour lunch break at noon. I don't know about you, but I couldn't do it.

Anyway. Stella slides into place at my right-hand side at one minute past nine o'clock, ripping off gloves and blowing her nose into a crumpled cotton handkerchief, and she whispers, "What gives with you, Kelly? Somebody told me she heard you been in the slammer."

"My mama died," I whisper back, and Stella mumbles a stunned apologia of condolence heaped high with exculpation, cut short by the arrival of Miss Atkins in the doorway of the typing room: plump, oval cheeked, wearing a navy blue suit and an expression of what you might call profound maternal concern, if your mother were Catherine the Great.

Stella stuffs her handkerchief in her jacket pocket and snatches a sheet of clean white paper, rolling rolling rolling around the cylinder.

Now, here's how it works in the underwriting department at Sterling Bates. Those crafty bankers, they convince some poor unsuspecting business that it needs capital, lots of capital, the kind of capital that can only be raised by an appeal to the public financial markets. And the business agrees, God knows why, too many gin martinis maybe, too many slick bankers using too many big words, and the next thing you know, the lawyers jump in and build a regular Swiss Alps of paperwork that needs to be typed up on the double, in triplicate, and that's where we come in, we girls of the typing pool. We arrive at our desks by nine o'clock sharp, by which time some poor sucker—maybe even Miss Atkins, for all I know she sleeps here—has laid a fresh, stinking new pile of underwriting documents with handwritten annotations to the left of the typewriter, ready for transfiguration into neat, evenly spaced sentences an investor might actually be persuaded to believe he understands, which are then laid to the right of the typewriter. All very simple. And this particular Monday morning, I have arrived at my desk a whole seven minutes before nine o'clock, fresh faced and suit pressed, in order to create the impression that I am ready, nay, eager to recommence the transfiguration of whatever documents the underwriting department has cooked up in my absence. Only to discover, I'm afraid, that the patch of desk to the left of my typewriter is empty. Nothing to transfigure. Nothing to do but sit rigid and conspicuously idle in my chair, typewriting paper wound around typewriter cylinder, hands poised, thumbs pressed together, while Miss Atkins surveys the room, eyes slitted keenly behind her round black-framed eyeglasses, and starts down the aisle toward me.

"Good morning, Miss Atkins," I say when she arrives.

"Good morning, Miss Kelly. Will you please have the goodness to follow me."

The question's rhetorical. All Miss Atkins's questions are rhetorical. She doesn't even bother with the formalities of punctuation, lifting up the tail end of the sentence. Just turns away and marches back up the aisle, expecting me to follow, and for the barest tick of a half second I imagine myself telling her, as a matter of fact and to my deep regret, I don't have that kind of goodness this morning. Fresh out of goodness. So sorry, Miss Atkins.

Instead, I leap from my chair, bang my knee against the corner of the desk, and hobble after her, because I've got another job here at Sterling Bates this morning, another job that's got nothing to do with typing, and I had better find a way to stick around until lunchtime or there'll be the devil to pay: the kind of devil that don't take checks.

2

Strictly speaking, I stand a good half foot taller than Miss Atkins, an advantage magnified by the two additional inches of height contained in my square-heeled leather shoes. No matter. She's got a way of looking down at you when she's really looking up, craning her lace-collared neck to sort of stare you severely into your place, until you find yourself shrinking, shrinking, like some sweet little English girl who's just swallowed herself the wrong kind of mushroom. Even me, Ginger Kelly, who never ate the shrinking kind of mushroom in her life.

And even though I'm following her just now— through the doorway of the typing room, traced by the electrified gazes of my fellow galley slaves, down the long corridor that runs the length of the fourteenth floor to the rarefied offices on the south side of the building, from which the underwriting partners peer out comfortably over New York Harbor and the gray-green lady who keeps watch over the shipping—I still have the strangest feeling that she's staring me down again. Taking the measure of me. Cutting me down to size right through the straight silver-brown threads covering the back of her head, which are gathered in the customary knot at the nape of her neck. She marches swiftly, little alligator legs churning up the carpet. Makes a sharp left turn and then a right one. Opens up some door that guards not an office but a staircase, cold and dark, and I clutch my pocketbook to my ribs—not a chance I've left *that* valuable object at my desk—and climb those stairs right after her, two flights up, out another door, and to the left, and now, *now,* when she opens a door and holds it back for me to enter first, she does fasten me with a stare, all right, but not to shrivel me. Just a blank, careful gaze, entirely without judgment.

I sidle right past that gaze and into the room.

A lean, middle-aged man looks up from a desk and says, "Is this the girl?"

Behind me, Miss Atkins says, "Yes, sir. Miss Kelly."

He lays down a pen next to a leather blotter and rises to his feet. "Thank you, Miss Atkins."

Door closes click.

The man rescues a pair of small, round spectacles from the bridge of his nose and gestures to an armchair, the kind of cushiony leather-swathed goods you ordinarily reserve for your more prosperous banking clients. The office is large and set on a fortuitous southeast corner, allowing you to keep your beady eye on not only Lady Liberty but most of Brooklyn as well, and yet for all its generous dimensions and expansive view, the whole place strikes me as Spartan. The man himself strikes me as Spartan. Decoration spare and simple. Clothing hung from a gaunt frame. A palette that spans the rainbow from dove gray to charcoal.

"Good morning, Miss Kelly. I appreciate your attending me so early."

I take my seat. Fix my pocketbook to my lap. "It's my pleasure. Mr. . . . ?"

There is an instant of confused hesitation.

"I—I beg your pardon," he stammers. "You *are* Miss Kelly?"

"I am. Typing pool, underwriting department."

The set of his cheekbones eases a fraction. "As I thought."

"And I do apologize for my recent absence. As I explained in my telegram to Miss Atkins, my mother was taken sick, and I'm afraid she—well, she expired altogether soon after—"

"Yes, I heard. Very sorry for your loss. But—"

"Are you really? Sorry for my loss?"

His head jerks. Those narrow, grayish eyes blink out some kind of Morse code. Hand reaches for the pen, lifts it, sets it back down. Knots together with the other hand, atop the paper on the blotter, and then moves back to the damn pen like it's a talisman. Fountain pen, made of gold, probably cost a fortune. "I beg your pardon. I didn't mean— Naturally you're heartbroken. Terrible thing. No doubt the two of you were close—"

"Not particularly, I'm afraid, but it was still an awful shock. The funeral took place Friday. If my absence has caused any inconvenience—"

"Your absence?"

"From my desk last week."

"Oh! Oh. Think nothing of *that,* Miss Kelly. Naturally a daughter must attend her family at such a dreadful time. Her—her devoted family. The bank is quite understanding of such matters, I assure you."

I observe the fiddling of his fingers around the pen. "How awfully comforting."

"You need harbor no concerns on that account, Miss Kelly. Your position at the bank is perfectly safe." He leans forward and fixes me with an earnest gaze. "*Perfectly* safe."

You know, it's terribly quiet inside this office. I suppose that's what prestige buys you in this buzzing, rackety metropolis: a sweet absence of sound, of vibration even, such that you can hang suspended over the tip of Manhattan Island and lock eyes with a saucy Appalachian redhead and not a single note will interrupt your private communion with her. Not a word, not the clickety-clack patter of a typewriter, not the guttural roar of an automobile engine, not the clang of a streetcar bell or the rattle of an El train or a siren or a scream or any damn thing. Just you and her, conversing in a silent tongue, until illumination dawns between you.

And the girl, she leans back in her chair and crosses her promising long legs and smoothes the pleats of her navy skirt that covers those legs, and she says—to your profound gratitude, because God knows you don't want to have to spell the whole thing out for her, word by word, in the vulgar language of commerce—

"I'm relieved to hear it, Mr. Smith. I *am* speaking to Mr. Smith, am I not?"

He closes his eyes briefly. "Yes, Miss Kelly."

"I believe I have a parcel for you, Mr. Smith."

"Yes. Yes, I—I am given to understand you might. Have a parcel for me."

He coughs.

I smile.

"Of course, I must beg from you some proof of authenticity, before handing over a parcel like this. Do you have such a proof for me, Mr. Smith?"

Mr. Smith nods and flips the pen vertical between his fingers, nib down, to write something on the topmost paper lying before him on the blotter, while an ocean liner emerges at that exact second from the corner of the window behind him, heading out toward the Narrows and to sea. Three stout funnels, steam flowing purposefully from the first one. Mr. Smith sets down the pen, waves the paper in the air to dry the ink, folds it in half, rises from the chair. He's a tall man, as I said, and I am reminded of an insect as he rounds the corner of the desk and approaches my chair—not your typical New York City bug, cockroaches and that kind of thing, overfed and scuttling, but an insect from back home. A daddy longlegs or a praying mantis, made of sticks and sort of awkward about it. He holds out the note and I part the sides. Read the single word written there in elegant block letters.

Mr. Smith falls back to his desk and braces himself against the edge. His fingers strum the underside in an anxious arpeggio. Those long, fidgety fingers. I keep my gaze on the paper before me, my brow knitted thoughtfully, and while I can't see out the window, I imagine that ocean liner making her way across the broad plane of glass, crossing past the base of Lady Liberty, forcing her way through the skein of watercraft doing business in the icy February harbor.

At last, I lift my face and smile at Mr. Smith.

"I believe everything is in order."

His shoulders slump. I think he even smiles.

I rip the note into a dozen dainty pieces, deposit the pieces on the oily brown corner of the desk, and open the clasp of my pocketbook.

3

I don't know what kind of message Duke gave him about me, but I'll swear he was scared out of his wits. Drink?"

I waggle the bottle over Anson's glass.

"Just water," he replies.

"*Water?* My goodness. I'm afraid you'll have to fetch that little old thing yourself." I set down the bottle and lift my glass. "Cheers, then. To my seamless initiation into a life of bribery and corruption."

He says nothing to that. I clink his empty glass, there on the chest of drawers, and swallow down my gin like medicine.

"Tell me something, Anson. Are you teetotal by nature, or on principle?"

"Because it's illegal, do you mean?"

"Have you ever had a drink, is what I mean."

"I have."

"When? The last time. Your last and final taste of intoxicating liquor."

He glances out the window. "In January of 1920."

"I see. You're the kind of fellow who likes to follow rules."

"*Laws*, Miss Kelly. I follow laws."

"An interesting distinction, I guess. Though I feel obliged to point out, as I'm sure you're aware, that it's not forbidden to drink this marvelous ambrosia." I hold up the glass for his inspection. "Just to sell and transport it."

"I'm aware of that. I choose to abide by the spirit of the law, not its letter."

"How admirable of you. I expect they can see the glimmer of your halo all the way over in Brooklyn."

He just looks at me. He's standing next to the narrow, grimy window that overlooks the rear garden—such as it is—of Mrs. Washington's boardinghouse: the same window through which he recently gained entrance to my bedroom, in the manner of a lover, if not the spirit of one. His idea. I wanted to meet at some joint or another, nice and smoky, plenty of sauce to settle my nerves, but Agent Anson is cautious of spies and eavesdroppers and wishes to keep our meetings as private as possible. So here we are, wedged rather intimately inside the four irregular walls of my bedroom, while the lamplight adds gold to his hair and underlines the strength of those barbaric cheekbones. I tip a little more gin into my tumbler and change the subject. "So what do you make of our Mr. Smith? I must say, he isn't what I expected."

"Oh? What did you expect?"

"Someone seedier, I guess. Not a respectable praying mantis in a corner office."

"A praying mantis?"

I make a few long movements with my arms. "Tall and skinny."

Anson props one sturdy hip on the windowsill and fingers the long vertical edge of the windowpane with great interest. "His real name is Benjamin Stone."

"Benjamin Stone. Sounds familiar."

"Should be. He's head of the municipal bond department. Deals with all the city officials, not just in New York but up and down the New England coast.

Boston, Providence, New Haven. Structures bonds, puts together syndicates. Connects municipalities with money. You might say he knows all the right people, if you're looking to transport a few quiet loads of merchandise past the noses of the men who ought to be watching for them."

"And Ben's on the take."

"Appears so."

I set down the empty glass. "So arrest him."

Anson lifts his head from his study of the window. "Now, what kind of good would *that* do, do you think?"

"Stop him in his tracks."

"And your stepfather, Miss Kelly? What would happen to him? What might he do to you, if he realizes you've double-crossed him?"

"He'd be arrested, too. For bribing a—bribing a bank official."

Anson regards me quietly for a beat or two and returns his attention to the window. "No proof. Only a fool would testify against him."

"A fool like me."

"Which is why I won't let you do it. This is just the beginning, Miss Kelly. Benjamin Stone—he's only a symptom, not the cause. Duke Kelly has the entire New York City prohibition office in his thrall, to say nothing of the police and city hall."

"But I thought Mr. Shevlin was supposed to be incorruptible. Why, Izzy and Moe are in the papers every day, making arrests."

"Sure, making arrests. Making arrests of people like you, Miss Kelly, people out having a drink and maybe the owners of such establishments, and even a few men supplying those establishments. But that doesn't make a difference, not a bean's worth of difference." He sticks his thumb into the windowpane. "Eight million New Yorkers out there, Miss Kelly. Eight million New Yorkers, and at least half of them buying and drinking intoxicating liquors, in public establishments and private homes—and that's a conservative estimate—and Messrs. Isidore Einstein and Moe Smith have arrested a thousand or two. And the New York papers call them heroes."

I consider the bottle of gin and my empty glass next to it, and I fall back a pace or two, away from immediate temptation, bringing me right up against the bed. I sit down and stretch my arms out behind me.

"The thing is, you don't need to have the head of the Bureau in your pocket," Anson continues. "You don't want the head of the Bureau. That's too obvious. What you want are the men who really run things."

"Such as?"

Anson rises from the windowsill and steps to the bureau, the one I've just left. He leans his elbow on the corner and lifts the bottle of gin. Inspects the label and the transparent curve of glass. "That's the point of this exercise, isn't it? We're going to let Duke Kelly lead us to each one of those men, until we've got what we need. Until we've got enough evidence that we don't need anybody's testimony. Until not even Kelly can wriggle free."

"You sound like it's personal."

"Maybe it is."

"Those missing agents?"

He sets the bottle back on the bureau. "I should be going. Let me know when he makes contact with you again."

"Now, wait a moment. Not so fast."

"It's late, Miss Kelly. I imagine you have more agreeable appointments awaiting my departure."

"Oh? You think so? You mean gentleman callers?"

"That's your business, not mine."

"Say. You're not jealous, are you?"

He fixes me with that gaze of his, all dark ice and packed with silent contempt. That's how he answers me.

I push myself up from the bed and step close, real close, so I am staring at the blunt point of his oversized nose and absorbing all that contempt like so much challenge. "As a matter of fact, I'm not expecting anyone tonight. Just you. I cleared my dance card."

"Then I guess you ought to get some rest."

"You're right. I ought. But I do have a little business remaining with you, Agent Anson, if you'll be so good as to oblige me."

"I think we've covered everything thoroughly already."

"Oh, it's nothing to do with the enforcement of laws. Heavens, no. I've had it up to here with those for one night. Just a little curiosity I believe you might have the power of satisfying for me. Sort of—well, returning the favor. I help you with your needs, you help me with mine. A custom we have, out there in the country, where I was bred up."

Without his expression shifting so much as a hair, the contempt flattens into a thoroughly enjoyable wariness. I don't know how he does it, communicating such ideas without benefit of human expression. Or maybe it's all in my own head. Maybe I'm just imagining what he's thinking, and the genuine matter of his brain contains something else. Truth be told, those blue eyes are blank and relaxed, and his mouth's set in the same straight line as ever. Might mean anything. I reach into the pocket of my skirt and draw out a button, which I hold near the corner of my right eye, not far from his own.

"Ever seen such a thing before?"

"A button? From time to time."

"You big lug. I mean a button like this."

A small crease appears in his forehead. He takes the button from me and tilts it toward the lamp. "There's a design on the face."

"No fooling, Sherlock. I thought you might be able to tell me what it was."

"Why me?"

"Because, to my untrained eye, it looks like a crest of some kind, and I figure you'd have seen all the crests there are to see in this city."

He turns his face to mine, and this time he really is frowning, no doubt about it. "Why would you say that?"

"Because you're a swell, Oliver Anson. All dressed up in your dour old Prohi agent costume, of course, but you can't fool me. I know a gentleman when I see one."

He turns the button between his fingers and examines each side. "How?"

"How what?"

"How do you know a gentleman when you see one?"

"Oh, a million things. The way he talks. The words he uses—"

"*You've* got a vocabulary, too."

"I learned mine at school. With you, it comes natural. And your clothes. Dull and all, but the material's fine, and the cut"—I whistle—"why, the cut's sublime."

"Where did you learn about men's clothing?"

"I work in the underwriting department of one of the most prestigious banks in the world, Mr. Anson. And I notice things."

He holds out the button. "Yes, you do."

"But you haven't said I'm right."

"Nor will I."

I grasp the button in his fingers, but I don't pull away. I like the touch of his skin. I like the shape of his fingertips and the trim of his nails. I like the way his breath just touches the tip of my nose. "And the button?"

"It's the Harvard crest."

"Harvard? You mean the college?"

"Yes."

I take my hand away at last and rub the ridged brass design with my thumb. There's not a hint of tarnish. I reckon Mama kept them polished. "A Harvard man, then," I say softly.

"It appears so."

"Don't you approve? Something against Harvard men?"

"I'm only feeling sympathy for poor Mr. Marshall."

"Oh? And how do you know it's not Billy's button?"

"Because he attends Princeton University. *If* I'm not mistaken."

I slide the button back into my pocket. "No, you're not mistaken. But the button doesn't belong to any lover of mine. My goodness. What do you take me for?"

"I don't take you for anything. It's not my business, Miss Kelly, to make any sort of judgment on your personal affairs."

"And yet, you just have. I guess I should be flattered. You must care a little for me, in that case."

He turns away. "Of course I care." His voice is hoarse.

The air goes quiet between us, that old Manhattan quiet, existing separately within the faint, constant cacophony of the house and the city around us: somebody's gramophone playing jauntily upstairs, the tinny reek of jazz from Christopher's down below, the thumps and the creaks and the muffled laughter and the arguments and the banging of stove lids. Anson's cheek is bathed in light, his nose outlined in gold, and for the first time I perceive that while his face has all the raw, prehistoric charm of a Viking skull, his ear is curiously tender, the kind of pink and elegant curve you want to trace with one finger while a hurricane rages outside.

"I found the button in a box on my mother's drawer chest," I say. "A whole box just full of buttons. I think they might have belonged to my father."

"To Mr. Kelly?"

"No. My real father. The man who sired me."

Anson looks back at me, and for an instant, you wouldn't know he was the same man. His face is soft, his eyes gentle. "May I see the button again?" he says.

I extract said button and hand it back. This time he gives the object his full attention, like a jeweler with a monocle, right there under the lamp. I step in close, next to him before the bureau, and watch the movement of those thick, careful fingers beneath the light.

"Well?"

"It's the Harvard crest, all right. But I'm afraid it doesn't help much. There must be thousands of Harvard men in New York, and that's assuming your father's in New York." He places the button on the wooden surface, where it wobbles and spins before us, like a small brass top. "Do you have more buttons?"

"Yes. About a dozen."

"Would you like me to examine them?"

"Might take hours."

"I could take them home with me."

There's something about his voice, saying those words, not demonstrably different from any other tone of voice—he tends to stick to the same one, you know, somewhere deep in the baritone register, lacking any form of what musicians like Bruno call dynamics—but still sort of intimate and low pitched. Again, maybe that's all in my own head. Sometimes your head's like that, finding things it wants to hear, even if they don't properly exist on the outside.

"Be my guest," I reply, touching the button with the tip of my finger, until it comes to rest. "Just take good care of them for me, will you?"

"Of course."

"You'll have to step aside for me. They're in the top drawer."

He steps aside, and I work the drawer open, offering him a fine view of my intimate articles. I remove the box and allow the buttons to spill over the top of the bureau, and he says urgently, *Let me see that,* and I say, *The buttons?* and he says, *No, the box, the box, by God.*

So I hand him the box, and that's when all that musical cacophony in the background resolves into a series of discrete and purposeful thumps, like the step of a man's boots on the staircase outside, and before I can even turn to Anson and offer some kind of warning, the thumping stops, replaced by a knock on the door of my bedroom.

And trust me when I tell you, dear reader, that no lady's feeble fist ever caused a knock of that size.

4

Now, you may have been wondering about Billy, all this time. I know I have! When I arrived home on Friday night, all cold and shriveled, sleet chasing me down the sidewalk and up the stoop, I confess I half-expected to discover my Billy-boy sitting there on the edge of the bed, wearing his college-boy duds, face turned toward me in a mixture of relief and reproach. Warm arms prepared to receive me.

But I'm afraid the room was plain empty. Just the radiator bubbling under the window and a thin fan of letters spread on the floor behind the door, not one of which was addressed to me in Billy's lopsided handwriting. And let me tell you, nothing's barer than an empty room when you were expecting somebody in it.

So I stacked all the letters on my bureau and opened

each one—as I said, there weren't many—and set aside those that needed replying to and those that needing paying for. I unpacked my valise and brushed out my dress and my spare skirt and set aside the underclothes for laundering. That kind of thing. By the time I climbed beneath the blankets, I had nearly forgotten that Billy was supposed to be there at all, filling the chasm inside my breast; I had nearly forgotten that a chasm wanted filling to begin with. Busy hands, you know.

I went on to fill my Saturday and my Sunday with all the usual things—you must keep to your routine, Anson instructed me on the train, you must pretend everything is just the same as ever—and today, as you know, I had my hands terribly full. First Mr. Smith, and then the stack of underwriting agreements waiting for transfiguration upon my return to the typing pool. And then arriving home to discover my bedroom crammed full of a bristling warm Prohibition agent, the kind of surprise that shouldn't have been a surprise: the parcel you had forgotten you were expecting. A reversal, really, of my disappointment Friday night.

So in all those things, but especially the last one, I had allowed the expectation of Billy to slip free from its foremost position in my imagination, right down into the murkiness of subconscious (have I got my psychology right?), from which it now springs forth like a demented clown at the sound of that urgent, uncompromising knock on the door of my bedroom, just exactly when I need it least.

5

Agent Anson has the reflexes of a feral cat, I'll say that much. Without any particular appearance of hurry, he simply disappears under the edge of the bed, enclosing all four limbs by God knows what kind of calisthenic maneuver. I untuck the blankets from one side, just to make certain, and call out, singsong: "Who-*iiiis*-it?"

"Geneva Rose? That you?"

It says something for the flimsiness of boarding-house carpentry that I can distinguish every word, as if my visitor's standing on the right side of the door instead of the wrong side. And I suppose it says something for my miraculous memory, too, that I can fling open that door and say, tone of relief: "Carl Green! What in blazes do you think you're doing here?"

6

M ind you, I likely shouldn't have been so glad to
see him as I was. It's just that I figured he *had*
to be Billy, and what a damned thing for Billy to walk
in right now, possibly expecting to stay awhile, possibly
expecting to stay the entire night, while my bed—at
least the underside of it—is otherwise engaged.

So, in my excess of relief, I usher my old friend Carl
gratefully into my bedroom, and that's when I discover
poor Mrs. Washington standing behind him, fluster
faced, wagging a finger and telling me ten minutes,
Miss Kelly, ten minutes and that cousin of mine must
go. She runs a *respectable* establishment, after all.

"Cousin?" I query when the door is shut.

"Well, now, I done had to say *some*thing, didn't I?
And I reckon we's cousins somehow, me and you." He
stands there awkwardly, holding his hat at his middle.
"How you been, Geneva Rose? I never seen you after
the funeral."

"I left pretty quick. Train to catch."

"You might could-a left Saturday instead. Train
runs on Saturdays, now."

"I might."

His hair is all slicked back, benefiting from a recent shearing. Cheeks all pink, suit all crumpled. He wears an expression of wary hope on that long, hollowed-out, handsome face—a country boy finding some point of refuge in the wicked city. I take pity on his confusion and ask him, for the second time, what brought him here on such an inauspicious winter's night.

(Well, as if I didn't know.)

"Done brought a parcel for you, from your daddy," he says, reaching into his pocket, and I take the brown-paper thing from his big hand and thank him for it.

"I expect you know what's inside," I say as I move to the bureau and tuck Duke's parcel in the bottom drawer, as far away from the hiding place of my mama's enamel box as I can manage.

"I guess I do. I never did open it," he adds quickly.

"Of course you didn't."

"It ain't none-a my business, after all."

"Oh, but it is your business, I guess. It's River Junction's business. And a good business it is, too. Drink?"

"Why, I just might! Thank you kindly, Geneva Rose."

"It's just gin," I say, slithering a few ounces down the side of Agent Anson's empty glass, hoping Carl doesn't start to wondering what it's doing there, side by side with my own, "but at least it's wet. And it's free."

"It is, too." He takes the glass, and of course I then pour another for myself—wouldn't be friendly, otherwise—and we clink glasses and commence to talking, as two people do when they share a bottle of gin between them, regardless of some fellow who might be hiding under the bed a foot or two away. Carl begins with some kind of observation on the luxury of my surroundings, and I shrug my shoulders and say, *It's home, isn't it,* and he says something about how I look different somehow, here in New York City.

"I've been working all day, Carl. Stooped over a typewriter for eight hours. I guess I might be showing the strain."

"No. Ain't that at all. It's the opposite. Looking all fresh and pleased with yourself. Your cheeks a-coming up roses."

"That'll be the central heating. Or the sauce, I guess." I brandish my glass.

"Well, maybe."

"You staying nearby? Can I get you a taxi or something?"

"Oh, I can find my way, all right. Mr. Kelly got me a room at a hotel. Real nice place on Fifth Avenue."

"The Plaza?"

"That's the place."

"Well, well! Carl Green's got himself a room at the

Plaza Hotel in New York City. A nice big one, maybe? Looking out over the park?"

"Nothing like that, Geneva Rose. Just a little old cupboard by the elevator. No more room'n a henhouse."

"You should have asked for a nicer one. I'll bet they thought you were some kind of hayseed who didn't know any better."

He laughs a little. "Why, Geneva Rose, that's just what I is. Simple fella from the country. I don't require myself no fancy hotel suite. Just a bed to lay my head on. Why, I don't reckon I might could sleep a wink in one-a your luxury accommodations. Room like this'd suit me much better." He starts to gesture, realizes how such a declaration must sound, and stiffens right up. Color starts spreading into his neck and over his cheeks. He stammers something, which I interrupt in soothing tones.

"Well, you just remember to tip for room service, now, or they'll find a way to get you back. Those Plaza bellboys."

He hides himself behind another drink of gin. "I reckon I been in a nice hotel before, Geneva Rose. I know myself some manners. What kind-a hayseed do you take me for?"

I squint a little, but I truly cannot tell if the old lummox is kidding me or not. He presents this face of angelic honesty, tinged with offended pride, which might or might not be the genuine article. Anyway. I can sense the proximate impatience of Agent Anson shimmering through the floorboards and into my shoes, so I finish off my gin and set it on the bureau with the air of a working girl who's done her bit for the day, thank you.

"Anyways. It's been fine to see you, Carl Green. I do surely thank you for fetching me this parcel through all that sleet and dark of night, like a regular postman. I reckon you'll be wanting to get on back to your room at the Plaza, now."

"I reckon so," he says, tone of indecision.

"Much nicer than this room of mine, even if it's just a broom closet. And I'm afraid I can't offer you any supper. Certainly not a nice hot one like they serve up at the Plaza."

"That's all right. I ain't hungry."

He stands there, toying with glass in the one hand and hat in the other, not quite looking at me. Outside the window, somebody's trumpet climbs up and climbs down, dizzy and melancholy, and the pluck of Bruno's double bass makes the glass thrum.

"Something else you want, Carl?"

"Maybe there's something."

"Out with it, then. We're old friends, aren't we?

Cousins, isn't that right? And I guess you don't have more than a minute left of your ten, before Mrs. Washington comes marching right up those stairs to evict you."

"I reckon that's true." He finishes the drink like a man inhaling courage and steps toward me. Sets his empty glass down next to mine with a resolute thump. "It's about your mama, Geneva Rose."

I think about Oliver Anson folded up under my bed, listening to every word. A wave of new sleet rattles against the window, overcoming the music.

"What about my mama?" I say softly.

"Weeellll . . ." Long, drawn-out syllable, and then, in a rush: "You knowed she and my mama was good friends. Near enough sisters, I reckon, most especially after you went away to school, and there was no more girls left around your place. Just Mr. Kelly and the boys."

And now my heart is beating strong, my breath is coming short, since the words *she and my mama was good friends* crossed his lips.

"I guess Johnnie told me something about it," I say.

"All right. And I reckon Johnnie told you how my own mama died two years back. Caught the influenza and it turned to pneumonia."

"I heard. I'm real sorry, Carl."

"Well, I reckon we was all kind-a shocked, you know, account-a my mama always was a strong woman, scarce sick a day in her life. And it came on so sudden. Not a thing we might could do except to watch her gasp for her breath and shake with the ague."

"Oh, Carl—"

"She didn't suffer long, though. No more'n a few days. I seen some fight it out for weeks, until they ain't no more than a pile-a bones in fits under the blankets—" He stops and looks aside, no doubt remembering how my own mama suffered and fought and finally died. Clears his throat, which doesn't really need clearing. "Anyway, before she passed, she called me to her and said there was a thing she required me to do. A charge laid upon her, which she now fixed to pass on to me. See, Geneva Rose, the two of them always reckoned your mama'd be the first to go, seeing as—as—well."

"Seeing as she was always the weaker one."

He picks up his glass and peers inside, as if expecting to discover some key to wisdom there. "That's about the size of it. And your mama—Mrs. Kelly—there was something she wanted you to have from her, once she was gone, excepting she was afeared there was no one to brung it to you . . . no one in the family, I mean . . ."

"So she gave it to Mrs. Green. She gave it to your mama."

"She did, Geneva Rose. And my mama done gave it to me when she died, and she said I was to pass it on to you when Mrs. Kelly found her end, and so I have brung this thing to you, Geneva Rose, I have borne it like a cross all the way from River Junction, and Mr. Kelly don't know a thing about it, my mama made me swan I wouldn't tell him, and the Lord knows I was a-going to give it to you after the burial, see, but you up and left so early—"

"What is it? Where is it?"

"Why, right here. Right here in my other pocket."

He reaches into a pocket, not the pocket of his overcoat but the one inside the lining of his jacket, right up against his chest, and he draws out a thick brown envelope bound several times over with twine.

"And I was a-wondering how I was a-going to brung it to you, account-a Mr. Kelly, see, he always knows who is coming and who is going in River Junction—"

"And then he asked you to deliver me this parcel."

"That's exactly it, Geneva Rose. So here it be." He presses the envelope into my open hands. "Take it. I don't want no more part-a this."

I fold my fingers around the envelope. Rough twine

scratching my skin. Smells of flowers, like it's been sitting in somebody's drawer chest, next to a sachet of old summer roses. "You don't like hiding things from Mr. Kelly, do you, Carl?"

"No, Geneva Rose, I do not. He liketa . . ."

"He owns you. Isn't that right? He about owns all of you."

"And you." Carl nods to the bottom drawer of the bureau.

"And me."

He sets the glass back down—he's been holding it in his left hand, all this time, while the right hand delivered me the goods—and he straightens out his jacket. "Fact is, he done a whole mess-a good in River Junction, Geneva Rose, and I ain't got no desire to say a word against him. And I don't hold with no government men, either, telling us what we can drink and not drink and what we can brew up and sell for the drinking of others. I would surely ruther take my orders from Duke Kelly than from some rich fellow in Washington, some swell with the dough to fill up his cellar before the axe set to falling, enough booze to last him until kingdom come."

"Then why didn't you tell him about *this*, Carl Green? Why didn't you?"

"Because I promised my mama, is why. Promised her on her deathbed, didn't I, and besides, I ain't stupid, I ain't blind, Geneva Rose, I know what—"

"You know *what*, Carl?"

He turns his attention to the buttoning of his overcoat, one by one. Lips moving to the rhythm of his fingers. He straightens and picks up his hat and smashes it down on his head, and his eyes are turned down at the corners, like the eyes of an old hound dog in front of a dying fire.

"Nothing. I know nothing. You take care of yourself, Geneva Rose. You take good care-a your dear self. You fix to get yourself out-a this racket as quick as you can, you hear me? You discover yourself some rich man to marry you and give you a nice, soft life. Life your mama wanted for you." He takes me by the shoulders, and before I have time to gasp or move my own hands or anything like that, he plants a kiss on my lips, the same kind of kiss he planted there back in the bushes by the old fishing hole, sweet and heartfelt, and just like that time he pulls away as I come to my wits, except this time he's quick enough not to get slapped.

"Good-bye, Geneva Rose. I'll see myself out."

And he does.

7

I believe I've had just about all I can take from this particular Monday, as I stand there listening to the echo of Carl Green's boots going down the boarding-house stairs, but I suspect Monday isn't done with me yet. Not when there's a man still stuck under my bed.

"You can come out now," I say. Still staring at the door.

There's some scraping and shuffling as Oliver Anson extricates himself from his predicament. I guess I ought to laugh, but all I can manage just now is a smile, and that smile only just turning up the far corner of the right-hand side of my mouth. I fold my arms and tell Anson he can just forget what he heard down there, every word.

He nods to the brown envelope half-hidden in my arms. "Is that what he gave you?"

"That's personal. None of your business."

"It *is* my business when you're as shaken as that."

"I ain't—I'm not shaken."

He doesn't bother to contradict me. I press my fingernails into my arms, hard as I can through the ivory crepe de Chine of my respectable Sterling Bates blouse, just to prove that I'm not trembling all over, not shaken in every bone.

"Has anyone ever told you," he says, not moving an eyelash, "that you possess an extraordinary ability to alter your voice and your language and your manner almost beyond recognition, depending on your audience?"

"Do I?"

"You're not doing it on purpose?"

"I don't know what you mean."

Anson moves at last, but only to brush the dust from the sleeves of his jacket. "All right, then. If you don't want to speak about it."

"Oh, now, that's rich, coming from a fellow like you. You've got no right to judge how I keep my secrets. How I keep my private thoughts to myself."

"I've already told you, Miss Kelly. It's not my business to make any sort of judgment on your personal affairs."

"But you do anyway. I can tell that you do."

"You're wrong."

"No, sir. I am never wrong, least about the inner speculations of the male sex. You might say I'm an expert. And do you want to know what I figure? I figure you're a clean, straight arrow, sharp and true in his course through the air, and I'm only a sly, crooked thing, and if there's one thing you can't stand, a straight arrow like you, it's a girl who drinks and breaks laws and shows every man a different face."

There is another one of those curious pauses, in which Anson examines me with his dark, steady eyes, and I just stand there and take it as best I can, like we're a pair of gunslingers out west somewhere, sizing up each other's parts. And then he breaks the standoff. Not, at first, by speaking, but by raising his right hand and cupping his palm about the line of my jaw, such that his fingertips straddle my ear.

"That's not quite true," he says. "You may have several *masks*, Miss Kelly, for reasons of your own, which you apply and discard at will, and I regard each of them with a deep professional admiration. But you have but one *face*, and I believe I admire that most of all."

You can't reply to a speech like that. You can but stand there and take those words, as best you can. Your own eyes open and unblinking to the stare of his. Your pulse drumming under his hand. Your two hands clutching a brown envelope full of something your mama gave unto your keeping. Your fingers tangling in the string.

"Your eyes are so dry," Anson says. "You need to weep a little, sometimes."

"I'm not one for weeping. No more than you are."

"We're not talking about me, are we?"

"No," I say, "I guess we're not," and I don't know whether it's me falling forward or him reaching out to catch me, but then the means aren't so important at a time like this, are they? Just the ends. The V of his gray tweed waistcoat, into which I shed about a pint of honest salt tears.

8

When I am done weeping, he gives me his handkerchief and pours me a tumbler of water from the faucet in the third-floor bathroom. Somehow I end up in bed, though I can't remember just how I got there: whether he helped me or whether I made my own way. I figure I never will ask him for certain. The gin has taken hold, though I believe I only drank but two glasses altogether. During that hour or so of my weakness, I never once looked at his face. Just the whites of his arms—he shed his jacket for my sake when I began to shiver, the way you do sometimes set to shaking after a long weep—and the gray comfort of his waistcoat. My armchair, in which he settled us, wedged between the bed's end and the wall's beginning. I believe I held my eyes closed, anyway, most of that time. Did not want to catch the horror of my reflection in some mirror or other.

In the morning, the sleet is gone and the sun does shine from a painful blue sky. My head's full of gin rocks, sharp and heavy, and while Mama's brown envelope lies on the bureau, strings still attached, the gray jacket and the enamel box and the half-dozen buttons are gone through the window, together with the man who bore them out.

9

Now, I keep a certain appointment on the first Saturday of every month: one I missed in February, on account of my mama's passing. But don't you worry, he's an understanding fellow, and when I apply my knuckles to his door at one o'clock on Saturday afternoon, the first of March, he opens right up and offers me an understanding embrace.

"How are you, Gin?" he says, once he's ushered me inside and handed me a drink, which he's already mixed in anticipation of my arrival. The little dear.

"Same as ever. Did you miss me terribly?"

"Terribly. None of the other girls are half so good as you, Ginger."

"Of course they aren't. I have a kind of *je ne sais quoi,* don't you know."

"Don't I ever." He sits intimately next to me on the sofa and places a hand on my thigh. "You've lost weight."

"A little."

"As long as you haven't lost anything in that glorious forecastle of yours."

"It's the fashion, you know."

"We gentlemen do not care much about the fashion, *ma chère amie.* We want the same things we have always wanted."

"And I suppose I have them?"

"In spades." He clinks my glass and drinks at last. His eyes fall on my bosom. "I don't suppose we—"

"Not on your life. It's just business between you and me, Anatole."

"That's not true. We have a beautiful friendship."

"If you say so. I call it business."

His hand retreats to the sash of his dressing gown. "You wound me."

"Oh, Anatole. If *only* I had the power to wound you."

He rises from the sofa and heads for the table next to his easel, where his cigarette case rests next to his paints and brushes and odds and ends. He offers me one, which I decline—he raises his eyebrows at that—and lights himself up with the kind of relish you ordinarily reserve for a juicy beefsteak in the comfort of a high-class restaurant. "You know," he observes, after a thoughtful drag or two, "I sometimes wish I had not made you what you are. There was something so deliciously wholesome about you in those days, with your round cheeks and that awful pink coat."

"Unspoiled, you mean?"

"Yes, exactly."

"So you figured you absolutely *had* to spoil me—"

"Before someone else did, *mon amour*! Some far more unscrupulous character than I."

He smiles with such satisfaction, I don't have the heart to explain to him that I was already spoiled, round cheeks and pink coat notwithstanding: that the rot in my middle had already taken hold, and he, Anatole himself, was the man I chose to obliterate it, or at least to replace the rot with something I could live with. We met on the Christopher Street IRT platform, on the evening of my second day in the typing pool, and he gave me a ticket to an art gallery of some kind, where he was shortly opening an exhibition of his latest work. I remember experiencing a real thrill at the curl of this ticket in my palm—an artist, a New York City artist, one skilled enough to have his own exhibition—but the gallery turned out to be some meager shop on Bedford Street, and the opening-night crowd consisted of me, Anatole, the gallery owner, and maybe a dozen or so of Anatole's discarded lovers, eyes dark with kohl and bright with hope. A futile hope, I'm afraid, for by then Anatole had come to some sort of decision about me, some kind of fury, and when Anatole grabs the bit in his teeth like that, there's nothing you can do but hold on and ride him to the end, so to speak. And I was eager for the ride—that was why I had come to New York, after all, why I had fled River Junction and made my way to the wicked city—so I climbed aboard, I let him sweep me upstairs to his studio so he could paint me, he said, paint me in all my glory! And the funny thing is, that's exactly what he did. Anatole's not a monster. He is not, as he said himself, altogether unscrupulous. Why, his paintings of me became the basis for an en-tirely new exhibition three months later, one that actually received a certain degree of critical attention, and it was only while celebrating this modest triumph that we became lovers. At the time, I was relieved and kind of naïvely puzzled to learn that I was—at least as a matter of strict physical status—a virgin, and I expect that's why I can never be sorry about Anatole, I cannot ever really renounce him. He returned to me some miniature piece of my soul that I thought I had lost.

Still, I don't have any wish to return to those days of early enthrallment, and anyway—well, there's the question of Julie Schuyler, isn't there?

10

I expect you've heard of Julie. She's that exact selfsame Julie Schuyler you've read about in the gossip pages, under those breathless headlines containing all the exclamation points and the simple, electric words: JULIE DRIVES FORD UP LIBRARY STEPS! JULIE STRIPS, DIVES INTO PLAZA FOUNTAIN! That kind of thing. You know whom I mean.

"Speaking of unscrupulous characters," I say, inspecting my glass against the light, "where's our Julie?"

Anatole makes this disappointed sigh and extracts his watch from the pocket of his dressing gown. (Anatole always wears dressing gowns indoors, and furthermore, he would rather die than own a modern wristwatch. He's that kind of fellow. You know what I mean.)

"Late," he says.

But she arrives a minute later, blue of blood and blond of hair, smelling of cigarettes and face powder and independence. She tosses her cloche hat on the sofa and says she's dying for a drink, would somebody please mix her a gin and tomato juice, and Anatole sort of starts.

"What the devil kind of drink is this?"

"It's all the rage in Paris right now—a thing I suppose you'd already know, if you were *really* French, instead of just pretending. Hemingway drinks them to chase away his hangovers." She notices me and frowns. "You've still got your clothes on."

"Only just arrived."

"Well, I guess we're all fashionably late today. The winter blues." She comes forward and takes my hands and kisses each cheek, very French—Julie spent the autumn in Paris, visiting friends, and it still hasn't worn off—and she asks me how I'm getting along.

"Fit as a fiddle."

"You've lost weight."

"Not where it counts."

"All right, then. Let's get down to business, shall we? Haven't got all afternoon, and my head's something vicious."

I step behind the screen and unbutton my blouse. "Bad night?"

"The worst."

She doesn't elaborate, and I don't encourage her. You see, a couple of years ago, Julie replaced me on Anatole's chaise longue (I'll tell you *that* story another time), an unexpected discovery that still inhibits the full flowering of our friendship, if you know what I mean. Not that we haven't tried. These are modern times, and Julie and I are terribly sophisticated women. The party, for instance, where I met Billy Marshall. That was at Julie's apartment, remember, or rather at her parents' apartment, given over to Julie's high jinks. She invited me carelessly that particular Saturday afternoon for a Saturday evening party, just as I was buttoning up my jacket, and I couldn't resist calling a bluff like that. The Schuylers, after all, are one of New York's oldest and best families, as I'm sure you're aware. I found myself disappointed by the apartment, however. I was expecting something grand, something kind of palatial, but the place owned but two parlors, and the library was closed to guests. No matter. We danced to jazz on the phonograph and the vintage champagne flowed all night. Julie introduced me to Billy, and you know the rest. So I suppose I owe her for that, among other things.

Now, Julie and Anatole are no longer lovers—come to think of it, I do wonder who Anatole's sleeping with these days—but I guess she does still regard him with a proprietary air. When I belt the silken dressing gown around my waist and step from the screen, I'm not surprised to find them tangled together in an almost erotic confederation, arranging the photography equipment and the chaise longue upon which I'm required to pose myself this afternoon. Above the chaise, affixed to the wall that serves as our backdrop, someone's hung one of the portraits Anatole painted of me three years ago, in which I'm arranged fruitfully atop that same piece of furniture, breasts catching a beam of light from the dirty skylight above, hair spilling down my shoulders in strange, abstract, carroty pieces. It's called *Redhead Under Skylight,* and it's the only painting Anatole didn't sell on that first night of the Ginger exhibition. Not because he didn't receive any offers—among the gentlemen, at least, it was his most popular work— but because he was so terribly in love with me then, and what better way to seduce a naïve girl from the far sliver of Maryland than with such a declaration of devotion? He used to prop that damn picture against the wall while he had me in bed, and I swear he preferred to watch his own representation of me than the genuine article laid out before him.

I turn around and plant my hands at my hips. "Whose idea was this?"

"Mine," says Julie. "It's Anatole's most famous work, and it's only been exhibited once. This card's going to be a sensation."

"What if somebody recognizes me?"

"Nobody's going to recognize you, pet. They never do. We always take the *greatest* care, don't we, Anatole?"

"Besides, my hair's bobbed now. Won't have the same effect."

"That's all right. We've got a wig for you."

"I'm not wearing a wig!"

"You've worn them before. And the better to disguise you, after all. You're so terribly worried about somebody recognizing you."

I turn to Anatole, who's fussing with the camera aperture in a naked attempt (you'll pardon the pun) to keep himself pure of the grime of commercial negotiation. "I thought you weren't ever going to make a dime from that painting. That's what you promised me. It was sacred, you said."

He straightens. Offers me a kind of ashamed smile. "My dear girl. Is this really so bad? It is only the scenery. Why, no one will even notice the painting behind you! It is only your lovely figure they see in these cards."

"I'm not an idiot, Anatole."

"We'll pay you double," Julie says. "A hundred dollars."

"Two hundred."

"One fifty."

"One eighty."

She smiles and holds out her manicured hand. "Done."

11

The cards were Julie's idea. Shortly after I applied a pair of scissors to Anatole's collection of silk dressing gowns and departed the premises, vowing never to return, Julie happened upon one of Anatole's portraits from the Ginger exhibition—*Redhead Eating Cherries,* I believe—on the wall of somebody's dining room. Apparently the painting was attracting a great deal of furtive admiration from the gentlemen present. Can't imagine why.

Anyway, the story goes, she stormed on down to Anatole's studio and asked why he had never painted *her* like that—after all, she's indisputably the more beautiful of the two of us—and he told her that as soon as she grew a pair of tits like mine, he would create an entire exhibition devoted to her, as well. Julie took this in the proper spirit. She found me at the Christopher Club that evening and made me the kind of indecent proposition you can't possibly refuse. She and Anatole would pay me to model for photographs—absent the customary drapery, but in perfect taste, she assured me—from which the two of them would produce, tinted and artfully printed, a series of cards, much like those made of professional baseball players. Why, I'd be the Babe Ruth of indecency!

Now, I had my own reasons for agreeing to this proposal, but I did impose one condition on my employers. In none of these images was my face to be identifiable as my own, and in order to ensure their compliance with this condition, I should have approval of each card before printing.

Done, Julie said right back, much as she said just now.

Though it was a shame, Anatole said at the time. *Her tits are magnificent, to be sure, but her face is something more. (Something more what?* demanded Julie, and Anatole said, *Something more interesting,* and apparently that mollified the dear old thing. Beautiful always trumps interesting.)

Naturally, the cards have proved a smashing success, print runs in the tens of thousands, each new release snapped up in every tobacco shop and newspaper stand in New York City, and I guess Anatole is one hundred percent correct when it comes to the male gaze: no one ever bothers to examine my face in those photographs, because I've never been stopped on the subway train or called into Miss Atkins's office or leered at in the Sterling Bates canteen—well, no more than usual—in short, never once recognized as the Redhead, even though her identity is a matter of intense public speculation. It's the funniest damned thing. I guess people see what they want to see. And I confess, I do wear a brassiere with a flattening effect, in order to achieve the fashionable profile.

Regardless. At the moment, I've got a job to do, and I need the dough for purposes of my own. A hundred and eighty clams are worth any amount of personal humiliation, I reckon, when you need them badly enough. I slip off my dressing gown and arrange myself on the chaise longue, while Julie applies the wig with maybe a little more force than is absolutely necessary. Anatole's busy with the lamps. That old skylight still exists, sure, but photography's a different world from oil paint, it's all trickery and make-believe, and generally speaking the more light the better. Above me, *Redhead Under Skylight* shifts under the changing beams, carroty hair against pale skin, and I think how plump that girl looks, compared to my present form, how pink and innocent. And yet while Anatole painted that portrait, while I sprawled my naked limbs upon this very article of furniture, I did imagine myself not bathed in white light but smeared with dirt: with the slick, rotting mud of a creek bottom. I remember that clearly, how dirty I felt, so that I was surprised to see the finished work hanging on the wall of the gallery a week later. That clean, lovely girl I didn't recognize. When I confessed all this to Anatole, later that evening, two empty champagne bottles tottering between us on the sofa cushion, he explained about perspective, and how he had painted all these portraits of me from a certain point of view, his own point of view, and this ravishing painting perfectly described that vision. After making this very beautiful speech, he came close and pushed the champagne bottles to the floor and kissed me for the first time, and I was so drunk and grateful, I put my arms around his neck and kissed him back. For a short while, I thought this was love.

12

Anyway. Julie arranges the scene and Anatole takes the photographs, and I hang around waiting while they process the film into negatives and that kind of thing, just in case there was a fly on the lens or whatever else. You'd be surprised what can ruin a good photograph of a naked woman.

By the time Julie's satisfied, it's past nine o'clock, and she's got some engagement uptown, and Anatole and I find ourselves sharing a table at the Christopher Club. It's the same table I used to share with sweet Billy-boy, right in front of the jazz orchestra, and I'm starting to develop that kind of restless itch in my middle that always leads to trouble. On top of that, I've got something to say to Anatole that requires a certain amount of lubrication.

"I'm done," I say. Setting down the whiskey, ker-thump.

"Done, my love? Done with what?" He's sitting far too close, and I guess I'm letting him. I don't know why. Maybe it's the absence of Billy, maybe it's the presence of whiskey. Maybe because I haven't received any parcels in a week, nor any kind of message from River Junction, and there's a fellow nursing a lowball glass at the bar right now who followed us here all the way from Hudson Street.

"Why, done with posing for you. I'm turning a new leaf."

Anatole frowns. "Does this concern that boy you are sleeping with?"

"In the first place, I'm not sleeping with him. In the second place, if I were, it's none of your business. And thirdly, since you're asking, no. It's got nothing to do with him." I turn my gaze to the bar and the fellow hunched over his drink. My old friend Millie the Vamp sits atop her usual stool, long legged and somber to-night in a fringed black dress, plucking a languid olive from her martini. "As a matter of fact, I haven't seen the fellow since January."

Anatole lays a hand over mine. "What a shame."

"Don't be ridiculous. He was nothing but a nuisance, really. A college kid."

"No, I mean a shame that you want to stop posing for us."

"Oh. Well, it's served its purpose. I've got enough dough saved up, and the fact is . . ." My attention drifts to Bruno's small jazz orchestra, ruminating some theme, Bruno on the bass and four others, drums and trombone and trumpet and a clarinet player I haven't noticed before, running up and down a minor scale with all the mesmeric dexterity of a squirrel ferrying acorns to a hidden den.

"The fact is what, dear?"

"The fact is . . . the fact . . ."

There's something about that clarinet player, isn't there? Dressed in a neat dinner jacket and a hat slung low on his forehead. Bristling mustache a shade or two darker than the golden-brown hair shining forth below the crown of his hat. In the course of a complicated riff, he tilts his head back a bit, lifting the shadow of his hat brim from his eyes, and his midnight gaze meets mine. I believe my heart stops.

"Beloved? Is something the matter?"

"Nothing's the matter, darling." I turn back to my companion and draw one index finger along the back of his hand that covers mine, and I just pray nobody notices that my finger's gone a mite wobbly. My voice a little breathless. "Just admiring the skill of that clarinet player. I can't help wondering when he joined Bruno's little band."

"Who knows? These musicians, they come and go."

"I'll say. I don't guess you could spare a cigarette for a girl in need?"

"But of course."

He withdraws the hand to make busy with the cigarette, and I lean forward and link my hands together beneath my chin to stop the wobbling, and I surely do *not* look back at that clarinetist, though the left-hand side of my face does burn with his proximity. Anatole slips the cigarette between my lips and lights me up. I blow out a great deal of smoke in a long, elegant curl and lean forward to kiss his mouth tenderly. "Thank you," I say.

"You are terribly welcome." Anatole's eyes go all bright and interested. He bends in to catch my drift, while my damn heart resumes its work at a wild, unnatural rhythm, flushing the blood right into my neck and cheeks and bosom. "Also terribly beautiful. Have I been such a great fool?"

"You've been an awful fool, and now you're too late. I never do make the same mistake twice."

"You will not offer me a second chance?"

I fiddle with his cuff. Insert my fingers along the skin of his wrist. "You don't deserve one, Anatole, and anyway we both know you weren't made for keeping to one woman."

"And this is an obstacle for you?"

"I believe I made that clear enough."

Anatole shakes his head and places his hand on my knee, underneath the table. "You pretend to be so modern, beloved, when really you are just a mere romantic. A quaint relic of an earlier age."

"Maybe I am."

"And we were so in love with each other once."

"For about a minute and a half, as I recollect."

"There's no reason we might not have another minute or two, you and I. It was such a very great pleasure the first time."

I lean forward to murmur in his ear, so close that my lips brush the cartilage at the tip. "Then let's not spoil the memory with another attempt, hmm?"

Now, I'm no musician—least no more than a dash of piano at the boarding school, while the nuns rapped on my disobedient fingers—but I could swear that clarinet misses a note.

Mind you, I've been an awfully good girl, up until now. I have followed Agent Anson's instructions to the letter. I've kept to my usual habits. I've kept to the hours of daylight, so much as I'm able. When I have craved a measure or two of something stronger, I've dutifully repaired to Christopher's, under the benevolent gazes of the musicians and the regular patrons and Christopher himself, who lets no other man fill my glass or offer me a sandwich. And true to his word, Anson has ensured that the Bureau of Internal Revenue has run no more raids on the establishment. No more bulls charging inside, breaking all the glassware: just a quiet, friendly business minding its own, safe as could be. During this time, since Anson last disappeared through my bedroom window, I have delivered six more envelopes, sealed up snug in brown paper, much like my mama's parcel she left to me, right up until a week ago, when the supply of said parcels shut off, like a spigot somebody's closed, like a well that's run dry.

And I have not seen Oliver Anson, not once. Not a single blessed time. On the bureau three weeks ago, when he climbed out the window before I woke, he left behind a note that I was to telephone him at his office with any new instructions, any new names, as soon as I received a parcel and before I was to deliver it. Which I've done, obedient to a fault, except that it's never Anson's voice that greets me on the other end of that telephone wire. I've left my message with some doll or another, likely the doll in the navy suit who made us coffee that first night, calling from the telephone in the hallway of the boardinghouse and revealing no details, just names and places and that's all, and the doll's voice replies, all matter-of-fact and professional, like a New York Telephone operator, that she will ensure Agent Anson receives my message forthwith. When I last spoke to her, three days ago, I just said that I hadn't had any news since last Saturday, and I would very much like to speak to Agent Anson personally, at his earliest convenience. She replied—calm as you please—that she would ensure Agent Anson received that message forthwith.

Well, maybe she did and maybe she didn't. Maybe she has and maybe she hasn't delivered that one or *any* one of those messages. Until this exact moment, here in the smoky, drinky confines of the Christopher Club, I haven't had the opportunity to discover the truth of the matter. Anson's made himself scarce as a firefly in January. I haven't talked to him. I haven't even seen him, even though I've looked for him every time I've left my door, every time I've boarded a train, every time I've entered a shop or arrived at my place of employment or, most especially, made a delivery of one of those little brown envelopes. (About those deliveries, more later.) I have craved the sight of Anson all the way inside my bones, the way you crave water to drink and air to breathe, not because I am in any way besotted by the walking, talking block of mountain granite, but because I am otherwise alone. Otherwise unarmed against the mighty skein of spies and protectors watching over the interests of Duke Kelly.

So I tell myself, as Anatole's hand inches up my leg, fingers climbing so nimbly as the notes of that damn clarinet: It's not exhilaration, you dumb bunny, it's not excitement or sexual arousal or any one of those things. It's *relief.*

You're just relieved, that's all.

Anatole's accent grows even more excruciatingly French. "And yet we might still make a better memory, don't you think? Since we know each other so well. Since I have made you famous."

"It's not *me* that's famous, it's my anatomy."

"For excellent reason. You don't know how I have admired that anatomy, these past two years. What a torture it's been, taking your photograph instead of your—"

"Tut, tut." I press my finger over his lips. "What gives with you? Haven't you got some other doll to keep you company these days?"

"Not a doll like you."

"Ah, I see. You've been left high and dry. Poor Anatole." I purr the words and lay my fingers atop Anatole's hand, somewhere at the middle of my thigh, in order to keep said hand from wandering into dangerous territory. Although I suppose, to outside eyes—say, the eyes of some musician playing a clarinet nearby— this gesture might have all the appearance of a caress. Nothing I can do about appearances, can I?

In any case, I'd say the disappearing bastard deserves a little vinegar in his teacup.

Right on cue, a shadow falls over the environs—both our linked hands above the table and our linked hands below—except that the shadow comes from the opposite direction I might have expected, and the clarinet continues to carry nimbly onward.

"Why, if it isn't my fellow jailbird," comes a smoldering voice, layered with irony and fringed in black. "Mind if I join you?"

13

Naturally, Anatole's delighted by the sight of our Millie. He jumps right up and pulls out a chair for her, and she styles herself upon it with all the customary grace, while a smile freezes hard upon my mouth.

"Ginger, darling," Anatole says, "perhaps you would be so kind as to introduce me to your friend."

"My friend?"

"This lovely young lady friend of yours."

"Oh, you mean *Millie*? Anatole, may I present Millicent Merriwether, late of the Sixth Precinct jailhouse, otherwise permanent resident of the stool at the far corner of the bar, so far as I can tell."

"You are serious?" He stares into Millie's face, eyebrows all stretchy. "This is your name?"

"Sure it is," I say. "To the same degree that you're actually from France."

The vamp shrugs effortlessly. Her shoulders are bare, and I'd swear they sparkle. "You can call me Millie, I guess. It's close enough."

"We got to know each other a few weeks ago, when the joint got raided by the Prohibition bureau. I don't suppose you know anything about that, do you, Millie?"

She regards me witheringly. "Oh, sure. I always call in raids on myself. Just for kicks. Who's the sheik? He's not the swell you used to bring around here."

"This? This is Anatole, an old lover of mine. We're just getting reacquainted."

"Anatole. Nice name. French?"

"It's a funny story, really," I say. "His mama named him Andrew. But you can call him Anatole, if you like. It's what he answers to. Say, now that I think about it, the pair of you have a lot in common."

"Anatole." She smiles. "Have you got another cigarette? I'm all out."

Anatole makes a sound like he would stop a freight train with his bare hands in order to obtain a cigarette for her. He would gather and bring to her all the cigarettes in the world. He snatches a gasper from his case and lights it with his own, like a kiss, and when the end flares orange he presents it into Millie's glamorous red fingertips.

She rewards him with a cloud of smoke. "Thanks awfully. Old lovers, you say? How sweet."

"This was quite some time ago," says Anatole.

"Was it? Because you look real cozy, the two of you."

"No, no. These days, we are business colleagues only."

"Oh, *business* colleagues. Of course. Say, what's your line of work, Anatole?"

"He's an artist." I tap my cigarette on the rim of the ashtray. To my left, the music ends abruptly on an upswing, and the musicians start breaking up. "You know the type."

"You don't say. An artist! And what? You mix his paints for him or something?"

"You could say that."

Anatole shrugs. "At one time, she did some modeling for me, that is all."

"Fascinating. I used to do that kind of thing. Artist's model."

"Perhaps," says Anatole, shifting the angle of his body so that he's entirely facing her instead of entirely facing me, "I could persuade you to do it again."

I stub out my cigarette and rise from my chair. "If you'll excuse me. I believe my nose needs powdering."

14

And so I find myself once more in Christopher's shabby powder room, gathering my nerves and my dignity. Staring at the reflection of my face in the mirror, which, as I've said before, is not a beautiful one. Certainly not now, cast into harsh, sallow shadow by the naked bulb hanging from the ceiling, my nose somehow extraordinarily large and my eyes all pointy at the corners. Like a cat's eyes, my brother Johnnie used to tease me, and that's how Anatole always painted them, only exaggerated, so that they really did look like the eyes of a cat. And not the domesticated kind, either.

I open up my pocketbook and locate a compact and a tube of Helena Rubinstein. Touch up the old lips. Powder to the nose, if only for the sake of honesty. Fingers to the hair, tugging this and tucking that. When there's nothing left to fix, nothing I can do to improve the appearance of what lies before me, no possible further excuse, I place my hand on the door-knob. God only knows what I'll do on the other side of it. I reckon I'll think of something. Ginger always thinks of something, doesn't she? Ginger always makes a flaming exit.

As I stand there, considering my options, weighing in favor of stalking right past Millie and Anatole and out the door, stiffing him with the bill, versus picking my way through the jazz orchestra and planting lips on the clarinet player, false mustache notwithstanding, the door opens beneath my hand.

And that's when I realize, what with one thing and another, discoveries left and right, teacups full of vin-egar, I'd forgotten all about that muscular fellow who followed us over from Hudson Street.

15

I guess it's fair to say that I never did discover much in common with the other girls at college. Maybe that's as much my fault as theirs. The choice of establishment wasn't mine; the nuns encouraged me to apply, but it was Mama—so Sister Esme told me later—who instructed them. Astonishing, isn't it? Mama, so preoccupied with her own troubles, yet had the desire and the sheer *will* to decide that I should attend Bryn Mawr College with all the daughters of the best families, the Philadelphia families and the Washington families and the New York families, girls who never went out without gloves and hat, girls who rode horses and wrote thank-you notes, girls whose brothers sailed yachts and played football, girls who wore white and came out into this thing called Society in big parties at fancy hotels. I guess Mama reckoned I would transform into one of those girls, if I only went to college with them. That Bryn Mawr could scrub the remaining stains of Appalachia from my skin and hair and hands and voice, and some horse-riding girl would introduce me to her yacht-racing brother, and hallelujah, Geneva's a lady. Poof presto. Poor Mama. I arrived at Bryn Mawr all by myself one hot morning at the end of August, nineteen hundred and nineteen, and the chip on my shoulder liketa gave me a hunchback. Inevitably one of those horsey girls decided she ought to knock it straight off.

She bore the unlikely name of Hyacinth—I don't recollect her last name, or maybe I never learned it—though I daresay she was nobody's flower. I think I heard once that her daddy divorced her mama when she was but little, and that he went on to have several more wives and children—*litters*, these girls used to call them, self-mocking—and whether or not that story was true, she wasn't a happy girl, Hyacinth whatever-her-name. She took to hating me straight off, and I made no scruple about returning that sentiment. Circled each other all freshman year like a pair of feral cats, while her friends sneered and snooted in approval, and my friends—well, I didn't have any, did I? Just Geneva Kelly from River Junction, Maryland, all on her own, not even a mama and daddy to see her settled in at college that first week. Come May, end of the year looming, Hyacinth made her move. Took umbrage at some remark of mine, some insult to her intellect for which I claim full responsibility, while we sat too close in a stale lecture hall to discuss the classical philosophers. Push came to shove, and as I turned the corner of the dormitory hall the next day, dressed in my tatty old robe, carrying my toothbrush, I'll be damned if that well-bred girl from a top-drawer family didn't just sucker punch me like no girl or boy in River Junction would ever stoop so low as to punch another girl or boy. I could do nothing but fall to the ground and wake up in the infirmary, and though the college president herself interviewed me later, I never would say who done it. I never would rat that Hyacinth out, even though she deserved ratting for a sucker punch like she gave me.

Because we may be poor as church mice in River Junction, but we are surely not rats. We take care of our trouble ourselves. And I took care of that Hyacinth, as soon as I came out of the infirmary.

Anyway, what I neglected to tell you before was this: I did not precisely drop out of Bryn Mawr College in the summer of 1920. I was kicked out, on account of busting Hyacinth's nose.

16

But that's not the point of the story. The point is this: I swore, in the time of Hyacinth, never again to allow myself to be taken by surprise like that. Never

ever again to turn a corner or walk through a door without expecting some kind of unpleasant surprise waiting for me. Someone lying in wait to do me an ill turn.

The thing is, though, that's a promise you can't keep, howsoever vigilant you may be. Sooner or later, you let your guard drop. Sooner or later you allow yourself to be distracted by the turnings of your own mind, by the slings and the arrows and the thunderbolts, and sooner or later someone's going to catch you when you're alone and vulnerable, when you've neglected to cover over your white nakedness before the world. When you're emerging from a powder room and your nerves and your dignity aren't altogether intact, and a fellow stands there in a dark pin-striped suit just about bursting from his chest, and he's got a heavy black revolver in one hand that he doesn't actually point at you. Just lifts up as if to strike you across the cheekbone.

And such is your shock, you can't even scream. Your throat freezes up, your hands rise to block this blow that can't possibly be blocked, not when delivered by an arm so powerful as that.

You stumble back, into the powder room, but you don't get far because the arm is swift, and you shut your eyes and try to dodge the blow, dodge down and around this mountain of manflesh, swinging his revolver in a damn sucker punch, except there's no chance, no room to dodge, no time to dodge in, and then you realize you're still alive. You haven't been hit. You're falling to the ground, sure, but not on account of some blow to your cheekbone. Just you, stumbling to the floor all on your own, and somebody grunting above you. You hit the chipped tile floor of the powder room kind of hard, knocking out a bit of wind from your chest, but a second later someone's lifting you up, and you open your eyes, and what do you know.

"Nice mustache," you say.

17

There's a back door at Christopher's, a door I never knew about, but Anson knows it. Back of the broom closet, behind a bucket full of mops. Might could-a come in handy at the end of January, when this whole mess began. Might-a stopped all this trouble in its tracks.

I tell him this as we duck through this doorway into the rot-laden courtyard behind the building.

"Wouldn't have made any difference," he says. "I'd have found you anyway."

18

In my bedroom now, where I'm daubing Agent Anson's knuckles with iodine, attempting to calm the furious rhythm of my circulation.

"So who in the Lord's name was that?" I ask.

"Who?"

"*Who.* That fellow who just about cracked my head wide open, that's who. Stop flinching. What are you, some kind of sissy? You can bust a man's jaw but you can't take a little medicine?"

"I have no idea who he is. I was hoping you might."

"Never saw him before." I reach for the roll of gauze. I figure if I can concentrate on these simple tasks, iodine and gauze, I can keep myself steady. Trick myself sane. He's got big, bony hands, Agent Anson, more long than wide, and this new scar across the knuckles of his right hand isn't the first. I take a firm grip on the pad of his thumb and wind the gauze carefully around his palm. "But he followed us all the way over from Hudson Street. My friend Anatole has a studio there."

"Yes, I know."

"He was waiting outside, I think." I tie together the ends of the gauze, nice and snug, and I give the knuckles a pat, just to make him wince. But I don't let go of the hand, and he doesn't pull it away. Just standing there, the pair of us, one paw stuck between the paws of the other. Moon coming in through the window, turning the gauze silver. I trace the edge of his fingernail with my thumb. "How long have you played the clarinet?"

"Since I was about eight, I guess."

"And when did you join Bruno's orchestra?"

"Two weeks ago."

"Does Bruno know—?"

"He knows I'm a friend of yours."

I look up into the wallop of his gaze.

"Anything else I should know about you, Tarzan? Since you seem to know so much about me."

"What do you want to know?"

"Anything. Maybe everything."

He withdraws the precious hand and turns to the bureau. Picks up the roll of gauze and winds it back up. "There isn't much to know, really."

"Oh, I think there's a lot to know. But you're one of those fellows who likes to keep his beans to himself, as I recollect. All I figure is that you're not married and you don't have any kids, and you come from some kind of money and know a Harvard crest from a crack in the sidewalk. And you can knock a man out cold in one blow, which is something a girl like me can respect, believe me."

"Look," he says, setting down the gauze, turning to face me, "let's get back to the business at hand. You're certain you've never seen that man before?"

"Positive." I tap my temple. "I never forget a face."

"He's not from Maryland?"

"If you mean is he one of Duke's pals from River Junction, he's not. Must be some local Duke's rustled up."

"But you're certain Duke sent him, is that right? Sent this man to hurt you."

"As sure as I can be."

"Why?"

"Because, as I told you, or at least as I told your secretary to inform you, Duke's cut me off. No parcels in a week. Truth to tell, I've been expecting something like this for days now." I jerk my thumb toward the moon outside. "He must have figured out I'm working for you."

"That's impossible. We haven't met in weeks. I haven't yet acted on any of the information you've given me."

"But you've been lurking around. Keeping watch on me."

He hesitates. "Yes. To protect you."

"So maybe somebody spotted you. Playing your

clarinet or something. Saw through that clever disguise of yours."

"That's unlikely."

"But possible?"

"Not *im*possible, I suppose."

I sit down on the bed and fold my arms. "So I guess it's over. The jig's up."

"No, it isn't. Not by a long shot. I'm going to get busy as soon as I'm out this window. Find out who that fellow is. Who he's working for. I don't think it's your stepfather." He moves to the window—just a couple of steps for those thick, tough legs of his—and peers out, as if contemplating possible routes of departure. A sound escapes him, and if I didn't know any better, I could swear that Agent Anson—straight as an arrow, pure as a bar of Ivory soap—just took the name of his Lord in vain.

"Why not?"

"Hmm?"

"Why don't you think he's one of Duke's men?"

Anson lets fall the curtain and turns to me. "Because he had a revolver. And Mr. Kelly's men don't use guns."

"Applesauce."

"It's true. Don't you know he doesn't hold with guns?"

"Of course I know that. But you can't run a bootleg racket without a Chicago typewriter in one hand and a revolver in the other. Nobody but a fool would try it."

"Oh, his men carry guns on the road, of course. In case of ambush. But anything else—when he sends someone out to deliver a message of some kind, settle a score—he does it the old-fashioned way." Anson lifts his hand and examines the bandage on his knuckles. "Because you don't hunt down a man like you would a mere animal."

"Lord Almighty."

"So I believe we can rest assured that your stepfather, for all his faults, isn't the fellow behind tonight's incident."

"Goodness me. What a terrible great relief. In that case, I'll sleep like a baby."

The fellow actually smiles at me. "Wake up howling every few hours, then?"

"Oh? And just what do *you* know about the sleeping habits of babies, Mr. Anson?"

"I know a little something about just about everything, Miss Kelly."

"Well, then. Maybe you can answer me this. Just out of idle curiosity, mind you. I don't suppose you've got any idea who else might be responsible for trying to darken my lights? If not Duke."

"I don't know the answer to that question at present. But believe me, I won't rest until I find out."

"And what am I supposed to do in the meantime? Lock myself in my room? Hire a Pinkerton guard?"

"You don't need to hire a Pinkerton guard," Anson says. "You have me for that purpose."

You know, I never did shift clothes after posing for Anatole and Julie. I'm still wearing my same plain skirt and blouse, my everyday clothes, nothing to catch a man's eye. Just the lipstick I applied in the powder room a half hour ago. Next to Millie, I reckon I must have looked like someone the dog drug home from the library. And a girl who isn't looking her absolute best, what shot has she got in this modern world? A girl all alone, what possible hope? Just her own wits. Her own strength.

So I am standing there atop my bedroom floor in my plain skirt and blouse, thinking someone is fixing to kill me, somebody wants me dead, I'm in trouble dire, a girl all alone like a sapling springing forth from a prairie field, and Mr. Agent Anson, he goes and says a thing like that. *You have me.*

"Have you found out anything more about my buttons?" I ask.

Agent Anson sticks his left hand into the pocket of his overcoat and draws out a small package wrapped in brown paper. He sets it on the bureau and unwraps the paper. Mama's box.

"Not much," he says. "Thought I recognized the decoration, but it turns out the shop was closed up long ago. I'll see if I can't find anyone who might know more."

"Don't go to any trouble, now."

"It's no trouble."

His hand falls from the box. He's only a yard away—you're only about a yard away from anything in my little room—and from this intimate distance I observe the comfort of his pulse at the side of his neck. The thrum of his tendons. Living and breathing and beating. I think, We are standing here just as we were a few weeks ago, just exactly like this, betwixt the bed and the dresser, right in front of the window, except it's not the same at all. It is somehow entirely different. Different tenor between us, different atmosphere, as if the earth has revolved its way into a strange new portion of the universe in the period since we stood together last. A moment ago I was occupying my brain with inconsequential games like jealousy, like vanity, like Anatole, and then a man swings a revolver and changes the whole world. Renders the previous world unrecognizable. Renders the thrum of Anson's tendons the pivot around which this new world whirls.

"The thing is," he says, entirely unaware of the new-found import of his tendons, "are you sure you want to know?"

"Why not?"

"Presuming the owner of these buttons is really your father—and that may not be the case—we already know he's the kind of man who seduces show-girls, gets them with child, and then discards them. You may not want to know him. He may not want to be known."

"I realize all that. I'm just curious, that's all."

"For what purpose?"

"Well, for one thing, you can't imagine the trouble, fretting about whether or not your present lover might turn out to be some kind of cousin."

His head jerks a bit.

"Oh, yes. Just think. Why, even you and I might be brother and sister, for all I know!"

"We're not."

"How do you know?"

"Because *my* father didn't go to Harvard."

"Well! I can't tell you how relieved I am to hear that."

He sort of catches himself. Turns his gaze first to my mama's enamel box, and then to the window. Puts his hand to the back of his neck. I believe the color of his skin warms to a delicate pink, though the light is too gray to properly tell.

Now, I can't say why I offered up this observation, the way I might offer up some mere scrap of flirtatious banter in the middle of a dull evening downstairs at Christopher's, or else uptown at some swank knees-up among the avenue set. I expect it has something to do with the relief of escape, the pure exhilaration of not finding yourself lying on the floor of a Village powder room inside a puddle of your own blood. And the fellow who saved you stands before you like some kind of conqueror, and Nature—which runneth deep inside the marrow of your bones, you know, and can't be ignored—now bangs in your eardrums, heats up your skin, demands you repay the debt you owe him. Offer up your frail human form as the spoils of war. No doubt the scientists have some clever name for this ancient instinct. All I know is that I have lost all recollection of any other man who might once have stood in this room with me, all thought of danger or mystery or hope of salvation: just this dear, blushing face, and those tendons, and that well-pressed lapel, and everything that lies beneath. Just the hot, living thrill of his blood, and the hot, living thrill of mine. Wouldn't you?

But that Anson. Maybe he's not like you and me. I don't know. I'm starting to think I don't know the first thing about men, and maybe I never did. He just stares out the window with grief in his eyes, and he starts to button up that overcoat, kind of clumsy because of the bandage on his right hand.

"Let me help you."

"I've got it."

I step forward and brush away his hands and button up that overcoat, and when I'm done I lay my palms on his lapels and look up into that face of his. Those eyes again. Grieved and snowy.

"Thanks for helping a girl out downstairs."

"There's nothing to thank me for. It's my job, that's all. I promised to keep you safe in all this."

"And you never break a promise, do you?"

"No."

Above our heads and somewhere to my left, the ceiling creaks. The pipes flush. We've been speaking in whispers, mostly, because the walls are so thin and the occupants so nosy. But a moment like this, you realize just how loud a few words can be. Just how easily overheard. I think about that word *no*, and how he might have said, *Not if I can help it*, or *So long as it's in my power*, or some other mealy qualification. But he didn't. He just said *no*. Clean and simple.

I hear myself say, terribly soft: "You can kiss me, if you like."

He takes in a little breath.

"Just a wee good-bye kiss to settle the nerves. Nobody needs to know."

His hands close over the blades of my shoulders. His eyelids grow heavy. I might swear the eyes behind them seem a little warmer, like someone's lit a flame inside his skull. If I rise to my toes, I can brush the tip of his nose with the tip of mine. I can press my lips on his and see if they soften.

But before I fix my resolve to do any or all of these things, he leans forward and touches his mouth to my forehead.

"Good night, Miss Kelly," he says.

His hands grasp mine and lift them away from his lapels, and you would not believe a pair of fists that crushed a man's jaw a half hour earlier could apply themselves now with such gentleness.

We stand there a minute, my hands folded between his, as if held together in some kind of mutual prayer. Not speaking. Just staring at our bound hands, his swallowing mine, bones and joints and skin, the smell of human longing.

"Good night," he says again, a true whisper, and he sets my hands to my sides and opens the window, and he's gone.

19

Now, it seems Agent Anson is correct in his speculations and assurances, at least insofar as Duke
Kelly's concerned, because Mrs. Washington hands me
a fat brown envelope the morning after next, just as I'm
stepping out the door for my bracing nine o'clock plunge
into the typing pool. Her expression is not best pleased.

"A gentleman left this for you, first thing this morning." (She renders the word *gentleman* inside a heavy
skillet of irony.)

"How kind. Thank you terribly, Mrs. Washington."

"And another thing. You were making a real racket
the other night, Miss Kelly. A real racket."

"Was I? A thousand apologies. I must have been
talking in my sleep."

"I thought I heard a man's voice, in there with you."

"A *man's* voice? But that's altogether impossible,
Mrs. Washington! Why, you know very well I received
no gentleman callers last night. What do you think,
I've got them shimmying up the drainpipe?"

"I know what I heard."

"How very strange. Are you certain? What was he
talking about, this fellow you think you heard?"

"Something about Harvard, Miss Kelly."

"Harvard! You mean that college in Massachusetts?"

"And Pinkerton guards."

"Pinkerton guards and Harvard! Now, that's salacious. I don't wonder you were shocked."

"It's what I heard! As if you didn't know."

"Mrs. Washington, I'm terribly sorry, but I'm afraid I haven't got time to wonder at your fertile imagination just now. Due at work any minute. But if this kind of thing goes on, hearing imaginary voices in the middle of the night, I think maybe you should see a doctor." I tuck the envelope into my pocketbook and turn for the door. "They've got miraculous pills these days, take care of all your troubles."

"Miss Kelly—"

But I'm afraid to say I let the door fall shut on the rest of that sentence. Wasn't going anywhere useful, was it?

20

According to the instructions inside the envelope, I'm supposed to deliver the sordid contents to a fellow named Macduff at some address on Broad Street at a quarter past twelve o'clock this afternoon. *Macduff*, I think. Lord Almighty. There goes my lunch break.

But when I arrive at said address at a few minutes prior to the appointed time, the place turns out to be a luncheonette, all cheap and new and white painted, trimmed in chromium steel, windows turning back the glare of the winter sun. You know the spot. Perched on the corner, hot soup for a nickel. When I open the door, a gust of steam rushes out into the street, smelling of grease and cigarettes.

Inside, the waitresses scurry. It's a young, lowly crowd, the kind that can't afford a nice juicy beefsteak at Delmonico's, stenographers and clerks and typists like me, hair bobbed and lipstick fading fast, suit jackets wilting in the artificial heat. The chatter comes fast and hard as the clickety-clack racket of a typing pool. I take hold of a passing waitress and ask her if she happens to know the whereabouts of a fellow named Macduff.

"*Macduff?*" she asks, harried. As in, *You putting me on, sister?*

"That's right. Mr. Macduff."

"Never heard of him. Go look for yourself."

She pulls her arm away, and as she's balancing four bowls of boiling soup on a small wooden tray, I allow her the privilege. Around me, the tables are filled, scarce an empty chair, and surely no crisp-suited gentleman who might or might not be on the lookout for a companion from behind a newspaper or something. Likewise, the dozen stools at the lunch counter stand occupied, except for a seat at the end now draped by somebody's lumpy charcoal overcoat. I make for the gap and tap its neighbor on the shoulder. "Pardon me. Do you mind removing your—"

A porcelain face turns up toward mine, so bare and plain I might not have recognized it, except for a single platinum curl dipping beneath the rim of a cloche hat to touch the arch of a perfect eyebrow.

"Not at all," she says.

21

I settle on the stool and take out a cigarette. "Macduff?"

"It's easy to remember."

"Millicent. Macduff. I don't suppose you happen to have a genuine moniker, do you? Something your mama used to call you."

THE WICKED CITY · 319

She lifts her coffee. "It's not important."

"Suit yourself." I signal for the counter attendant and make my hand like a cup of coffee. "So what's a nice girl like you doing mixed up in a business like this?"

"I might ask the same of you."

"Isn't it obvious? I need the dough."

"I doubt it. You've already got a nice little income, haven't you? Smiling for the camera."

"Not anymore. I quit the indecency business yesterday."

"Oh? For what reason?"

"For one thing, the money's better in the bribery racket. Do you want your envelope now, or do we enjoy a nice civilized lunch first?"

She stubs out the last of her cigarette. "There's nothing in the envelope. Just blank paper."

"Oh? And how do you know that?"

"Because I sent it to you myself."

I swear. The coffee arrives in a clatter. I reach for Millie's cream and sugar.

"Aren't you going to ask why?" she says.

"I'm waiting for you to start. I reckon you've got something to say to me, don't you? That's why we're here."

Millie makes a noise of maybe assent and extracts another cigarette from the silver case reclining against her saucer. Her fingers are long and nimble and bony, her nails varnished in crimson. But it's her face that fascinates me. The change in her. Unpainted, she looks all faded and monochrome, even her eyelashes, like somebody unplugged a drain beneath her chin and emptied her of color. She lights the gasper and enjoys a long, pensive drag, and by the time she pauses to consider the pattern of smoke curling forth from her lips, I've more or less run out of both coffee and patience.

"Well? What's the news? I haven't got all afternoon."

"You sure like to cut to the chase, don't you, Miss Kelly?"

"So would you, if you were due back at the typing pool in thirty-eight minutes, or else. A ham sandwich and a cup of tomato soup, please," I tell the counter attendant, who's just returned with the cream and sugar I don't need. He nods and turns away. From behind us comes a crash of china, a brief vacuum of silence, a trill of laughter. The resumption of clickety-clack chatter. "Let's begin with you, Miss Macduff. Since we have to start somewhere. Just who's pulling your strings? My stepfather?"

"Goodness, no. What an idea. I'm with the Prohibition bureau, sweetheart."

"No kidding. You and Anson, together?"

"No," she says. "Just me."

I set down my cup and pluck the end of my cigarette from the ashtray, holding it betwixt my thumb and my forefinger while a large gray crumb breaks away and crashes into the porcelain. "You don't say."

"Oh, I *do* say."

"Then I'm afraid I don't understand."

"My dear girl. Don't you see? You've been tricked. You've been bamboozled. Our dear Mr. Anson doesn't work for the government. He's in business for himself."

"Get lost. What kind of rube do you think I am?"

"Look, I don't blame you for falling for him. I'll bet he took you to his office, didn't he, made it look all official. Fed you the best story in the world. But the truth is, he was kicked out of the New York City agency a few months ago."

"Baloney."

"No, it's true. He was on the take, see. Feathering a nice little nest for himself."

I laugh. "Now I *know* you're feeding me a line. Anson on the take. I never saw a straighter arrow than that one, and I know from scoundrels, believe me."

"Look. I'm not going to waste my breath. I just wanted to warn you, that's all. He's not what he seems. It's all a front, see."

The ham sandwich slides into place before me. The soup in its cup, steam rising, butter melting to a small, speckled yellow pool in the center. I glance up to thank the counter boy, and he's giving me a strange look, brows all bent.

"Everything all right, miss?" he asks.

"Just fine, thanks."

"Look," says Millie, "you just think about it, all right?"

"I don't need to think about it. For one thing, why isn't he in jail? If he was caught on the take, like you say."

"Because he's got mighty friends, sweetheart, mighty friends. The kind of friends even the Bureau doesn't dare to cross. You don't think he came from nowhere, do you? So they kicked him out, but they couldn't throw the book at him, and they didn't. And when Duke Kelly asked him to bring you in, why, he was more than happy to oblige in exchange for a cut of the action—"

"Says you. Didn't he pick me up from the police station? After that raid on Christopher's. You saw everything, you were right in that cell with me. Say, I'll bet it's all the other way around, isn't it? I'll bet *you're* the rat working the double-cross. Staked out the joint, called in the raid. Or else maybe you're trying to rat out Anson, because he raided your daddy's joint and hauled you off to jail—"

"What, me and Christopher? You think we have a thing together?" She laughs. "Look, I guess you've got no reason to believe a word out of my mouth. That's fair. I'm working my own angle, and maybe I should be glad it's got you fooled, a smart girl like you. One thing's for sure, I shouldn't be *here* right now, wasting my time, blowing my cover like a silly fool, on account of I've got a soft heart and hate to see another girl wander into trouble like this. But that's what he does, you know. Fucking Anson. If I had a nickel for all the girls he's taken in, that square jaw and those thick shoulders, all the girls who think he's a fine upstanding fellow just about *made* of virtue—"

I snatch my pocketbook from the countertop and hunt for a dollar bill. My fingers are trembling, my ears roaring. The brown envelope keeps getting in the way, so thick as it is. I pull the damned thing free and toss it in Millie's lap, and the roll of bills appears at last, wedged in the bottom next to the rip in the lining. I strip away an ace and lay it on the counter, crumpled greenback against bright new aquamarine blue. The ham sandwich sits untouched on the plate, turning my stomach.

"Keep the change," I say. "And go to hell."

She shrugs. "Fine, then. Have it your way. Don't say I didn't warn you."

"Oh, you warned me, all right. And trust me, I'll be passing along this interesting information right where it belongs."

"You do that. See what he says. Although you might want to start by visiting those offices of his on Tenth Avenue." She stubs out her cigarette in the ashtray and inspects my ham sandwich. "I'd love to know what you find there."

22

I'm not the least bit inclined to follow Millie Macduff's advice. For one thing, I'm due back at the typing pool in—check watch—twenty-seven minutes, and for seconds, who wants to give the dame that kind of satisfaction?

On the other hand. Here I am, striding not toward the familiar corner of Wall and Broad but southwestward, toward the Battery, tossing my cigarette stub on the cold pavement and fishing for a nickel in my jacket pocket. What do you know.

I tell myself, as I inhale the sharp, sunlit atmosphere and listen for the telltale sing of the elevated tracks, that I'm making this journey out of caution, not suspicion. I've got to warn Anson about this Millicent Macduff: warn him in person, not over the telephone to some kind of doll who might or might not be the kind of doll you can trust. And maybe he'll be sitting at his desk and maybe he won't, who knows, but the urgency of the situation demands my best efforts, does it not? I owe him that much for saving my life. For almost kissing me in my bedroom last night, I mean on the forehead like a gentleman, when he might have claimed any reward he wanted, and what fellow kisses a willing girl on the forehead in the privacy of her own bedroom, unless he's an honorable fellow and he's maybe a little in love with her? So Anson's a fellow I can rely on, and Miss Macduff is made of rotten phonus balonus, and by the time I've spilled off the train at Twenty-Third Street and descended to the hubbub of Ninth Avenue, I can just about taste the indignation at the back of my throat: sort of like the homemade variety of gin, only more sour.

By now it's almost one o'clock, and I should be sliding into place before my typewriter this exact second, tucking gloves and hat into the drawer and straightening my collar for the benefit of Miss Atkins's patience. Quite possibly I'll lose my job over this little whim, unless that praying mantis upstairs sees fit to protect me. The wind shrieks off the Hudson River and down the sharp, straight streets. Finds the cracks in my coat, turns the legs numb beneath their stockings. I turn up my collar and smash my hat closer over my ears, and I set out westward through the fragrant confluence of manure and garbage and gasoline exhaust, in the direction of that shrill whistle floating over the wind and the dirty brick buildings: the sound of the New York Central traversing Tenth Avenue, up the Hudson shore and down to the West Side Station, all the livelong day.

23

Now, I haven't experienced this corner of Manhattan Island since that startling night at the end of January when a certain Mr. Anson first intruded my notice, and why should I? Nobody sets out in this particular direction unless she's got dirty New York business to transact, or else an ocean liner to board. But I remember it well: the cobblestones crusted with slush, now gone; the boarded-up saloon on the corner of Tenth Avenue and Twenty-Second Street. The tarnished brass plaque outside, which I now take time to read: H. L. HEWITT, LEGAL ADVICE AND PRIVATE INVESTIGATIONS. SECOND FLOOR.

I try the doorknob. Locked, of course. I bang on the door, just like my old friend Brooklyn did that night, only this time nobody comes to open it; no noise of any kind reaches me from the other side of the stoop. I crane my head one way and another—as if that will help—and step back to crane my head upward. Windows closed and dusty. Abandoned aspect overall. No sign of occupation by any members of the New York office of the Bureau of Internal Revenue. No sign of occupation whatever.

Bang, bang. Desperate now. *Bang bang bang.* I step back and cup my hands around my mouth and holler upward. "HELLO THERE! ANYBODY IN?"

"What the hell you doing, lady?"

I spin around. Man standing there on the sidewalk, dressed in a cheap brown suit, lunch pail dangling from one hand, staring at me like you stare at a leper.

"There's an office here," I say. "On the second floor. Nobody's answering the door."

"An *office,* ma'am?"

"Yes! I was here a month ago. A regular office."

"You mean the dick? Why, he moved out a couple-a years ago."

"No. The Prohibition bureau. They've got an office here."

He starts to laugh. "Prohis? Not here, ma'am. You got a bum steer. Nobody been in them rooms for years, not since the dick left. Building's up for sale."

"You're wrong. I was inside that office at the end of January."

"Sure you were, ma'am. And my uncle's the mayor. Maybe you need to lay off the sauce a little."

"Oh yeah? Maybe you need to mind your own potatoes, buster."

"Suit yourself." He shrugs. "You just keep on banging and see if anybody opens up. I gotta get back to work."

"Yeah, thanks for nothing."

"Anytime." He pauses. Gives me the old up and down. Pats his right front pocket. "Say, I get off at five, if you're still around. Buy you a drink or something. Got paid yesterday."

"Get lost," I say, and I turn around and bang on the door again, just as if I'm expecting somebody to open it.

24

Ten minutes later, I'm around back, climbing up the fire escape, because that's the kind of optimistic broad I am. Determined to discover some kind of life inside this damn building, determined to prove the perfidy of Miss Macduff.

At the second-floor landing, the window is locked tight, but when I climb up to the next floor, my luck is in. The wooden sash groans and gives way under my urging. I work it up a foot or two and lever my body inside, head and shoulders and hips, like going forth from the womb, I guess, except this world I'm entering is cold and damp and smells of mold, and as I tumble free onto a hideous rotting carpet, a strange feeling mushrooms inside me: the same gut sickness that used to warn me when it was time to skedaddle, back home in River Junction.

But I am not cowed. Nobody and nothing cows

Ginger Kelly. I scramble up from said carpet and brush my skirt. Straighten my hat and my collar and my pocketbook over my elbow. The hall is dark, not a single lamp lit, and quiet as death, except for the noise of Manhattan streaming under the window sash and through the pores in the brickwork. To the left runs the stairway, battered and dirty, leading up to God knows and down to Anson's office, the office into which Brooklyn dragged me at the end of January, desk and chair and hot coffee brought in by a navy-suited doll of some kind. And Anson himself, still and stern and mountainous, clean and straight and true. Draping his jacket over my shoulders against the chill in the air. Driving me home through a whirling of new snow.

You know, up until this point, I don't believe I've properly understood just how far I've fallen. Just how goofy I've gone for a pair of reliable shoulders and a glacial gaze that might or might not contain a small amount of tenderness for me, Ginger Kelly, bastard Appalachia hillbilly, red haired, smart-mouthed, whose bubs could be bought for a dime a time at any old newsagent in town. The enormity of my crush on Special Agent Anson, its exact mass and dimensions, such that the possibility of betrayal seems to threaten the smooth operation of every single last vulnerable organ of my body. As I stand there in that hallway, regarding the shadowy length of the staircase, its dark ending at the second-floor landing, the sensation of sickness grows and grows. Vibrates the delicate molecules of blood that runneth along my veins and into my heart.

I tell myself, stern-like: Don't be a coward, Gin. Get ahold of yourself.

And maybe my blood obeys that command and maybe it doesn't, but I guess enough will remains pulsing inside said veins to engage my gams in the terrible act of walking down the staircase toward the darkness at the end. Because that's what I do. Walk down the staircase, step by step, until I'm standing inside that shadow and it's not so bad, really: like any other shadow, dissolving by the light from the dirty window. I turn up the hallway—Anson's office, remember, lay on the front side of the building, overlooking the street—and I tread down the mildewed carpet until I reach the last door, swinging easily open under my touch, room empty, desk bare, no paper or pens or telephone or anything. Just nothing but a few sticks of familiar furniture, covered in a layer of dust. Cold, damp air. A sliver of light finding the edge of the window as the winter sun slides west.

I sit down on the armchair before the desk and stare at that sliver of sunlight. The ghost shapes of the buildings on the other side of the glass.

25

For some reason, I'm not surprised to find a familiar yellow Hudson roadster parked on the street outside the Sterling Bates building on the corner of Wall and Broad when I return for work a half hour later.

"Billy-boy," I say as soon as I can extract myself from between the lapels of his overcoat. His face is sweet and bright, his smile wide, his brown eyes open for business. "What the devil are you doing here?"

He takes me by the shoulders, kisses me; takes me by the hands and kisses those too, one by one. When he lifts his head again, his cheeks are as pink as two fresh hams.

"Why, isn't it obvious, darling? We're eloping."

New York City, 1998

All the articles, all the books, the whole humming database of girlfriend wisdom: everyone said the same thing. You should know if your husband's cheating on you. Why? Because most men aren't James Bond. Not skilled at the meticulous art of covert operations. The secrecy, the evasion, the unexplained dinners and business trips. The call history on his cell phone. The mystery charges on his credit card. Any alert wife knows when she has something to fear. All she needs is proof.

But until that evening four weeks ago, Ella never suspected a thing. Everything seemed perfectly normal, perfectly married and domestic. They'd just made love the night before; there was nothing weird about the way he touched her or kissed her. Same Patrick as ever. Except they'd been officially trying for a baby for a year now, and she wasn't getting pregnant, and after he pulled out she rolled over and turned her back to him so he wouldn't engage her in the usual desperate, awkward postcoital banter about this one *definitely* doing the trick. So maybe it was her fault, turning her back like that, after a round of perfectly good sex. Maybe he felt lonely and hurt and disconnected from her, from the whole mechanical business of baby making, from the failure of any of Ella's eggs to accept the amazing gift of Patrick, and that was why, the next evening, he slapped Ella's knee and insisted on being the one to collect the delivery pizza from downstairs.

Except he always insisted. That wasn't new. He was such a gentleman.

But this time, fatefully, Ella had risen from the sofa to fetch a glass of water from the kitchen, and in doing so she'd passed the hooks in the entryway and realized she'd left her laptop bag in the residents' gym.

So she'd taken the stairs down to the gym (she always took the stairs) and when she turned the corner of the stairwell in between the third floor and the second floor, where the gym lay, she heard some noise coming from below: the damp, breathless efforts of two people screwing. She got flustered and turned to bolt, but then the perv in her spoke up and demanded to catch a glimpse of this interesting, furtive act and see who it was—who among her neighbors was maybe cheating on a girlfriend or boyfriend or wife or husband; she could tell Patrick all about it when he returned with the pizza—and *even then,* my God, even then it never occurred to her, when she peeked around the edge of the concrete slab, that it might be Patrick's pale, muscular buttocks, Patrick's ragged breath, Patrick's hands around the wrists of some pneumatic Lycra-clad woman with long, fine, fried blond hair— Ella could still remember the exact color and texture of that hair—bracing her against the cinder-block wall while he humped her furiously from behind. Shorts around his ankles. *Oh baby, oh baby,* the woman said, and Patrick shouted, *Fuck! Fuck! Here it comes!* and shoved one more time, sticking himself deep inside the woman for several seconds, releasing one of her wrists to grab a tanned, enormous breast. Groaning like he might die. A couple of final twitches. Shoulders go slack. Then withdrawal in a rush. Panting hard. Semen dribbling from the end of his bare penis. Parting slap to a bottom like a navel orange. And that was when Ella turned back around and climbed the stairs in silent, fairy steps. Sat down on the sofa and stared at the flickering television. Not even ninety seconds later, Patrick bounded through the door and said, "Hey, babe! Pizza's here," just exactly as if he had not been fiercely fucking another woman two minutes earlier, had not just ejaculated inside another woman's vagina. He opened the box on the kitchen counter, pulled out a couple of plates, put a slice on each one, and asked her if she wanted salad. She said no. He brought the plates to the coffee table and set hers down before her. Picked up his slice and started eating, pitched forward, elbows resting on his thighs. Fixed entirely on the flat, colorful images on the screen before them. She stared at the hair on his nearby knee—he always changed into shorts when he got home—and she rose from the sofa and said she had to go to the bathroom.

When she walked out a few minutes later, she took a path behind the sofa, so he wouldn't see she was carrying a gym bag. "We're out of milk?" she said in a perfectly normal voice. "Be back in a sec."

So absorbed was Patrick in whatever it was they'd been watching—*ER,* probably, since it was Thursday night—he didn't even consider how strange it was that she would leave to buy a quart of milk while her pizza went cold on its plate. He just said, "Sure, babe," and she walked out the door, just like that, and those were the last words they spoke.

Until yesterday. Until now, sitting across from each other, a round, blond Starbucks table between them. Ella arrived early so she could buy her own drink. She was going to order her usual latte but decided on a double espresso instead, in a small, ceramic mug. No milk or sugar. Patrick nodded at the cup. "Changed your drink."

"I'm changing a lot of things."

"Good for you, good for you." Like he hadn't actually heard her. He tapped the plastic lid of his own cup. Jiggled his knee. "So where do we start?"

She spread her hand. "You were the one who wanted to meet."

"We had to meet. We're married, for God's sake."

"Oh, *now* you think of that." Before he could open his mouth to reply, she went on, "So I had myself checked for STDs. Full screen. Came back clean, thank God. Dodged that bullet. But I'm supposed to go in again in a few months."

"Come on, Ella—"

"You should probably get yourself checked, too. Riding bareback with prostitutes is pretty risky."

"Shit, Ella." He looked down and mumbled, "I made sure she was clean."

"Um. How, exactly? Did you *ask* her first, before you screwed? Well, surprise, surprise. She tells you she's good to go! What about the others?"

"There weren't any others. It was a one-time thing, I swear."

"A one-time thing?"

"I swear. I was so stressed out. Stuff going on at

work. And the whole baby thing. Everyone pregnant but us."

"Seriously? You're seriously telling me you hired a prostitute because you couldn't get your wife pregnant?"

His face went sharp and pink at the edges, like he was about to snap something back. Which was what she wanted, really. She wanted him snapping, she wanted him just as mad as she was. But he wouldn't give it to her. He took in a deep breath instead. Sipped his coffee. Said, quietly, "I know it doesn't make sense. I just—I wanted this so bad. *Want* this so bad. Want us to be a family, Ella. Watch my wife growing our baby and kids running around all over the place. And I didn't want you to see how stressed I was that it wasn't happening and, like, blame yourself or anything. I felt like I was going to explode. And it was stupid, okay? Stupidest thing I ever did. I have no idea what made me do it. But it won't happen again." He was speaking fluently now, in short, rote sentences of contrition. "I started seeing a therapist, right after you left. I'm working through everything. So it's done. Finished. Over. Happened once, never again."

He reached across the table, but Ella moved her hand away.

"Do you really think," she said, in slow, careful words, "I'm actually that stupid?"

Patrick's uncertain eyes stared back at her. For a man whose wife had just left him, whose marriage and life had just imploded, he looked remarkably well rested. Skin clear, eyes fresh, hair shining. His lips were a little chapped—they always were—and now hung open. The expression was somehow familiar; she couldn't place how.

She leaned forward a few inches. "Just because I didn't see this coming doesn't mean I can't see the whole picture, now that the shades are off, okay? That wasn't the first time. Are you kidding me? What are the odds, the *one time* you cheated I miraculously happened to catch you? Come on. You were fucking her like an expert. You knew exactly what you were doing. Slapped her ass afterward for good luck. Then you pulled up your shorts and waltzed into that apartment and *lied to me* like you'd been practicing *that* all your life, too. And I'll bet you have."

Now she could identify the expression on his face. That of a dog, caught on the kitchen table, eating a sandwich left behind while the owner went upstairs to put the laundry in the dryer.

"Haven't you, Patrick? Come clean. She wasn't the

first. How long have you been hiring hookers to help you with your stress issues? And it's probably not just hookers, either. That's the quick and easy solution, right? When you have your choice and a little more time on your hands, you go to some bar after work and find a cute girl to pick up and have hot sex in the bathroom, or else go back to her place and hump on the futon while her roommate watches TV. Am I right? And why stop there? So many young analyst bunnies at the bank, so little time. An office affair is a great way to keep some nookie on standby, whenever you need a little help with your *stress*."

Now he was turning pale. She could actually see the blood draining from his face, while the adrenaline pummeling through her own veins at this unparalleled act of confrontation made her almost dizzy. Stoned out of her mind. Her legs and fingers twitched, like she could run a marathon at a full sprint.

"Poor Patrick. You're stressed. I get that. I was stressed, too. But I didn't go out and pick up some guy from a bar and screw him in the alley, did I? I mean, that never even occurred to me. Because I'm married to *you*. I'm supposed to have sex with only one man for the rest of my life, and that's you, and I knew that was the deal when we got married and I accepted it *joyfully*.

I plighted you my fucking troth. So are you saying it's now okay for us to have sex with other people?"

"No, of course not. I mean—I mean, what I did was *wrong,* I admit it—"

"Because there's this really hot guy in my new building. I bet he'd be amazing in the sack. Young and super fit. He could go all night. I should really try him out after work. Take care of my stress and all."

Patrick leaned his head into his hands, like he was about to throw up.

"Anyway. You go on sitting there, trying to figure out some new lie to spin to me. Starts out with a confession—*Right, fine, you got me, there were others, I just didn't want to hurt your feelings*—and then the revised version of events. *I've only been doing it for a month or so, it was a cry for help, I actually wanted you to find out so we could resolve all our unspoken issues.* But you don't need to bother, Patrick. It's okay. The when and where and how many doesn't matter. You've probably been screwing other women all along, since we first started going out. It's who you are. It's in your DNA or whatever. You're a cheater. You just are. There's nothing you or I or some fucking psychiatrist can do about it. We could talk about it all day, you could tell me every detail, we could spend a million dollars on therapy, we could probably have you castrated and you would still find a way to spread a little bit of Patrick around. Let's be honest about that, at least."

Patrick just stared at the table. Fingers speared through his hair. Around them, the ordinary business of Starbucks went on, line ebbing and flowing, grind of coffee beans overpowering the air, wet whir of steaming milk. Dull chatter. Some kind of Sinatra music laying itself on the walls. The smell of strong, burned coffee. Ella finished her espresso, which had grown sweet with age.

"So that's where we stand, Patrick. That's our current status. And the only question is, do I try to understand what it's like to be inside your skin, to sympathize with this biological destiny of yours, and the guilt and pain it's probably causing you, you know, loving your wife while still needing to screw around with hookers and whatever. I mean, unless you're a complete psychopath—"

"Of course I feel guilty! Jesus, Ella! I've been tearing myself apart. Everything we built together—"

"Everything we *built*? News flash. You destroyed it, Patrick. You did. It's gone. I'm sorry, but this wasn't the deal. Forsaking all others, that was the deal. So I just have to decide whether it's worth trying to negotiate a new deal, or whether we shake hands and walk away."

Patrick's fingers still pressed against his skull, but he was now looking up. Peering at her from under his brows. "So that's it? A month ago, you loved me. Now you don't? You're that cold? Switch it all off like that?" He pulled away his right hand and snapped his fingers.

"Well, that's the question, isn't it? *Did* I really love you? Because I'm looking at you now, and I don't feel anything except disgust. And pity. Maybe I'm still in shock, I don't know. But the thing is, the moment I saw you in that stairwell, having sex with that woman, you changed to me. You became a different Patrick. The husband I thought I knew just died. Or maybe he never even existed. So, no. I don't think I do love you. I just love the person you were. The person I *thought* you were, the one who existed in my imagination. I miss him a lot, actually. My imaginary husband." She checked her watch. "I really have to go."

"Wait." He caught her arm. "What if I *am* that man, Ella? What if I can be that man again?"

Ella patted his hand. "But you can't, Patrick. You never could. That man, he isn't in you."

She rose from the table and carried her cup back to the counter. As she walked out through the door into a chill, sunny March afternoon, she thought that Patrick wasn't the only person she didn't recognize anymore. She didn't recognize herself.

And she kind of liked the new Ella better than the old.

What with the double espresso and the catharsis, Ella settled into a manic groove, back inside the Sterling Bates conference room that had been turned over to the Parkinson forensics team. Yesterday, the two junior accountants had finished entering all the raw data from the stacks of printouts and invoices and receipts in the Sterling Bates files, allowing Ella to do what she liked best: construct a spreadsheet of such breadth and detail and complexity, she could model just about any possible scenario, she could detect the smallest anomaly between these accounts and the official books provided by the municipal bond department.

Another thing that had dug a narrow yet unbridgeable gap between Ella and her girlfriends, such as they were: math. Beautiful, elegant numbers. Ella never could understand why the other girls at school—even the clever ones, even the ones who soldiered along with her in algebra and trig and calculus—couldn't grasp the *beauty* of math, its breathtaking logic. Like a crystal, each complicated molecule connecting delicately to the next, so that if you were able to abandon all other thought, if you just walked out of your world and sank yourself into the math world, you could see the whole universe around you, humming in all its infinite perfection.

Ella loved that world. She occupied its soaring hallways right now, while the two juniors, sensing her absorption, brought her coffee after coffee, like they were feeding quarters into an arcade game and sitting back to watch her play. Until there wasn't any more coffee, and Ella looked up and saw it was eight o'clock and the room was empty except for her and the blue computer glow. Someone had even turned off the fluorescent lights, and she hadn't noticed. She put her hand to her back, just in case someone had taped a note there—DO NOT RESUSCITATE, like some joker had done when she was a lowly second-year—but it was empty.

Ella rose and yawned and glanced into the hallway, through the door that was cracked open. Still lit, of course. At eight o'clock at night, the young cubs in the Sterling Bates analyst program were only getting started in the febrile competition to see who could stay awake the longest, who could pull in the most hours, who was future managing director material and who would get tossed into the moldy reaches of the back office—banished across the river to Jersey City, even—or worst of all, passed up for that precious offer to continue to business school and then return as an investment banking associate, making two hundred thousand a year with nowhere to go but up. Like Patrick had done.

On the table, next to Ella's laptop, rested a yellow legal pad, on which she'd scribbled notes to herself as she went. Not about her spreadsheet, which she perceived as a whole, three-dimensional object, needing no mnemonics, but about data. Missing data, information she meant to hunt down when she came up for air. She lifted that pad now and squinted at the letters and numbers—her handwriting got really sloppy when she was in the zone like that—and then looked again at the clock.

She could call it a night. No particular urgency here; just curiosity. Something nagging her, the old buzz in her gut that told her she was getting close to the hole in the middle of that three-dimensional object in her head. She didn't want to stop, not yet. Because of something. Something nearby that wanted to be found.

She looked again at the name on her legal pad: FH Trust, LLC. She wasn't sure what the FH stood for; she'd never even heard the name, which was odd to begin with. Between her job and Patrick's job and the jobs of all his friends, she'd thought she knew the name of just about every financial institution in New York and Boston, and most of those in the rest of the country. Of course, new funds seemed to be popping up all the time these days. Still. The commission revenue from FH Trust—whatever it was—had been coming in regularly, month on month, the exact same amount, during the entire period of the investigation. Not a huge figure. Nothing to raise anyone's interest. But so regular. So precise. That morning, she'd sent an e-mail to one of the Sterling Bates staff members who'd been assigned to assist the team, asking which bond salesman was responsible for the FH Trust account. No answer yet. And it probably had nothing to do with the fraud on the underwriting side. But she was curious. Anomalies always aroused Ella's curiosity.

On the other hand. Sleep. She needed it. The caffeine hangover was about to hit hard—already that telltale ache was beginning to surround her brain, warning of an incipient crash—and the fatigue of all that insomnia, all that stress and pain and deprivation of ordinary habits, seemed to be leaching into her bones.

She could go home. She should go home. Hector was home.

No! Bad brain. Hector was off-limits. Hector had Claire. Hector—

Her cell phone buzzed against the table.

For a second or two, she stared warily at the device as it rang and rang, sliding a few millimeters to the right at each long vibration. The squat antenna hummed with purpose. It was a new phone, a blue Nokia to which she'd upgraded a few months ago, and Patrick had entered all her contacts and speed dials, putting himself at number one. It lay facedown, so she couldn't see the caller ID. Somewhere between the fourth and fifth ring, the point of decision, she picked it up.

A Manhattan number. Not Patrick. She pressed her thumb against the green button.

"Hello? Ella Gilbert speaking."

"Ella, it's Travis. Travis Kemp."

"Oh! Hi, Travis. I was just thinking of emailing you, actually. There's this firm I've never heard of—"

In her relief, she hadn't noticed the note of unleashed thunder in his greeting, such as it was. She wasn't expecting thunder from Travis; he was the reasonable one, the partner you wanted to work with because he never lost it, never had tantrums, never even raised his voice, no matter what the heat from the client. No matter how badly you'd screwed up. Some of the other associates thought he was kind of cold, actually, but Ella admired his sangfroid. She really did. You might even say that she trusted his sangfroid—trusted that Travis could keep his cool, would protect her from any client pissiness, unlike the other partners who happily hung you out to dry when the client was pissed.

His interruption therefore shocked her.

"Never mind the fucking email, Ella. You're off the account."

Ella felt as if she were falling. Her fingers went cold, her head went dizzy. "I'm sorry," she squeaked. "What did you say?"

"What did I say? I said you're off the account! You told me, Ella, you told me you had no conflicts of interest at Sterling Bates"—she could hear him actually spitting into the phone—"and today I get a call from some—some—I don't know, some guy at the SEC that your fucking husband works for them!"

Ella opened her mouth and tried to speak.

"Well?" Travis's voice rose up to some kind of outraged octave. "Is that true?"

"Yes—I mean, he works—he's not in munis, actually, so I thought—and I thought you knew—"

"Cut the stammering, Ella."

"And we're not together anymore. We're separated."

There was a strange, cold pause. "You're separated? You're saying this is all okay because you're separated?"

"He works in a completely different department. Nothing to do with muni bonds. And you knew he worked there; I know I told you that. Several times.

At the Christmas party, I know I told you then. So I figured you wouldn't have asked me to—"

"For Christ's sake, Ella. I'm not going to remember what you told me at a fucking Christmas party! Didn't I tell you what a high-profile case this was? And now the fucking SEC is calling me to let me know that my lead associate is fucking married to a Sterling Bates managing director!"

"But I thought—"

"You're off the account, Ella. Wipe your laptop. Leave the files on the conference table and lock the door. When you come into the office Monday morning I'll let you know if you still have a job."

Ella opened her mouth again, but there was a sound in her ear like the bang of a gun, like Travis had slammed the phone into his desk, and instead of speaking she lowered the dented Nokia to the conference table and folded her hands in her lap. Her eyes stung. Her throat ached. There was some grave injustice here; she *knew* that Travis had known that Patrick worked at Sterling Bates. It was on her list of disclosures, for God's sake, the one that every associate kept on file. How could he *not* have known? And Patrick was a technology banker. About as far removed from the snoozy world of municipal bond underwriting as you could get.

Injustice. Life wasn't fair, Mumma had always told

her, like every mother had told every child since Homo sapiens first conceived the abstract idea of fairness, and yet Ella never could accept injustice. When you followed every rule, tried your best to please, and still somebody accused you of wrongness. She wanted to scream. She wanted to cry. She wanted to demand the name of this hairy idiot at the SEC and pull out his fingernails. Her hands were shaking. She picked up the phone and touched the buttons and set it down again. Outside the window, across the street, Manhattan blinked its fluorescent office eyes at her. A million people at work, but not her. Not her. She rose and sat down and rose again. There was a sob rising in her throat; she pushed it down. Turned to her laptop and began dutifully erasing files. Stacked all the documents in a neat pile in the center of the table. Gathered up her things. Put on her navy wool coat. Left behind all the Sterling Bates documents, because she always did what she was told; she hated the disorderliness of disobedience.

Of course, Travis didn't say anything about her own notes. Her own yellow legal pad, tucked into her laptop bag, containing all the interesting scribbles of the past week.

Ella took a taxi home—she was calling it that now, *home*—and changed into sweatpants. In the kitchen, all the bottom cabinets had been ripped out. The pots and pans and food sat in a cardboard box next to the wall. There was a note attached. *Hey, Sherlock, we need to talk re your awesome new kitchen. Knock when you get home. H. PS: water's on!!*

She smiled a little, from the corner of her mouth. Walked out the door and went upstairs.

But when she knocked on Hector's door, nothing happened. Not a sound, not a note of music drifting from within. She waited a minute and tried again. Stepped back and checked the bottom of the door for light. Nothing.

So she turned around and trudged back downstairs, and as she turned the corner of the landing the woman in 4B, who was just locking her door, looked up and smiled. She had a slight Southern lilt and impeccable brunette hair, and Ella had been looking for an excuse to see if some kind of friendship might be possible between them. Except she couldn't remember the woman's name. Something with an S. Sadie? Sarah?

"Looking for Hector?" she said, in the kind of between-us-girls voice that said, *I know what you're after, bless your little heart, and I don't blame you for trying.*

Or maybe Ella was only hearing her own guilt. She blushed and pulled out the keys from her pocket. "He was supposed to meet me to talk about the flood damage? You know, from that burst pipe yesterday?"

"Oh, yeah. What a pain. So sorry. Weird, though. I mean, they just did some major plumbing work there when the last tenant moved out. I thought the pipes were all new."

"Really? Hector said . . ." Ella's voice trailed off. Trying to recall exactly what Hector *had* said yesterday.

"Anyway, you're out of luck, honey. He went out a couple of hours ago. I think he was meeting Claire or something. Friday night and all."

Something about the way she said *Friday night* made Ella conscious of her own sweatpants, her own conspicuous lack of plans. Her catastrophic failure in the conference room at Sterling Bates; the job she had possibly lost entirely. The tense, empty weekend ahead. She turned the knob and pushed the door open, into the cramped, odorous darkness of her apartment.

"Good for him," she said.

The light was blinking on her answering machine. She held her finger over the playback button and counted the small, red pulses. One, two, three. She counted all the way to fourteen before she squeezed her lips together and pressed down.

Her mother's voice. "Darling. Not sure where you are. I'm at Vivian's. Just arrived. Horrendous traffic. Remember we're on for Maidstone Meadows tomorrow morning. Nine sharp. I expect you've probably forgotten, so do try to clean yourself up a bit. [*Slight pause.*] Hope you're well, darling. Daddy's meeting us for dinner afterward at the—what was it, Vivs? [*Offstage murmuring.*] Oh, Balthazar. Only the best. Should be laughs. See you tomorrow. Kisses."

Well, Mumma was right. Ella *had* forgotten about the pilgrimage to Maidstone Meadows, where Great-Aunt Julie held court in a kind of elite dormitory for the WASP ancien régime, a couple of hours' drive from midtown Manhattan at the eastern end of Long Island. Third Saturday of the month. Mumma always came up from Arlington to join Aunt Viv and whichever cousins happened to live in New York and had regained liver function by nine o'clock on a Saturday morning. Aunt Viv packed two Thermoses—one full of coffee, one full of Bloody Mary—which she administered as needed. Usually Ella looked forward to the trip. First, there was Mumma and Aunt Viv, who could pack more entertainment into five minutes' conversation than most women packed into a year. Second, there was Great-Aunt Julie, who had pretty much lost whatever remaining damns she'd ever given about anything.

And third, nobody could mix a Bloody Mary like Aunt Viv.

But tonight, the idea of dressing up—Aunt Julie always required appropriate dress—and meeting the Glamour Sisters for a four-hour round trip in a ten-year-old Mercedes station wagon that smelled of wet Labrador and Chanel No. 5 held about the same appeal as an acid peel. Especially if there were any cousins involved. Ella loved her cousins, but everyone knew each other's business, discussed each other's business, had fucking *opinions* on each other's business.

In short, she was going to need a hell of a lot of Bloody Mary to get through this.

Unless she didn't go. Unless she picked up the phone and called her mother's cell (which Mumma never answered) and left a voice mail (which Mumma rarely checked) to say that she wasn't feeling well. That she had to finish cleaning out the debris from her flooded apartment. That the last place she wanted to visit in the middle of March was the gale-beaten tip of Long Island, for God's sake. She could do that. She could just . . . *not go.* What did she have to lose anymore? What had being a good, dutiful little girl gotten her, after all?

Do it, she thought. Do it now, before you talk yourself out of it.

She picked up the phone.

By midnight, Ella had filled two large green garbage bags with ruined objects and humped them down the stairs to the bins in the back courtyard. The sky was still clear, the air as cold and fresh as it could be in the middle of New York City, inside a communal courtyard where everybody kept their trash. Ella swung the bags mightily over the edge of the bin—twinge of guilt, so much landfill—and stood for a moment, hands on hips, catching her breath. Tasting the metropolitan flavors of garbage and rotting vegetables from some nearby grocery.

Except the nearest grocery was a couple of blocks away.

The faint, reedy, intricate voice of a clarinet touched her ear.

Almost by instinct, she looked up. Canted back her head until she found the window of the fifth floor, the top floor, and saw that it was dark. Because Hector was out. Out with his girlfriend, Claire, as he had every right to be. As Claire had every right to expect.

The clarinet grew a little louder, as if feeding on her melancholy.

Ella looked back down at the pavement, at her feet in their L.L.Bean slippers: the ones Patrick hated. She looked at her hands, long and workmanlike, nails bitten, knuckles bony, bearing no rings whatsoever. Whoever played that clarinet was really good. Not just technically good, but expressive, too. Like he had a lot to say, all bottled up inside him, and this was how he was going to say it.

She turned her head in the direction of the neighboring building. The heavy steel door next to its own garbage bin. The clarinet's voice seemed to be floating from that direction, and as she squinted through the sodium haze of the security light, she thought that maybe it looked ajar.

There was no railing, no division between the two properties. Ella turned and stepped off her own back stair, the back stair belonging to 11 Christopher, and took a few paces toward the back stair belonging to the building next door.

Just close enough to see that a thin plastic wedge held the neighboring door open by a couple of inches.

Um, that would be trespassing, the old Ella scolded in her ear.

Let's check it out, said the new Ella. The reckless Ella. Clubbing the old Ella over the head.

And the real Ella stood in the courtyard, torn between the two Ellas inside her skull, the good girl and the wicked girl, the one who stayed virtuously in her apartment and the one who went out hunting, until the clarinet shifted into some strange, inviting melody that circled her thoughts in large, sensuous loops, strangling both voices. She began to walk toward the wedge of space in the crack of the door. Her arms felt light and unburdened, her thighs like jelly after the effort of carrying the garbage. She reached for the handle. The door was heavier than she expected, resisting her strength, almost as if someone were trying to hold it closed from the inside. But Ella fought back. She braced her foot on the doorjamb and gripped the lever with both hands and pulled, pulled, until the door gave way in a sudden rush and Ella stumbled backward, landing on her knee.

All right, she thought. If that's the way you want it.

She picked herself up and charged through the doorway, taking care to close the door on the plastic wedge, just in case. The clarinet quickened, grew louder, eager, like it was welcoming her home. Some home. Not a hallway, but a broom closet, damp and cramped, reeking of bleach. Ella thought, What the hell? Who leaves their building through a broom closet? She spread her fingers out before her and felt for the wall, for some kind of opening, yarn mops and brushes and metal pails, claustrophobia gripping her chest like a panic—and she wasn't even claustrophobic, damn it!—until she felt a small knob, turned it, burst out into an old tile vestibule, open door to a bathroom opposite, metal stairs leading up in a spiral, solid cinder-block wall where the rest of the basement should have been.

And the sound of the clarinet, filling the air nimbly from nowhere in particular.

The phone rang at six in the morning, startling Ella from a dream about rain that turned out to be real, battering her window in furious waves. She picked up the receiver without thinking. "Hello?" she said, an instant before thinking, *Oh, shit.*

"Got your message, darling," her mother said. "I sympathize, I really do. But I'm afraid I'm going to have to ask you to be a big girl. We'll be outside your building at five minutes to nine."

"But, Mumma—"

"Ta-ta!"

Click.

ACT IV

We Have a Change of Plans

(ain't that the truth)

LONG ISLAND, NEW YORK

1924

1

The sun may shine fierce from its cradle of blue, but the air don't care. I instruct Billy to lay on the brakes and put the rag back up on his breezer, and he obeys me. Whistling some tune between his happy lips. He climbs back in and delivers me another kiss. And I kiss him back, with maybe a little more strength than he was expecting.

"Miss me, did you?" he says.

"More than I can say."

Billy grins and puts the car back in gear. "Just you wait, darling. Just you wait and see what I've got planned for us."

The roar of the Hudson's six-cylinder engine precludes my reply, or maybe I just choose not to speak. Huddle down deep in my coat while the atmosphere slowly warms in the combined heat of our two human bodies. We cross the Queensboro Bridge and work our way eastward. The sun drops behind us, the air turns gold. I press my knuckles together and watch the buildings blur past, the storefronts and houses, the parks turning into meadows, brown skeletal trees and dead winter hills. How terrible a time is the beginning of March. In a month there will be daffodils and the sudden blossoming of orchards, but you wouldn't know it now. You have to take spring on blind faith.

When the last tendrils of New York City disappear behind us, I speak up. Ask Billy what he's been up to this past month.

"This," he says, reaching for my hand.

"And you couldn't telephone? You couldn't write?"

"I wanted it to be a surprise. I wanted to amaze you."

"Well, you did that. I thought you were gone for good."

"Really? You didn't look all that surprised when I turned up. You looked like you were expecting someone." His hand goes still on my fingers. "Say. You haven't taken up with some other fellow, have you?"

"Of course not."

"Because if you have, I—well, I'm not going to force you into anything—"

"Applesauce. I'm here in this car of yours, aren't I? Nobody forced me into anything."

"Then you mean it? Really? You'll do this with me? On the level, now."

"Do what, exactly?"

"What I said before. Run away with me. Start a new life."

"In the land of milk and honey, where the sun always shines and the lilac blooms all year long?"

"Ginger," he says, "be serious for once. Don't lead a fellow on."

His hand still rests atop mine, inside the hollow of my lap. I lay my thumb over the joints of his fingers and lift his hand to my cheek. "Oh, Billy. Just drive, all right? Take me somewhere safe and warm. And for God's sake, feed me. I haven't had lunch."

Billy chucks me on the cheek and returns his hand to the steering wheel. "Hungry, are you?"

"Famished."

2

We don't say another word until Billy turns left off the main road onto a smaller one, following a signpost that says GLEN COVE 4 MI.

"Glen Cove?" I inquire. "This is your idea of a country retreat?"

"What's wrong with Glen Cove?"

"Nothing's wrong with Glen Cove. Full of rich folks, I hear. Nice spot, if you can afford it."

"If you're asking whether I can look after you—"

"I'm not asking anything."

"Just you wait, Ginger. I know where I'm going."

He seems to know where he's going, all right. The Hudson bends confidently into the curves in the road, into the turn down a narrow lane, the turn down a narrower one. Here and there, you can glimpse a house or two, big and rambling and nestled in gardens. I imagine, in the coming of spring, the landscape will take on a wholly different look: lush and verdant, leaves bursting out every which way, softening the edges and disguising those beautiful bricks from view. But for now, it's all bleak and sort of ravishingly exposed, like a lady who's shed all her clothes and her cosmetics. For some reason, I think of Millie Macduff, bare faced and monochrome in the unforgiving light of a noontime luncheonette.

The Hudson slows and makes a steady right turn between a pair of stone pillars. There's a word carved into one of them, stately Roman capitals, but we flash past so quickly, I only catch the first letter: P.

"We're staying here?" I say. "Some mansion?"

"No, not the main house. Friend of mine is letting me have the old gamekeeper cottage. I've spent the last month fixing it up with my own two hands." He holds up one of them for inspection.

"What about college?"

"I quit college. Two days after we last met, I marched right in and tendered my resignation."

"Quit college! What the devil were you thinking?"

The drive is gravel and hasn't been raked since September, probably. Since all good families returned to their metropolitan homes in time for the Metropolitan Opera. Billy grips the wheel to keep the Hudson steady. Ahead of us looms a castle, turrets and all, lonely and magnificent, but Billy turns the car at the last second, down a track leading away from said castle and around the side of a hill.

"I was thinking about you," he says. "I was thinking about how you need a fellow you can trust, a fellow who's ready to give up everything for you. As soon as I woke up and saw you in the chair that morning, all curled up like a lost kitten, why, I knew what I had to do."

"Oh, Billy. You darling thing. You didn't need to do anything of the kind."

"Yes, I did. There comes a time when a fellow needs to decide if he's a boy or a man, and I figured that time had come for me. My bell was tolling. Look! There it is. Our new home."

Well. I don't know much about gamekeepers or their

cottages—River Junction being the kind of town that likes to cut out the middleman in such matters—but I have to admit, the place has got some charm. Made of the same old gray stone as the castle up the lane, big mullioned windows, tree out front that might just prove to be a lilac, in the coming of May. A gigantic rhododendron looms next to the door, pregnant with about a thousand buds. Billy brings the Hudson to a stop on the drive, sets the brake, and rests his hands on his knees.

"Well? What do you think?"

"It's beautiful."

"Wait until you see the inside. Come along."

He hauls himself free of the car and swings around to open my door. I allow him the niceties; they mean so much to him. He tucks my arm into the crook of his elbow and leads me forth past the probable lilac, branches scratching the cold wind, and when we reach the stoop he releases my arms and swoops me into the air.

"Billy! What in God's name—"

"It's tradition, isn't it?"

And my stomach lurches as he we dive over the threshold, my pulse goes all nuts in my neck, and I squeeze my eyes shut and think, *It's perfect, you need a place to hide out, Billy adores you, you adore him, let's play lovebirds until this whole sorry affair dies out of mind, until Duke's in hell and Anson's maybe with him. Let's live in shabby comfort, let somebody take care of you for once.* Billy kisses the top of my head and whispers something, I can't hear what. When I open my eyes a few seconds later, we're standing in the middle of a cozy parlor strewn with cushions and afternoon light, everything my childhood home was not, and Billy sets me on my feet and wraps his arm around my shoulders.

"I'll get the fire started, shall I?"

3

The wood's already laid in the inglenook fireplace, and while Billy sets the whole thing ablaze I wander through the rooms. There aren't many. The parlor, the kitchen. A kind of small den lined in shelves, containing a desk messy with papers. Upstairs, two bedrooms and a small bathroom. The larger bedroom's got a tall four-poster, all made up in fresh white linens and a paisley counterpane, topped by a half-dozen plump pillows. You can imagine its purpose. The second bedroom's got two twin beds: the natural outcome, I guess, of the first bedroom. I stand between them for a moment or two, caressing an old wooden bedpost with one hand. My chest hurts. There is a panic rising inside me, the old panic. The window looks west, where the sun is just beginning to touch the treetops, and distant Manhattan gathers its breath for an evening of no good.

But I am not thinking about Manhattan just now. I am thinking of my mama, and the time she nearly died giving birth to Angus. Though I was but six or seven at the time, still I recollect every detail of those terrible days, every terrible second counting down on the clock in the kitchen. How Duke sat beneath that clock, chair pulled right up to the edge of the kitchen table, and drank bottle after bottle of rye whiskey, rising only to visit the outhouse. How his eyes glassed over and his hair lay in greasy pieces about his forehead, the most untidy I have ever seen him, before or since.

At one point the scene grew so desperate, so hopeless, that Laura Ann Green did bring me up to Mama's bedroom to say good-bye. The place was a dump. Bloody rags in the corner, bloody water in the chipped blue-and-white bowl on the washstand. The sweet-sour smell of sickness. Wee Angus inside the cradle in the corner, howling his lungs out for want of milk. And Mama on her bed she shared with Duke, except now there was only her, my thin, pale mama, spread in the middle of four stout bedposts, like they was some kind of medieval instrument upon which you might persecute a traitor, stretching his four limbs until you tore him clean apart. That was the picture I kept in my head, anyways: Mama's bed as a rack of torture, killing her inch by inch.

She wasn't properly awake. Kind of delirious, as I now understand, and I could not then comprehend the words she said to me. I said how I loved her. How she couldn't die. And she said something about God's will and *penance*, that exact word, which I went to the library to look up afterward, because we kept no dictionary in our house. *Penance* meant punishment for sin. Meant you had done wrong and now you was paying for it. And though Mama did get better, by some miracle, some act of mercy—not mercy for *her*, mind you, only for us who did love her—I never could banish that sight of her on that bed. Those four posts, stretching her to death.

4

By the time I return downstairs, the fire's lit up like Christmas and crackling hot. Billy stands back and sets his proud knuckles on his hips. "Now, that's better. Warm enough for you?"

"Yes."

He looks more slender than I remember. Slender and tallish, golden hair polished. Skin smooth as satin over those rounded, even features. He's taken off his overcoat, revealing a vest of brown cashmere wool over his starched white shirt, the sleeves of which are rolled up his forearms as a man settling into his evening chores. His mouth tilts upward as he watches the wild dance of this fire he built himself.

I slip my arms around his dear woolen waist and say his name.

"Do you like it, Gin? Do you really?"

"It's wonderful. Awfully homey."

"I cleaned it all up, painted the walls. Brought in some furniture."

"Where did you get the furniture?"

"Fuzzy let me raid the attic in the Big House."

"Who's Fuzzy?"

"Pal of mine. It's his parents' place. They're here in the summer, mostly."

"Of course they are. But do they know we're here in the spring, Billy dear?"

An infinitesimal pause, and then: "Of course they do."

"Oh, Billy," I sigh out.

"Don't you worry, Gin. Don't you worry about a single thing. I just couldn't let my parents find out, not yet. Not until—well, until things are settled."

"*Settled.* Now, that's an interesting word."

"Darling." He turns me in his arms so we're face-to-face, and the chocolate light of sincerity just beams out of his eyes. "Don't you see? I've built us a nest, you and me, just like I said I would. That dream I had, the one I told you about. You and me in the countryside. No more slaving away in a typing pool all day and then cheapening yourself in gin mills at night. I'm going to write, and you're going to keep house and—well, whatever you like. Whatever makes you happy. I'll do anything for you, Gin. Keep you safe and warm and happy."

"Until your parents turn up and talk some sense into you."

"Well, now. I figure if we stay here long enough, why—well, they can't argue if there's a grandchild on the way, can they? They'll just *have* to welcome you in. And once they get to know you—"

"A *grandchild* on the way?"

His ears turn red. "We could try, couldn't we?"

"Dear Billy. And if they don't welcome me in, after all? Your parents?"

"Well, of course they will."

"I mean if they take one look at my hair, listen to me mangle my vowels and my verbs, and they say to you, *William Marshall, you're the damnedest fool,* and there I am, all knocked up and nowhere to turn—"

"Why, where did you get an idea like that? My parents aren't like that, not a bit. They're not so snobby as you think. Anyway, you sound just fine. Why, you could hardly tell that—well, that—"

"That I be some rough-cut stone the old mountains done cast off, is that right?" I reach behind me and find his hands. Pull them gently away from the small of my back. "And then Pater takes you aside for a stern chat and tells you he's writing you out of the will—"

"Aw, he'd never do that! And I don't care if he does. I'll marry you anyway, Gin. That's right. I want you to marry me, with or without their blessing. I'd marry you this second, if I could."

"Would you? Would you really? Have you got a ring and everything?"

"Not yet. But I will. As soon as I save up enough—"

"Save up from what? There's no money in poetry, Billy-boy. Even I know that. And sooner or later you'd get the itch, you'd get sick of babies squalling while you're trying to write, you'd get sick of all this rustic charm and say to yourself, Lord Almighty, Billy-boy, you might have had yourself a grand ten-room joint on Fifth Avenue and a nice blond wife with a lockjaw accent, and instead you're living in sin in a gamekeeper's cottage on a dollar a day, kids crawling over your lap, your faded-up hillbilly doll withering before your eyes, nagging you about your dirty socks—"

"Don't talk nonsense, Gin. That'll never happen." He takes me up again. "I love you. I love you madly. This past month, why, it's been torture. Getting this place ready, making all these grand plans, and then expecting to hear any day that you had taken up with some rich fellow who was showering you in diamonds, like you deserve. All I've got is this place, and my heart, and these two hands to labor for you. And I hope that's enough, darling Gin. I hope you'll accept them."

Well, what are you going to say to a speech like that? I'm not made of old gray stone. I'm made of tender woman's flesh, and what's more, I've just had a dreadful shock, a dreadful disappointment, my beating heart liketa broke in bits. My poor arms yearn for some kind of comfort. Billy looks on me with his soft, handsome young face. Skin all warm and gold. Eyebrows crooked to a plaintive peak above his nose. Arms wrapped around my ribs. Hands cradling the back of my head. So terribly, terribly close. Within easy reach.

"Billy," I whisper. "Sweet Billy-boy."

His lips are pink and round. I close my eyes and

think of that bed upstairs, and me and Billy atop that bed, locked between those four posts, underneath the paisley counterpane, skin against skin, Billy's lean chest rising and falling in the light of the moon. Nights and days and weeks and years of me and Billy; kids with Billy, one after another; cooking and cleaning for Billy, keeping house with my Billy-boy in the lilac-scented Long Island countryside while my true heart lies in bits on the floor of an empty Tenth Avenue tenement. The pain in my chest grows and grows, until I'm sick with it. The back of my throat turns bitter. My eyes sting.

"Gin, you're crying. What's wrong? You're not unhappy, are you?"

"I don't deserve you, Billy."

"Gin, don't—"

"I've made a terrible mistake, Billy. I've been awfully selfish. I shouldn't have come here. I shouldn't have—have taken you up to begin with. Like you were some kind of toy."

"Gin!"

He calls after me. Runs after me and snatches my arm and demands to know where I'm going, what I'm doing. What he's done wrong. His expression's so distraught, I can't stand it. Choke up. Can't speak. Just shake my head, and maybe that's enough, maybe the sight of my wet face repels him entirely, for he does drop my arm like a lit match and turn an elegant shade of pale. I dart for the door, throw it open, run down the stony path to the Hudson parked outside. Billy keeps the key in the ignition; he's that kind of boy.

5

I leave the motorcar at the Glen Cove railway station, keys under the seat, and take the train back into the city. The sun falls, the buildings light up. The carriage is nearly empty, the atmosphere saturated by stale cigarettes and perspiration, and I peer out the window at the glitter assembling ahead. Just before we plunge beneath the East River, a sensation of panic seizes my breast once more. I clutch my pocketbook and try to breathe until it eases: breathe and breathe under the dark, soothing weight of the tunnel. In the steely, rhythmic clack of the wheels on the tracks, like the operation of a typewriter.

We throb to a halt at Pennsylvania Station. I gather up my pocketbook and my composure. Buy myself a ham sandwich and eat it right there in the center of that dirty, glorious space, standing next to the big brass clock, surrounded by a mess of harried suburban businessmen, of working girls, of housewives hurrying home to Long Island after a hard day's shopping in the city. Staring at the sooty columns, wondering where on God's crawling earth I'm supposed to go next. What I'm supposed to do, now that I've got no job and no lover, no safe harbor left. The sandwich is as stale and tired as I am, the last one left on the automat shelf, salty enough to sizzle your tongue, and I'm too hungry to care. I finish the last crumb, smash the waxed paper into a ball, and toss it into the trash.

What I really need is a drink.

6

Maybe I'm making another big mistake, taking a seat at the far end of the Christopher Club bar. Laying my pocketbook on the counter and asking Christopher for a gin martini, dry. I cross my legs at the knees and contemplate the shelves of empty, immaculate glasses—they keep the bottles tucked away from view in joints like this—while mine host mixes my drink in silence.

I say silence because it's utterly still, there inside that familiar room, just me and Christopher and the empty tables. Too early for business, see, and in fact he's only opened up on my account, because he's a good fellow and because I'm his best customer. He sets down the glass—strange to hear the clink, which is ordinarily drowned in music and conversation—and gives me a look that says, *What's eating you, sister?*

"Aren't you going to pour one for yourself?" I ask. "I won't tell."

"Naw, I don't take liquor."

"Not at all?"

"Not a drop."

"Well, now. That's irony. Cheers, anyway."

Christopher nods. Wipes down the counter. Asks, grudgingly, if I've had a tough day at work.

"You could say that."

He's got a young face, our Christopher, terribly young. Did I ever mention that? Plump and fresh as a new peach. Medium height, square frame, dark hair wet and slick. Always wears a black vest and white apron, shirt forever crisp, collar as sharp and neat as if his own mama straightened it for him before he left for work. On his left jawbone there is a small, black mole, his only remarkable feature, which I study for some time before I pipe up again.

"Say. I've got a question for you."

"No law against that, I guess."

"What do you know about that platinum doll who sits on the stool at the other end? The one with the stilts all the way to China."

"I don't know nothing about nobody, Gin. Not in this business."

"Because I always figured she belonged to you."

"Now, why would you think a thing like that?"

"I don't know. Just a hunch. Air of coziness about the two of you." I open up my pocketbook and locate a packet of cigarettes, nearly depleted. Light one up, but my heart's not in it. Like some old morning ritual that now turns your stomach, like you went and upchucked your porridge one fine day and can't ever eat porridge again. I allow myself a shallow breath anyway, it's something to do, and I watch Christopher's wary face as he replies.

"We ain't cozy, Gin. Not like that."

"But you maintain some kind of understanding betwixt you, nonetheless."

"Don't ask me that. You know I hate to lie to you."

"I'm not asking you a thing. I'm stating a fact. You know all about how she works for the Bureau, don't you, and everything that goes down here goes down on her say-so. Isn't that right? In exchange for a little official protection, which is something a joint like this stands in need of, during these desperate times."

Christopher glances at the door. Glances back to me.

"That's right. Tell me the truth, now. Nobody can hear you. Why, you don't ever need to make a sound, in any case. Just nod your head *yes* if I'm onto something. If what I say sounds familiar."

He fixes me in the eye and makes a small nod *yes*.

"Good. And as for that bastard Anson—"

But I am not allowed to inquire after Anson, it seems. Not because Christopher's disinclined to continue this interesting conversation—though I expect he right enough is—but because the door does swing open wide at that exact second, and a man staggers into the room, skull cracked open like an egg, orbitals swollen fit to burst. He sways, stumbles, catches himself on a chair. Stares at me like he knows me, like he's been searching for me all his life.

"Why, Carl Green!" I cry, starting forward from my stool.

"Get going," Carl says, like a man with no teeth. He spits something out, or rather dribbles some piece of something from his lips. "Get on out-a here, Geneva Rose," and he pitches right forward, over the seat of the chair, and bleeds himself dry all over Christopher's nice clean floor of checkerboard tile. Black and white and red all over.

7

And I am kneeling there on the tiles over Carl Green's body, yelling for more dishcloths, cradling his poor split-open skull, when that bastard Anson strides in from the back hall and makes a noise of anguish.

"You! What the hell are you doing here? Get on out, do you hear me? Get on out before I take up a stool and bash you where—"

He steps forward and snatches my arm. "Come along, Gin. Right now!"

"I ain't going nowhere! Don't you see what you done to him?"

"Come *on!*"

"You get your hands off-a me! He's a-dying, can't you see?"

"He's a dead man, Gin! You can't help him."

"He ain't dead, he's alive, he wants saving—"

A pair of hands closes around my shoulders and lifts me upward and into the chest of Oliver Anson.

"You do as he says, Gin Kelly," says Christopher. "You get the hell out of here *now!*"

I'm no match for the two of them, and anyway there's this mad urgency packed into Christopher's voice—a voice so ordinarily laconic it couldn't possibly care less about my troubles—that stuns me into acquiescence. The blood-soaked dishcloth drops from my right hand, while Anson's paw clamps around my left hand. I stagger after him, eyes kind of blurry, head kind of light, down the back hallway and through that door in the broom closet. Up the narrow, wet brick staircase and into the courtyard that smells of garbage, where Anson scales a wall as nimbly as a six-foot squirrel and lifts me after him, over the top, scraping my knees on the rough edge and then landing on the pavement, stumble-thud.

"Wait!" I gasp. "My pocketbook!"

"Christ, Gin! Let's go!"

I want to scream *No,* I want to plant my feet and wrest my arm away, but Anson's bicep is eight sizes bigger than mine, his strength is insurmountable, and instead of making my stand I clatter along in his lee, down a narrow alley and into a street, I don't know which one, where a black motorcar sits by itself in the shadow betwixt two street lamps.

"No! Are you out of your mind? Ain't getting inside any kind of automobile with you—"

Anson just bends down and hauls me up into his arms like you would haul a sack of grain, like you would haul a barrel of moonshine, and he turns the handle and kicks open the door and dumps me into the seat. Levers himself over me and starts the motorcar so fast, roars from the curb so fast I don't have time to unscramble myself and open the door. I just set to swearing at him. Pummel his arm as I turn the air a bright shade of Appalachia blue. He sets his teeth and pays me no mind. Just drives down one wet street and another, round a mess of corners until we squeal to a stop somewhere in the Manhattan gloom. And he sets the brake and grabs my wrists and says, "Now, you calm down, Gin, you calm down one minute. What the devil's wrong with you?"

"You bastard! I know what you are, that's what's wrong. You are no more Prohi than I am, that's what's wrong."

"Who told you that?"

"Millie did!"

"Who the devil's Millie?"

"The blonde, you bastard! The stinking blond vamp

from Christopher's joint. Met me today at lunchtime and told me to look up your offices on Tenth Avenue, and there was sure enough nobody there, because I am a damn fool and *trusted* you—"

"Damn," he says, and lets go of my wrists.

And I am not so shocked by Anson's use of the word *damn* that I can't now spring forth from the automobile and sprint down the cobbles for some kind of freedom, though he catches me in seconds and says, whispers, right in my ear: "Well, you've got to trust me now, Gin, you've got to come with me now or you're next."

"Next for what?"

"Next for dead. Next for having your skull split open like that poor fellow back on Christopher Street."

"By whom?"

"By Kelly, that's who."

I strain against his arms and he lets me go, without warning, such that I lurch forward until he just saves me by the elbow.

"You were right about that fellow the other night," he says. "I should have listened. You were right."

"I'm always right. Except about you."

He swears again. "I'll explain. Just come with me now, all right? Just let me get you somewhere safe."

"Do I have a choice?"

"Not really."

A cold rain falls upon us, somewhere between a drizzle and a mist, and I realize I've got no coat, either. No coat and no pocketbook. No gloves nor hat. We've landed near the docks, I can smell it in the air, salt and fish and oil and rust and rot, the flavor of maritime commerce. The steam drifts from my lungs and his, dissolving together into the gloaming. Some kind of hullaballoo sounds from a nearby street, but it seems to belong to another world entirely. A world of people going about ordinary business, people whose skulls stand in no danger of bashing. Anson's hand is warm and snug around my elbow. His heart beats a few inches away. I start to shiver.

"Come on, Gin. You're cold. Let's get out of here."

I close my eyes and Carl Green's head appears before me. The contents of his skull, leaching out onto a nice clean black-and-white floor.

"I'm going to kill him," I say. "I'm going to kill him with my bare hands."

And the thing about Anson is, he doesn't have to ask me whom I mean. Just lets his hand fall from my elbow and says, kind of soft and yet so hard and straight as a steel rail: "You don't have to kill him, Gin. You have me for that."

8

Now we are spurting out past the Narrows, white wake trailing from behind us, aboard some boat that Anson magically unmoored from a dark, rotting dock not far from where the ocean liners fill with coal and stores. The rain's blown out, the moon bursts free. The draft freezes my cheeks. He's wrapped me in some kind of blanket, pulled from beneath the seat behind me, but that doesn't stop the shivering, which derives from a source far beneath my skin.

"Are you all right?" he asks at last, over the noise of the motor.

"Course I am."

"You're still shivering."

"It's a cold night."

He says something under his breath and starts to maneuver his coat from his shoulders, switching the wheel from one hand to another.

"Don't bother," I say. "You'll freeze to death in this draft."

"So will you."

"So I'll find another blanket. You just stay put and keep us on top of the water, all right?"

He exhales and nods over his shoulder. "Under the seats. With the life belts."

I bend down on my shaky knees and poke around underneath the seats, until I find a stack of wool plaid blankets identical to the one I'm already wearing. The boat pitches violently; I sprawl on the slatted wooden deck.

"Sorry!" calls Anson. "Keep hold. Crossing a wake."

Another wild pitch, and another. I brace myself against a seat until the jolting settles back into what I suppose is the ordinary rhythm of a small, sleek motor-boat skimming across a calm sea. Not that I've ever had the pleasure. My stomach lurches in time to the swell. I set my hands on the edge of the hull and lever myself up, clutching the blanket under my arm, and then I stagger back to where Anson steers the thing, one hand on the chromium wheel and one hand on some kind of throttle, like he was born to do such things.

"Sorry," he says again. "You're all right?"

"You might have warned me."

"If I'd seen it in time, I would have. You weren't hurt, were you?"

I unfold the blanket and lift it over my shoulders, atop the first one. "I'll live."

"Seasick?"

"Now, why would you ask a thing like that?"

"Because I don't want to see your dinner all over my clean deck."

"Don't worry. No dinner here. Just a ham sandwich and a dry martini."

He doesn't answer. The boat skips happily along the black water, while the moon strikes a silver path before us. Nearby, a few dark spots suggest other ships, and I guess if I look hard enough, I can distinguish their shapes by the meager light of the night sky. But I don't want to look. I stare dumbly ahead, listening to the drone of the engine, smelling the brine and the gasoline exhaust. Trying not to think, trying not to blink, because each time I close my eyes, I see Carl Green's head spilling onto the floor. His blood the color of wine. Brains the color of jelly.

"How much farther?" I sort of choke.

"Far enough. You should sit down. Just sit down and hold on to something."

I sink into the passenger's chair, made of oiled, salt-stained leather. The sea ahead disappears from sight, hidden by the long wooden bow. I watch the glimmer of moon on the polished wood. Hear myself asking whose boat this is.

He answers me with some kind of reluctance. "My father's."

"Does he know we're borrowing it?"

"He won't care, if that's what you're asking."

"And just why does your father keep a motorboat tied up on the Hudson River?"

"He doesn't. I brought it in myself."

"From where?"

"From where we're going."

"Which is?"

"Don't ask so many questions, Gin. I'm just doing what I have to do. Once I realized we had a leak—"

"Millie?"

He pauses. "No, not her. I'll explain later."

"No. I want you to explain now."

Anson heaves a sigh so deep, I imagine I can hear it above the noise of the motor and the water slapping our sides. I turn my gaze to his fingers, gloved in leather, wrapped around the throttle, and the moonlit hairs at his wrist. My stomach falls and falls. He pulls on the throttle, and the entire boat seems to rear up like a damn stallion, and I thought we were going fast before, but now we're racing. Tearing across all that black water. I clutch at the side of the boat and find a handle right there, just for the purpose of keeping your body anchored to the seat. They think of everything, rich people. I clutch this thin metal bar with one hand and the blankets with the other. My eyes sting. The tears stream out across my temples. I think, Wouldn't it be lovely just to race and race along the track of the moon, Anson silent by my side, wind freezing my lungs. Salt spray dashing like needles into my cheeks. Race on forever, no shore in sight.

Inevitably, the boat slows. Makes a long, graceful curve to the right. Anson's hand eases the throttle to a low putter, and the great thrust below my feet dies away into a kind of drifting.

"What are those lights, ahead of us? The shore?"

"No," he says. "That's Rum Row."

"Rum Row?"

He reaches for my arm and pulls me gently to my feet. Points all the way to the right and then across our front, in a long arc, all the way to the left. An endless string of lights, like somebody's hosting a midnight party in a giant garden.

"Ships," he says. "Anchored six miles out from shore, where the legal jurisdiction of the United States ends. They're full of liquor, Miss Kelly. Like floating warehouses. You and I, in our motorboat, if we wanted a case or two of genuine Scotch whiskey, we'd sail out to meet one of those ships and shout up for what we wanted. And they'd sell it to us. And we'd hurry back to shore, before the Coast Guard could catch us."

"You don't say. As easy as that?"

"More or less. Depending on the state of the weather.

Of course, most of the boats taking advantage of this service are bigger fry than a man and a woman searching for a drink. The New York rackets, the gangs who keep the clubs and the speakeasies running."

"And my stepfather? Where does he fit in?"

"I suppose you might say that Duke Kelly's organization finds itself in something of a competition with the ships of Rum Row. Imported liquor against the native variety. But New York's so thirsty, it doesn't really matter. There's room for everyone, you might say, if nobody decides to get greedy. Everybody sticks to their territory."

I stare out at the string of twinkling lights. What an innocent beauty; what a fairy show. "This line of ships, how far north does it go?"

"Up Long Island and Massachusetts. Down south along the New Jersey coast. Maryland, Delaware. All the way to Florida, with some breaks in between. Like a sort of blockade, I guess, only the opposite direction. Bringing goods in instead of keeping them out."

"Then why doesn't the Bureau just sail out and arrest them?"

"Can't. It's perfectly legal, what they're doing. International waters. It's the motorboats we try to stop—the Coast Guard does, that is—except we haven't enough boats and men and guns."

"We?"

He makes a little movement, as if catching himself. Rests one wrist on the top of the wheel. The casing of his watch glints softly by the light of the moon.

"Well? Which is it? Are you a genuine Bureau agent, or not?"

"Not at present."

"Not at present. You quit?"

"They fired me. Two months ago. Two and a half. Just before Christmas."

I whistle softly. "So Millie's right. Hand in the cookie jar, was it? And I thought you were such an honest fellow. What happened? Gambling debt you couldn't convince Papa to cover?"

His hand moves against the wheel. He curls his fingers around the lacquered wood, making a fist. "No. I guess you might say I was sniffing too close to somebody else's cookie jar. That's what I surmise, in any case. I was working on the Kelly racket, as I told you, trying to follow the trail of money, and they called me into the office one morning and told me they had evidence I was taking bribes. Photographic evidence, paper evidence. I remember his face. Shevlin's face; he's the head of the New York bureau. I could tell it was killing him. He's a good man. But he had his orders."

I turn to face his profile, lit by the moon. "His

orders? Are you trying to tell me this entire affair—my stepfather—are you saying it goes all the way up to the top?"

"I don't know about the top. Higher than Shevlin, certainly. It seems your stepfather's got a protector of some kind. One prepared to do just about anything to keep his name clear and his bank account fed."

He stands erect, Mr. Anson, his spine so straight as a rail of steel track, so straight as an arrow from Robin Hood's own bow. Shoulders thick and level. One hand fisted around the ship's wheel. Eyes narrowed into the distance.

"And I imagine that's where I came in, isn't it? You wanted to find out who this protector might be. You cast about. You discovered Duke Kelly's own baby girl lived right there conveniently on your doorstep, right there in Manhattan, just waiting to be plucked up and fashioned into a doll of your own using. Some kind of puppet, some marionette with her strings all in a heap—"

"You're wrong."

"Am I? Explain to me, then, how you couldn't just tell me the truth from the beginning. Why you had to put on such a hoax, just to get me to play along."

"For exactly that reason. You wouldn't have believed me. Even if you did, you wouldn't have thought it worth your while, a slim chance like that, without the Bureau behind me."

"Ah, so it *isn't* worth my while. There's not a thing you really can do to Duke, is there? I'm just the stakes in your little poker match. No, that's not it. I'm the stooge. The dumb stooge holding the bag when—"

"You're not a *stooge,* for God's sake. You're not any of those things."

"Then what am I? Tell me! What the hell am I to you, Oliver Anson?"

He lifts his right hand and does something to the throttle, I don't know what, kills the motor entirely. The sudden absence of manufactured noise unnerves me. The slap of water against the hull. He turns in my direction, and his face is all shadowed and bony. His eyes are the same color as the moon, except hotter.

I swing to my feet and push my chin up to match his. "Well? When you staked me out—isn't that the word?—when you watched me and followed me and made yourself an expert on Ginger Kelly and her squalid little life, what was your angle? What were you thinking?"

"Does it matter?"

"It surely does."

The boat rocks beneath us, but he doesn't make a grab for anything. Just balances there on his two braced feet, hands down against his sides. I wish I could see his face better. Wish I could divine some clue to this long, silent contemplation he's making, this terrible gaze upon me with his eyes the shade of the midnight ocean reflecting the moon.

"Well?" I demand.

He says softly, "I was thinking you were the most extraordinary woman I'd ever seen."

The boat pitches, catching some sort of broadside, and I lurch forward straight into Anson's right shoulder. Hard, too, such that he makes an *Oof!* and staggers back, snatching at me while we tumble together into his seat, the way they do at the pictures, except that instead of kissing him I sort of trip off his knee and land on my buttocks on the narrow, wet boards of the deck.

And it's the last straw, damn it, falling on my buttocks at Anson's feet, catching glimpse of his horrified, silvery expression above me. I make a sound of rage and rise to my knees. I swing my right fist into the bottom of his iron rib cage and then the left fist, and I reckon it hurts me more than it hurts him but I don't care. Feels too good. I hit him again and again, and he just lets me swing away, taking those fists to his middle, grasping me gently by the blades of my shoulders as if to support me in my singular rampage. "All right, now," he says, like you might say to a fretful pony, while my swinging slows and stops and I start to list forward into the same belly I've just abused. "All right. Deserved that, I guess."

"You did. You did. Old Carl—"

"All right. All right."

Seems I'm crying now, too. Why not? Back shuddering against his firm hands. Soft wool fibers of his overcoat stuck to my cheeks. Now he moves, holding me carefully by the shoulders while he slides down from the seat to the deck beside me and gathers me up whole, just scoops me up and presses me snug into the wide, soft plane of his chest.

"I oughta keep a-belting you. Would, if I'd had any dinner."

"You should. I guess I deserve it."

"Opening that door on Tenth Avenue. Realizing that Millie was right."

"I'm sorry."

"Gave me my first kiss, Carl Green. Now he's gone because-a me."

"Wasn't your fault."

"All that *blood* . . ."

I want to express more, but the terrible words won't

form. The blankets have come undone from my shoulders, but the steady warmth of Anson's arms replaces them. We are just a tangle of blanket and overcoat and great, damp, bony limbs. Exhausted skin and the punch of two heartbeats.

"I found those agents of mine last month," he says. Words hitting me somewhere atop my bare head, stirring the hairs there. "When I was keeping watch over you in River Junction. They were in those woods near the cemetery. Buried about a foot deep under the snow."

"Why didn't you tell me?"

"I just didn't." He shifts under me. "They looked like your friend Carl, you know. Smashed up around the head. They'd buried the two of them face to foot, like a pair of horses in a pasture. Shoes still laced. The animals had got to them a bit; that's how I discovered the grave."

"The bastard."

"It's a bad business, that's all. A terrible business. Maybe I shouldn't have brought you in. But you were the only way, you see. There was no other way inside his racket. No one else he might possibly trust, except someone he already knew. Someone in the family, someone who might yet have a reason to dislike the man. Someone with brains and spirit. Who else but you? So I had to see it through. I couldn't let myself be swayed by . . ."

"By what?"

"By sentiment," he says softly.

The air's dark down here. The moon's safe over the ridge of the bow. My head lies comfortably against the lapels of Anson's overcoat; my legs nest into the hollow betwixt the two of his. The boat bobs helplessly. A half mile or so away, a line of floating warehouses lies at anchor, bow to stern, packed to the rafters with any kind of hooch you care to drink: an industry, a city almost, constructed with elaborate human ingenuity in order to circumvent human law. What chance have we got against all that? The two of us, draped upon each other at the bottom of a single motorboat, atop the wide, cold black sea.

"Why do you do it?" I whisper. "People are going to drink, that's all. People are going to get fried, whatever the government does. What's the use?"

"Because it's the law," he answers.

I wait for him to continue, but he doesn't. That's all he has to say. I consider all the questions I ought to ask him, the outrage I ought to feel, but instead I find myself overcome by something else, something softer. Pity. Not for Anson himself, but for the entire world, this whole rotten state of human affairs, first war and now this. You can't win anymore. You can't get ahead. You shouldn't even try.

"I told myself it would be all right," Anson says. "I made a bargain with myself, that if I kept you from harm, kept the closest possible watch over you, then it didn't matter that I was deceiving you. That the ends were noble enough."

"And *I* wasn't, I guess. Noble enough."

"That's not true. You're the noblest part of this whole business, Miss Kelly. The only one of us worth the trouble."

I lift my head from his chest and squint at the tip of his nose. "The trouble of what?"

"Redeeming." He says the word without the customary irony. Calm and reverent, like he actually believes in such things.

"And what if I don't want redemption? Saints never do have any fun, it seems to me. Never know any earthly joy."

"That depends on what you mean by joy, doesn't it?"

I lift myself a little more, so my face is next to his, and my breath and his breath curl together in the darkness. "I don't know. What do *you* mean by joy, Mr. Anson?"

He makes a little noise in his throat.

I place my bare hand on his cheek. The skin is warm and springy beneath my palm. A little scratchy, if I care to stroke my fingers against the wedge of his jaw. Strange how I can feel his skin, while I can't quite see his face. I run my thumb along the seams until I find the corner of his mouth. The blankets have fallen away from my shoulders. The boat sways around us, the stars wobble on high.

"Here's what I think, Mr. Anson," I whisper. "I think that if you're lucky enough not to get your head bashed in by some lunatic bootlegger, lucky enough to survive another day in this brute modern world, lucky enough to be sitting inside the measure of somebody's warm arms at the bottom of a boat where nobody can find you, where you're safe from harm for just one *moment* at the end of a terrible day—"

Anson leaps to his feet. Gin goes *kerplop* against the deck.

"Stay down!" he shouts, and the motor growls to life, and that's when I realize there's another sound buzzing in, another motor drawing near, and as the boat rears up and shoots across the water, the air explodes into *pop-pop-pop-pop-pop:* the wicked noise of a Chicago typewriter beating hell out of somebody near.

9

Of course I've got no intention of obeying Anson's command. I climb on my hands and knees and start to rise up, and his hand comes down on the center of my back and presses me in place.

"I said stay down!"

The motorboat starts to bank into a turn. I sink down low where he can't reach me and crawl to the back of the cockpit, or whatever you call it, and prop myself up on the seat behind Anson's. Just sort of poke my head over the parapet while the boat skips crazily beneath me and the unseen chopper spits out its rapid *pop-pop-pop-pop-pop-pop* like a mouthful of nails.

At first, I can't see anything on that dark water, except the faint glimmer of the lights on shore, bobbing up and down against the horizon of the boat's stern as we tear the sea apart. And then I recognize that the particular flash of one particular light represents the *pop-pop-pop* firing of that Thompson submachine gun, and that it weaves back and forth across the phosphorescence of our wake, nimble as a water bug, droning like a skeeter.

"Who is it?" I scream over my shoulder.

Anson doesn't answer. I guess he's too busy steering

this beast of ours through the night air. The noise of the engine builds and builds, the deck slants at an unnerving angle. The force of our speed presses against my skin, weighing down my arms and legs as I creep back upward to the front of the cockpit, anchoring myself on the seats.

"Where's your gun?"

"What?"

"Your gun!"

"Just get *down*, Gin!"

He must have a holster, right? Surely no special agent of the Bureau of Internal Revenue—present or former—goes anywhere without some kind of insurance policy underwritten by the likes of Smith and Wesson, and especially not to a place like this, crawling with bootleggers and gangsters and pirates of every stripe. I run my hands up under his overcoat, ignoring his shout of outrage. Find the edge of his jacket and reach up under that.

"Gin!"

Superfine waistcoat. Buttons. Abdomen twisting away from my touch.

"Hold still, will you?"

"For God's sake! Get down."

"Aha! There it is!"

I slide gun from leather. Work the object back

down under jacket and overcoat and into the open air. Anson makes an angry noise. Takes one hand off the wheel to make a grab for the gun, but that kind of maneuver's easily avoided, if you've been reared up in the company of three hillbilly brothers like I have. I turn about and take a second or two to weigh the revolver in my two hands—a .38 Special, and I hope to God it's loaded—and I stagger back down to my previous post and aim the gun over the edge of the cockpit.

Now, as you no doubt recollect, my stepfather don't hold with guns, not even the kind you use to stalk down a deer in the woods or shoot a plump new bird from the sky. He never did enjoy a spell of hunting like the rest of the River Junction menfolk. He professed a love for animals in a state of nature, you see, and the thought of spoiling all that noble fur and keen muscle by the unjust advantage of human machine made him sick to his stomach. He did begrudgingly consent to the raising of dumb livestock, which he butchered himself with a long, sharp knife, but he would not hunt an animal in the wild, not ever, not beast nor fowl nor even fish, and not once did he allow the barrel of a gun to invade the threshold of his house and his land beyond it.

But my brothers, now. My brothers found themselves more susceptible to the allure of a bolt-action
rifle or a long-barreled shotgun or a short, loud pistol.
Around the kitchen table, they did nod their heads
wisely while Duke held forth on the abomination of
shooting God's creatures, but in the woods with their
friends, why, they showed no such tender scruples.
And before I left for the convent, I knew the smooth
texture of a rifle's stock beneath my arm, and the calm
that settles over you as your finger caresses the curve
of the trigger. Not that I especially enjoyed hunting
for prey—I shot at made-up targets in the wood, or
at objects launched in the air for that purpose, not
any living thing—but because of the sensation of
power a gun conferred upon me. I might be a weak
female, born wanting the heft and muscle and timbre
of a man, but I surely could kill him, if I needed to. I
surely had the advantage over a fellow, if I held a gun
and he did not. If I had the resolve to aim the barrel
and press the trigger before he had the opportunity to
touch me.

I haven't felt the shape of a gun in my two hands
for many summers, but it's the kind of thing you never
quite forget. Once done, always remembered. I don't
bother to check that Anson's revolver is loaded; I can

tell by its weight that it is. Just close one eye and settle my soul on that dancing, erratic flash before me, and then, when I find the rhythm of the motorboat's thrust, sense the pause in its motion before it plunges back down, I do squeeze that trigger in the loving embrace of my right index finger.

Gun fires *BANG*. Kicks back like an angry child. Shout comes out across the water, and the *pop-pop-pop* stops dead. The flash winks out.

I call back over my shoulder, "Think I got him!"

Anson swears. The boat starts a sudden turn to the right, banking so hard that I teeter sideways and collapse on the other seat.

"Hey! What's the big idea? Didn't I just shoot the bastard for you?"

Anson swears again, and the word is so uncharacteristic of him that I actually turn and look out past the bow.

And that's when I hear a shout out over the water, and perceive the regular flashing of a large, determined lamp. The boom of an official gun. The motorboat slows in defeat, and while I am no expert in these affairs, I reckon I know the arm of the law when it clasps me to its chest.

And unless God Almighty now descends from the sky to intervene, the jig is right enough up.

10

Obedient to the orders of the United States Coast Guard officer calling us through a wooden cone, we fall under the lee of the gray-painted cutter and await further instruction.

"Should I ditch the gun?" I whisper to Anson.

He fiddles with wheel and throttle. Maneuvers us close. "Give it to me," he says, and I hand the revolver to him behind his back. He tucks it into the pocket of his overcoat and hails the deck of the cutter in a voice that knows no master.

"Special Agent Marshall, Bureau of Internal Revenue! In pursuit of known subject."

"*Marshall?*" I whisper. (Anson replies with a dig to my ribs.)

"By whose authority?" somebody replies.

"My own, damn it!"

There is a brief silence. I have the impression of profound professional annoyance, like when a girl from the typing pool in the commercial loans department takes it upon herself to point out some error made by the typing pool in the investment banking department, under such public circumstances that nobody can pretend it didn't happen.

A slight commotion ensues. Somebody shouts down a maritime instruction, Greek to me, and Anson brings the motorboat to rest right next to the painted steel hull of the Coast Guard boat. Blood goes whoosh in my veins. Nerves sing out under the premonition of trouble.

"What in the hell are you doing?" I whisper. "We could outrun them in this thing, I'll bet."

"And they'll be searching for us all night and all the next day."

"But now they'll arrest us for certain!"

"Just let me do the talking, all right? Don't say a damn word."

He must mean it, or he wouldn't have added that telltale *damn*. A regular blossoming garden of profanities this evening, our Anson. I clam up and cross my hands behind my back. Try not to shiver in the sharp air. The blankets lie in a heap at my feet, like an abandoned nest, once warm, and for an instant I ache all over. Most especially in the kisser.

Marshall. What kind of game's he playing now?

A series of metallic bangs strikes my ear as a rope ladder uncurls against the cutter's hull. A moment later, a pair of legs descends along that ladder, topped by a dark coat and an officer's hat. The legs spring deftly from the bottom of the ladder into our snug little motorboat cockpit, and somebody shines down a flashlight from above, revealing a dark mustache attached to a middle-aged face, not best pleased.

"A Revenue agent, you say? Where's your badge?"

"Right here, sir."

To my great amazement, Anson unbuttons his overcoat without hesitation and reaches inside his jacket. Hands the officer a piece of paper.

"Marshall, you say?"

"Yes, sir. Oliver Marshall, New York Bureau."

The officer motions to me. "Who's this?"

"Civilian deputy. She's been assisting me with an investigation."

"Name?"

"Can't reveal that, sir. I'm afraid you'll have to appeal to the Bureau. And if everything's in order, we'd like to return to our pursuit, although I suspect our man has already got away."

The officer's gaze shifts from me to Anson's badge to Anson's face. To me again, sharp and kind of narrow, in the manner of a predatory bird. (You know the look.) Says dryly: "Seemed to me as if *you* were the one being pursued, agent."

Anson replies in kind. "As you may have noted, sir,

the fellow happened to be in possession of a Thompson submachine gun, with which he proceeded to fire upon us. My colleague had just returned fire and struck the gunman."

"That was *her*?"

"Yes, sir. She's an expert marksman."

"Well. The night is full of surprises."

I dig my fingernails into my palms and knit my lips firmly together, just like Sister Esmeralda taught me to do when my mouth threatens to get the better of me.

"I assure you," says Anson, "this woman is one of the Bureau's most trusted and valuable associates. I can think of no other partner I would rather have by my side on a dirty night like this."

The officer frowns. The old moon's disappeared, gone behind a cloud or something, and the cutter's light is harsh on the ridge of his brow. He holds his balance on the small, bobbing deck without thought or effort. Leather hands still clutching that Bureau badge of Anson's.

"Look," Anson says, "it's been a hard night, and we've already lost our man. I've got to get back to port and make my report. And boy, am I going to get hauled over the coals for this one."

"You should have let us know you were carrying

out an operation in these waters. It's our watch, out here."

"I'm sorry about that. Began in spontaneous pursuit and turned into a damned ambush. I'm just sick to death of these fellows slipping through our fingers, that's all."

He says this so sincerely, so brimful of professional dejection, I almost believe him myself. The officer glances back at me, and I assume an air of identical world-weary regret.

"You really did shoot that bootlegger, from a racing speedboat?" he asks.

"I surely did, sir. On the first try. Learned how to aim a gun from my brothers, out the western side of Maryland."

He shakes his head and hands the badge back to Anson. His fingers find the buttons of his thick woolen overcoat.

"Shame on you, Marshall," he says, taking off that rich garment and laying it over my shoulders, "letting a lady shiver like this without thinking to offer her your coat. What the hell kind of gentleman are you?"

"I've often wondered that myself," I say demurely.

The officer steps back to the rope ladder and places his hands on the rungs. Moon comes out again, touching his cap as he turns his head over his shoulder, chin just edged against the cutter's hull.

"Carry on, then, Marshall. Sorry for any inconvenience."

11

You never told me you were an expert marksman," Anson says as we shoot out over the water, away from the twinkling lights of Rum Row and the diminishing shadow of the Coast Guard.

"I thought you already knew everything about me."

"Not everything. Not a thing like that."

"Well, now you know. Where are we headed, anyway? Back to New York?"

"That depends on what you mean by New York."

"I mean the city, of course."

"Then no. We're not going back to the city. City's too hot for us right now. I'm taking you somewhere safe."

"Oh, brother," I say. "Long Island again."

"Again?"

"It's a complicated story. I'll tell you sometime. Say,

that reminds me. What gives with that badge of yours? Taking Billy's name like that."

He doesn't reply. The motorboat's skimming along at a fair clip, headed for the glimmering shore of Long Island, Rum Row parked to our right, and a wave smacks our bottom, sending us airborne for a second or two. We land with a hard bump, and Anson grunts.

"You all right?" I ask.

"Fine."

He grips the wheel and lifts the throttle a bit more, and I start to wonder just how much juice we have left in the can, racing along like this, gulping down gasoline in such a reckless fashion. The geography of Long Island is gray to me, but I guess we're some distance to the east, hurtling toward shore at an acute sort of angle. Anson shows no hesitation in his navigation, no veering whatsoever from our course. He tilts forward as if that might somehow increase our speed, as if by narrowing his eyes and clenching his stomach, say, he might propel our slim, aggressive craft into safe harbor. Safe harbor, some cottage on Long Island, except this time, when I imagine a cottage like that, snug inside the walls of somebody's grand estate, or else tucked into the lee of some fishing village, some farm, some anything, I don't feel that ache in my chest as I felt in Glen Cove. I feel something else. Some kind of warmth. Some kind of lightening of the blood. I stuff my fingers into the pockets of my Coast Guard overcoat and listen to the thud of my heartbeat against the rip of the engine, and a rare somnolence settles over me. Like on that terrible day when I ran across the wet grass from the old fishing hole and boarded the next train out of River Junction, and no sooner did I fall into the clasp of that ungentle seat, and experience the surge and the thrust of a steam locomotive bearing me to safety, than I went to sleep. I slept right the way to Baltimore, and a conductor had to wake me up so I might not miss the connection to New York, and I remember how, for an instant upon waking, I did not know where I was. I could not have said my own name. Only that I was bound for Manhattan, I was fixing to plunge myself straight into the bosom of the wicked city and never come out again. That was all I knew. The horrors of the hour before, why, they had buried themselves, as I slept, under the kind of rich, foot-thick cushion of unconscious thought that would do any psychiatrist proud.

And it's the same thing now. That sharpness that overcomes your mind in moments of peril, the perfect acuity that guides your ideas and your actions when your life's at stake, it just wears away as we race for safety on the Long Island shore. Slides from my skin like an old coat. The horror of the previous hour replaced by something that is nothing at all.

12

Anson wakes me when we reach land, or maybe the land wakes me all on its own. I open my eyes to the changing rhythm of the engine, the boat maneuvering into some kind of port. Sky still black and cold, moon somewhere behind us. Man beside me says *Welcome back.*

I uncurl my stiff body from its strange position and try to summon back the shades of memory. A blanket slides from my chest. "Welcome back to what?"

"You've been out cold."

"Since when?"

"Since about three minutes after we parted company with the Coast Guard."

Coast Guard.

Of course. Big boat, small Ginger. Fear like a bucket of ice emptying on your chest. And something else. Something so terrible you can't even think about it just now. You need to think about present needs, just this one moment you're living now, or else you'll never make it. Black night, strapping warm fellow leaping from boat to dock, carrying a rope.

Anson.

I place my hand on the hull's edge and push myself upright. He secures the rope to a piling and holds out his hand, gloved in leather. The strength of his grasp startles me. "Watch the edge," he says, low and rumbly, and I suffer my legs to leap.

"Where are we?" I ask. Marveling at the solid way about the boards beneath my feet.

"Southampton, New York."

"And what's in Southampton, New York?"

"A place I know where we can lie low for a bit, until I've figured out our next move." He's working a knot into the rope, and there's something a little wrong with his movement, something I can't quite pin down. He finishes and turns to me. "Don't worry, you'll be safe here. I know the owners."

"Oh, brother."

"What do you mean?"

"Nothing. And these owners, they won't mind our tramping through the gardens at midnight?"

Anson consults his watch. "It's only ten o'clock, as a matter of fact. And no, she won't mind."

"*She?*"

"*Me,* I presume."

The woman's voice shoots through the darkness from the edge of the dock, causing us both to jump. Anson's left hand catches my elbow, and again I'm struck by the strange notion that something's gone wrong in the regular operation of his knobs and spindles, something's not quite right, but the notion's overcome by the sight of the woman now striding up the dock toward us like a bizarre, moonlit ghost, dressed in a white bed gown trimmed by long, downy feathers.

"Hello, Mother," Anson says, calm and clear as you please, just before he topples straight forward onto the planks.

13

Well, I won't bore you with all the details. How, between the two of us, we manage to convey him—protesting at every step—to what Mrs. Anson calls the *pool house;* how she lifts the receiver of the telephone inside the foyer of said building and asks the operator for a Dr. Somebody, exhibiting all the urgency of a woman making an appointment with her decorator, while I unwrap the overcoat—which I now perceive to be badly torn under the left sleeve—from her son's body. How I discover a neat charcoal-gray suit jacket wet with blood; how he mumbles at me not to make such a fuss. How I swear and yell that I'll make all the damned fuss I want; how I run for the kitchen and fill a bowl with hot water and return to find the two of them, mother and son, locked in some kind of low, intense argument, from which Mrs. Anson extracts herself with the observation that her son appears to be in excellent hands, and she'll just head for the drive and wait for the doctor, so the fellow doesn't come barging right into the Big House and wake up all the staff.

"Oh, of course," I mutter, unsticking Anson's bloody shirt from his bloody skin. "For God's sake, don't wake the staff. Would you stop flinching, please?"

"She's right about that, however. Can't have anyone talking."

"Lord Almighty. Liketa bled to death, and your own mama can't think but for the gossip?"

"Not because of gossip. Because of our safety. And I'm not bleeding to death. Bullet just grazed my ribs, that's all."

"How do you know?"

"I already checked."

Sure enough, a thoroughly red handkerchief falls free as I unwrap the last of his clothing. I set the gory thing aside—Mrs. Anson can spare a dime or two for new upholstery, I do reckon—and fish the cloth from the bowl of warm water.

"Poor Gin," he says softly. "I expect you've seen enough blood for one evening."

"Think nothing of it. I was reared up with a mess of boys. I don't ever faint at the sight of blood."

"No. But I'm sorry nonetheless."

"Are you actually apologizing to me for getting shot?"

"For all of it, I guess."

"Well, in that case," I say, busying myself with rag and water and skin so he can't form a good look at my eyes, "I expect it's a good thing we've got all night."

14

While the doctor attends his patient, I wander outside. Some things ought to be kept private, I believe, and anyway I could use a mite of air after all that reek of copper blood filling the cavities of my head. To my surprise, I am not alone. The lean, ghostly figure of Mrs. Anson frets about the stonework, smoking a cigarette.

For a moment, I imagine she doesn't notice me. I stand fixed, fingers curling by my sides, while the moon touches her profile and the top of her bare, immaculate head. She exhales a bit of a smoke and says, without turning, "How is he?"

"All right, I guess, for a fellow missing a chunk of his left side. Bullet went straight between the ribs."

"Well, that's a mercy, I suppose," she drawls. Another taste of her cigarette, and then: "You must be one of his colleagues at the Bureau."

I hesitate only an instant. "Yes."

"How lovely. Do you enjoy your work, Miss . . . ?"

"Kelly."

"Miss Kelly. Do you enjoy all of this? Running around New York with my son, capturing gangsters and getting shot and all that sort of thing?"

"Not particularly. I'm more in the amusement line, myself."

She laughs harshly. "Are you? A girl after my own heart, then. I suppose I ought to ask you how you got into the enforcement business, in that case, but at this hour of the night I frankly don't care. Adventure, no doubt. You young things are all terribly mad for adventure."

"Adventure. That's it."

She turns at last, and I wish I could see her face properly, because I have some idea that she must be beautiful. She's the kind of woman who carries an air of beauty around her, carefully cultivated, like a waft of rare oil. Delicate and chiseled. Skin as marble in the moonlight. The smoke trails from the end of her cigarette, and she shakes her precious head and says, "Just like Ollie. First football, and now this. Smoke?"

I start to decline, but my lips tingle. "Why not?"

She pulls a silver case from the pocket of her dressing gown and tosses it to me. "Never have sons, Miss Kelly. They're nothing but trouble. You take the most tender care of those little limbs, and then they go off into the world and spend the rest of their lives trying to break them."

"Girls find other ways of getting into trouble."

"Yes, they do." She watches me fumble with cigarette and match. There's a bit of light glowing from what Anson called the *Big House,* a hundred or so yards away, and maybe it's just enough to pick me out, there in the country midnight. Just enough to see me by. She goes on, more softly: "I have a daughter, too. Just two years old now. I expect she'll prove a great deal of trouble when she's older. But my oldest son went to war and died of the 'flu, and Ollie seems determined to get himself killed even more pointlessly. At first I thought he should break his neck on the football field. When he finished Princeton intact, more or less, I thanked God—"

"I'm sorry. Did you say *Princeton?*"

"Yes. He graduated, oh, I suppose it's four years ago, and instead of taking a nice safe job in a bank or a place at law school, like any sensible boy, he tells me he's going to work for the Prohibition agency. Can you imagine? *My* son, enforcing temperance. The irony." She laughs again. "He was in Florida first, chasing all those fellows running rum from Nassau, and then they sent him back to New York, and there isn't a day, Miss Kelly, not a day or a night I don't worry about him turning up on my doorstep, dripping blood from some wound or another. Of course, I never expected him to bring a woman home with him."

I've been drifting in bemusement, smoking fiercely, ever since the word *Princeton* crossed those elegant lips, delivered in an accent that reminds me of the Bryn Mawr girls, mouths all stuffed with marbles. The sharpness of her last sentence yanks me back to the present. "Why not?" I ask.

"Because he's such a monk, you know. Tommy, he squired about every deb in town, he was in *such* demand. Darling, charming, golden boy. But Ollie. There never was such a serious child. Even worse since Tommy died. He worshipped Tommy, of course, but the two of them couldn't have been more unlike. Ollie couldn't stand parties. All those girls in white dresses. They threw themselves at him, of course—girls adore all that dark tragedy—but he never paid them the slightest attention. Never brought anyone home, that is. First football consumed him, and now this." She drops the end of her cigarette into an urn of some kind. "Listen to me. I suppose you're hungry and that sort of thing. I'll make up sandwiches. Cook's gone to bed, poor dear. Ham or chicken?"

"Chicken," I say.

She turns toward the Big House and pauses. "You know, I believe I rather envy you."

"You shouldn't."

"No, it's true. I might have liked a little adventure, when I was your age. Instead I got *this*." She gestures. "And you've got my Ollie."

"He's your son. He loves you."

"Yes, he's awfully loyal. The kind of boy who would die to protect you. Would take anything upon himself to lighten your own burden. But I never quite felt as if we understood each other properly. My fault, I suppose. It's always the mother's fault, isn't it?"

"That's what the shrinks say."

"It's a terrible burden. Poor Ollie. He arrived so soon after Tommy, whom I worshipped. And then there was Billy, who was my last, my baby, until Claire was born, and Billy was so much more . . . more . . . oh, he has a sweetness to him, my Billy, for all his mischief. But Ollie. So quiet and grave and orderly. Kept his room neat as a pin, even as a child. You could see he was thinking huge, fierce thoughts behind those eyes, but of course he wouldn't tell you about them. Music, that was what he liked. That was how he told you things."

"Plays a fine clarinet."

"He plays everything. Piano, trumpet. Used to practice for hours, until he discovered football. And I never tried, you see, I never tried hard enough. Tommy and Billy, they were so much easier to love. Now it's your turn to try. Imagine. A sharp-chinned redhead from— where *are* you from, Miss Kelly? You're certainly not one of us."

She says the word *us* with such a note of strange disgust, I don't take insult. Instead, I say simply, "Maryland."

"From Maryland. Well. I suppose Ollie wasn't going

to fall in love with a debutante. Take good care of him, please. He really is rather tender on the inside, I believe, though he hates to show it."

She starts to move away, toward the house, skirting the dark form of what I believe to be the swimming pool. Her fine, pale feathers shiver in the draft, like the hair of a Persian cat.

I call out after her, "Thank you, Mrs. Anson!"

She starts and stops. Turns her shapely head to the moon. "Anson?"

And maybe I said that on purpose. Maybe I called out the name Anson as a test, because I already knew what she would say. Maybe I'm expecting what comes next, the way you expect a wave to crash upon the beach, after watching it build and build to a mighty crest offshore. My stomach is sick, my eyes a little blurred. My head still turning her words over and over, sorting them into some kind of order.

"Yes," I say firmly. Sort of desperately. "Anson."

And she answers me as if she's been expecting something like this. As if she's playing a part, as if she's been guiding me homeward all along. Voice gentle and sure and terribly, terribly weary.

"Anson is Oliver's *middle* name, Miss Kelly. After the great naval captain. Didn't he tell you? Our family name is Marshall."

15

I stand there, smoking my cigarette outside the pool house, for some time. Until the cigarette's finished and the moon drops behind the roof. The door opens, the doctor appears. "Miss Kelly?" he says, squinting into the darkness.

"Right here."

"Ah. I've bandaged him up. Nasty gash he's got. I've given him brandy—"

"I beg your pardon. Did you say you've given him *brandy?*"

"For medicinal purposes, of course," he says in a tone of slight offense. "It's perfectly legal, you know."

"And he drank it?"

"Why, yes."

"Lord Almighty. How much?"

"Four ounces. He wouldn't take more." Aggrieved sigh. "I hope it will help him sleep. A good night's rest is *essential.* I've left another eight ounces on the nightstand. He should have another two ounces in the morning."

"I'll see to it personally, doctor."

"And no exertion of any kind, Miss Kelly. We can't have that bandage becoming dislodged. He lost a great deal of blood, a great deal. You may give him another two ounces if he becomes restless."

"With the greatest pleasure."

He seems to be peering at me, underneath the brim of his hat. I link my hands modestly behind my back.

"Yes. Well. Rest if you can, Miss Kelly. It may be a long night. You may ring me on the telephone, of course, if there's any change. Any difficulty whatsoever."

"Of course."

He makes a gruff noise in the back of his throat and wishes me good night. I wait until his shadow disappears into the maw of the Big House before I straighten away from the giant stone container against which I'm leaning and slip through the doorway into the pool house.

I'll say this about the rich: they know how to live. I judge this building is designed for summer entertainment, if the wicker furniture is any indication, to say nothing of the absence of any source of central heat. Large parlor, lined with French doors. White, sanitary new kitchen to the side. Bathroom of bright clean tile. In contrast, the bedroom's small and made for napping— or possibly something else that has nothing to do with a good night's sleep—containing only an armchair and what I believe they call a daybed, done up in white sheets and a counterpane of blue-and-white toile. Summery and feminine and much in contrast to the man who sits stiff beneath that counterpane, propped by pillows, thick chest altogether bare except for the wide white gauze swathing his ribs. I find myself a hollow next to his left knee. He gazes warily at me.

"You could use a shave," I say.

He lifts his right hand and touches his jaw. "I apologize," he says, without a hint of irony.

"I suppose, on an ordinary night, you'd have shaved before dinner. A good, thick beard like you have. Isn't that right?"

"Usually I do, yes."

"Is there a razor in the bathroom?"

"I expect so. But—"

I rise and fix my stride for said bathroom, and when I return with soap and towel and razor and hot water, the wariness in his navy eyes has transformed into horror. "Don't you worry," I tell him, busying brush into soap. "I have three brothers. I can surely shave a man's chin, when I must. And this is a fine new steel safety razor, besides. You couldn't cut yourself if you tried. Just you lean back against those pillows, Mr. Anson, and allow me to do the rest."

For good measure, I press the tips of my fingers into his right shoulder, and he obeys me. Sinks his back against the pillows and aims his gaze at the ceiling as I swirl suds over the planes of jaw and chin. The shaving soap's of a fine, expensive grade, producing rich lather that smells of bergamot or something. I never was good at perfume, never could certainly tell the scent of one rare substance from the scent of another. The bedside lamp casts a quiet glow over all that skin, his face and his neck and his beautiful wide shoulders. I don't know how he endures the chill like that, without a shiver nor even a goose bump. The air's so heavy and cold, you could almost put out your hand and lift it.

"You don't look much like your mother," I observe. "So delicate and pretty as she is."

"Thanks very much."

"You're something else. I don't know what it is. All squares and blocks and dark angles. Did you get that from your father?"

"Not really. My father's fair. Elegant, like her."

"So you're a throwback of some kind. Barbarian ancestors. Reckon that's why you liked football so much, isn't it? My brother Johnnie's like that. Lives for football."

He flinches. I take his chin in my left hand and lift the razor in my right. Commence to stroke his cheek in long, sure movements. "Your mother told me," I say. "Mothers do spill all the beans, don't they? I guess

Mama spilled more beans in the past five minutes than you've spilled in all these weeks I've known you. How you played football for Princeton, for example, and then joined the agency after graduation. Something to do with your brother's death, I think. Another golden boy, your brother, just like Papa. And you were the dark, silent one. Murder on the football field. Despair of debutantes everywhere. The exact opposite of— what was his name, again?"

"Tommy."

"Tommy. I'm awfully sorry about all that. Poor Anson, losing a brother like that, when you was scarce more than a kid yourself. I truly am sorry."

He doesn't say a word. Just stares a hole in the ceiling and endures the way I rasp carefully along the line of his cheeks, his jaw, his chin, his neck. Orderly rows, uncovering his skin from its thick layer of foam, one stroke at a time. His breath smells of warm brandy. His thick lashes lie dark against his eyelids, so near I could count them. Study each gold tip.

"But you have another brother, don't you? A younger brother."

"Yes," he whispers.

"Let me guess. The young lad's still in college. Your own alma mater, in fact. The good old orange and black. All the men in your family go to Princeton. Don't they, Anson?"

"Yes. Generally speaking."

I dip the handsome silvery razor into the bowl for the last time and swish, swish. His face lies before me, immobile, still flecked with soap. There is this beautiful golden cast to his skin, this pink freshness blooming in his cheeks, and he is so young and ancient, both at once, so raw and beautiful and sort of pure, making me think of water running over stone, like when I was young and rambled by myself in the hills around River Junction, and there was nothing but me and the mountainside and the rush of fallen rain hurtling down the stream beds. A state of nature. State of grace. My throat aches. I rise and carry the bowl to the bathroom, where I rinse it out and fill it with hot water. Sink the towel inside. Return and set the bowl on the nightstand and wring the hot cloth in my hands. I can feel Anson's gaze upon my face as I capture his jaw. His breath on my skin, smelling so opulently of brandy.

"You might have told me you were Billy's brother," I say.

"I couldn't take that chance."

"Why not? Were you afraid I'd tell you to go to hell?"

"No. I was afraid you might tell someone else. Let the fact slip. And then my brother would be in danger. My parents would be in danger."

"Danger? What kind of danger?"

"Because your stepfather understands the importance of family, Miss Kelly. If he knew I was still on the case, knowing where I came from . . ."

I lift the towel away, wiping his chin as I go. Peer this way and that, as if inspecting my handiwork, when really my heart is smacking hard inside the cavity of my chest. My breath is coming in short, shallow bursts. I look up at last and find his eyes, and there's an odd, unsteady quality to his gaze, a warmth I don't recognize, and I remember he's just had four ounces of perfectly legal medicinal spirits poured down his throat by a doctor, though he is lately but a stranger to the consumption of liquor.

"So. You were afraid I'd blow your cover. Is that the only reason?" I say.

"I don't know what you mean."

"Yes, you do. You know exactly what I mean."

He closes his eyes.

"Tell me something," I say. "When did I come in? Was it the chicken or the egg? Did you discover me because of Billy, or was it the other way around?"

"Does it matter?"

"I don't know. Maybe it does."

He opens his eyes again. "Can you really think," he says slowly, "I've only known of you since January?"

"I've only known of *you* since January."

We are awfully close, he and I, there on that bed. My left leg presses against his right. The towel grows cold in my hand, dampening my skirt. Takes all my strength to sit still, locking eyes with this man, absorbing the warmth of his breath, the thrum of his blood rushing under his skin. This knowledge laying itself upon me, waiting to be understood.

He speaks hoarse, like something's gone wrong with his throat. "They assigned me to the Kelly case last spring. Found my way to you by summer. But I couldn't—it wasn't right, drawing you inside, when you were innocent of it all. The more I learned about you, the more I discovered I just couldn't use you like that. Couldn't risk you. I thought I'd find another way. I would track down every shipment, every payment. Go in with my best men."

"And your men got killed. And you got canned."

"Yes."

"And in the meantime, I met Billy. Coincidence?"

"It wasn't *my* choice."

"Then whose was it?"

"Julie, I guess," he says bitterly.

"Julie *Schuyler?* But how do you—"

Another silence falls upon us as I end that sentence that doesn't really need ending. Because of course he knows Julie Schuyler. Why, Marshalls and Schuylers are practically related, aren't they? Live on the same avenues, shop at the same uptown department stores, dine at the same restaurants, belong to the same clubs. When Julie Schuyler came out into society in a floating white dress at a grand party at the Ritz-Carlton or someplace, Oliver Marshall's name no doubt appeared on the dance card that dangled from her precious wrist. And when Special Agent Anson needed a little help tracking down a certain wayward stepdaughter of an Appalachia bootlegger, and discovered a connection between a certain indecent Redhead and same, and furthermore discovered a connection between that indecent Redhead and the thoroughly decent Miss Schuyler, why—

Well, that sentence hardly needs ending, does it?

Anson says softly, "When I saw you leaving that party together—"

"What party?"

"At Julie's place."

"You were there?"

"Yes, of course."

"But I didn't see you!"

"I didn't want to be seen. Anyway, I could see Billy was enamored. I didn't blame him, I guess."

"You should have said something. You should have introduced yourself."

"You know I couldn't. It was fair and square, your going off with Billy. I had no right."

"I'll say you had a right. You've got a right right now."

He doesn't reply. Just looks at me with those steady eyes, sometimes navy blue and sometimes almost slate, now strangely green in the yellow light of the lamp. His pupils are dilated, black and round. Maybe it's the pain of his wound, maybe it's the liquor that was supposed to make it better.

"Does it hurt?" I whisper, and he nods a little.

I lean for the nightstand and the medicinal brandy left behind by the good doctor. "Just a little more," I say, unscrewing the cap, pouring out a wee dram.

"No, thank you."

"Doctor's orders. He told me himself. Two more ounces. Perfectly legal."

He frowns. I press the glass to his lips. Possibly there are more than two ounces inside; I don't know. I never was any good at estimates of such kind.

"Be a good boy," I say, "and take your medicine."

His lips part. He lifts his hand to support the glass. When the liquor hits the back of his throat, he winces a little, and then his whole face sort of relaxes, like he's gone to heaven and seen his Lord before him, shimmering in holy raiment. Empties the glass. I pry it from his fingers and suggest that wasn't so bad, now, was it? Makes you feel a bit better, when your side's been cut open by a bootlegger's bullet?

"Yes," he says. Eyes still closed.

I lean forward to whisper in his ear. "You're at my mercy. Half-sauced as you are. All bound up in nice white bandages."

"Ginger . . ."

"I like Billy. He's a dear boy. But I'm not in love with him, and I never was."

"He's in love with *you.*"

"It's over. He'll find some other girl, a much nicer girl than me. We'll all have a good laugh about it, when we're eighty."

"What are you doing?"

"Taking off my blouse and skirt. You don't mind, do you?"

"Ginger . . ."

"And my stockings. Can't sleep in those."

"Sleep?"

I clamber carefully over his legs, the way you would clamber over a pair of felled trees, and find the edge of the counterpane. "It's bedtime, Anson, and there's only one bed. You wouldn't want me to sleep in that old armchair, would you? Why, my neck'd liketa break, all bent out of shape like that."

"But it's—it's—"

"Indecent? Improper?"

He takes my wrist. "Don't make me say it."

"Say what, Anson? I've still got my knickers on, haven't I? You surely don't think I mean to *seduce* you, in your drunken state. I have my standards."

At the word *seduce,* he releases my wrist like you might release a hot cinder from a bonfire. And *bonfire:* that's another word, all right, a good word for the temperature underneath this counterpane of elegant blue toile. Anson's eyes are shut, his hands now folded behind his head in a sort of self-entrapment. My camisole is made of silk and peaches, the brassiere beneath rather less frivolous. I take advantage of my companion's momentary blindness to remove it. You can imagine the discomfort of a brassiere like that, meant to confine one's natural bounty into fashionable adolescence. I lean over Anson to drop the old thing off the edge of the bed, and then I grasp his upright shoulders with my two hands.

"Ginger," he whispers. Kind of slurry.

"Now, just you lie down, nice and easy. You need your sleep, after a day like this. Gently does it. That's the way."

He mumbles about how I'm trying to kill him, how we shall both burn in hell or some kind of thing, while I ease him down the pillows into a more or less horizontal predicament. His chest is heavier than I expect, his shoulders like boulders under my hands. I arrange the pillows beneath his head. Reach across him to extinguish the lamp. Ask him how he feels, whether his wound troubles him.

"I'll do," he says.

I curl myself by his side. Trace his profile with my finger, down his forehead and along the bridge of his nose and that furrow above his lips, I forget what it's called. All by sight; I can't see his face. A pure, decent blackness cloaks us both. My camisole is silky against my skin; my breasts fall against the sheets, heavy and warm. The desire I feel for the man before me takes on a mighty power, unbreakable, like the magnetic force binding an atom together, depending not on the angles of his profile or the size of his shoulders or anything to do with his skin and bones and teeth and hair, his luminous eyes or his strong fingers, though I crave each one as you crave water to drink and air to breathe. Just him. The humanity within. That sliver of eternity bearing his name. Whatever it happens to be.

As I reach his lips, his fingers find mine and hold them in place for a terribly long time. His hot breath travels along my nerves, right bang into my solar plexus. Not a sound escapes us, such that the faint, slow pulse of the ocean actually reaches my ears through the walls of the house. The day's memories slide past, belonging to another lifetime. I cannot even summon the pity of them. Just the present. Anson and me, touching slightly, singeing each other at a few delicate points. My knees tucked up to his hip. His sternum cradling my elbow. Lips and fingers.

"He's my brother," Anson says. "My baby brother."

"It's a terrible shame."

"Practically raised him myself."

How satiny his mouth feels. His soft words forming against my thumb.

"Here's the thing," I tell him. "I'm not in love with your baby brother. I'm in love with you. And you're in love with *me*, God help you."

His head rustles the pillow. Turns toward mine, I think.

I continue: "And every baby's got to grow up sometime, doesn't he? Every baby brother needs to learn that he can't have a toy just because he wants it."

"His heart would break, Ginger. Would break in two."

Such a curious thing, lying so close to another human being, breathing his own breath as it leaves his mouth, sharing the heat of his own flesh, and yet you can't see a thing. The cold darkness blinding you from the sight of his face. Like you are babes tucked inside a single primordial womb, you are alone and naked in the middle of the universe, and there be nothing else existing outside the two of you. Not light nor life. Only truth.

I drag my hand southward to lie upon his breast.

"Lord God Almighty," I whisper. "I do swan, the only heart I care about is this one."

The heart in question thuds against my palm. The ocean sighs nearby.

He whispers, "How is it possible you can forgive me?"

"Oh, I don't know that I forgive you. That's an awful lot to ask, at the present moment. I just understand, that's all. I understand you, top to bottom."

"Ginger," he slurs softly, "you are something else."

"Aren't I, though."

"You are the berries. The cat's whiskers."

"Why, Oliver Anson Marshall, I do believe you're sauced."

"That's impossible. Only drank a drop."

"Sure you did. Don't move, now. You'll hurt yourself."

"I am already hurt, love. Can't get any worse."

His hands find the supple skin of my waist, under the camisole of silk and peaches. And we kiss.

16

I wake only once, under the slight gray arrival of dawn. The sight of Anson's sleeping face takes me by surprise; not because I've forgotten he's there, or what has gone between us during the night, but because it's the same exact face I recollect from yesterday. Hasn't altered a bit.

He stirs and opens his eyes. We meet as a pair of interested cats, sizing each other's intentions.

"How's your head?" I ask.

"Like murder."

"Your ribs?"

"Worse."

"Well, that's a shame." I draw myself close. Tuck the counterpane snug around us both. Kiss the meeting of his ribs, above the uppermost edge of the bandage. "Because I am positively berries, myself."

17

I sleep all the rest of the morning, and when I wake, Anson's gone. The sheets are cold where he ought to be. Only his scent remains trapped in the pillow, which I gather to my face to block out the brilliance of the sun through the tall French doors facing the ocean.

But a mere pillow can only comfort a girl for so long, and anyway I am beset with a fierce hunger that has nothing to do with the absent man in my bed and everything to do with the dinner I never ate last night, to say nothing of the breakfast lost from my morning. So I rise from the bed, gathering the counterpane around me, and there on the nightstand, propped against the lamp, is a note that says *Ginger* in a dear black scrawl.

(The remaining bottle of medicinal brandy, I perceive, has not been touched.)

Going into town for news. Stay here. Trust Mama.

(Then a brief space between lines, inside which I can picture him frowning, chewing on the end of the pen, pressing his thumb into his temple. Searching for words to express this delicate, newborn understanding betwixt Ginger and Anson.)

Trust me as well.
Yours, A.

18

In the living room, a plate of sandwiches rests on the cocktail table, thoroughly stale. From the look of it, Anson snatched a couple of them on his way out. I imagine Mrs. Marshall in her long, feathery dressing gown, observing the state of the door to the bedroom, setting the plate down silently. Floating back out into the night, wearing a private smile. She's that kind of woman, I do suspect.

I eat three sandwiches without stopping for breath, regardless of crumbs, and then I lean back on the sofa—counterpane still wrapped about my shoulders—and contemplate the last line of Anson's little love note.

Trust me as well.

Now, a reasonable person—you, for example—might well point out that I have no reason whatsoever to trust this man. Didn't he meet me under false pretenses? Present himself by a false name? Withhold vital facts, all for his own particular purposes? How could any girl forgive a man for such a plan of deceit as he has practiced upon me? Forgive him, moreover, in such a manner as I have done during this night, fulsome and irrevocable?

I, who have never yet trusted another human being on this earth?

I'll leave you to mull that one for yourself. In the meantime, I'll rise up from the sofa and dust the crumbs away from the counterpane—discard the counterpane entirely, for all that the air is just as chill in the early March afternoon as it was during the dead of March night—and amble back into the bedroom, naked as a shorn lamb. I'll discover my cami-knickers down the other side of the bed and slide them back into place, and I'll do the same as regards my blouse and skirt at rest on the armchair. My jacket. The overcoat given me by the Coast Guard captain. As for that instrument of torture my brassiere, I'll toss it into a drawer.

Now. I don't know about you, but I could use a cup of coffee, after all that hard work.

In the kitchen, I find a kettle and a miraculous tin of java. Boil myself a potful and pour the liquid into one of Mrs. Marshall's expensive porcelain cups, careful not to disturb the spent grounds settled at the bottom of the kettle: a trick taught me by none other than Duke Kelly himself, when I was but small. (The cup, in that case, was made of tin instead of porcelain, and lest you imagine Duke was impelled by the selfless spirit of instructing the young, let me make clear that he intended the coffee for himself.) As I sip the resulting brew, which ought to fill me with pleasure, I am invaded instead by a slow, black-edged melancholy. By the unforgiving light of day, I stare at my hand and imagine not the heart that beat underneath, a few hours ago, but the terrible blood running from the busted skull of Carl Green, and I startle in such haste, the coffee spills painfully over my knuckles and the tears follow, a regular damn flood, because I'm alone, hidden, trapped in an expensive little hut at the tip of Long Island, and I cannot see a way out, howsoever mightily I am loved inside it. Howsoever mighty the man who loves me, who has gone into town in search of news.

19

The tears do run out, however. Don't they always? You can't cry forever. I dry my face and freshen myself up in the bathroom, ignoring the bloodstained bandages in the wastebasket. Finish my coffee and hunt inside the pockets of my suit jacket until I find the small packet of papers my mama bequeathed unto me.

Yes, those. Have you forgotten? I surely haven't. I've carried them everywhere, work and play, nestled against my ribs where I can actually feel them. The only place I haven't conveyed that packet is the open air. I have not broken the string that holds the brown envelope together, nor yet read a single paragraph of what lies inside. I can't say why. Only that the thought of those words fills me with dread. The possibility of perhaps seeing my father's own hand, the contents of his private mind, his opinion on the subject of my mother and maybe even me, sets my stomach to vomit.

As I said, I can't say why.

But I do take comfort from the presence of that lump, nestled next to my heart. The square edges and stiffness of it, like a passport or a checkbook, an object that testifies to my origins and importance, to the incontestable fact that I have a father at all—or, at the very least, a flesh-and-blood fellow who took the trouble to sire me. I stare now at the brown paper, the faded red twine that binds the envelope at each edge, and the usual bile sloshes queasily in my belly.

Now, you may think that I lay claim to a long and undistinguished history of immoral dalliance, from Anatole up to the present day. I guess I can't blame you for that conclusion. After all, I'm the kind of girl who accepts money to bare her naked bounty to the gaze of thousands of strangers, aren't I? Moreover, I admitted young Billy to my bed, and now Billy's brother, and that's just the lovers I've taken the trouble to mention.

But the fact is—believe me or no—my personal roll of dishonor is less populous than the fingers of one hand. And what is more, upon every occasion except the one just past, I have paid the most rigorous attention to ensure that nothing more derives of these unions than pleasure and friendship, if you know what I mean. Why, I lived in the utmost fear for two months after my departure from River Junction, supposing I might be laid under sentence of life; I then paid utmost attention to the hush-hush chatter of the girls on their lunch breaks, learning how such a possibility might be prevented. And when I lay with Anatole that very first time, I inquired after the matter, and then I made myself explicit. I might have been naïve, but I knew where babies came from. Because why? Because that was how I came into the world, that's why. That was how my mother returned from the wicked city in a state of disgrace, and enslaved herself to the likes of Duke Kelly, to be laid out upon her rack of penance. And now, in our enlightened modern day, just about every drugstore on every corner of Manhattan Island will sell a fellow a state-of-the-art vulcanized rubber condom with no questions asked, and in that case I'll be damned if I pay for my sins as my mother did. I'll be damned if I return to River Junction in a state of disgrace, and enslave myself to the likes of Duke Kelly.

Except this past night. Except when Oliver Anson Marshall curved his broad back and hollered my name into the darkness like a man at revival, wearing nothing whatsoever but a white bandage about the middle of his chest: an omission for which I have no sensible excuse. No conceivable explanation. Only the reckless-ness that comes of tossing your heart over the moon, the audacity of love.

And maybe this act of foolish trust has something

to do with the way I pluck my fingers upon the string holding my mama's treasured papers together, like Bruno plucks his fingers upon the strings of a double bass to elicit some kind of noise. Maybe the night before gives me some inkling as to the possible innards of this plain brown envelope. Maybe I do glimpse why my mama might have acted so reckless as she did, when the century was new and full of hope, and so was she. Maybe if I part these strings and open this envelope, I will discover the story of how I came to be.

And it will be beautiful instead of squalid. Right?

20

The brown paper packet bequeathed to me by my mama contains a series of pages, all folded up snug, likely notes or letters. Certainly they have the feel of notepaper, the expensive kind, trim and glossy, each one identical to the next. There are no envelopes at all. I don't know if that's because they were lost or they were thrown away, or because they never existed at all. Maybe the United States Postal Service bore no witness to the commerce of my parents.

Now I spend too much time altogether in running my fingers over said notepaper, like I am Sherlock Holmes trying to discover somebody's age and employment and history of sickness from the quality of the stock and the angle of the folds. Sip my coffee and swallow back the bile wanting to rise from my belly. It's only a few letters, after all. A few letters written by some Manhattan cad to my poor dead mama.

I finish the coffee and unfold the topmost.

Best-beloved,

All morning I have been staring out the window, at a busy metropolitan street that cares nothing at all for my little sorrows. I can see only your darling face and your soft hair and the delicate skin of your legs which I kissed again and again in such rapture! Thank you for ever, darling girl—for the privilege you have at last afforded me—for an ecstasy more sublime than any mortal man deserves to know— for (above all else) that pure jewel with which you so generously presented me—the most fortunate man alive—a sacrifice for which I shall always honor and venerate you. I returned to the apartment—I now reserve the word home for that sweet nest I departed in such regret—as in a kind of dream. Have the flowers yet arrived? I am picturing your face as you bury your dear nose among the blooms. And then my imagination wanders into more secret gardens, and a bed upon which those flowers are artlessly strewn, and you lying atop all—your exquisite pale limbs open to my embrace—your fragrant breasts crested by petals of infinitely greater fascination. I am wild to see you again—wild to clasp you once more—wild to press my lips in worship upon your beauty! This separation of our two souls, which was once only painful, is now intolerable. This very moment, I am forming plans for our reunion—a meeting which, I promise, shall know no such cruel end as oppressed us this dawn.

I suppose, in the eyes of the self-righteous, we have done something wicked. But how can acts so sacred signify anything but goodness? God will forgive us—He must forgive us—for He alone reads our hearts and knows what is written there. On mine, there is nothing but love, now grown a thousandfold for my dearest, dearest girl, who has bound herself to me more securely than any bride. Wait for me. Believe in me.

Your own,
Tiger

The strangest feeling steals over me as I read these lines once, and then—because words like that sort of swim in your eyes, the first time—read them again. I think, first of all, *What nonsense.* Nobody writes a letter like that, certainly not anymore; words like *clasp* and *venerate* and *rapture,* ideas like *sacred* and *honor,* have been trampled over and soiled in the mud of French battlefields and modern science, and after such a terrible mucking, you cannot ever retrieve such words again, not in poetry and not in prose, not letters nor conversation.

I think, *Mama, you poor sucker.* You didn't stand a chance, did you? Not a chance against a swell fellow like that, with such language at his command. You must have thought he meant it. You must have thought he actually cared you were a virgin, that he really did imagine your innocence as a pledge of trust instead of a prize to be captured.

And then I think, Haven't I just committed the same damn act? Haven't I just fallen for a swell fellow, opened my exquisite pale limbs to his embrace, because I thought—like Almighty God Himself, I guess—I could see what was written on his heart?

I rise from the sofa and make my way to the bedroom, the bedside table, where I lift Anson's note and hold it next to the one written by the man I must presume to be my father: a man apparently known to my mama by the interesting nickname *Tiger*. The authors are likely separated by about a quarter century, so near as I can judge, and I reckon it's been a real doozy of a quarter century, because these two letters might as well belong to different eons. Different wings of a museum on the history of the epistolary arts. One trailing long vines of floral verbiage; the other one . . . well. Anson.

Nothing alike at all, except perhaps for the final lines. *Trust me. Believe in me. Yours.* The old story.

My breasts ache, my stomach churns. I sink my bottom onto the edge of the mattress, atop the twist of bedsheets and the mess of pillows. Rest my hand on the spot where Anson's head lay. Where, not twelve hours ago, hot of skin and tingling of nerve, I settled him carefully back in the comfort of his mama's pool house mattress and told him not to strain himself, not to risk those brand-new stitches holding the side of his hide together. Where I mounted high and sank him deep inside me; all in the dark, all without seeing, only *feeling* the tremor of his muscles at each fresh stroke, each beat of the rhythm that held us together. I confess I used him hard as he used me; I held his fingers to my hips and showed him how to carry us both to the shivering brink. At the instant of culmination, his ecstasy was mine. His holler of sacred joy came in chorus with my own, rising directly upward to the ears of the Almighty. And I sank down upon his slick chest, skin for skin, pant for pant, and his hands, now free, roamed over me as if in worship of this beautiful sin we had just committed, this act of trust, this sacrifice of a pure jewel, for which I would always venerate him.

Because there does exist one singular difference between my mother and me, in our reckless orisons, besides the letters our lovers wrote us afterward.

The virgin in *my* bed wasn't me.

21

At which point, the door bangs open in the living room, and I spring to my feet, drying my eyes, tossing aside my opposing letters.

"Anson!" I cry, bounding through the bedroom doorway and into the other room, where I stop so short, I liketa tumble over my own feet.

"Well, now," says the platinum goddess standing there in the sunshine. "I guess that's the last time I'll bother to give any poor girl the benefit of my well-meaning advice."

New York City, 1998

Ella felt the strangest sense of déjà vu as they throt-
tled down the Long Island Expressway, having
just parted company with the eastern edge of Queens.
Not because she'd been making this exact journey every
month for the past three years—ever since Cousin Lily
finally booted Aunt Julie out of her Gramercy duplex
for the crime of strolling through a baby shower in the
living room in order to pour herself a gin and tonic,
wearing nothing but a negligee made of sheer peach
silk—but because of something else. A memory she
couldn't quite pin down. Fleeing the city, dirty tenements skidding past the windows. A March rain clicking on the glass.

In the front seat, her mother and Aunt Viv were
talking about summer plans. Aunt Viv's youngest was
getting married over July Fourth weekend at the beach
place in East Hampton, and the two of them were
scheming to pull in as many cousins as possible for a
family reunion—*Before everybody kicks off,* Mumma

said cheerfully—that sounded as if it was going to last a week at least. The problem was accommodation. Too many cousins.

"But I don't think half of Tiny's brood will make it," Aunt Viv said. "They hardly ever do. She never should have moved to California."

"Honestly, Vivs, can you blame her? Those in-laws of hers."

"The Horrid Hardcastles. I know. But children should grow up with *family* near. It's just wrong, Schuylers heading west like forty-niners."

"Her husband's sister is out there. Plenty of cousins on *his* side."

"That doesn't count. I need more coffee. Actually, I need a Bloody Mary, but you always make me drive."

Ella's mother unscrewed the lid on the nearest Thermos. Sniffed. Replaced the lid and opened the other one. "It's your country, out here. I never liked the Hamptons."

"Speaking of family traitors."

"Well, it worked out well, didn't it? At least we didn't have to fight about who got the summer place when Mummy died." Aunt Viv held out her ceramic commuter mug, and Mumma unscrewed that lid and refilled it from the Thermos. She glanced in the rear-view mirror. "Everything all right back there, darling? You're awfully quiet."

Ella met her aunt's familiar tip-tilted blue eye in the mirror. That beautifully arched eyebrow she'd always envied. Ella's brows were thick and straight; she'd somehow missed the Schuyler genes in that respect, as in so many others. Her own eyes tilted downward at the ends, instead of upward. Hooded instead of deep-set. Only their color matched the irises of the two women in the front seat, except that her blue eyes took on a lighter shade, like someone had mixed white paint into the can. "I'm always quiet," she said. "Especially when you two glamour-pusses take the stage."

Aunt Viv smiled back in the mirror. "Oh, we're just a couple of old broads now. Aren't we, Pepper? Husbands and kids and grandkids crawling around."

"*You've* got grandkids," Mumma said.

There was a little silence. "Darling," Aunt Viv said in a low voice.

Ella turned to the Labrador sitting on the blanket beside her and caressed a pair of soft, chocolate ears. The dog looked up and sighed. There were several new gray hairs around her eyes. Ella touched them with her finger. "Poor Bundle. She's looking old."

"Like all of us, I guess," Aunt Viv said.

"Speak for yourself, Granny," said Mumma. "Ella? How's your apartment? Have you finished unpacking yet?"

"Sort of."

"Sort of. What's the latest on that dishy fellow up-stairs? The musician."

"I never said he was dishy."

"Not in so many words. Well?"

"Mumma, we're just friends. He has a girlfriend."

"And? Is he happy with her?"

"Mumma!"

"Well, is he?"

"It doesn't matter, okay? He has a girlfriend. He's off-limits."

"Darling, what a terribly sexist thing to say. As if he's just some helpless being who can't resist tempta-tion. He's got a right to make that decision on his own. To choose between the two of you."

"Yeah? And how does that make me any better than the women Patrick slept with?"

"That was Patrick's choice."

Ella released Bundle's ears and turned to look out the window. "Anyway, I think I'm moving out, as soon as I can find another place."

"Moving out? But you just moved in! And I thought you liked it. Why on earth?"

*Because I may have lost my job. Because the build-
ing next door is probably haunted. Because I'm falling
stupidly in love with the man upstairs, and I can't seem
to stop.*

"I just realized it's not right, after all," Ella said.
"Not the right place for me."

By the time they pulled into the parking lot at the
Meadows, the rain had leveled off to a steady drizzle.
There was an ambulance out front, lights pulsing in
resignation. There was almost always an ambulance
out front at Maidstone Meadows; you pulled up hoping it wasn't intended for the person you were visiting.

Mumma and Aunt Viv both wore neat, fitted trench
coats, belted at the waist, reaching just above the knee.
Identical Thoroughbred legs shod in graceful, expensive pumps: alligator for Aunt Viv, patent leather for
Mumma. Aunt Viv extracted an enormous golf umbrella from the rear of the station wagon and put it up,
so they walked in a strange, awkward huddle to the
front door, which was automatic because of the wheel-
chairs. Inside, the smell of vegetable soup and lemon
oil rolled over them. The receptionist looked up and
smiled. "Oh, hello, Mrs. Dommerich! Mrs. Salisbury!
She's already in the private dining room, waiting for
you."

Ella was used to going unnoticed in the company of her mother and aunt. She unzipped her Barbour coat and shook out her hair, which—despite the umbrella— had managed to collect an assortment of raindrops and was already starting to crimp. Mumma bantered a bit with the receptionist while Aunt Viv stowed the umbrella in the stand and hung up her trench coat on the rack. The Meadows was that kind of place: you bantered with the receptionist, you made yourself at home. Why not? Nobody here was making do on Social Security and Medicare; you bought your own apartment and filled it with your priceless artifacts, your décor of dull, studied, elegant shabbiness. The exterior of gray cedar shingle and crisp white trim looked exactly like all the clubs and mansions in the Hamptons, such that people often mistook the Meadows for an especially roomy private residence.

Actually, Ella liked the place. If she had to admit it, she wanted to end up here one day. Everyone at the Meadows had been born in the early part of the century, had gone to war at least once, had survived depression and nukes and the death of the world as they knew it. They'd started out practically on horseback and watched men land on the moon. Now they sat, as Aunt Julie did, in reproduction Sheraton chairs while waiters served things like tomato aspic or deviled eggs or watercress soup or shrimp cocktail, followed by sirloin tips in mushroom sauce or lobster salad or calf's liver with onions. Complaining—as Aunt Julie did, in her quivering ninety-six-year-old voice—about the weakness of the cocktails.

"They came for Bitsy today," she said, nodding at the window. "Poor thing. Went just like that, right after breakfast. I expect I'm next. Remember what I told you about my navy Chanel suit, Vivian. And the pearls."

"Julie, I've said it before and I'll say it again," said Aunt Viv. "You look much better in the green."

"Also," said Mumma, "those pearls are *mine*."

"I'm not passing into eternal rest wearing imitation pearls, Pepper darling."

"You'll never know the difference."

"I *will* know," Aunt Julie said, banging the table with her skeleton fist, "and I'll haunt you both, the rest of your miserable days."

"Aren't you doing that already? Besides, darling, where *you're* going, the poor things will only burn to a crisp. Real or fake."

"Ouch," Aunt Julie said, sipping her gin.

Ella sat and listened, as she always did, listened and

observed, lifting her voice only to ask for salt or more wine. Say yes or no, chuckle on cue. Aunt Julie had her figure to maintain, so the main course was a scoop of tuna salad, heavy on the celery, served on a lettuce leaf with tomato and avocado. (Or, as Aunt Julie called it, avocado pear.) Ella and Mumma and Aunt Viv shared a bottle of white Burgundy, while Aunt Julie stuck to gin. Afterward, there was strawberry shortcake and flaccid coffee. Aunt Julie scraped up the whipped cream with her fork and said, in her old-lady vibrato, "Poor Bitsy. Her husband died eight or nine years ago. I slept with him once." She frowned and dropped another lump of sugar in her coffee. Her hand trembled. "No, twice. There was that time on the *Rotterdam*."

"I don't know how you keep track," said Mumma. "You slept with everybody."

"That may be true. But we were discreet in our day. Everything was so amicable." She looked at Ella, for the first time since the powdery kisses had been exchanged an hour ago. "Wasn't it, darling?"

"I don't know," Ella said. "Maybe it feels that way in hindsight. I don't know if poor Bitsy would agree."

"Hmph," said Aunt Julie. "Look at you. You've gained two cup sizes. You're not pregnant, are you?"

"God, no," Ella said. "It's just this jacket."

Aunt Julie looked at Ella's mother and then Aunt

Viv. "Off you go, the two of you. I've got a few things to say to my niece."

"Grand-niece," said Aunt Viv.

"*Great*-grand-niece," said Mumma.

"Honestly," said Ella, "I really don't think—"

Aunt Julie waved her hands. "Go on. Scat! And tell them to bring me a brandy Alexander, while you're twiddling your thumbs in my parlor. I have a feeling I'm going to need it."

Ella crossed her knife and fork on the plate and sat back in her chair. "Make it two," she said.

"Divorce." Aunt Julie made a sound of disgust. "Is it really necessary to do something so vulgar?"

"For God's sake, you divorced three times."

"Yes, but we could afford it. Now everybody's divorcing. It's become dreadfully middle-class, Ella." She patted her legs, which were covered in blue wool bouclé to the knee, and sheer nude panty hose below. The legs, as she was fond of saying, were the last things to go, and Aunt Julie always made the most of what she had. She dressed her lips in the same magenta she'd started wearing in 1960, and every three weeks a dutiful hairdresser visited her apartment to touch up the gold in her hair. She disdained maquillage—*at my age, it only makes you look worse*—except for a clump of mascara on each of her remaining ten eyelashes and a dusting of Max Factor loose powder all over. "Damn it all," she said, "here I am, looking for my cigarettes."

"But you don't smoke."

"Not since 1972. But I still miss them. Especially at a moment like this."

"What kind of moment is that?"

"Passing along the benefit of my vast wisdom to some young thing who probably thinks she knows better." Aunt Julie hacked out a rheumy cough and inspected the bottom of her coffee cup. "Your mumma says you caught him with his pants down."

"That pretty much sums it up." Ella paused. "Actually, they were shorts."

"Well, I'm not surprised. I knew right away he'd be slipping it elsewhere, if he wasn't already."

"What? How?"

"Darling," Aunt Julie said witheringly, "I know the type, believe me. It was somebody's wedding, when I first met him. Your cousin Margot? I think that was it. At the beach house. He was dancing with one of the bridesmaids, and I could see it, plain as day. Oh, my, yes. There are men who flirt a bit, just because they like women so much, but they don't mean any harm. And there are men who flirt with purpose, because they want to get laid."

"Aunt Julie!"

"Oh, don't be shocked. I know the difference, all right, and your Peter—"

"Patrick."

"Whatever. I wouldn't be surprised if he slept with that girl, that bridesmaid—awful lilac dress—I wouldn't be surprised if he slept with her sometime during the evening. So many dark corners on a beach at night."

Ella, who remembered that wedding well—the first time she'd brought Patrick to a family event—also remembered going looking for him at midnight, when the band picked up again after a break and started playing some Jim Morrison song that she and Patrick liked. How he emerged suddenly from the shadows near the pool, looking handsomely disheveled and bright of eye. They'd danced to the song. They'd gone back to the hotel and had hot, drunken wedding sex. Terrible hangover at brunch the next day. That was the end of June, a few months after they'd met.

Ella pushed her plate of half-eaten shortcake out of sight to the left.

"Anyway," Aunt Julie said, "you probably knew that already, if only at a subconscious level. The subconscious is terribly perceptive."

"That's not true! I was shocked when—when it happened. When I caught him last month."

"Baloney. You were in denial, that's all. But that's not my point. What *was* my point? Damn it. I had something awfully brilliant to tell you."

"Take your time."

"Don't get smart with me. You'll be old too, before you know it. Forgetting every damn thing. Some terribly wise point to make, and your thoughts all scatter at the critical moment. What were we talking about? Oh, that's right. Fidelity. It's overrated! What the hell difference does it make if he pokes his pecker where he shouldn't?"

"It makes a big difference to me."

"That's because you're young. You think everything's about sex. God knows I did. But I also know a lot about husbands. I've had three of them, for God's sake, and not one of them to grow old with, and why? Because I cut the bastards off whenever they disappointed me. Now I can't for the life of me remember what they did to disappoint. I'm sure it was awful, at the time."

"Had sex with a hooker in the stairwell of your own apartment building?"

"Oh, is that what happened? Your mumma wouldn't give me any details."

"More or less," Ella said.

"Ha. Well, I've known many happy marriages that

survived worse than that. You must know these women don't mean anything to him. God knows I never meant anything to poor Fred."

"Who's Fred?"

"Bitsy's husband, darling. It was just for fun. It was—I don't know—a little adventure to start the blood going. Some of us need that, you know. The thrill of novelty. It's got nothing to do with the sanctity of marriage."

"Aunt Julie, this is all a little—"

"I realize we old folks aren't supposed to talk about sex," she said, "but believe me, we had it. *Lots* of it. How do you think this country got so damned crowded?"

"Immigration? Immaculate conception?"

"Don't sass. But it's a funny thing, you marrying a type like that. You're supposed to marry a man like your father, aren't you? And that father of yours was never disloyal a day of his life. I don't think he ever looked at another woman, after your mumma. She was *it* for him."

"Yes. She was. She is."

"I adore your father. When's he coming to visit me again? He doesn't visit me nearly enough. And God knows there's few enough handsome men around this joint to begin with. Except Ricardo, here, bringing our brandy at last. Ricardo, I need your opinion, as a man under the age of forty, I believe. My niece here just caught her husband with another woman. A chronic condition of his, a bit like psoriasis. Should she take him back or boot him out?"

Ella put her head in her hands.

Ricardo set down Aunt Julie's brandy Alexander with a flourish, and then Ella's. He straightened his waistcoat and started taking away the dessert plates. "A pretty girl like that?" he said. "I think she must find a man who treats her right, Miss Hadley. That's what I think."

Ella waited until the door closed behind Ricardo before she tossed down her napkin, stood, and stared down at Aunt Julie's watery blue eyes. "*Aaaand* that's a wrap. You seriously had to say that?"

"Of course I did. I'm old and don't give a damn. Anyway, I find Ricardo's advice invaluable. He keeps me in touch with the times. Would you sit down, please? I've got something else I want to discuss with you."

"What is it?"

"You know, you're being terribly impolite, looming over me with that terrifying expression. Your husband was unfaithful. Like millions of other husbands. Wives, for that matter. It's not the end of the world, by any means. But if you can't live with it, divorce him quick. Get the sorry business over with and start fresh."

"You know, you're the second person in two days to give me that advice."

"So take it."

Ella crossed her arms. "I started proceedings yesterday, as a matter of fact. Mumma gave me the name of a lawyer."

"Well, then. If Mumma approves, I guess that's all there is to it. She's the one with grandkids at stake, after all. And you've got a good job, haven't you? Something to do with Wall Street, isn't it? So you can afford a little moral superiority, since you seem to want it so badly."

"Actually," Ella said, blurting really, "I've probably just gotten fired."

Aunt Julie lifted her brandy. Her eyes had gone a little soft, like she was looking into another dimension. "That's nice, dear," she said.

"Didn't you hear me? I said I'm going to be fired."

Now the eyes sharpened. "*Going* to be fired? They let you know in advance?"

"Sort of."

"But why? Why you're being fired, I mean. Not why they're letting you know."

"It's kind of complicated. It's called a conflict of interest. Except it isn't, I mean I haven't actually done anything wrong, but someone called my boss—"

"Made enemies, have you? Good girl. If you're not making enemies, you're not getting anywhere."

"Enemies?"

"Someone who wants you out of there, darling. Probably because you're on to something good. But don't worry. A girl like you, you'll find another job like whistling. Or another husband, whichever comes first."

"Honestly, Aunt Julie? Not helpful."

"Why not? So you failed at something. You—what's that word? You screwed up. The world keeps spinning. Try something new. Try someone new."

"You don't understand. You don't know what it means, losing your job in a town like this. It's worse than divorce. Splitting up is like—well, there's two of you. You can blame the other person. If you lose your job, it's just *you*. Everything's on you. It's who you *are*." Ella's voice made this sobbing sound on the last word. She turned her head and stared at the painting on the wall, a reproduction Degas, pair of ballet dancers in wide blue tutus like the opening of flowers.

"Fine, then. Wallow in misery. My God, you young people, you take everything so damned seriously. Life's a gas, Ella. Just stop and breathe it in, once in a while. Believe me, it's gone before you know it."

"Again, not helpful."

Aunt Julie waved at her. "Oh, enough of this. You're boring me. Sit down, will you? I had something else to talk to you about. Something *important* to discuss." (There was a gimlet emphasis on the *important*.)

"What?" Ella asked. Still standing. Eyeing the ballet dancer on the left, whose legs alone were visible and seemed to be caught in the middle of a fall.

"I don't know. Something. Something. Damn it. Oh, that's right. About this apartment you're renting."

The change of subject was so abrupt, Ella actually turned from the picture and sat down. Reached automatically for the brandy, which was topped with more whipped cream and constituted a dessert in itself. "It's just for now," she said. "Until I can find something more permanent. Once the divorce is settled, probably."

Saying the word *divorce* was easier than she'd thought. Maybe it was because the breakup seemed like the least of her troubles now. Or maybe it was because of the lawyer, whom she'd called right after returning from coffee with Patrick, before she could lose her nerve. Who was so factual and unsympathetic. Whose lack of sympathy actually made her feel better: she was just another wronged wife, just one among millions. The same old story. Better luck next time. Don't get mad, get—

"Your mumma said it's on Christopher Street. Number eleven."

Ella blinked herself back to the present. "Yes. Number eleven. I'm on the fourth floor. It's all right. Kind of small."

"I know it well. Well, the building. Not the apartment itself."

"Really? How?"

"I used to go dancing there, back in the twenties. When the basement next door was a speakeasy."

Ella choked. Coughed. Grabbed her napkin. "I'm sorry. Did you say *speakeasy?*"

"Yes. Oh, it was terrific. Absolutely the best jazz. Used to go there every week. At least, until it went under."

"Went under?"

"Yes," Aunt Julie said. She set down her glass and dabbed her lips, which had lost most of their magenta to the tuna salad and had faded to the color of Pepto-Bismol, leaking gently into the wrinkles around her mouth. "Something terrible happened there, and the place shut down and never opened again. I believe I heard that both buildings were bought up later for cheap, and the bar was bricked in. All very hushed up and mysterious, and naturally I've forgotten the details. But I always did wonder what became of Ginger."

"Ginger?"

Aunt Julie's pocketbook lay next to her brandy glass. She lifted it and unhooked the clasp. "A friend of mine who lived at number eleven," she said, rummaging inside the pocketbook until she produced a postcard bearing a photograph of a naked woman lying on a Victorian chaise longue, face turned up and away toward an abstract portrait of another nude. The picture was black and white except for the woman's hair, which had been tinted a brilliant auburn. "I dug this up when your mumma told me. God knows why I kept it. A real dish, wasn't she? I've never seen another pair of knockers to equal those."

ACT V

We Lift Up Our Eyes
to the Lord
(hallelujah, hallelujah)

RIVER JUNCTION, MARYLAND

1924

1

About ten minutes after we cross the Delaware River into Pennsylvania, I realize I've left behind my mama's letters on the wicker table of Mrs. Marshall's pool house in Southampton, New York.

Luella notices my distress. (Luella Kingston—that's our Millicent Merriwether Macduff's real name, don't you know. At least she says it is. Frankly, I prefer Macduff.) "Something wrong?" she asks, casting me a sideways glance as she points the automobile down the darkened Lincoln Highway at a steady fifty-one miles per hour.

"Nothing."

"Nothing?"

"Just something I left behind, that's all."

"Your virtue, maybe?"

I open my mouth to snap back that it's not *my* virtue lying among the tangled sheets a couple hundred miles behind us, by God, but I stop myself just in time. "Whatever you say, Macduff."

She reaches for her pocketbook with one hand. "If

I've seen one woman throw herself at that bastard, I've seen a hundred. And he chooses *you*."

"I wonder why you care. You don't happen to count yourself among the unlucky hundred, do you?"

"God, no." She fumbles with a pack of cigarettes, steadying the wheel with her knee. She's wearing a pair of men's trousers in checked brown wool and a Norfolk jacket, like she's off to the countryside to shoot pheasants or something. Her pale hair's caught up under a wool cap. Not glamorous but tremendously capable. The kind of woman who can drive a six-stroke automobile with one knee while extracting a thick, masculine cigarette from a cardboard box. "I'm just puzzled, that's all. Like they say, there's no accounting for taste, is there?"

"Do you want a hand with that? Before you wreck us inside a tree somewhere?"

"Nah, I got it." She holds matchbook and wheel in the left hand, strikes the match with the right. Lights the stick, which is stuck between her faded pink lips. "So how was it?"

"How was what?"

"You know. Shacking up with Mr. Marshall."

The word *Marshall* jars me. I turn my head to the window, though I can't see much. Just the shadows of trees, flipping past in a dark blur. The reek of tobacco burning fills the air.

"That bad, was it?" Luella says. "Or that good?"

"Just watch the road, will you?"

"My God. You're dead gone, aren't you? You are just plain cuckoo for that block of damned wood. I'd laugh if it weren't such a tragedy."

"He's not dead yet, for God's sake."

She sucks hard on her cigarette and hauls down the window a few inches. A gust of wet air pours through the crack. "I guess we'll find out soon, won't we? Try to get a little sleep, carrots. You're going to need it."

I wad up my jacket and stick it between head and window. "Call me *carrots* again, Macduff, and you'll be picking your teeth from the steering wheel."

2

The automobile is a Franklin two-seater, racing green, six muscular cylinders. Belongs not to Luella, I hasten to add, but to Mr. Marshall himself, lord and master, who wasn't exactly around to sanction its requisition by the New York City Prohibition enforcement agency, though Mrs. Marshall assured me he won't mind. We didn't tell her the whole truth, of course. How could you tell a woman who's already lost one son that her remaining two boys are now the property of one Duke Kelly, hillbilly bootlegger? I couldn't do it. Not least because the fault lies with me.

Even the sanguine Luella is rattled, though she hides it all behind a bravado of wool trousers and cigarettes. She can't fool me. I can see the tremor in her fingers holding the smoke; the small, nervous pulse of her lacquered thumb against the steering wheel. I have a thousand questions I need to ask her, but it seems they're all stuck in my throat. Maybe I don't desire to know the answers.

The miles pass. The towns pass, bleeding into the northern reaches of Philadelphia, the western suburbs. Bryn Mawr, against which sight I shut my eyes. Wayne.

Well. The good Lord hates a coward, Gin.

I unstick my forehead from the window and say, "How in the name of God did they take Billy? That's what I want to know. Last I saw him was a parlor in Glen Cove, Long Island."

"Didn't I tell you to get some sleep?"

"Not the way you're driving."

She tips her cigarette out the window. "Just what was he doing in a parlor in Glen Cove?"

"Proposing to me." (I can't resist.)

Luella whistles. "How you get around. Engaged to one brother and going to bed with the other, all in the same night. I guess you can take the girl out of the hills—"

"I told him no. Not that my private affairs are any of your beeswax. That's how I ended up back in the city. Where Anson found me."

"Anson. You mean Marshall?"

"Not to me, he's not."

"No," she says thoughtfully, hunting for another cigarette, "I guess he's not, at that. Anyway, young Billy seems to have gone back into town in search of you, because that's where they snatched him. In that boarding-house of yours. A big to-do. Christopher telephoned me with the news."

"Did they hurt him?"

She pauses. "I expect he put up a struggle, poor fool. They always do."

"So you went to find Anson."

"He wasn't home."

"Home? Where's home?"

"He's got a little place near the river. Away from his family. They've got a position, you know, a life on the society page—"

"I know who they are."

"Anyway, it's a shabby little apartment on the West

Side, not much to speak of. One of those beds that folds out from the wall." She speaks with conscious familiarity, flicking a bit of ash out the window. "He wasn't there. No sign of him. But when I went back to my own place, the landlady had a telephone message from him. Where to find him, if something came up. So I telephoned back, first thing in the morning, and made Mrs. Marshall fetch him for me. Poor dear."

"And what time was that?"

"I don't know. Six or seven o'clock, I guess."

Six or seven o'clock. When I was fallen back asleep, no doubt, bone-weary after our second bout at dawn. Side by side, faces and bodies illuminated by the sunrise. Hands soft in idolatry. My leg thrown over his hip. His eyes, now thoroughly sober, in which my reflection lay clear and torrid. How strange and how electrifying, to look into someone's eyes and see yourself. I don't recollect the pulling apart afterward, nor falling into slumber. But somehow Anson heard his mother's knock on the door and found the strength to rise. I clutch my fist under the shelter of my overcoat. "Say, how did he get word to you in the first place, anyway? I was right there with him the whole night, except when the doctor was stitching him together."

"Mrs. Marshall, of course. She rang me up about half past ten o'clock last night."

I consider the urgent conversation between mother and son, while I was in the kitchen getting the water hot. "I see. You've done this before, then?"

"We've got a history, if that's what you mean. I was the one who stood by him when the Bureau kicked him out. Trying to win back his good name. We started out partners, you know. Spent all day together, sometimes all night. We got so close, we could tell what the other was thinking, without saying a word. We would lay down our lives for each other."

"I see. No wonder you warned me off like that."

"Don't be jealous."

"Don't need to be."

"Whatever you like, doll. Any beans, I told him the news, and he went straight out in that motorboat. They caught him in New York Harbor."

"They?"

"Your stepfather's men. They sent us word, I jumped on the next train out to Southampton to fetch you—"

"Because of course poor Billy's just the bait, isn't he? Both of them, Billy and Anson. I'm the one he really wants."

"Exactly. Don't feel bad, honey. It's only business."

"It's not business to him. *I'm* not business. It is personal, between Duke and me. About as personal as it could be."

"Oh, don't flatter yourself. He wouldn't go to this much trouble for a little family affair."

"You don't understand—"

"Don't I? What kind of bunny do you think I am? What do you think I've been doing these past three years, while you've been dancing and drinking and posing for photographs? I've been flirting with these fellows, fighting them, sleeping with them when I had to. I know them inside and out. And no boss risks good men for the sake of a private argument. No, ma'am, no matter how much he hates a girl, no matter how sore he is. Duke Kelly wants you for the same reason Marshall wanted you. Because you're the only person alive who can take him down."

"That's not true. Passel-a men know enough about Duke's business to put him in jail."

"But not one of them cares to turn against him, doll. Only you."

We are nearing some kind of town. A pair of yellow headlights grows and grows, bursting on our windshield like a double sun, and Luella slows the car. Worries the top of her cigarette with her thumb where it clutches the wheel, causing a small crumb of ash to fall from the end. A signpost flashes by, almost too fast to read. Some town named Coatesville. A few meager buildings rise up along the side of the road. Though the interior of the Franklin is chilly, a raw draft streaming in through the crack of Luella's window, still she perspires from her temples and probably her armpits. I can see the gleam on her skin in the light from the other car as it roars past. I can smell her feral scent, overlaid by traces of a familiar, expensive perfume I can't quite recollect the name of. Something she must have put on before she left New York City to fetch me. Something left over from the night before.

I wait until we pass through the town—rows of worn, paint-chipped storefronts, waiting for a boom—before I speak again. "So the idea is, you give me up to Duke and get your man back."

"That's about the sum of it, as far as I'm concerned. Of course, Marshall's going to have other ideas."

"Oh?"

Luella shifts gears smoothly, sending the Franklin to a high, even speed, flying westward along the Lincoln Highway. The cigarette's gone, lost out the window, and she doesn't light another.

"The bastard never could resist trying to be a hero."

3

I guess I do fall asleep, because at some point, leaning back against the window, jacket crammed between ear and glass, I leave off thinking and commence to dream I am back in bed with Anson. Except in this dream he looms above me, gargantuan, uninjured, hips rocking against mine, and though we can't see each other I am absolutely overpowered by the brawn in his limbs, by his mass, near enough suffocated, while a most powerful climax builds up a head of steam in my parts like an express locomotive. Faster and faster we go. Thrusting like a piston. Nearly there. Too much to bear. I lift up my hands to what I suppose is Anson's face, because I am plain afeared of the strength of this mounting explosion, scairt to death, need something dear to hold on to, but what I find is wet, hot and soaking wet, his head is split open and the blood pours over me, my neck and breasts and belly, while his body moves furiously on mine like a snake still moves after it be cut in twain. And I open my mouth to scream and I can't say nothing, can't see nothing, my throat is frozen and my eyes are blind, and I startle so hard I bang my head on the roof of the car.

"Jesus!" says Luella, swerving a little. "What's eating you?"

"Nothing." I open my hands and stare at the bare palms. Dawn's starting to break, just enough light that I can see there's no blood soaking me, only pale, cold skin. The shameful veins still throb between my legs, kind of painful, seeking the promised release. Feel as if I'm going to vomit.

"Some nothing," she says. "Let me know when you see a service station. Almost out of gas."

4

We drive all morning and into the afternoon, under a sky made of cold Pennsylvania steel. I ask Luella why we couldn't take the train. We'd have arrived by now, aboard the good old B&O.

"There's no hurry," she says. "The party doesn't start until you arrive, does it? Anyway, surprise is the only chance we've got. Only card in our hand."

"You've got a plan, I hope?"

"Sure I got a plan. The plan is, you do just as I say."

"Yeah? I don't like your plan. This is *my* country. I know how to deal with these fellows. I know who I can trust and who I can't. I know who my step-daddy is, how he thinks and where to find him—"

"Oh, shut your gums. You know nothing. Worse than nothing, because you think you're so damn clever, so damn irresistible. You can't just waltz into a gang of bootleggers like you waltz into a juice joint, carrots. All your sex appeal doesn't count for beans when men are bent on business."

I grab the wheel, elbow her in the side, and steer us into the grass by the side of the road. Car bumps and rolls and stops while Luella tears at my skin. I wait until the tires stop rolling and the engine cuts before I let go the wheel, settle back in my seat, and say quietly, "What did I tell you about calling me *carrots*, Macduff?"

"You've got some kind of complex, sister. You want to get us killed?"

"I said don't do it. So don't." I wrap my hand around the bit of her hair falling below the cap and bring her ear next to my mouth. "I'll do what you tell me. I allow you've got more experience than me. But as soon as there's trouble, as soon as your nice plan falls apart, it's my rules, all right? My country, my rules. My life at stake."

"And Marshall's." She yanks her hair away.

"That's what I meant."

She starts the engine back up and sends the car back to the pavement, swearing as she goes. But she doesn't say another word, not when we stop for gas and sandwiches in Gettysburg, not when we turn off the Lincoln Highway and head south into Maryland. The clouds dim and turn to rain. At some point past sunset, she pulls off the road and switches off the engine again. Tells me it's time to get a few hours' sleep, before we roll into River Junction at dawn.

5

So long as I inhabited the town of my rearing, I can't ever recollect driving there in an automobile. There is but one road, finding passage betwixt a pair of low-sloped mountains, mostly following the line of the creek bed. In summer, said creek runs scarce more than a trickle, cold and mountain-fed, wandering past the grazing kine and the fields of billowing rye, gathering tranquilly in the fishing hole where I once liketa murdered my step-daddy for his crimes against me.

Now, though the world is still dark and sightless, I hear the voice of that creek as a raging god, swollen high by melting snow and late downpours. How it roars over the rocks. A fall of new rain smacks the windshield so hard, the automatic wipers can scarce keep up, and still the water bellows downstream, so loud and fearsome as I have ever heard it.

I turn to Luella. "Creek's high."

"What's that?"

"Creek's high! Might could flood!"

"Over the road?"

"No, not here. Other side of town, maybe. Where it crosses the bridge."

She makes a single nod. Grips the wheel with her two long-fingered hands (no more steering by insouciant knee, no more lighting of cigarettes) and peers hard through the windshield, past the frantic swish-swish of the wiper blades, to follow the streaming patch of road illuminated by the headlights. Around us, the mountains press close, coal-black and unseen; the sky bears no trace of the coming sun. Just rain and more rain, the Lord Jesus weeping down pity for our sins, like my mama used to explain when I was but small.

6

B ut the rain does lift when the road bends into the holler and the first houses creep past like solitary ghosts. Recedes to a mere drizzle, as a brash spring downpour is wont to do. Luella switches off the headlights and I guide her off the road toward what used to be an old barn but is now something else: a still, I dare swan, by the smell of rye mash and smoke. We make for the orchard instead. Leave the Franklin there between the dripping trees, poised to run.

Unlike Luella, I possess no hat and no mackintosh, just the overcoat bequeathed me by the Coast Guard captain. I turn up the collar and huddle inside as we trudge through the dark in the direction of Duke's splendid new mansion. Drizzle splintering through my hair. Tip of my nose numb with cold. Belly wet with fear. Some kind of fragile childhood map guiding my steps, together with the noise of the rushing creek.

Now, according to Luella, the message from Duke came to her through our mutual friend Christopher, whose role in these affairs seems like that of Switzerland, so far as I can tell. And said message was about as brief and straight as the firing of a pistol: the Marshall boys now under protection of one Duke Kelly, whose stepdaughter better make her way home to River Junction should she wish to see either man alive. But so small as River Junction always seemed to me, from the vantage of the great metropolis, there are yet many places to hide a pair of men from those who seek them. Luella and I, we have already discussed this point. How we must therefore discover some kind of ally from within, somebody who might know where this particular pair of men has been stashed away. Which nook or cranny or outbuilding of River Junction conceals these men, *my* men, my two lovers, past and present, brother and brother, Billy and Anson.

If they're still alive.

But I'm going to ignore that possibility. Cut off its bad head right now, before it takes root. Of course Anson's alive. You can't unite with someone so fiercely as that without exchanging some kind of sympathy in the marrow of your bones, whether you welcome this barter or no. Wouldn't I know the stopping of Anson's heart as the stopping of mine? Wouldn't the hurt of his body recall itself in my body? The shock of his pain cause me similar shock? And I feel only queasy now, queasy with anxiety, that's all. So I stride forth—guided, as I said, by noise and intuition—a half step ahead of Luella's gamine pace, making for the back of Duke's house.

The kitchen entrance, which might yet stand unlocked at this hour, for the convenience of Duke's help.

Though the air is still dark, the sky has taken on a promising transparency. Not long before dawn. We tread across the soggy ground, the queer half-familiar landscape of my youth, small, broken-down houses replaced by great houses, trees snatched away to appear somewhere else, fences repaired, new garages erected to contain new automobiles: all of them as shadows against the wet, charcoal world. Closer and closer, the creek roars hard, fighting its banks, and I consider what a good thing it is that Duke's ancestors had the wit to build atop the slope of such a hill, a comfortable height away from all that hurtling water. Even here, on the high ground of the ornamental garden, the rain stands in deep pools around the shrubbery, and the grass has turned to swamp. By the time we reach that corner of the house occupied by the kitchen, my shoes are soaked through, my stockings squishing against the leather insoles.

I think, *Damn it all, Billy, could you not have stayed put in Glen Cove? Could you not have just sat and sulked before that comfortable fire in the inglenook fireplace, the fire that you built by your own hands?*

I have no proof, of course, that this door exists, linking the kitchen to the outdoors. But it stands to reason,

doesn't it? And we've reached some kind of stone beneath our feet, smooth and puddled, suggesting a path
or a courtyard. I find the brick wall with my hand and
crawl along, Luella in my lee. Already the garden is
exposing a little more light and shape. Around the far
corner, I distinguish an irregular shadow that might be
the tops of the trees shading the fishing hole. My fingertips hurt from the rough brick; the damp tobacco
smell of Luella's breath fills my head like a fog. So chill
as it is, we might stand but a few degrees from snow.
Worse, an ice storm. Had one of those when I was six
or seven, before I went off to the convent, and I never
will forget the sight of the world glazed in ice. The
terrible beauty. Walls all coated, locks all stuck. Trees
and shrubs all dipped in glass. We were lucky. Over
McCurdys' way, the limb of a giant elm crashed right
through the upstairs, killing Mr. and Mrs. McCurdy in
their bed. Left their three children orphans. I believe
Laura Ann Green took them all in, poor mites, though
I don't recollect for how long. Whether she adopted the
three little McCurdys as her own or gave them up to
some kind of institution.

My left hand finds wood. I stop and motion to Luella.
Run my fingers over the panel until they encounter a
knob, dead cold. Won't turn. I jiggle carefully, trying
not to make a racket, but the lock is surely bolted.

"Move aside," Luella whispers, and I step to the left, blowing on my fingers, which burn from the coldness of the metal. She draws something out of her pocket, an object like a pencil, and inserts it slowly into the keyhole, lovingly, feeling her way as might a midwife confronted with a baby in breech. The lock gives out, the door opens. She steps back to allow me in first. Can't see her face so well, but I expect she's smiling.

And yet an uncommon understanding seems to have opened up betwixt the two of us, Ginger and Luella, which requires no words. Like a pair of oxen in yoke, I guess, who might despise each other in pasture. I step past the threshold into the unlit entry, troubling not to see if she follows. Some kind of pantry, seems like, except lined with the tools of housekeeping. Brooms and mops of all kinds, hanging on rows of hooks. I can just make out their shapes. A few more steps, and we pass into a pantry proper, cabinets bumping along my fingertips, and then the room opens up to the kitchen as I remember it, except empty of bustle, empty of cook and kitchen maid and God knows, massive Garland range squatting mute along the wall. Icebox and sink over there. Worktable in the middle. I throw out my hands to find my way to the remembered door at one end of the opposite wall. A swinging door, as I recollect, so as to render the carrying of trays and dishes more efficient. I can't hear Luella's footsteps behind me on the sleek linoleum floor, but I know she's there. Her scent, the warmth of her breath. There is a perilous passage from the end of the worktable to the wall with the door. I can't quite picture how it lies; the room's too dark to really see. You can only sense the presence of furniture and cabinet and wall, by something closer to instinct than sight.

Except when you can't.

My foot finds the leg of a chair; I lurch forward, snatching for balance. Chair legs scrape against the floor. Gin falls to one knee, bites back a cry of pain and surprise. Then silence. Only the knock of our two hearts, the delicate whoosh of air from alveoli into throat into warm kitchen atmosphere, and back again.

We remain still for many seconds, counting breaths. Listening hard for any stirring. Luella's hand grasps my elbow and urges me up. Disapproval flows from her flesh into mine. I shake her off and strike forward, around the chair, this time reaching the wall and then the door. Passing through without a squeak into the short hallway to the dining room.

The light's a shade better here, on account of the great windows. I skirt the massive table, the ducal chairs, the fireboard of dark, mottled marble, and come out the door on the other side. Here be the grand hall, the staircase curving upward in its double tracks, exposed to maybe twenty-five feet of empty vertical space. You might suggest I should have tried the back stairs, but that particular hall leads past Duke Kelly's private study, which I aim to avoid, because my step-daddy is an early riser and always has been, even before he had any fixed occupation to rise to.

The white marble gathers up the dawn. I have no trouble at all stealing soundless up those stairs, Luella padding in my wake, all the way to the landing above. Blood runs loose, such that I ought to feel dizzy but do not. The queasiness has likewise disappeared. There is only purpose, sharp and singular, filling my head and chest, galloping along my limbs. *This* landing. *That* hallway. One door, two doors, *three* dark mahogany doors beneath my hand.

Stop.

Seems my heart is pounding hard. Breath rushes low. Run my fingers over the third door, looking for I don't know what. A sign of some kind. A detail re-called, to assure me my surmise is correct. Something to counter this small surge of doubt that assails me in-conveniently as I touch the brass knob, caress it with-out turning, eyes closed, ears open.

"Are you sure this is it?" whispers Luella, so low as to make me strain.

"Course I am," I whisper back, "unless he's gone."

"Then what are you waiting for?"

"Nothing."

I turn the knob all quiet, and the door swings wide, and I call out in a hushed voice: *Johnnie?*

A figure rises up from the dark bed. "Geneva Rose? That you?"

But it's not my brother Johnnie's voice, oh no. Similar, maybe, but Johnnie ain't lived enough years on this earth to collect that much mountain gravel in his throat, disturbing all the honey.

I turn and push Luella back from the doorway. "Go!" I shout. "Run!"

And she does run, sprinting back down that hall like a spooked horse, but it's too late for me. Dumb out of luck this new spring morning. Or else the Lord seen fit to abandon me altogether, for the greatness of my sins.

7

Now, I did make earlier mention of the springhouse, did I not? I feel certain that I did. Small room built of stone atop the running creek, just above the place where it widens out to form the fishing hole, in the absence of an actual spring bubbling up from Duke Kelly's land. It's been there so long as ever I can recollect; from the time of Duke's granddaddy, or even before, judging from the general degradation of stone and shingle roof. Used to store meat and milk and butter and such precious things, for we had no ice delivery in River Junction when I was small, nobody rich enough to pay for ice. Certainly no modern electric refrigeration machine, which we still modestly call an icebox, like there now stands in Duke's fancy new kitchen. In summer, we small fry might head down the slope of the hill to fetch a bit of butter for Duke's bread, or a couple of eggs, or a plucked chicken for frying. Sometimes I might seek out the springhouse on my own, for no other reason than to obtain an hour or two of quiet, cool peace during a hot summer's afternoon, for all that there was no window and no light to read by. Just privacy.

And sometimes we did play in that springhouse, during our childhood adventures. We might make like it was the Alamo, to be defended to the last man, or else seek shelter there during some game of hide-and-go-seek. Some sudden break of thunder.

So I happen to know every last stone of that springhouse, maybe fifteen foot by twelve foot, wooden shelves to one side, channel cut into the floor along another side, no windows and no light to speak of, though I confess I'm surprised to see it still exists. Surprised to see this humble crib intact, built into the bank astride the narrow, raging creek this March morning, near enough engulfed by the torrent; even more surprised that Duke Kelly should lead me here, of all places, when he has now an entire mansion at his command. An entire town.

Dawn has come, but the sun hasn't risen so far as to breach the ridge to the east. We are yet in shadow, the same as we were that last morning in River Junction, four and a half years ago, when I did give my step-daddy the white scar that streaks downward from his temple, and he bestowed on me a scar of another kind. Whether Duke recalls this particular geographic detail, I can't say. We neither of us utter a word as we sidestep down the last of the slope, slipping a little on the wet grass. He's wearing a pair of handsome, shiny black shoes and a thick felt hat and a sturdy mackintosh, belted at the waist, like any businessman on his way to work. On his mouth there is a pleasant smile.

"You bastard," I say, as our destination becomes clear, "you've got them freezing in the springhouse, haven't you? Why, they might could drown if the creek runs any higher!"

"Then I reckon it be good work you showed up in time, Geneva Rose," he says calmly, reaching inside his pocket, and now I do notice a recent alteration to the springhouse's construction. A door at the entrance, bearing a small window barred with iron, and a thick, heavy lock.

"Lord Almighty," I whisper. Feeling a little sick.

Duke withdraws a small object from his pocket, a key, which he inserts into the lock on the springhouse door. Scarce does he turn the bolt and draw back the door but I push him aside, into the raw darkness, creek roaring against the stone outside, and call out Anson's name.

"Ginger?" someone says in a thready, exhausted voice, belonging not to Anson but another.

"Billy!" I exclaim.

And while this short exchange is taking place, Duke lifts a lantern from its hook near the door and lights it, and the flame slowly takes and spreads a circle of illumination along the dim stone walls and shelves, the floor now sloshing with a good foot of icy water. The three men held by their wrists to one wall, from chains fixed to the stone at such a height that they cannot stand upright. Can only kneel on that hard stone floor, taken over by the rising creek that rushes in through the open channel.

Anson, Billy, and Johnnie.

I scream and plunge forward, down the three steps from the door and into the pool, splashing my way toward them. The wall's not long, and the three men are packed shoulder to shoulder like sardines in a tin, Johnnie nearest, head canted toward his massive chest at a strange angle. I grasp his cheek and try to turn up his face to mine, but his eyes remain closed, his skin cold, his neck too stiff to budge, and that's when I see the thick purple bruises at his throat, the black eye, the smashed and blood-crusted jaw.

The cold, lifeless skin.

"Ginger," Anson says softly, next to me.

I start up a keening, cradling Johnnie's broken head. His wide, strong shoulders, which could once bear any weight. "You killed him! You killed him!" I wail, smoothing back his poor hair, kissing his poor white forehead.

"Not myself, I did not," Duke says calmly.

I turn to face him, still holding Johnnie's head. "You ordered it done, which is the same thing. Your own son. You had your own son killed. And you call yourself a Christian!"

"God Himself did sacrifice His only begotten son, to cleanse the sins of man."

I don't even recognize the noise in my throat as my own. I just let go of Johnnie and launch myself at Duke, pounding and scratching and biting, while Anson shouts at me to stop in a voice like the breaking of glass.

But Duke only laughs at my onslaught. Laughs and jerks my right arm behind my back; grasps the hair at the nape of my neck and twists it around his fist so that my scalp about bursts into flame. "You play nice, Geneva Rose," he says. "You play nice or I pick one-a these fine young fellows to go next. You want that, baby girl? You want to watch these poor boys die on account-a your wickedness?"

"No," I whisper, so soft you can't even hear me above the noise of the creek outside.

His face is so close, his chin nearly touches mine. The same sleek, handsome face as before, skin of smooth olive, eyelids low and lazy. Lips red and full. His black lashes cast a furry shadow against the sockets of his eyes.

"Now, you be soft and attend to me. Attend to your step-daddy that reared you and loved you like you was his own, even though you be but a bastard, begotten in sin betwixt a harlot's legs."

"She was your *wife*."

He tightens his fist in my hair, setting my eyes to sting.

"She were a harlot, Geneva Rose, though I did take her to wife and redeem her, until the Lord saw fit to summon her to His side. As I did take you to my own bosom, but instead-a cleaving to me as you should, you turned on me like a snake. Ain't that right?" He puts his mouth to my ear and yanks back my head. "You turned on me, and you turned my own son against me, and by your wiles you did lure that poor fellow Green. You done broke my heart, near enough, and so I got no choice, Geneva Rose, no choice but to take an eye for an eye, as the Lord commands. Break your heart as you broke mine."

"You are the devil's own, Duke Kelly."

There is no movement from him, no word at all. Just that hot breath in my ear. Behind me, someone mutters something, kind of agonized, and Duke lifts his head.

"What you say, son? Was you fixing to join Miss Geneva in blasphemy?"

Billy's voice, young and defiant. "I said, take your hands off her!"

"Be quiet, damn it!" Anson snaps.

"That's right, boy," says Duke. "You attend to your big brother. He knows better 'n you. He knows there be a dozen good men among them trees outside, like an army of righteous salvation, just a-waiting for my word."

I draw breath sharply.

"That's right, now. They be waiting with blades sharp and eyes full-a glory, hearts full-a vengeance against this Delilah who has abased herself in the eyes of the Lord Almighty, who has betrayed her own people that did nothing but welcome her and her harlot mother to their bosom. So you just keep that tongue-a yours inside your pretty head, boy. You keep your eyes open and your mouth closed. You attend to what I say. You just watch how I wield the hand of God against them harlots that turn against their people. Turn against the good men and women that reared them up from the cradle."

And he releases my hair and spins me around and tears the Coast Guard overcoat from my shoulders and arms, and he throws that coat to the stone floor, now covered by a foot of cold water.

I close my eyes, because I cannot watch the faces of the two men before me, as I stand there in Duke's arms, realizing what I realize, understanding what he is fixing to do. The nature of his vengeance upon me, for my crimes against him.

The air is stone cold on my skin, on my arms and my chest through the thin, delicate material of my crepe de

Chine blouse, which I have now worn for three days running. Duke's hand curls around my throat, caressing the long tendons.

"She always were pretty," he croons. "Not so pretty as her mama, maybe, but pretty enough. Don't you two gentlemen agree? You surely do, I swan. By word and by deed."

Billy cries out: not a word of any kind, just agony.

"Don't look," I say.

"Now, you fellows know better 'n that. I told you both to keep your eyes open, I believe, and I surely don't want to have to hurt all this pretty white skin any more 'n I need. You watch, or I will make her bleed. You hear?" There is a little pause, and then: "That's right. That's good. Now watch."

His fingers find the collar of my blouse and rip downward.

As I said, I wear but my cami-knickers under my clothes, for my brassiere still lies in the drawer of the pool house bedroom in Southampton, New York. And that camisole is made of nothing but silk and peaches, and the air be as cold as stone, and I might just as well stand bare-naked just now, for all the modesty this scrap of gossamer confers upon me. My face is hot with shame and hatred and grief and something else, panic or what have you, because we are all at Duke's mercy,

all of us, and when he has had his way with me, tortur-
ing Anson and Billy by the sight of my degradation, he
will kill all three of us, one by one, by the might of his
bare hands. So I have nothing to lose, have I? Only a
few minutes of life lost, and those minutes not worth
the trouble of enduring them: not for me nor those men
who hang in chains before me, who hang for the sake
of me.

So I come to some decision. I move fast as a pistol
shot. Dig my elbow into Duke's middle, spin about,
and drive my knee into his groin.

He grunts and totters back, nearly falling into the
edge of that channel through which the creek runs, re-
frigerating the stone interior of the springhouse. I press
forward, raising my fists, while someone roars behind
me, and Duke's head snaps up just as I fix to swing that
fist toward him, into his thick jaw.

And though my fist strikes home in a satisfying
thwack, sending a shock up the bones of my hand and
wrist, radius and ulna and humerus all the way into my
shoulder, I perceive I have caused no such shock among
the bones of Duke's skull. He shakes his head once, as
if to discard the sensation of my touch, and reaches out
to snatch my arm as it draws back to punch again. He
bends that arm backward, near enough snapping the
elbow, smiling quietly as he goes, until the joint folds

behind my back and my brain goes white with pain. My body limp and pliant in Duke's hands. We are caught in a terrible embrace, face-to-face, while he holds my arm bent behind my back, and his head looms over mine, smelling of stale tobacco and hair cream and lust. The noise of the creek does rush in my ears, yet louder than before, and above that din I hear somebody groan like it's dragged out the devil's own throat. Anson. And I wonder, sort of inconsequential, because your mind is apt to strange frivolities when you can't reason for pain, if that's the last sound I shall hear on this earth. Anson's voice, sending me into eternal rest.

But seems the good Lord is not even so merciful as that. Duke's voice intrudes on this meditation, calm and conversational, saying something about how he always did admire my spirit, though it were such temptation to the devil that old Beelzebub done bought it for his own.

"Go to hell," I reply.

To which command he only sighs. Curls his fingers around the fringe of tiny lace at the décolletage of my camisole and pulls downward, so that my breasts spill free into the open air.

For an instant, even the raging creek seems to hold its breath. Or maybe I simply cannot hear it anymore; maybe my senses are all wound up into such a knot that nothing can slip through, not sound nor sight nor touch.

There is Duke's hand on my bosom, sure, but I can't say how I know it's there. Only that my flesh curdles, and some flurry of activity takes place along the wall.

"Take your paws off-a me," I whisper. Try to lift my hand, but my arm don't obey me. Like a wing dragging behind an injured bird.

"Would you look at that," Duke says slowly.

The world commences to tilt around me, and then I perceive that I'm the one tilting, that Duke is catching me and holding me upright. Digging his hands at the waistband of my skirt, so that it falls away, hands on my knickers tearing those too, and my vision is grown blurred, my head is too light to remain fixed on my neck, and I am floating away somehow, away from his hands, except I'm not, of course. I'm stuck here on earth. Some kind of present hell from which I cannot seem to wake.

"Now, *this* be interesting," comes Duke's voice, from somewhere nearby. "Mighty interesting. What shall we name this particular work-a art, gentlemen? *Redhead Sunk in Shame?*"

I guess the gentlemen are having trouble arriving at a decision on the spectacle of my bare-naked bosom in the cold springhouse air, while the creek fixes to flood, the water so cold as it creeps up my legs that I can hardly breathe for the pain of it. The pain in my arm where my step-daddy near to broke it. Duke holds me in place and turns me to face the wall, the horrified expressions of Anson and his baby brother, Billy, and he presents me to them like you would present a prize sow at the county fair.

"All them pictures as she took. Baring her harlot's skin afore the eyes of man. Surely we can summon up a name for this-un, betwixt the three of us. *Redhead Afore Her True Redemption?*" He brings his arms around my front and gathers up my two breasts in his hands. "*Redhead Submits to the Embrace-a Her Lord?*"

Billy cries out. "You're a damned monster!"

"Quiet," Anson says.

And I cannot look upon them, the faces of these two brothers who have each, in their turn, lain with me in the heat of bed. I, Ginger Kelly, on whose bare-naked photographic image a hundred thousand lustful men have feasted, cannot meet either gaze: not that of the dear boy whom I once adored, nor of the man for whose sake I would barter this poor body in an instant, did I imagine Duke Kelly would keep that bargain. I look upon my own brother instead, my beloved Johnnie whose eyes lie evermore closed, and I think, *He has won, Duke has won, he has sunk me in shame at last, he has surely made a harlot of me.*

"Of course," says Duke, "I might could think of a

better name. One that does surely fit my darling baby girl in her interesting new situation."

I go on staring at Johnnie, and a prayer starts up in my head for his soul. *Dear Almighty Lord, though You did abandon me here in my hour of need, I beg You, find mercy in Your everlasting heart for Your servant Johnnie, who did but sin for the love of me . . .*

Duke continues. "What? Speechless, the both-a you? Ain't you understood my meaning? Ain't you got eyes in your heads? Look upon this fair skin. Look upon this fair bosom-a hers and speak me the truth."

His right hand moves to the flat of my belly, all rough and pink with cold, while his left hand does pluck the nipple of my breast.

"Which one-a you two sinners has got this harlot with child?"

8

Now there is silence again, but a different kind of silence altogether. I don't guess I can explain its particular quality, really, except to observe that while the sudden baring of my breasts might have occasioned shock, we were none of us in any doubt that said bosom did exist. And if you could wet your finger and test the air for wonder, you might feel it now, rushing and swirling among us like the water that rises up against the thick stone wall of the springhouse, spilling inside through the cooling channel.

I rasp out, "You're a liar, Duke Kelly, and always have been. I'm no more with child than you are."

"Now, why should I lie about a thing like that, with the evidence a-laying right here under my hand? I do surely know the look of a woman's bosom when she be commencing to breed."

"And I say you're a liar."

"I don't guess you been feeling poorly of late, baby girl? Maybe missed your monthly sickness?"

"Course not!" My teeth now start to rattling, my whole naked body to shaking in the damp cold as fills that stone room.

"Now, you just look those two fellows in the eye, Geneva Rose, and say that thing again."

"Don't need. It's impossible, that's all."

"Well, now. Might be I done put this question to the wrong sinner. I guess any fellow could reckon whether he be the father of a harlot's babe, or no. Ain't that right, boys?"

Silence, save for the hullaballoo of the creek outside,

clamoring to fill the channel, to drown us as we stand. Water's near up to my knees now, and I'm shivering and rattling under Duke's fingers. Going a little mad. Altogether too weak even to raise my hand against him.

"Come, now," Duke says. "Confess your sins to save your souls. Tell me which one-a you has had to do with this hoor. Left behind your wicked seed to take root between her legs. Or is it the both-a you?"

"You're a villain, Kelly," Anson says.

"You best fess up. You best fess up afore I take my fist to her sinful womb. Afore I commence to cleanse her-a wickedness and prepare her for holy redemption."

"You're wasting our time, Kelly. Wasting your own time. The water's rising. Miss Kelly is freezing to death. Leave the damn woman alone and do what you came for."

"*Came* for?" Duke sort of roars. "You think I been to all this trouble for *you*, son? Why, you was just doing your job. I ain't got no particular quarrel with that. Done earned yourself a good soldier's death, Mr. Marshall, and I do swan you shall have it. But this one. This dirty hoor-a mine, this Judas that betrayed her daddy and her people. I called all you all here on her account, see, to punish her as the Lord does instruct us to punish those who turn against their own."

"Only a coward toys with a woman."

"You calling me a coward?"

"I'm saying you and I have a reckoning, and it seems to me you're putting it off. You're tormenting a defenseless female, instead of having the courage to match yourself against men."

Duke takes my hair again and yanks back my head, exposing my throat. "Then I reckon you fine gentlemen oughta put her out-a her present misery and answer my question. Be a simple one, after all. Which one-a you boys did sire a babe inside this harlot's womb?"

And Billy blurts out, "Stop it! Let her go!"

"Is you confessing at last, Mr. Marshall? You did plant this seed?"

"Yes! It's mine, she's mine!"

Shut up, Billy! Anson shouts.

"You did have to do with this hoor? Take her to bed and fornicate with her?"

"Yes!" Billy sobs.

"Yes, *sir?*"

Shouts Anson, *Billy, no! Damn it, wait!*

"Yes, *sir!*"

Duke releases me so sudden, I lose my footing. Fall kersplash on the floor of the springhouse, which is now so deep and as frigid as a penitent's bath. I look up to find Duke removing something from his pocket and affixing it to the knuckles of his right hand.

"They Lord! *No!*"

Duke takes a single stride forward—we are that close, inside this miniature space—and releases his fist like a piston, into Billy's young cheek.

I don't know if you've ever seen the effect of a set of brass knuckles on tender human flesh. I don't recommend that you do. I do expect I shall see it always, scored on my memory, the slow explosion of blood and flesh and the sound of splintering bone. Billy just grunts and goes limp. So I scream for him, I scream from deep in my chest, force my numb limbs upright to strike down the devil that is my step-daddy, but he does anticipate the blow, I'm afraid, and his elbow meets my stomach to send me stumbling against the opposite wall.

But in doing so, he brings his body closer to the wall on which the prisoners hang, and in turning his vain head to witness the result of his labor, he misses the movement of the man in the middle. The way Oliver Anson Marshall does gather his puissant body into a steel spring and balance all that power on the balls of his feet, under the rising water. How he does wait in this coil until Duke takes one more careless step in my direction, and then brace his hands in their cuffs and unleash all the force in those legs, mass times velocity, right square into the midsection of Duke Kelly.

And so great is the mass and the velocity of Anson's strike, translated by these laws of physics into a nigh-unstoppable force, my step-daddy liketa broke that stone wall as he hits it.

In that instant of impact, I realize that the Lord Almighty has not abandoned me after all. Has not wholly abandoned this earth to the imperfect justice of man, for Duke's eyes remain open, his brain remains certainly conscious of what has occurred, even as he drops like a gunnysack into the channel that flows beneath the springhouse walls and into the hell-bent creek.

And you will surely recollect what I told you before: that Duke Kelly cannot swim, no more than he can read the words in the Good Book.

9

For some few seconds, I continue to stare at the wall, on the spot where my step-daddy struck, as if he might somehow reappear. A faint whimpering starts up. Anson says my name atop it. I turn and set to crawling toward him through the icy water, and then I consider the whimpering and remember my Billy-boy.

"Get the key," Anson says, voice so rough as the walls around us.

"Key?"

"On the ledge."

I look at him. Fix Anson full in the face for the first time, and the sight of him shocks me, so bruised and swollen as he is. Cry out in pity. He just nods to the right, over the body of my brother Johnnie, and I summon the strength in my limbs to crawl in that direction, through maybe two foot of swirling, icy water, toward the stone shelf where we used to keep butter. I run my hand along the plane and find a small steel key.

"Handcuffs," Anson says.

I splash back to him, key in hand. My numb, shaking fingers cannot seem to stick the damn thing in the keyhole. His hands are white, the wrists raw. *I'm sorry, I'm sorry,* I keep saying, over and over, and he says nothing at all, just sits there patient and warm and hurt while I work to free him.

I think, *The bastard, the damn bastard, keeping that key in sight.*

The key finds its mark, the lock turns. Handcuffs fall free and Anson makes a sound at last, half grunt, half sigh, like he's been holding his breath the whole while. Then he says *Billy,* and I turn to his brother.

"My God," I whisper, and this time I find the keyhole at the first strike. Lift away the chains from my dear Billy-boy and gather him in my arms, caressing his bloodied hair, keening in agony. Anson sticks something in my hand, a cloth, my sodden skirt, and I hold it to Billy's face and try to clean the blood, try to find the start and end of his wounds. I look up and meet Anson's terrible gaze, and I say *Forgive me.*

He just fishes the key from the water beside me and commences to unlock Johnnie's body from its chains, working swift and stiff, like he is made of wood, like his joints stand in need of oiling.

"How do we get him out of here? Woods are full of Duke's men."

He answers, "Just run and trust to God."

He lays his hand on Johnnie's still head and murmurs something soft, and he turns back to the pair of us, Ginger and Billy, his broken brother Billy, who is waking up and starting to moan. Straightens and finds the buttons of his shirt and slips it from his shoulders. "Put this on," he tells me. "Quick, now. Not much time."

I take the shirt and put it on, quick as I can, while Anson, chest clad only in undershirt, undershirt lumpy with soiled bandages, slides his brother carefully onto the bridge of his own shoulders.

"You can't!" I gasp.

"No other way. Hurry up. Can you get your skirt on?"

I find my skirt and wring it. Cold's penetrated me so deep, I can't even think. Just follow orders. Cover my nakedness. Anson hoists his brother a little higher on his back. Flinches just a bit.

Shot rings out, so faint you can scarce hear it above the creek's roar.

"Goddamn," I whisper. "They're outside!"

Anson goes still, considering. He starts to slide Billy back down from his shoulders. "Stay here."

But before he can lower Billy to the ground, the door flies open.

I stumble back. Splash on my bottom before the towering figure of Luella Kingston, wrapped up warm and comfortable in her hat and mackintosh, revolver gripped in her right hand.

10

You're late," I tell her.

"Had to stop and kill a fellow on the way. Where's Kelly?"

"Downriver," Anson says. "Let's go."

She looks at him, and my God, the bitch doesn't even flinch. Like she has seen this man in such a condition before. Just reaches into her pocket and pulls out a second revolver, which she holds in my direction. "Can you shoot straight?"

I stand up, snatch the gun, and inspect the barrel. Fingers so stiff and cold, I'm as near to drop it as fire it. "If I have to."

"Don't worry about her." Anson hoists Billy, and even so gentle as he is, Billy lets out a cry. "Come on."

But I cannot leave without pressing my lips on Johnnie's poor head, before it reverts to the possession of River Junction. His soul I do trust to the possession of the Lord.

11

Luella goes first. Me next, revolver in my right hand, ready to fire.

The rain's started up again, cold pellets against my wet clothes, though I scarce feel anything at all. Don't know how I stand, don't know how I contrive to walk across the wet grass, up that slope, waiting for the shot that kills me. But no sound flies above the noise of the running creek, no bullet strikes my chest and sends me to earth. Maybe Luella's shot the sentry. Maybe they've discovered Duke's body downstream, caught in the footbridge or maybe the wreckage of said footbridge, and we have stolen some lucky sliver of opportunity.

Regardless. There we go, panting uphill toward the ornamental gardens that now stand atop the site of the old henhouse—I daresay the roses do grow abundant in such soil, come June—and the great house built from the spare change of thirsty lawbreakers. Behind me, Anson grunts out the mighty effort of carrying his limp brother. The sound of the rain now overcomes that of the roaring creek. Luella leads us past the back corner, the kitchen corner through which we snuck in an hour ago, now ghost-lit by the gray sunrise, and I guess she means to make for the orchard and the waiting automobile that will carry us free of River Junction.

And at that instant, passing the kitchen corner, some kind of bee stings the back of my hand. The exact same spot as before, in Mama's bedroom.

"Wait!" I call out.

Luella turns around so sudden, I nearly smack her chin. "What? What's wrong?"

"Patsy," I say.

12

She's still asleep, poor mite. Out cold in the great French canopy bed in her white-and-gilt room. Slept right through the murder of her big brother and the torture of her big sister. The just vengeance wrought upon her daddy, leaving her an orphan.

I lay my hand around the top of her soft, warm head. "Patsy. Patsy-pet."

Her blue eyes open.

"It's me, darling. It's Geneva Rose. Your sister, Geneva."

"Ain't you in New York City?"

"Not now. I'm visiting. Just for the day. And guess what? You're coming to visit me."

"Visit you? When?"

"Now."

She studies this. Struggles upright under my hand. Hair falls over her face, and she pushes it back in a ges-

ture that reminds me of our mama. "What about Johnnie?" she asks.

I gather her up in my arms and lift her from the bed.
Drag the blanket from the sheets and drape it over my
shoulder and around her body. I am so weary, eviscer-
ated, each muscle and bone and tendon drained of life,
and yet my arms find the power to carry her, I don't
know how. "Johnnie'll meet us later, darling."

"You're all wet."

"Got caught in the rain."

I don't know what it is with children. She just snug-
gles right against my chest and believes every word I
say. Because why? Because I am her sister, her own
Geneva Rose, and Johnnie has taught her to love me,
though she knows me but little. Her warm body nestles
deep in my bones, lending me the strength to carry her
down the hallway to the back stairs. Into the kitchen,
where the kitchen maid has just arrived, sprinkled with
rain.

"Miss Geneva!" she exclaims.

I put my finger to my lips, and I guess the poor girl
hasn't heard the news, doesn't know that Geneva Rose
Kelly has betrayed her step-daddy, has betrayed the
town's great savior and sunk River Junction directly
back into the misery and squalor of harder times. She
just stares as I carry my sister to the pantry and out the

kitchen door, covering her body with my body against the rain that does rattle down upon us.

Just so far as the orchard. I can carry my sister that last half mile of sodden ground before I give way. Just so far as the orchard, and the automobile that will carry us away.

13

In the orchard, the Franklin is gone. Patsy has fallen back asleep inside her cocoon of blanket and Ginger, and my arms are so exhausted, I am near to dropping her. I collapse against a trunk and look around me, while the rain tumbles from the leaves upon my head.

"There you are."

I turn my head sharp, just to see Anson step from the trees behind me, wearing nothing but his undershirt and trousers and a tired face covered in bruises. He reaches for Patsy.

"Where's Luella? Where's your brother?"

"Gone for the hospital. Wasn't enough room for all of us. Didn't dare wait."

"But *you* did."

He lifts Patsy gently from my arms, blanket and all. "Let's go."

"Go where?"

"Out of town. There's a path through those woods, the other side of the orchard."

"But it's miles to the next town! All the way over the ridge. They'll find us for sure. Hound dogs'll track us down in a minute."

He starts off anyway. "Are you coming?"

"Didn't you hear me? It's hopeless! We're goners without that car!"

"Don't you *dare* give up!" (Over his shoulder, not even breaking stride.)

I stand there a moment, drenched in despair, while Anson walks away, bearing my sister in his strong arms, just as if he did not spend the night chained to a stone wall inside a springhouse while the creek did flood its banks around him. My own strength is plumb gone. Every last ounce drained away into the soggy earth, to which I now fall on my knees, so cold and wet and exhausted I can't even feel the striking of my bones against the turf.

"I can't. I can't."

He stops at last. Turns and stares at me. Walks back

slowly, until he reaches the ground before me. Settles
Patsy on his shoulder and drops to one knee. "You can,
Gin."

"Where do you get your strength?"

"The same place as you."

"I'm out. I'm done."

"You can do this. You have to do this. I can't leave
you behind."

"Yes, you can. You have to, because of Patsy. I'd
slow you down. So cold and weak as I am. Five or six
mile at least, over the mountain ridge. And you can't
carry us both. Not even you be so strong as that."

He reaches out one hand to my shoulder, like he
means to try, by God. And I pull away. Can't have his
touch on my skin, not anymore. Break me in twain.

"Ginger—"

"Go on. Take my sweet baby sister away from this
place. I'll find a way. Always do."

His eyes are dark and narrow in the shadows. Flesh
around them all swollen and blackened, just as ugly as
sin, as beautiful as sunrise. And the look inside those
poor dark slits says he knows I'm lying. No way I'm
fit to elude those men and their canny hound dogs, my
people I have betrayed. Not the state I'm in.

"Leastways," I continue, "I can distract them, can't
I? Distract them so the two-a you can get away."

"The Ginger I know wouldn't lie down and give up."

"I ain't giving up for *my* sake."

"That's what I mean."

"Well, maybe that girl is dead and gone, and this time you can't save her, everhow you try. Only waste time you can't spare."

His face is too beat up to show any kind of expression, not that he was ever so expressive as that. But I have the idea he is hung with mourning.

"Go on," I say. "Keep my sweet baby sister safe from harm, will you?"

I guess any other man would rant and storm. Tell me he can't live without me, tell me he's bound to protect me; impossible to leave me behind for the mob and the hound dogs, he'll die fighting by my side. Not Anson. I do reckon he knows me better than that. Well enough to understand what I'm asking of him. Well enough to grant me that boon, though the cost do break him in twain.

"Ginger," he says again. Just my name. But I reckon I know what he means to say. All the words crammed into that one little sound.

Water's puddling around my knees. Smell of wet spring grass fills my nose. I crumple down on my sore calves. Reach up and lift the blanket from Patsy's face. "Reckon your mama will know what to do with her."

And he starts leaning forward, like he's about to kiss me good-bye, when a noise reaches my ears. Noise like the engine of an automobile.

"Go!" I shout, and I push him off. Away to the cover of the woods.

14

From where I'm crouching, tucked behind a tree, I can't see a thing. Engine grows louder and angrier. Peek out and discover some movement on the nearby road, a black shape slipping in and out of the rows of trees, coming to a sudden, squealing stop.

I turn my head into the rough bark of the tree. Apple tree, what will soon burst in blossom, soaking up all this cold rain and then stretching its long, thin branches to the inevitable sun. My right hand falls to the waistband of my skirt and draws out the revolver. Flicks back the safety latch.

"Geneva Rose!"

The voice carries among the trees, high and female.

"Geneva Rose! I know you's in there! You come out-a cover right now!"

Peek around the edge of the tree again. Try to find movement. Some flash of color.

"Geneva Rose! Be Ruth Mary Leary! You come out-a them trees right now!"

Squeeze my eyes shut and press my forehead into the tree.

Ruth Mary Leary. Of all people. Ruth Mary, whose beloved brother Carl got his head split open for my sake, just like my own brother did. Ruth Mary, whose precious babies have been fed and clothed by the generosity of my step-daddy, whose new house and new hearth have all been bought and paid for by Duke Kelly.

Voice coming closer now. "You better come! You better show yourself!"

I think, *I will give myself up to her.* Why not? I'm a goner already. Give myself up so that Anson and Patsy gain some kind of chance.

I take a step away from the tree.

"Stop!" calls out Anson, farther back. "Stop there! I've got a gun!"

"Who's that there?" Ruth Mary calls back.

"Just go!" I shout. "Anson, take Patsy and go!"

"Not going anywhere!"

I bring the gun up to my temple. "Swear to God, Anson, I will blow my brains directly out if you do not take my baby sister and make for those woods right now!"

"They Lord, Geneva Rose! You tetched? Put that gun down!"

Ruth Mary's voice is weary and exasperated. I see a bit of movement between the trees, maybe twenty yards away, and then Ruth Mary herself, wrapped in a coat, marching toward me as if we was joining each other for a Sunday picnic.

"Put that gun down and attend to me, before you get yourself killed!"

I lower the gun.

She keeps on marching, marching, hands in pockets. Right hand gripping something there. I can see the bulge of her fist.

"You stop right there!" shouts Anson. Strides up fast, Patsy in one arm and gun poised ready in the opposite hand.

"Shut that fellow up and attend to me!" She draws her right hand from her pocket and opens up her fist. "Take this. Go on, git!"

"What is it?"

"The keys, Geneva Rose. Ain't you got eyes in that fancy head-a yours? Keys to Carl's flivver. You get yourself inside and make tracks. Go on!" She thrusts her hand forward.

I stare at the keys. At her face. White and haggard, eyes all hollow. Fine, fair hair straggling away from her cloche hat. To my left, Anson stands still, bearing my sister in her blanket. Patsy begins to whimper.

I guess Ruth Mary recognizes my amazement. She shakes her head a little, sending drips flying. "Had my brother killed, didn't he? Cut off his damn ear and left it on my doorstep to warn me against speaking."

"Who did?"

"Your step-daddy," she spits. "All for Carl's bearing your mama's letters to you, like he was charged to do. Now git. Git yourself gone before they make out what I done here this morning."

And my childhood friend Ruth Mary Leary does then toss the keys to her brother's Model T Ford on the wet grass before me and stride away betwixt the trees, back into town, to her four wee babes with no father and no uncle to keep them.

New York City, 1998

Another hour in Aunt Julie's parlor, as she called it, and then another hour making a circuit around the barren grounds when the drizzle let up at last. Bundle accompanied them on a lackluster leash. At three o'clock, Aunt Julie consulted her watch and said they'd have to leave, because she had a mah-jongg engagement in half an hour.

"Mah-jongg." Aunt Viv rolled her eyes.

"You laugh, but I've won four thousand dollars off that fool Soamy."

"I sometimes wonder if you're not having the time of your life," said Mumma, kissing her cheek.

"My God. Why do you think I strolled across Lily's living room in my negligee? I was at my wit's end. She's a dear thing, but that apartment bored me out of my mind. All those books." Aunt Julie turned to Ella. "Remember what I said, now."

Ella kissed her cheek. "Which part?"

"All of it. And keep hold of that photograph, will you? I expect it's worth a fortune. It's an antique. Like me."

Keep hold of that photograph. As if Ella needed to be told.

She'd kept her composure throughout the torturous two hours of socializing at Maidstone Meadows, as Julie's friends popped in and out of view in knit suits (female) and navy jackets (male). She'd kept her hands from shaking as she tugged Bundle along the asphalt path, as she walked back to the car and belted herself in and watched the frail trees and the changing blue-and-white sky swallow up all those cedar shingles and the white trim, until the station wagon turned a curve and everything was gone.

She feigned sleep all the way back to Manhattan, though her heart rattled and her mind spun, keeping one hand immersed in Bundle's fur to anchor herself to something living. When they arrived back at Christopher Street, she made as if to wake, starting and stretching, eyes racing all over the old bricks and the railing and the stairs and the windows and the doors. "Guess I'd better head upstairs and finish the cleanup," she said. She gave Bundle a last pat. Kissed Mumma and Aunt Viv.

"Don't forget about dinner," Mumma said. "Baltha-zar. Eight o'clock."

"You've got no idea who we had to sleep with to get that reservation," said Aunt Viv, "so you'd better be there pronto."

"I'll do my best," Ella said, and at the time, she actually meant it.

Then she hurried up the stoop and through the door. Hurled herself along the stairway, one floor two floors three floors four. One more flight. Around the stair railing.

Hector's door.

She lifted her fist and knocked three times, like the release of firecrackers.

"Hector?" she called. "It's Ella!"

The building was quiet. There was the distant groan of pipes, the bang of a radiator. Ella lifted her hand again, and the door opened almost under her fist. But it wasn't Hector; it was Sadie. Sarah. Whatever her name was. Her eyes were red, her face pale, her brown hair pulled back in an untidy ponytail. Ella must have looked at her in amazement, because she managed a small, tight smile.

"Don't worry, I was just leaving," she said.

Hector appeared behind her and laid a hand on her thin shoulder. "You'll be all right, Sade?"

"Sure I will. Thanks for the pick-me-up. Travel safe, okay?"

"Always. Let me know if it comes back, all right?"

She lifted his hand and held it to her cheek for a second. Ella stepped back, and she rushed out suddenly, in a whir of wiry limbs, smelling of dainty floral perfume.

Hector looked at Ella. "Is this about the flowers?"

"What flowers?"

"Um, the ones inside your apartment, maybe?"

"I haven't been inside my apartment since nine this morning."

"Oh. Jeez. Well, you're in for a surprise. Everything okay?"

"Everything *okay*? I don't know, Hector. I *think* everything is probably *not* okay, but then I don't seem to *know* much about anything these days. Like, for example, the speakeasy next door? The one that shut down in the 1920s—"

Hector's arm came out of nowhere, scooping her up around the shoulders and practically flinging her inside the apartment. The act was so sudden and almost violent, so completely uncharacteristic of him, that she staggered forward and covered her head with her arms.

"Shh, it's okay," he said, taking her by the shoulders. "Sorry. I didn't mean to scare you."

"What the *hell*, Hector?"

"Shh. I'm sorry. It's just—you never know who's listening, right? Ella. Jeez, you're shaking. Don't shake."

Ella stepped away from his hands and turned around. He'd shut the door and now stood before it, wearing clothes that were equally uncharacteristic: a navy blazer and striped button-down shirt, tan slacks, calfskin loafers, as if he were going out to dinner with his parents. A scrabbling of small claws came from the direction of the bedroom, and an instant later Nellie hurtled into her legs. Ella crouched down mechanically and smoothed her ears.

Hector said quietly, "I'd never hurt you."

"I know."

"But?"

"But you have to tell me what's going on," she whispered.

He'd gotten a haircut, she thought, or else he'd taken a lot of care with a brush, taming that forelock and all the rest of it into dark, curving order. His arms hung by his sides, as if he didn't really know what to do with them. Pull her up into some kind of embrace, or cross them across his chest. "Okay," he said slowly. "I'll tell you. What I can, anyway. Let's just sit down, all right? Can I pour you a drink?"

"No. And I'd rather stand." She straightened away from Nellie.

"Then let's at least get out of the doorway, all right?"

He stepped forward and took her hand and led her to the kitchen. There was a suitcase next to the counter, a dark green carry-on wheelie bag. He went to the open shelves, took down two tall glasses. Turned to the refrigerator. Nellie followed him, a little subdued.

"Where are you going?" Ella asked.

"LA. Meeting with the director."

"When's your flight?"

"Eight o'clock. Are you sure you won't have something? Water? Juice? Tea?" He was pouring something into one of the glasses, some kind of liquid the color of cantaloupe. "Or stronger? I don't drink before flying, but I can get you something."

"No, thank you. I just want the truth."

Hector picked up the juice or whatever it was and drank rapidly. His Adam's apple rose and fell, rose and fell, mesmerizing. He set the glass down slowly, like he wasn't ready to part with it, and stared at the rim. "What have you heard? I mean, how did you find out?"

"I was out in the Hamptons today, visiting my aunt. She used to hang out here, back in the day."

"Your *aunt?*"

"Great-great-aunt. She's ninety-six. She was some kind of flapper, I think."

Hector nodded. "She would've had to have been a flapper. It was a pretty hip spot. You couldn't just walk in wearing a work suit. You had to be dressed up, you had to be part of the scene. You had to know people."

Ella's heart was moving in long, slow crashes. Her blood coursed with adrenaline. She laid her hands on the counter to steady them, the reclaimed-wood counter that Hector had made himself.

Hector.

The astonishing Hector, man of all talents. Musician. Carpenter. Consoler of weeping women. He looked back at her the same way he'd looked at her in the laundry room, that first day, with his old brown eyes and his face that said, *We know each other from somewhere, don't we?*

I know who you are.

Ella curled her fingers and stared back. "And just how do you know all that, Hector?"

"Because my grandfather played music here. He was the orchestra leader. It's where he got his start. You might have heard of him. Jazz guy. Bruno."

"Bruno? Wait, *the* Bruno? He was your *grandfather?*"

He shrugged and finished the juice. "So they tell me. I never met him. He died before I was born."

"But your father owns the building."

Hector came around the edge of the counter and sat down on the stool next to her. Pried one of her hands free and tugged her gently to the other stool. "True. My dad owns the building. Both buildings. The owner passed them on to my grandfather, who promised to keep them in the family. Not to sell. Not to allow anyone in to snoop around. For a hundred years. That was the deal."

"You're, like, the watchmen? The guardians?"

"I guess you could say that."

"Guarding *what?*"

"Whatever's behind that wall in the basement."

"Don't you know?"

He shook his head.

"Don't you *want* to know?"

"At first I did. And then I figured, whatever's in there, it's best kept where it is, right? Not hurting anybody. Just playing music. Like an echo, you know. Echo from wherever. Or whenever." He leaned his elbow on the counter and rested his cheekbone against his knuckles. His other hand still held hers, very gently. "Sometimes, I get the feeling they're watching over us, instead of the other way around."

They. Ella shut her eyes. "You believe that. You believe there are—ghosts, or whatever, in that basement."

"I don't know what they are. But something's making music down there, something's making sound and vibration. Life. But it's not life. You can't get inside that basement, behind those walls. Believe me, I've tried."

"Holy shit."

"Hey. It's okay, all right? Nothing's going to hurt you."

Ella opened her eyes. "But who? What happened here? That woman screaming, I can't get it out of my head."

"Well, I went to the library once. Tried going through the newspaper archives, looking through books and magazines. I never could find anything. Not a word ever written about the place. I called up the *Times,* the *Post. The New Yorker. Metropolitan.* Zero. Nada. Nothing, never, not in the entire period of Prohibition, ever written about a speakeasy on this part of Christopher Street. Let alone a raid or a shootout or murder or whatever it was. My grandfather knew, but he never said a word. Took it to his grave."

"So there's no way of knowing?" she said. "No way of finding out what happened? What's really there?"

"Does it matter?"

"Of course it matters! Aren't you curious? Don't you care about the truth?"

"I guess I used to," he said. "But then I started to wonder if I had the *right* to know the truth. I mean, it's not my secret, is it? The truth belongs to the people who lived it. I guess if they want me to know more, they'll show me the way. Everyone's got a right to privacy, I guess. I listen to them down there, the echoes of them, whatever they are, and I think, It's enough. Let them be. What difference does it make, who they are? They're not hurting anyone. They just *are*."

Ella pulled her hand free and rose from the stool. The apartment was dark, except for the pendant hanging above the kitchen counter. The sun had set; a violet sky hung above the buildings outside the windows. She walked toward the piano, which was closed, lid down, keyboard covered, ebony so black and shiny it was like looking into a pool of oil, and rested her hand on the cool, curving edge.

"So have I completely freaked you out? Moving out of the building first thing tomorrow?"

"I don't know. I don't—I don't even believe this. I don't believe in—" For some reason, the word wouldn't come. Ghosts. Or spirits. Souls? She felt queasy. "You know what? Maybe I'll have that drink after all."

She heard the legs of the counter stool scrape softly against the floor. Some clinking, the rattle of bottles. Outside, the world was perfectly normal. The rooftops in their usual order. Lights going on in a hundred rooms, a thousand, a million across Manhattan. She thought, So many old buildings. So many lives. So many girls starting out here in the big, wicked city, falling in love with the right man, falling in love with the wrong man. Falling in love with a woman. Going out dancing and drinking and falling into bed after. Going to work, flapping frantically after some grand dream. Getting into pickles. Getting into grooves. Dying old, dying young, dying somewhere in between. All this packed into twenty brief square miles. Was it any wonder you could still hear the echoes?

Or had she known this all along? The first time she lay on the table in the laundry room, listening. Waiting. Observing.

Hector came up behind her shoulder and handed her a drink. She sniffed it.

"Gin," he said. "Theme of the evening. It's what they're serving down below, after all."

She laughed. And laughed. Set the glass down on the piano because it was shaking so much, threatening to spill. Kept on laughing until Hector put his arm around her, then suddenly moved his hands to her waist and hoisted her up onto the piano while the hysteria shook her chest and bent her over. She put her hands over her face.

"I really hope you don't, though," Hector said, when the spasms subsided.

"Don't what?"

"Move out."

"Oh, come on. With the harem you've got here? And Claire."

"Harem?" He looked shocked.

"Sadie and Jen and the others."

He braced his hands on either side of her legs and bent his head. "Jesus, Ella. Mind in the gutter."

"Well?"

He looked up. "They're my *cousins*, Ella! Actually, that's not true. Sadie's my half sister. The rest are cousins."

"Not all of them."

"All of them."

Ella spoke slowly. "Are you saying I'm the only person in this building who isn't a family member?"

"That would be correct. We had a meeting about it, actually. Mike left to get married—his girlfriend was too spooked to hang out here, anyway—and we'd basically run out of cousins. Nobody wanted the job. What's the matter?"

"I'm just . . . just trying to get my head around all of this."

"You know, you're not in any danger or anything. I hope you know that. Swear to God, nothing's going to hurt you."

"How do you know that?"

"Because I do. Because do you think I'd take a single chance like that with you? The smallest chance you might be hurt?"

Ella said nothing. Somewhere below the edge of the piano, Nellie whimpered a little: not in anxiety, she thought, but some kind of eagerness. For what, who knew?

Hector picked up the gin and handed it to her. "So, my turn. What's with the flowers? Are you getting back together with that asshole?"

"No! Of course not."

"Glad to hear it."

"Actually, I talked to a lawyer yesterday afternoon. Started proceedings. Should be pretty straightforward, he said. Not asking for alimony or assets or anything, just to get back what I put in."

"Well, your apartment looks like Kew Gardens at

the moment, so I'm guessing what's-his-name didn't get the memo."

"Please. Give me credit."

"Oh, I have total faith in you," Hector said. "From the moment you spilled your underwear all over my feet. Said to myself, Hector, this one's for real."

"That is total bullcrap. I know for a fact I looked hideous that morning."

"You were sublime in your hideousness. I couldn't take my eyes off you."

"Because your taste runs to sweaty women with unwashed hair and lurid underwear."

"Actually, you were radiant. I dig that glow of yours, when you're just back from running. And your eyes. You've got this thing you do with your eyebrows that knocks me over. Remember how you dumped the soap on top of your clothes and you turned around and said to me, *Are you happy?* You did the eyebrow thing. And I remember thinking, I am so happy, I could sing. I could stand here and belt out 'Oh, What a Beautiful Fucking Morning.'"

"So glad you didn't, Curly. I would have run so fast . . ."

"Naw, you wouldn't. You would have given me that stunned look, and then you would have smiled and joined in, you would have known every word and every note, and that, Ella, *that* is why I want to compose a symphony to your eyebrows and then build you the best damn kitchen in Manhattan."

"Because I know all the music to *Oklahoma!*?"

"Because, when you sat down at my piano, everything made sense, right then. You belonged there. You belonged *here*." He spread his open palm over the middle of his chest. "And I haven't thought of anything else since."

"Stop." Ella finished her gin and crashed the glass down to the piano lid, just missing Hector's fingers. "Just stop. You can't do this to me. I just left my husband, and you have a girlfriend."

"*Had* a girlfriend. Claire and I broke up last week, actually. Right after we watched that movie together."

The air left the room. For a moment, Ella thought her heart had stopped, too. Hector's arms were braced around her, his face close. His skin turned to indigo in the shadows. Too close and too much. She closed her eyes. "No. Please don't say that. Don't say it was me."

"It wasn't you. It was mutual. Overdue. A lot of stuff, going way back. For one thing, she hated the apartment, and I can't imagine living anywhere else. For another thing, Nellie just kind of tolerated her, which is the same thing as another dog hating her guts, and we all know you should listen to your dog in matters of the heart. And finally . . ."

Ella waited for him to continue, but the words just hovered there, balancing carefully between them.

"And finally, what?" she whispered.

"And finally, you can't keep a girlfriend if you're falling in love with someone else."

"Oh, damn."

"*I* can't, anyway. Maybe certain assholes can. I won't mention any names."

"Oh, damn. Oh, Hector."

He pushed away from the piano. "Anyway. There it is. Just threw that bomb out there and blew everything up. But I couldn't *not* tell you, Ella. I was going to wait until I got back from LA, but—well, I suck at pretending. And it's all I can think about. Everything I've been playing, writing lately. You're in every note."

"Hector, you *jerk*."

"I know. Incredibly selfish of me to say all that. I acknowledge. But when I saw all those flowers being delivered—"

"Hector, please—"

"Everything out of season. I can't afford flowers like that. I'd like to think I *could,* one day, but for now—"

"Just shut up. Shut up a second, so I can think."

"All right. Fine. You think, and I'll just wash up these glasses."

Hector plucked her empty gin glass from the piano and walked back to the kitchen. She opened her eyes and stared at the wall, but really she was watching him, admiring the compact grace of his stride. Not strutting. Just . . . at ease. Inside an apartment he'd renovated himself. Filled with the things he loved, the objects that constituted the physical manifestations of his dreams. Which Claire had hated. Or maybe it was just the basement she hated, the voices from the past. The clarinet that followed you when you took out the trash at night. Hector turned on the faucet and rinsed out the glasses. Set them in the dishwasher. Wiped his hands on a striped towel. Looked up and saw her watching him, and this time she didn't look away. Didn't close her eyes.

"You jerk," she said. "You have laid so much on me tonight. You have no idea."

"That wasn't the plan. You were the one who pounded on my door, demanding explanations."

"And another thing. You were supposed to come into my life in a year or two. Not now, when I'm like the walking wounded. Bleeding all over the place. Hitting bottom so hard, I've shattered the fucking pavement. And now completely freaked out by this ghosts-in-the-basement thing."

"You're not freaked out. Not really. That's not you, Ella."

"Maybe not freaked out, exactly. But this—all of this—it's just . . . big. It's like I was living in one country a month ago, and now I'm living in a different one. And I don't know the customs and the food's weird and the ancestral spirits keep beating their drums in the wilderness, and the locals are incredibly sexy but I've only just arrived, I haven't even unpacked yet."

"Life is stupid that way."

Ella drew in a long breath and turned to address the wall. "Also, I think I've just lost my job."

There was a brief, strange silence. The slight jingle of Nellie's collar as she moved her head.

Hector said, "You *think* you've lost your job?"

"Actually, I'm pretty sure of it. Pretty sure the axe will fall when I walk in Monday morning."

"What the hell? Why?"

"It's complicated. Politics, I guess. But the official reason is that I didn't tell them Patrick works at another division in the bank we're investigating. Which I did, by the way. But when you want to get rid of someone, any excuse will do."

"Jesus. I'm sorry."

"Yeah. Me too." She paused. "At least I think I am."

"You're not sure?"

"I don't know. I actually—it's kind of funny, because I love my job. I thought I loved my job. But right now . . ."

"You don't give a shit?"

Ella stared at her hands and thought of the yellow legal pad in her laptop bag. "Maybe I don't," she said. "Or maybe I do. I'm still in shock. Kind of numb. Kind of pissed off. I guess I'll find out Monday morning."

"If you want the job, you should fight for it. Fight for what you love."

"Yeah, well, they don't give you much choice in this town. I've seen it happen. Escorted downstairs by security. It's ugly. It's like you get erased."

"So don't let them do it. Make a plan. Talk to a lawyer. Decide what you want and fight like hell."

"But it's just me against them."

"No, it's not. You have us."

"Us?"

"Us. Here. Me. All of this," Hector said. "And either way, whatever you decide, we'll work something out. You're safe here, okay? You can stay as long as you want. Figure out whatever needs figuring out. If you want to start a new life, start a new career. Fight for the old job or look for a new one. The world's your oyster. The world *should* be your oyster. Don't let the bastards get you down."

But they already have, she thought. The bastards. All of them. Patrick, Travis, FH Trust, the SEC, whoever else. A few swings of the hammer, and everything was broken, her old world, her old life. "Sure thing," she said. "World's my oyster. How does it go? *Which I with sword will open.* Falstaff, right?"

"I mean it, Ella. Use this place. Just use it. Lick your wounds here. Plot your comeback. You've got all the strength you need, right here."

She looked up. Hector's face was grave, sincere, except for one well-groomed piece of hair giving up and sinking over his forehead to spoil the effect. She wanted to lift that curling hair. She wanted to kiss the skin beneath it. Not because her heart was beating gratefully at his kindness; not even because of the dizzy sense that her overturned life was revolving in pieces around her. Only because he was Hector, and the pieces seemed somehow to be revolving around them both.

What had Aunt Julie said? *Life's a gas. Stop and breathe it in.* Or something like that.

She said, "You know, you were supposed to time this right. You were supposed to wait for the exact right moment. *After* I put everything together again."

"Hey, I can wait. I can wait forever. Well, maybe not forever. I might have to march over and drag you upstairs like Tarzan after a decade or so. But otherwise, as long as it takes. I have stamina. Perseverance. Self-control, unlike Mr. Priapic, who sends you flowers to make up for being a cheating loser asshole. Sorry. That just came out."

Ella started to slide off the piano.

"No, don't. Stay right there," he said. "I want to think of you on top of that piano, all the way to California."

"You're going to lock me in?"

He set down the hand towel, reached into his pocket, and walked back toward her. "Actually, the opposite. I'm going to give you the key. You can stay here while I'm gone, if you want. Because first, your apartment has no working kitchen—sorry, I'll get on that when I get back—and second, it's currently crammed full with lyin', cheatin' flowers." He set the key down on the lid. "There. But only if you want to. No pressure."

"No *pressure?*"

He spread out his hands. "Seriously. I'm a patient man. Just crash here. Make yourself comfortable. Go through my drawers. Sniff all my sweaters. Nothing to hide. Just Sadie coming in to take care of Nellie."

Ella took hold of his hands. Her heart was galloping now. "I think I'm going to barf," she said.

"Bathroom's right through there."

She yanked him between her knees, laid her hands on his cheeks, and kissed him. She meant to be brief and hard, but he wouldn't play along. His mouth was too soft, his breath too sweet. His hands, sliding up her back to cradle the curve of her head, too gentle.

"Better?" he said, pulling away at last.

"Better."

"Because I kind of have a flight to catch."

"I have dinner with my parents at eight. At Baltha-zar."

"So you definitely can't cancel."

"No way. Neither can you. Meeting with the direc-tor."

"Not a chance. Besides, I don't just want to be your revenge fuck. Or your comfort fuck because you're getting fired."

"*And* freaked out by the ancestral spirits in the base-ment."

"Which, by the way, are completely benign. But I want more than that. I don't know. Maybe a lot more."

They were silent. Holding his cheeks, cradling her head. Brows touching.

"You know what?" Hector said. "Scratch that. You want revenge, I'm here for you. Use me."

Ella lifted her head. "No."

"No?"

"I don't want to be your rebound fuck, Hector. I want more. Maybe a lot more. Now get your mind out of the gutter and scram, before you miss your flight. Go on. Git."

Hector kissed her again and stepped back. Straightened his jacket. Stepped forward and kissed her once more and turned away quickly, grabbing his wheelie bag without even pausing.

"Not going to look back," he called over his shoulder.

"Break a leg. Or finger. Whatever."

"Will do! And, Ella?" From the hallway.

"What?" she called back.

"One more thing!"

"What?"

Hector's voice echoed bountifully up the stairwell.

"Don't fall in love with anyone else while I'm gone!"

Ella slid off the piano and stared at the door. The silence rushed in like a tornado. At her feet, Nellie rose and whimpered. Looked up anxiously with those round, black King Charles eyes. Silky, curling face.

"It's for the best," Ella said. "It's the sensible thing, not to go rushing in. I'm incredibly susceptible to sexual contact."

Nellie rose up on her hind legs and pushed Ella's knees.

"Look, I've just left my husband! I've just lost my

career, maybe! I'm *vulnerable.* I can't just jump into bed with the first guy I meet, can I? No matter how amazing he is. That's how I got into this mess in the first place. Sleeping with Patrick on the first date. It clouds the judgment. Too much oxytocin. Not going to repeat *that* mistake, believe me."

Nellie tilted her head in bemusement.

"That's because you're a dog with absolutely no morals at all," Ella told her. "I'll bet you'd be pregnant every twelve weeks if you weren't fixed. You'd be letting every alpha in the Village hump you on the way to the park."

Nellie barked and ran to the open door.

Ella followed. Moved her hand to the doorknob and let it hover there, while the longing rose in her throat until she could actually *taste* longing, could actually feel its bittersweetness on the back of her tongue. Nellie scrabbled her paws at the door's corner, trying to work it open farther.

"Look, Nellie, he said to listen to *your* dog in matters of the heart. And you're *his* dog. You work for him. How do I know I can trust you, either?"

Nellie whined and scrabbled harder, and the gap in the doorway widened. Ella put her hand on the knob and started to push it closed, and it was like someone jabbed a hot pin into the back of her hand.

"Ouch!" she hissed.

Somewhere down the stairwell, a faint thumping made her pause.

"Hector?" she called. "Are you still there?"

"What's up?" he called back.

Ella sucked on the back of her hand. Nellie darted through the doorway and turned, looking up anxiously, expression of absolute supplication.

"It's too soon," Ella whispered. "It's a leap of faith. A whole new country. What if I get lost somewhere?"

Hector's voice. "Ella? You okay?"

Ella found herself walking out the door to the landing. Placed her left hand on the banister. Her pulse crashed so hard in her neck, she felt the skin move. She felt the blood whir in her ears. Some kind of otherworldly electricity skittering along her spinal cord, as the old Ella and the new Ella threw sparks off each other.

You belong here. Did she actually hear those words, or did they echo between her ears? The back of her hand tingled urgently.

You belong here.

Ella called down: "I'm fine. I just forgot to ask you something."

"What?"

"Do you mind if I sleep naked in your bed?"

The air turned to glass. Not a sound came up from

below; even the ordinary background clang of Manhattan seemed to disappear into another dimension. No music floating from the basement. No voices. No sirens. Just the sound of her own heart slamming against her eardrums.

And then.

Thump, thump, thump. Pause. *Thump thump thump thump thump.* (She walked to the end of the landing and stood thrumming at the top of the stairs.) *Thumpthumpthumpthumpthumpthumpthumpthumpthump* and Hector swung around the last curve of the staircase, dark hair flying apart, and ran up the final flight and lifted her up in the air.

"This is a huge mistake," he said.

"Huge."

They staggered down the hall and crashed through the door.

"Also, the sexiest thing anyone's ever said to me. Were you doing your eyebrow thing, too?"

"Probably."

"Dream girl." He stopped kissing her to shut the door behind them. Cupped her jaw with his hand. "I'm kissing you. We're kissing, Ella. This is actually happening."

"What about your meeting?"

"He'll understand. Your dinner?"

"No contest."

He kissed her. His hand wandered down her hand and found her fingers. "Husband?" he whispered.

"History."

He kissed her chin, her jaw, her ear. Moved down the side of her throat. "Are you sure? Sure you want to do this?"

"No. I'm scared to death."

"We can stop. We can wait."

"Wait for what?"

"You tell me, Ella. You tell me what you want."

Ella leaned into his chest and inhaled his soap, his skin, his wool, his dog, his everything, and it seemed to her she had known this scent all her life. The smell of home. Music and laughter and bourbon and honest wood shavings. All this could be hers. Just say the word, Ella.

"I don't know," she said. "How good are you in bed?"

"For you, dream girl? I can be off the charts. I can keep you up all night and make you breakfast in the morning."

She lifted her head and took in another kiss. Looped her fingers around the back of his neck. The back of her hand had stopped hurting or even tingling; in fact, she was buzzing all over with the kind of dizzy well-being you ordinarily feel after a long, expensive massage in a hotel spa. She pressed her hips against his, and instead of feeling daring, she felt safe. She felt warmth. A promising firmness. Connection. Agile musician hands sliding down her back to round her bottom.

A snatch of Gershwin floated through her head. *And the living is eaaaasy.*

"Let's go," she said.

ENCORE

We Make Like a Banana
(and split)

DIXIE HIGHWAY
March 1924

We drive almost until nightfall, stopping only for gas and food and hot coffee, for a set of dry, warm clothes for each of us. Roll of new gauze for Anson's chest, which I wind carefully upon his bare skin, while he does close his eyes against my touch. Then I curl up on the seat and sleep, while Patsy, so fully alive as only a five-year-old child can be, sits on Anson's lap and asks him a thousand questions. He answers each one with grave patience—at least those I'm conscious to hear. At six o'clock Anson pulls over at a motor inn and pays for a room. I don't bother asking where he got the money. Sewn inside his trousers, probably. Or else given him by Luella, right before she drove out of River Junction in that two-seater Franklin, bearing Billy to help. Against her own wishes, probably. Anson forcing her to the same sacrifice I asked of him.

I can't stop shivering, no matter how much coffee I drink, no matter how many clothes Anson piles upon me. When at last Patsy falls asleep in her cot, I crawl into my narrow bed and draw the covers around me and curl into so small a ball as I can, and still my teeth set to chattering in my head. Maybe they will chatter forever. Maybe cold is my permanent condition, in consequence of my sins.

Anson speaks softly from the other bed. "Still chilled?"

"Thought I told you to get some sleep."

Soft creak of bedsprings.

"You can't sleep here," I say. "Bed's too narrow."

He just lifts the covers and slides in, resting his weight on his good side. I turn my face to his chest and suck his warmth into my skin. Breathe in the store-bought smell of his wool sweater. Man's like a blast furnace, burning high-grade Pennsylvania anthracite to a pure, noble hotness. I think of my mama and her last fever, and the difference between that sickly heat and this one. I ask him where we're going.

"Away," he tells me.

"New York?"

"No. Farther. They're going to be looking for you in New York. We're going to Florida. Fellow down in Cocoa Beach owes me a favor."

I nod. The wool of his sweater scratches my nose. My hurt arm slows to a dull, stiff ache at my side. He asks me if I'm still cold, and I say not anymore.

We are quiet. Not touching, except for my nose and

his chest. Clothes on. The sheets are thin and cheap; the bed smells of must. I want to sleep; my head aches, my stomach roils, the way you feel after a night of gin and beefsteak and dancing, all clangy and drained, your bones stiff. But there is no more sleep in me. If I shut my eyes, I see blood and splintered bone, I see sloshing water and rain and the certain knowledge of annihilation. I see Anson's bruised face. I hear his rough, beat-up voice. So I open my eyes and stare at the blur of dark knitting before me, only just visible because there's a light on somewhere outside our window, and the glow streaks through the shabby curtains.

"Billy be all right?" I whisper.

"I guess so. Going to take some healing."

"His poor face," I say, "his lovely face."

Anson puts one arm around me. Doesn't tell me not to cry or anything stupid like that. Just allows me to sob, muffling the sound with his own body, so Patsy doesn't hear and wake herself. I put my hand on the back of his soft neck and my sobs turn into hiccups.

"All right?" he whispers.

"Sure I'm all right. Never better. You?"

"Just fine."

And my hiccups turn to giggles, and his chest shakes a little too, though it must hurt like the devil. "Lord

Almighty," I say, between spasms, "I am going to hell. What's wrong with us?"

"Just shock, that's all. The grief comes later."

"It's just too much. It's too much."

"It's over now. He's gone."

"Duke's gone."

"He is. He's dead, Gin. Saw his body myself, floating downstream. No life in him at all."

I think about that spot on the wall of the spring-house, the sound of bones snapping. Brief and violent. Look of amazement on Duke's face as he prepared to meet his Maker. My heart sets to thumping. I tilt my face to the ridge of Anson's chin. Can't see the bruises in this dark, but I know they're there. I know that jaw is swollen and purple. I touch it with my finger and he flinches.

"Sorry," I say.

He takes the finger and holds it there against his skin. "Try to sleep. We'll be driving all day tomorrow."

"Can't sleep. Head won't stop thinking."

"Thinking about what?"

"Everything. Pair of fugitives, aren't we? No past remaining to us. Everything left behind. Just what lies ahead."

"Regrets?"

"Maybe," I say, and then, "No. Everything I hold

dear is right in this room. Except maybe those things my mama left me, I guess, the buttons and the letters, but that doesn't matter like it did."

"Doesn't it?"

"No. What difference does it make, who my daddy was? You can't yearn for what was never yours to begin with. I would a million times ruther have Johnnie back than some old buttons. Million times ruther have Billy untouched. So I am grateful for what's left. My mama's in my heart. My baby sister's sleeping safe nearby. And you. Alive. Lying here against me. Everything plain between us."

He doesn't speak. I wonder whether he is recollecting those things Duke said in the springhouse, considering the possibility of something else lying between us. The state of his body, I perceive, is so tense as a coiled spring. So taut as his legs curled up beneath him in that springhouse, ready to strike. The gentle touch of his hand against my back belies something else, something akin to the craving I keep inside my own skin, like you crave water to drink and air to breathe. Garments to clothe your nakedness. Balm to heal your wounds.

I slide up a few inches, so we are face-to-face. Lips touching but not kissing.

"Are we sinners, Anson? You and me."

His thumb, which had been circling some knob of

my spine, slows to a stop. We sink into contemplation of each other, and I recollect how we first lay together, blind as moles.

"Yes," he says. "God forgive us."

"What are we going to do?"

"I don't know, Ginger. Find a way, somehow. Wake up in the morning and find a way home."

As I told you before, a narrow bed does foster intimacy. Nowhere to spread your limbs, nowhere to hide. You lie conjoined as babes in the womb. Life in flood between you. Cells multiplying and dividing.

Thus you fall asleep, and your flesh rests content against him.

Author's Note

Driving through rural Maryland to a bookstore a few years ago, I passed by a town that startled me. Instead of the modest farmhouses of other villages, several imposing homes lined the main street, made of brick and stone and clearly dating from the earlier part of the twentieth century. I asked the bookstore manager what industry had driven this apparent boom in wealth. She told me it was bootlegging money, and *The Wicked City* started to take shape in my head, right there. From the beginning, however, I saw Ginger belonging more to the mountain culture of the Appalachians than the hills outside of Washington, so I moved her hometown to the northwest corner of the state, where Maryland drags a hand into West Virginia.

The Appalachian dialect is a complicated, variegated work of human language, and while I spent a considerable amount of time researching its unique syntax, pronunciation, and vocabulary, I make no pretense to reproducing it here. For one thing, there are so many arcane phrases and word usages that would either misdirect readers or pull them out of the story altogether; for another thing, the dialect has evolved since the 1920s, leaving very few surviving examples of its earlier forms, which makes historical accuracy virtually impossible. For example, most (though not all) current maps tend to place the northwest counties of Maryland in the Midland dialect group, but sound files of older residents intriguingly suggest the more Southern speech patterns indicative of classic Appalachian usage; I suspect that mobility and industrialization have had their way during the past century. Meanwhile, Ginger herself is a chameleon who has journeyed through a variety of different environments, all of which have influenced her speech to varying degrees. Taking all these factors into account, I gave the residents of my fictional, isolated town of River Junction a proud mountain twang, and in doing so have tried to remain faithful to the sense of Appalachian English—its extraordinary poetry and rhythm, its almost Shakespearean rendering of sentences—without losing either myself or my readers in its specifics. I hope linguists and native speakers will forgive me for any errors and inconsistencies, intended or otherwise.

Acknowledgments

My name may be the one on the cover, but *The Wicked City* was really brought to you by a number of unsung heroes whose passion it is to turn manuscripts into books. Thanks are forever due to my dear and fabulous agent, Alexandra Machinist of ICM; to her assistant, Hillary Jacobson, who sadly has no clone; and to my badass editor, Rachel Kahan, and all her fellow miracle workers at William Morrow whose support has meant so much to me, both professionally and personally.

I owe so much to the booksellers and librarians who have loved and championed my novels, and to the readers who have then taken these books to their hearts. Your enthusiastic words feed me daily, and most especially on those days when both words and enthusiasm come hard.

Last and always, I'm grateful for my family— husband and children, parents and sister, in-laws and outlaws—and my beloved friends with whom I share coffee and champagne, as needed.

About the Author

A graduate of Stanford University with an MBA from Columbia, Beatriz Williams spent several years in New York and London hiding her early attempts at fiction, first on company laptops as a communications strategy consultant, and then as an at-home producer of small persons, before her career as a writer took off. She lives with her husband and four children near the Connecticut shore.

HARPER LUXE

THE NEW LUXURY IN READING

We hope you enjoyed reading
our new, comfortable print size and found it
an experience you would like to repeat.

Well – you're in luck!

HarperLuxe offers the finest in fiction and
nonfiction books in this same larger print size and
paperback format. Light and easy to read, HarperLuxe
paperbacks are for book lovers who want to see
what they are reading without the strain.

For a full listing of titles and
new releases to come, please visit our website:

www.HarperLuxe.com